Praise for the novels of E. E. Knight

Dragon Avenger

BOOK TWO OF THE AGE OF FIRE

"Knight breathes new life into old conventions. . . . Here is no warmed-over Tolkien playground, but a new world breathed to life and populated with fascinating characters we long to hear more from. . . . Knight, a master plotter and world builder, alternately surprises and delights, keeping us on the edge of our seats. . . . Knight has written a classic here, a kind of *Watership Down* with dragons—a book that will be cherished for generations to come. It is, simply, a grand tale, full of the mystery and wonder fantasy readers long to discover and too often find absent in modern fiction." —*Black Gate*

"[A] gritty coming-of-age story. . . . Knight makes the story complex enough to entertain readers of all ages." —*Publishers Weekly*

"Knight offers a thoroughly crafted fantasy world. . . . For a lushly unique fantasy read, look into *Dragon Avenger*, as well as its predecessor, *Dragon Champion*. You'll never look at dragons the same way again."
—Wantz Upon a Time Book Reviews

Praise for Dragon Champion

BOOK ONE OF THE AGE OF FIRE

"Smoothly written . . . a bloody, unsentimental fairy tale."
—*Publishers Weekly*

"*Dragon Champion* is an enchanting story of a young dragon's search for answers to help him understand what it is to be a dragon. This is a heartwarming story full of adventure, where good deeds and friendship always succeed. The characters are wonderfully endearing, and the adventures that Auron experiences as he grows into an adult dragon are exciting and entertaining. A superb introduction to what I hope will be a wonderful series."
—The Eternal Night

continued...

"The author of the Vampire Earth series has crafted a series opener with a refreshingly new protagonist who views the world from a draconic, rather than a human, perspective. A fine addition to most fantasy collections."

—*Library Journal* (starred review)

"Knight did a great job of hooking me into the story.... This concern and attention to the details illustrate how strong the overall feel of the book is— Knight clearly is building something more in this world, and the amount of back story to the characters and creatures is very impressive.... Very entertaining—the characters were genuine and the world full of depth. With the ending Knight gave us, I am very interested to see where he takes these characters next."

—SFF World

"E. E. Knight makes the transition from the science fiction of his Vampire Earth series to a fantasy saga with an ease that is amazing but not surprising with someone with his enormous amount of writing talent."

— Paranormal Romance Reviews

TALE OF THE THUNDERBOLT

"An entertaining romp rife with plausible characters; powerful, frightening villains; suspense; romance; and monsters ... everything good fantasy and science fiction should have."

—SFF World

CHOICE OF THE CAT

"David Valentine is ... a true hero. I found myself rooting for him on page one."

—SF Site

"Memorable."

—*Midwest Book Review*

"Strong characterization, excellent pacing, [and] believable depth in world building."

—SFF World

"Impressive ... sure to delight all fans of dark fantasy and hair-raising heroic adventure ... a unique and wonderfully entertaining novel."

—Rambles

"I highly recommend *Choice of the Cat* to speculative-fiction fans who enjoy science fiction/horror hybrids, and especially to fans of apocalyptic fiction."

—SFReader

"I dare you to try to stop reading this exciting tale of human resistance in the face of impossible odds."

—SF Reviews

"Knight's style made me think that if *The Red Badge of Courage* had been written by H. P. Lovecraft, the result would have been something like this."
—Paul Witcover, author of *Tumbling After*

"A winner. If you're going to read only one more postapocalyptic novel, make it this one." —Fred Saberhagen, author of the Berserker series

"Knight's dark book of wonders is a marvel—simultaneously hip and classic, pulpy and profound. Evocative of Richard Matheson as well as Howard Hawks, Knight's terrifying future world is an epic canvas on which he paints a tale of human courage, heroism . . . and, yes, even love."
—Jay Bonansinga, author of *The Sinking of the Eastland*

"This is one of the best books I've read in years. If you like action books (or horror or military or suspense . . .), just buy it."
—Scott Sigler, author of *Earthcore*

"Four stars. . . . Lays down a strong beginning for what promises to be an engrossing series. The author handles traditional motifs in fresh and often unsettling ways. Fans of slipstream fiction will definitely want to read this. It also holds great appeal for readers who enjoy any of the component genres: dark fantasy, horror, or adventure. Highly recommended."
—Infinity Plus

"One of the most impressive debut novels I have ever read." —Rambles

"The style is compelling and skilled. E. E. Knight manages to blend battles and violence with the gentler side of his characters, allowing them to . . . experience a wide range of emotions. . . . Stunning! I am looking forward to the next installment of the adventure!" —The Eternal Night

"I have no doubt that E. E. Knight is going to be a household name in the genre before he's done." —Silver Oak

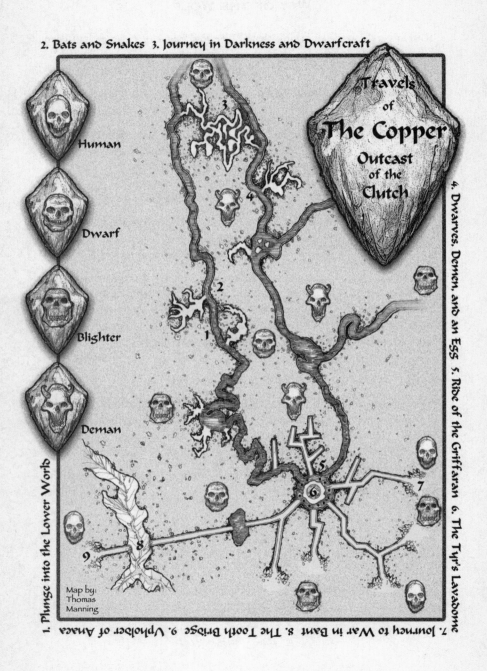

2. Bats and Snakes   3. Journey in Darkness and Dwarfcraft

Human

Dwarf

Blighter

Deman

Travels
of
The Copper
Outcast
of the
Clutch

Map by:
Thomas
Manning

1. Plunge into the Lower World

4. Dwarves, Demen, and an Egg   5. Ride of the Griffaran   6. The Tyr's Lavadome

7. Journey to War in Bant   8. The Tooth Bridge   9. Upholder of Anaea

Dragon Outcast

BOOK THREE OF THE AGE OF FIRE

E. E. KNIGHT

A ROC BOOK

ROC
Published by New American Library, a division of
Penguin Group (USA) Inc., 375 Hudson Street,
New York, New York 10014, USA
Penguin Group (Canada), 90 Eglinton Avenue East, Suite 700, Toronto,
Ontario M4P 2Y3, Canada (a division of Pearson Penguin Canada Inc.)
Penguin Books Ltd., 80 Strand, London WC2R 0RL, England
Penguin Ireland, 25 St. Stephen's Green, Dublin 2,
Ireland (a division of Penguin Books Ltd.)
Penguin Group (Australia), 250 Camberwell Road, Camberwell, Victoria 3124,
Australia (a division of Pearson Australia Group Pty. Ltd.)
Penguin Books India Pvt. Ltd., 11 Community Centre, Panchsheel Park,
New Delhi—110 017, India
Penguin Group (NZ), 67 Apollo Drive, Rosedale, North Shore 0632,
New Zealand (a division of Pearson New Zealand Ltd.)
Penguin Books (South Africa) (Pty.) Ltd., 24 Sturdee Avenue,
Rosebank, Johannesburg 2196, South Africa

Penguin Books Ltd., Registered Offices:
80 Strand, London WC2R 0RL, England

First published by Roc, an imprint of New American Library,
a division of Penguin Group (USA) Inc.

First Printing, December 2007
10 9 8 7 6 5 4 3 2 1

Map by Thomas Manning and Eric Frisch.

ROC REGISTERED TRADEMARK — MARCA REGISTRADA

LIBRARY OF CONGRESS CATALOGING-IN-PUBLICATION DATA:
Knight, E. E.
    Dragon outcast / by E. E. Knight.
        p. cm. — (The age of fire ; bk. 3)
    ISBN 978-0-451-46185-8
    1. Dragons—Fiction. I. Title.
PS3611.N564D736 2007
813'.6—dc22   2007022537

Set in Granjon   •   Designed by Elke Sigal

Printed in the United States of America

PUBLISHER'S NOTE
This is a work of fiction. Names, characters, places, and incidents either are the product of the author's
imagination or are used fictitiously, and any resemblance to actual persons, living or dead, business
establishments, events, or locales is entirely coincidental.
    The publisher does not have any control over and does not assume any responsibility for author or
third-party Web sites or their content.

To Dawn,

WHO KNOWS ABOUT GROWING UP DIFFERENT THAN OTHERS

Acknowledgments

Each novel requires effort from a platoon of professionals work-ing behind the scenes, represented by nothing more than the chip-sized graphic of the publisher's imprint. Sharp-eyed copy editors and imaginative artists, painstaking typesetters and overloaded editorial assistants, plus the agents, sales staff, law-yers, accountants, and executives . . .

I thank you all.

One important face behind that little orange-and-black icon has gone missing, however. Liz Scheier recently moved on to a different publishing house. This volume represents the last of our efforts together. She was (and is) a clever wordsmith, an in-spired advocate for my work, an ally in success as well as adver-sity, and a patient "boss." Her flair and polish is woven into this saga. Like the young Copper fellow you're about to meet, I feel like I've got a bad leg and a bum wing without her.

Thanks, Liz.

Dragon Outcast

BOOK ONE

Hatchling

"A BAD START IS STILL A START."

—*Tyr FeHazathant*

Chapter 1

No pleasant dream, this. Discomfort and darkness, cold and cramp, clinging tendrils binding. The restrictions vexed him.

The hatchling struggled against his torment, twisting his neck to a more comfortable position, for his head kept jerking uncontrollably.

Suddenly his nose tore free of its bonds with a startling crack that ran down his body to the tail-tip. A membrane gave way, air tickled at his nose, and his lungs greedily pulled in its enticing freshness and a comforting, musky odor that filled him with longing.

A weight dragged at his belly, and he knew he had to be free of it. He reached up a rear claw and tore it away, the small pain worth the greater freedom.

The pain brought an additional benefit: His mind cleared of dreams and confusion and doubt. Instinct took over his little body, from deepest fiber to smallest hatchling scale. He pushed in every direction at once, head twisting and battering at the gap as his nose worked out.

Then it all gave way and he sprawled, whipping his tail around and fighting to right himself in a mass of clinging membrane and white shards. He opened his eyes, but the light pained and confused him, so he shut them again.

A wet web hung on him. It stuck everywhere in his scales, in the folds of hide and bone behind his jaw, his crest, his claws.

Strange, strange, strange. No clouds or currents or friendly sun, yet he was not frightened at the newness. The musky smell told him that all was well. He was safe.

He brought up a forelimb and wiped the web away from his eyes and off his crest. Now he could go to work with his long, flexible neck and sharp teeth, getting it off his limbs.

"We've done it; oh, thank Susirion and the four shapers, he lives." The voice, the mind, more than half his own, had spoken to him in the egg. Through it he had seen brilliant sunlight and hot, flowing gold, blended and poured into his consciousness. This was the voice of his dreams, the spinner of images bright but vague around the edges, sunlight, crashing ocean waves, herds of blotch-backed beasts thundering below, leathery wings flapping and a proud, booming voice shaking the mountainside with song.

"Open your eyes, my jewel. See your mother and your world!"
Mother!

He opened his eyes, and it took a moment for his vision to clear. Too much to take in: a wall of green scale, curled-down head with its sniffing nostrils and shining, wide-open eyes, darkness filled with strange columns bathed in a glow from pools of light gathered on the floor, even a gentle, probing tail-tip as thick as his midwaist flicking bits of . . . of . . . *shell*, his brain supplied . . . flicking bits of shell off his haunches.

Wave after wave of love, delight, contentment rolled out of her and over him. This was better than any of the dreams before. The hatchling basked in it, a tiny thrumming deep in his throat answering her powerful one. They *prrum*ed to each other. The ground almost vibrated with the low, resonant thrumming.

Two other eggs stirred. One rolled into the other with a soft tap.

The shifted egg opened like a jagged-toothed mouth, and a

powerful red form spilled out. Its back legs outdrove its front, and it collapsed forward for a moment, jaw flat against the hard ground.

It squawked. He listened to the echoes and determined that they were in a confined space, but a very large one, and that a vast distance—to his few moments of experience—yawned behind, like his body, far longer than it was high.

The hatchling hardly noticed its smaller forelegs, its powerful neck, the clinging goo trailing from its rear limbs and bits of egg flying off its whipping tail. He had eyes only for its crest, a short rise of flattened horn sweeping back from its eyes.

Every instinct screeched: *Threat, threat, threat!*

The Red snorted liquid out of his nose. He opened his eyes and blinked. The tiny sharp spur crowning his nose turned toward the hatchling. The Red gathered himself, short flaps of armored skin behind his jawline rattling angrily against the base of his crest.

The hatchling found his own flaps answering the sound.

Tchkka-tchak tchkka-tchak tchkka-tchak!

The Red lowered his head and exploded toward him in a flash of glittering scales, mouth agape, fans wide and menacing.

He shifted to dodge him, but the clumsy new body didn't react the way it did in dreams. They reared up on hindquarters, claws scrabbling and mouths biting—

—suddenly they were suspended in space.

Falling, but not for long.

They hit hard, the hatchling atop the Red, the Red's crest striking first and absorbing much of the blow.

The hatchling brought up a rear limb and raked the Red's flank. When the Red shifted he bit, but his jaws closed on air as the Red lurched away.

The Red swung around, rushed him, used his weight to roll the Copper, got atop him. Bit down—

5

He put up his left forelimb to protect his neck, and the Red's jaws closed on it rather than his neck and they rolled again. They clawed and scratched at each other's scales. He tried to push the Red away and right himself. A tearing pain in his forelimb, and the Red tightened his grip, braced those massive rear haunches, and began to pull, jerking his head back and forth, rending muscle and joints as the hatchling squawked and tried to bite at the Red's neck.

Craack!

The hatchling didn't know what caused the Red to drop his limb. Then the Red jumped off him and climbed up, up, toward the eggs and another crested head.

The hatchling jumped after him—*no foe is getting away that easy!*—but he sprawled as he took his first step, hurt forelimb not where it should be. It seemed to be folding itself against his breast, claw turned inward.

He wobbled on three limbs and tried to climb, but fell on the first attempt. He heard high-pitched, angry cries from the vicinity of the eggs.

His second attempt at a climb went a little better, as he braced himself with his tail. But he fell again when he shifted his rear limbs and his tail slipped on the hot, wet liquid dripping from his limb.

The third time he used his jaws, gripping a projection with his teeth when his tail could no longer support his weight. Panting, he heaved himself over the edge, up among the eggs again.

His vision blurred a moment and he felt dizzy from the climb. When it cleared again . . .

The Red fought another hatchling, a slight gray thing compared to the Red's bulk. It had leathery skin rather than scales. The Red used his weight to upset the Gray and managed to get his jaws around the Gray's neck.

The hatchling saw his chance. He coiled and jumped, throwing himself on the Red's back with his powerful back limbs. He got his jaws around the Red's neck, where it was thinnest just under the jaw. . . .

The Red thrashed, used his weight to knock him over, and scrabbled. The hatchling bore down, feeling the Red's panting breath and pounding neck hearts through his teeth. . . .

The Red stiffened, every muscle in his body aquiver, and went limp. The hatchling closed his teeth on his throat, feeling the neck hearts rattle and die.

The hatchling went as limp as the Red.

Movement. The Gray was on his feet, facing him crest-to-crest.

Kill it! Kill and eat!

The Gray sidestepped to get around the corpse of the Red and rushed him, aiming straight for the bloody wound on his injured limb. The hatchling shifted to protect it, and the Gray drove his crest into his side, pushing, pushing. . . .

He squawked as he went over a second time, grabbed for the Gray, but the hatchling danced out of the way of his rear claw and he fell. . . .

Right on his bad forelimb.

The pain blinded him; it took him a moment to recover, and when he opened his eyes again he was alone at the base of the egg shelf, listening to more cracking sounds.

More?

He couldn't even beat the lighter Gray. Suppose another such as the Red . . . ?

But though he did not know it, he was the son of a powerful line, and his young hearts knew no despair. And he had his mother's wit still intact. He rested, gathering strength. He'd let the others weary themselves tearing one another to bits and then come up fresh. . . .

Except he felt so weak. He licked at his wounded limb, and the blood-tang left him both hungry and revolted.

No cries of battle greeted his ears. Maybe they were all bled out. He examined the wall to the egg shelf first, looked for an ascent with plenty of good grips.

This time, when he began to slip, he just tightened his grip and searched for a rest for his tail until he found the strength to climb on. He passed over the lip. . . .

Nothing. Just two sprawled green hatchlings, uncrested and therefore innocuous, digging into the corpse of the Red. The blood smell inflamed his appetite.

My victory! My feast!

Others enjoyed his kill. He jumped on the Red's corpse, claiming it, baring his teeth at the hapless Greens.

One, shorter of length and powerfully built like the Red, backed away. The other, longer and thinner even than the Gray, tripped, thrashed weakly.

Drive her away, his appetite roared.

He jumped on her, pushing, nipping her at the shoulder and hip points. She squeaked in alarm, pulled away.

He tore free a piece of fleshy tail she'd been gnawing at.

The other Green intervened with a growl, opening her jaws, glaring at him like the combative Red.

He caught a flash of motion off his weak side. It was the Gray again, bounding up from a trickle of water at the other end of the egg shelf.

The Green advanced, covering her sister with her own bulk.

He couldn't fight them both at once. He mouthed the chunk of tail and fled, finding he could use the elbow of his injured forelimb when running, though it pained him. He jumped back off the egg shelf. If they tried to jump down after him, he'd get them at a disadvantage when they alighted.

The Gray yapped down at him, but showed no sign of plunging to the cave floor. The Copper gnawed at the meaty tail, feeling the energy entering his bloodstream from the swallowed hunks of tissue.

The Gray's head disappeared, and the battle fury left the Copper. He felt cold, alone, and wandered over to the trickle and lapped a little water. He cooled his injured limb in the pool. Above, Mother started to sing. He crept closer so he could catch the end of the song:

. . . and the long years of dragonhood are sure to be thine.

He tried to climb up to the egg shelf, but failed, the pain in his throbbing limb overcoming him. He lay in the cold, hearing Mother's soft throat music, half song and half *prrum*.

He made one more attempt at the climb. Not to fight this time, but to be by Mother, safe and warm, wrapped in music and belly heat. Mother's great tail dropped over the edge and pushed him down. She looked down at him from the heights of her neck.

"No, little one, Auron has won the egg shelf. If you come up again he will kill you."

He tried to reply, but the only noises he seemed to be able to make were squeaks, not words. He tried, came close, tried again:

"Fwhy?"

"I'm sorry, hatchling. You are an outcast. You must learn to overcome on your own."

He huddled against the base of the egg shelf, cold and alone.

No pleasant dream, this.

Chapter 2

Loneliness was a constant companion to the outcast. Often hunger tagged along throughout the day, gnawing at him from belly to tail-tip, but hunger wandered off at night as he dreamed of warm, rich feasts. Loneliness would not be so easily seen off.

> *Only loneliness is mine to hold,*
> *Scale-edge sharp and dreadful cold.*

The outcast rhymed to himself, in imitation of the songs he heard from the egg shelf.

He made his first kill almost by accident. While sleeping, tucked into a crack lest the Gray attack him again with a pounce and a triumphant squawk, he felt an odd tickle at his tail. A wide, flat thing, rather like his tongue save for a questing projection that stuck up from its front—he knew the front judging by the direction it slurped—had touched his tail and recoiled.

He fell on it without really knowing what he was doing and tore it open as he landed. It still writhed, so he batted it about some more before biting off the head. It mindlessly crept down his throat, seeking tight, wet safety, and he instinctively swallowed.

It tasted vile and slimy, but filled his belly. He ate the other half and suffered no ill effects save for a hunger that came back all the fiercer for having once been assuaged.

Hunger drove him out into the cave when his belly sagged, empty, and loneliness forced him back to the crevices under the egg shelf.

He explored the cave from the egg shelf to the entrance hole, knew its drains and its hollows and its patches of shining green moss that brought light to the blackness, thriving on dragon waste and bat droppings.

Often he clung to the side of the egg shelf, straining to pick up mind-pictures from Mother as she taught the rest of her clutch. Stories, lessons, songs, rhymes, she bubbled like the trickle at the other end of the egg shelf whenever she didn't sleep.

The Gray was named Auron, he knew. His noisy sisters were Wistala and Jizara.

And then he met his father.

Father was a massive bronze mass, frightening in the quiet with which he moved. One moment the outcast was following a slug trail in the hope of another ephemeral meal of slug meat, and the next it seemed as though the cave wall had shifted next to him, a startling mass of sliding scales approaching the egg shelf.

He keened up at Father, tried to form words, sat up on his hindquarters and yapped until his head swam.

Father stared at his stiff, maimed limb, snorted, and continued his journey toward the egg shelf. He had to dodge Father's swinging tail by retreating into a crevice.

Of course, he and Mother began to discuss Auron, the Gray Rat. To the Copper his brother was rather like an oversized rat: quick, quiet, and vicious.

Thus the pattern of his days was set.

He managed a grubby sort of survival, living off slugs, rats, and the bit of hoof or tail that he could sometimes filch by sneaking up onto the egg shelf when the others were sleeping.

How he longed to join them, basking in Mother's heat!

Once he tried to settle up against them, under Mother's protective wing, but she began to shift and rumble and woke Auron. He had to scramble off the egg shelf, pursued by his brother's angry yaps.

He sat at the base of the egg shelf, picking up a stray mind-picture or two from Mother as she taught the others in dreams. He hugged the memory of Mother's attention at his hatching. Would it be too much for her to stretch her neck and give him a lick, breathe a few bars of one of the long songs she sang to him in the egg . . . ?

Tell him his name?

Little crying coughs escaped his body.

He learned to differentiate his sisters. Wistala was quick of tongue, Jizara long, elegant, and with a melodious voice.

He avoided Auron. The Gray seemed vulnerable, with a thick, pebbly skin instead of scales, but was fast and alert and hard to hear coming. And he was growing strong on what he and the sisters hunted and the choicest bits of whatever Father brought back.

But soon the Copper realized he only thought he knew unhappiness and longing.

It happened during one of Father's longer visits to the cavern. Every now and then he spent a period between hunting trips inspecting every nook and cranny with eyes, ears, and nose. Coming to a crack that the outcast knew contained nothing but dark, Father nevertheless stuck his nose deep inside and drew a long breath. He snorted out dirt and mucus.

"What do, Fazer?" the Copper said, greatly daring. The dragon-smell made his hearts pound against his skin.

The huge, six-horned head lifted and turned. "Ah. It's you."

Which wasn't much of an answer.

"What name I? I name how?"

"You're not of the nest, cripple. You don't need to be named. I'm not even sure you can be called a dragon in the lifesong."

That just made him miserable, and he lowered his head.

"That's no way to look, hatchling. You're unique, as far as my family memory goes. None of my line of sires ever saw a second male survive. You're not of the clutch, yet you're of our kind, and the cave's so big Auron can drive you away, but not out, so to speak. Neither scale nor claw, son nor stranger."

The Copper formed his next words carefully, and they came out better. "You my father. That prove me your son!"

"You may be lame in body, but your wit's quick enough. That's your mother speaking with your tongue. If you've got her brains, I expect you'll survive at least until you leave the cave."

"To light?" The Copper knew that tidbit from egg-dreams.

"Yes. The Upper World is a dangerous place, and your wings are still a full clawset of winters off. Look at your scales! Poor little blighter. You need a bellyful of coin. Follow me."

The Copper almost danced in Father's wake, the dragon's dangerous smell no longer terrifying but thrilling. Father approached a small ledge, descended, and approached a heavy stone resting in a small sink. A dead trickle of water was thick with dried dark moss.

Father grasped the stone with his front *sii* and wrestled it out of the rock.

"I've been meaning to give the girls some play-pretties. But you need something more substantial. Can't do more; there's little enough as it is."

He stuck his head down the hole, and the Copper smelled something he'd never experienced before: an aroma hard and rich and metallic. He felt his scales bristle and his *griff* descend and flutter against his jaw and neck, giving a faint rattle.

Father's head came back up. His eyes burned.

"Indeed, little enough! Why should I part with any to a wretched nothing? Cripple! Outcast!"

The Copper backed up, half-terrified and half-furious. The gold smell made him want to leap and claw.

Father tilted his head back and forth as though gauging distance; then he suddenly relaxed. "Serves me right for depriving myself." He swallowed something that clinked. Then his bristling scale relaxed and he gave a brief, satisfied *prrum*. He reached down again and spit out a few gold and silver coins, thick with slime.

"That's to get you started. All there'll be, I'm afraid, unless I get lucky."

The Copper sniffed a silver disk. He needed its light, its brightness. His mouth went thick and wet all over. He gobbled it down, and then the others, quickly, as though they were a nest of rats about to escape.

Father's feet stamped restlessly.

"I suppose no harm's done. Auron won't need it, after all." Father exhaled in a whoosh that flattened the Copper's scale. "Maybe we'll have better luck with males in another clutch."

The Copper smelled more gold down the hole. He hurried toward it, following the smell, which seemed to have seized hold of his brain.

The boulder came down, and he ran nose-first into it.

"A dragon must win his own hoard, outcast," Father said, moving off toward the egg shelf.

Chapter 3

The Gray Rat and he made a sort of peace. The Gray kept to his hunting perches, keeping an eye out for slugs, and as long as the Copper avoided the usual spots they'd go long stretches without seeing each other. Wistala, the chatterer, seemed always to be talking to her mother or brother or sister, and was the most successful hunter.

Of course, they were usually hunting the best spots, so the Copper had to make do with trying to catch the white, long-whiskered cave rats in the offal pile while the others slept. They were smart, quick, and vicious, and to get on he had to be smarter, quicker, and even more vicious. He tried piling bones and loose rocks in such a way that they loomed over a juicy bit of dragon-waste, then toppling them when he heard noises in the pile, but he found that the rats would worm through the bones and hooves easier than if he tried to catch them on the hop.

He found that if he smeared himself first with slime from the receding pools and then with dragon-waste, they couldn't smell him, thanks to the wet, and would often get within a jump's distance. But he learned an enervating lesson when he overhunted the garbage pile, for the rats quit coming. He took to visiting it only after the other hatchlings ate something Father brought back, for sometimes they missed a tail or an ear or a bit of marrow. Then he hunted the pile with an appetite that would have taken many, many rats to fill, but took away only one or two for all the filth and bother.

Of course, this necessitated a good deal of washing afterward.

While scrubbing off after one meal he heard a high, pleasant trilling coming from the egg shelf above. The words and tune warmed him like the sunlight he dreamed of. The running, splashing water devoured the words, so he climbed up the egg shelf and peeked over.

Farther down the egg shelf, almost out of the mosslight, his mother slumbered, and he saw the tail of the Gray Rat wrapped around her tail-tip. Wistala's nose peeped from under Mother's tail.

The longer and thinner of his two sisters lay across the trickle, arching her back in the water cascading down the side of the cave, warbling to herself:

> Paint my wings, as a stranger in paradise,
> Take me not from the city's light,
> through white towers I long to soar . . .

"Oh," she squeaked, seeing him. She shrank against the cave wall.

"Why did you stop?" he asked.

"Do you want to use the trickle?"

"Use it?"

"The cascade. It's marvelous for cleaning under the scales, especially that bit that falls all the way from the ceiling."

"Your name is Jizara," he said, marveling at how easily the word formed in his mouth.

"That's just for songs and such. Zara rolls off the tongue so much easier. You don't speak very well. I suppose you don't get much chance for talking."

"Will you sing more?" He felt the clumsiness of his words.

She uncoiled a little. "You like my singing?"

"It's beautiful." He edged up on the other side of the trickle.

She turned a little deeper green as her scales rose and fell. "You won't . . . you won't jump on me?"

"Why should I?"

"Auron does it all the time."

It felt so good to talk, he was wondering if he wanted a song to interrupt. "I'll stay on this side of the trickle."

"What do you want to hear?" she finally asked.

"What was that you were singing before?"

"A song of Silverhigh, the ancient. They made such beautiful songs. I can only sing them when I'm alone."

"Why?"

"You sound just like Auron! Mother said it was a wicked place full of foolish dragons."

"But they made beautiful songs. Sing."

She went on, and he found himself relaxing, joint by joint, claw by claw, lulled by the music. Then he was asleep.

He woke in glorious warmth. Jizara lay wrapped right around him, nose-tip to tail-point. But then she had an extraordinarily long neck.

A golden eye opened. She yawned. "You're rather small. Almost like a new hatchling of my own," she said. "You fell asleep, so I came over to your side." She looked away. "Oh, Mother is stirring. I'd better get back. She gets angry when we wander while she sleeps."

"When will you sing to me again?" he asked.

She retreated from the intensity of his words, jumping across the trickle. "I don't know. A day? Another day after that?"

Why couldn't she be more precise? *Day* had no real meaning in the Lower World. "I'll wait for you."

"And I'll sing for you, brother. A-la, now."

Her voice calling him *brother* settled in his head like a mother dragon on an egg perch.

He lurked about the base of the egg shelf too much, waiting for her to return, growing even hungrier. They met twice more, but one hardly counted, for Auron woke and the Copper had to run as soon as he saw him stretching his neck. After each meeting he hugged the moments to himself, played them in his mind so it seemed they'd never parted. They had played a game as they talked, trying to mirror their tail-tips, and he would go to his pool and play against himself, pretending the vague reflection was his sister.

Sister. Brother. Such lovely words to a lonely little dragon.

But the fourth time he saw her, she looked down into the water between them and wouldn't meet his eyes.

"I'm not to sing to you anymore," she said.

He was shocked into speechlessness. Everything appeared as usual at the other end of the egg shelf, Mother apparently asleep—

"You're nameless. Outcast."

He found his voice. "Zara, you are all I have."

"She says that if I truly care for you, I'll do this and you'll go up out of the cave on your own and find more food and grow strong. Don't you see how weak you are? You look positively hag-ridden. You've no chance at metals. Your scales are thin as an eyelid!"

A glubbing sound came out when he tried to reply.

"Mother says Auron is growing. He may kill you in an attempt to drive you out of the cave."

"I hate being alone! I'd rather die."

"Mother has a message for you."

"She does?"

"She told me that you can overcome this. You've got a gift, in a way, a chance to establish your own line. A whole new family of dragons, all tracing their songs back to you! Not even Auron has that. Go, and maybe one day we'll meet again in the Upper World."

Chapter 4

He lingered in the cave, however, keeping to the edges, avoiding the others. Once or twice he ventured up the passage Father used on his hunting trips, but they smelled of old dragonblood, and he found broken pieces of scale.

He was tempted to try eating it for the metals it contained, but the smell disgusted him and he wondered what the sharp edges would do to his insides.

The trickles of the cavern dried up into practically nothing, and the slugs ceased roaming. He became hungrier than ever— his appetite grew and thrived and seemed to tap insistently at the backs of his eyes, and he worried the edges of his claws with sharp little teeth, pulling up dead skin until he bled.

He drank and bathed at a little pool in a far corner of the cavern. Once it had been fed by a fall that made the trickle on the egg shelf seem like a rainy bit of nothing, but now even the cascade had dried to a thick dampness on the cave wall.

While licking at it one day he noticed air moving around a projection. Even better, the air carried with it the smell of slugs.

He squeezed around the rock and found a crack, a jagged projection that narrowed at the bottom like a claw. Some water trickled from the bottom, carrying a more definite slug smell. He wormed through the crack and heard a few loose scales—it seemed all his scales were loose these days—fall into the water.

19

The air in here was wetter, and the cave moss still grew thickly in a ring around the pool, offering some light and playing on the bubbles that popped up now and then through the pool, which had spongy pads growing on the surface. He saw slugs squeezing themselves between rocks and under the pads and fell on them, and upset one of the pads in his thrashing.

The other side of the pad held little white spheres, clustered together so it was hard to tell where one began and the next ended. He sniffed them and they smelled delicious.

He tried swallowing one and almost immediately felt better. Eggs! They were probably slug eggs; they certainly smelled like the slugs. He devoured six more before he remembered how he had overhunted the rats in the offal pile. *Eat up too many eggs and there'll be no slugs. . . .*

He tongued down two more anyway, and let out a soft burp. His blood flowed with new life.

He watched the water flow into the pool from a crack at a slightly higher level, less of a waterfall than a water step, and a little flowed out into "his" pool on the other side of the crack. The volume coming in and the volume going out seemed out of balance; a torrent came in but a trickle flowed out.

Of course—the bubbles. Water was going down, as it always did, and air wandered up, each always looking for company of its own kind.

He dove, followed the bubbles, hoping for another chamber with more slug eggs to raid. Though so little light filtered down that it was the next thing to black, he couldn't get lost; the bubbles would guide him back up. He found another shelf, with the bubbles gathering momentarily before sliding up and out.

But a distinct glow came, not from the source of the bubbles, but from deeper within the shelf. He swam toward it, his whole body moving in an easy, back-and-forth manner, though the cold made his hearts beat hard.

Then the light burned above him and he rose.

The pool top had more of the spongy pad growths, but only partially covering the pool, like a half-closed eye. He grabbed onto one of the pad stalks to arrest his rise and stuck his nose out among the pads.

Instinct made him take a small, cautious nostrilful. The air smelled good. He half emptied his lungs and drew in fresh air, then examined the scents of the room. He smelled mosses and some slug trail and rats and a strange rich, dry smell and dirt and a dirtier, sweaty smell, like horse hoof and ... *metal*!

He took three more breaths and found some more slug eggs under the pads. Then he risked popping the ridge of his head up.

Cave moss, brighter than any growths he'd ever seen, lit the room from a big mound next to the pool. The chamber was shaped rather like a dragon's head and neck, with the pool resting at neck level, a high rise above that had air moving up it, and then it seemed to narrow off in one direction, like his snout. The pool next to the chamber had been cleared of the spongy pads, and a metal tube like his own neck rose out of the pool and turned at the top.

The metal came from what looked like flats and pits carved into the stone. The artificially straight lines on the metal and the worked stone set off some inner alarm.

Go back. This is not for you.

But the maddening, metallic smell made his mouth go thick and slimy. He had to find it.

He swam across the pool and heard rat claws *scritch* as he rose dripping from the water, sniffing and listening. The passage led off downward, narrowing even further. The sounds of anything coming up it would be forced in a single direction toward him, and he'd have plenty of warning, so he relaxed a little.

The metallic column rising from the water smelled delicious, but was too big to swallow. It made a loop above and turned back down over a big stonework hollow. It had a vaguely greasy smell to it, like food.

Strange, fashioned objects of a rough, dry, wholesome-smelling substance—*wood*, some old memory echo told him—held growth of some kind. The wood had bits of metal embedded into it.

Ah, here's the metal. And here. And here.

The flats and pits of the chamber had bits of metal, some with wooden handles, many of them redolent of meats and scorching, and even better, a few were small enough to be swallowed. He found a hollow tube sealed at one end, the same color as his scales, and found that if he stood on it he could crush it. He folded it in half and smashed it down again—he enjoyed compacting the metal more than he'd enjoyed anything since listening to Zara sing—and soon he had it in a shape that could fit down his throat.

Most satisfying.

Now food.

Where the moss grew thickly there was a garbage pile so rich in tidbits it felt like a gift. He broke up a few bones and extracted the marrow, found several chunks of rat-gnawed gristle and delicious, charred skins with the hair conveniently burned down to a stubble.

Now, this is a feast worthy of a dragon!

With nothing but some gassy burps to keep him company, he explored a pit where some kind of fire had burned recently and found more wooden holders, some with metal bands. He decided the vaguely greasy, dirty smell was some manner of hominid. Didn't dwarves spend a lot of time tunneling and mining?

He heard a clattering echo from deep down the passage and decided to leave the chamber, filching one more tube of metal on his way out. He'd have fun flattening and devouring it later.

———

While hunger gnawed at him back in the home cave, he argued with himself about going back. Certainly the metals he'd eaten would be missed, and the dwarves, if they were dwarves, would be put on their guard.

He visited the cave a second time, and lurked long in the pool before emerging. He spent most of the time rooting in the garbage heap and hunting rats. He very much doubted the dwarves would miss a few rats. He did find a single coin, fallen and rolled into a shadow behind one of the wooden boxes, and gobbled it eagerly. Coins were a perfect size to slide comfortably down a hatchling's gullet.

But the metallic tang nagged at him, wanting company. He worked one of the metal talons driven into the wood loose with his teeth—there were so many others he didn't see how one would be missed.

Since the second trip went so well he planned a third, though he waited what felt like ages, just in case. He kept himself in practice hunting up slugs. The trickles into the egg chamber increased day by day—evidently the dry period above was ending. The other hatchlings had all grown substantially, ranging over almost the whole cave now, and he couldn't avoid them with his usual paths. Luckily he could hear Wistala, for she was always talking to Jizara.

Quick, quiet Auron was something else entirely. The Gray Rat almost killed him with a pounce and chased him all the way across the egg cavern, and the Copper had to dive into the rising pool to escape him by wiggling through the crack, now underwater again.

Auron wasn't satisfied with having Mother and Zara and the chatterer and food and Father's horded gold. Rich in everything, he wanted even the lightless edges and holes and cold corners of the egg cave.

But Auron had a weakness, and in his arrogance didn't see his own faults. The Gray Rat had no scales. If the Copper could build up his strength a little, thicken his scales, he could close with Auron and take back the clutch.

The thought made his fire bladder boil.

With the waters rising again it meant a little longer swim to the treasure chamber. He took extra time smelling the air and certainly smelled no dwarves, though there was a dirtier scent, of the kind he associated with bits brought down from the Upper World.

The garbage pile had some meaty tidbits, and he lingered at the edge of the pool, ready for a fast dive, slowly nosing drier garbage aside while he extracted the meaty joints.

Then he smelled the silver.

It wasn't a strong smell, and leather masked the aroma. He investigated next to the benches and cubbyholes—they smelled of the recently cooked meat—listening, always listening, and probing with eye and ear before he placed a foot.

The silver-and-leather smell came from pegs driven into a wooden wall hung with bits of woven fabric, most of which smelled like either grease or charcoal. Farther down the tunnel were stacks of fragrant wood, and many roots and herbs hung up and drying—perhaps the dwarves were replenishing supplies as the season changed above.

He found the source of the enticing smell. A leather bag containing a few coins—copper, silver, and even a faint aroma of gold—hung there. The top had some kind of binding on it, evidently to close it, and had been left loose, allowing the smell of coin to escape.

The Copper salivated. The dwarf would pay for his forgetfulness. . . .

He nosed the bag off the peg.

Ka-thunk!

The peg, relieved of the coin's weight, sprang up in its wooden slot.

Hairy masses of rope engulfed him. Festoons dropped from the cave roof, weighted with chains, and his eyesight went white as one of them struck him across the snout. The boxes to either side exploded open, throwing more lines that sprang from them. He felt weights and hooks and slick little circles of metal skittering across the floor.

When his eyesight returned he saw shadows all around, their beards glowing faintly. He felt tugs at his limbs as they attached lines.

He'd never been so terrified. His hearts felt as though they'd burst out of his chest or from behind his *griff*. Auron's leaps and sudden pins were nothing to this.

One was trying to extract the purse from his mouth, grunting as he pulled. The Copper sawed at the purse strings and the dwarf fell back. Defiantly, he swallowed the silver. The dwarves might win a three-limbed hatchling, but they'd lose their silver.

The dwarves made noises that all seemed to be some variety of *yak* or *grumt* or *phmumph*.

They drove metal claws into the rocks and tied him, snout and tail, and set bands of leather about his limbs. A massive dwarf with an ax watched the whole thing, gurgling to his companions, ready to sever his head if he wiggled free.

But the dwarvish hands seemed made of rock and iron, and he was soon covered with their greasy smell.

Then the beatings began.

They took iron bars and smashed them against his vulnerable pinioned tail. The pain ran up his body, fired in each digit, sparked yellow in his eye sockets, whirled about his organs so that each breath brought agony.

He whimpered; he cried; he sent mind-pictures begging them to stop.

That pain was nothing to what came when they stopped, gave him time to sleep and heal, and then started in on his tail again. During the second beating his teeth came together and tore at mouth edge and tongue until he spit blood.

Even through the pain a clarity took over and he wondered at the dwarves. *What sort of creatures cause pain just for the sake of pain?* There was no contest for control of a cavern, and they weren't killing him to eat him. The torture was its own end.

By the third beating the pain wasn't so bad, just dull warmth with the occasional jolt, like a fading cramp.

He heard a heavy step and shifted his body, felt scales give way. His skin had stuck to the floor with his own dried blood.

He did his best to tuck his tail. It moved clumsily, stiff and heavy, unable to curl. He rolled an eye upward, saw a vague sort of shadow, a hominid huge and dark looming above. The hominid smelled of dogs.

The tall one grunted and turned away, almost as an afterthought giving him a swiping kick to the nose with the side of his heel. Pain shot across both eyes.

A warbling broke out, and another hominid fell to its—no, her—knees in front of him. Her flat face was scarred on one side, and she wore an eye patch. A light brown eye, with just a touch of Mother's gold and a hint of green, looked into his.

"Oh, how they've hurt you, young one," she said in intelligible Drakine. "Poor thing."

His hearts woke to the words, the sympathy of her tone, even if the Drakine was nasal and harsh. She reached out and rubbed him between the eyes. If his snout hadn't been tied shut, he would have brushed her with the tip of his tongue, so grateful was he for the sympathy.

"Worthless little scut," the tall, broad, dog-scented man said in far worse Drakine. He lifted his boot again, and the Copper shut his eyes.

The one-eyed one interposed her body, and he noticed that she had leaves in her hair. That should mean something, he felt, but the aches in his body kept whatever vestigial memories he'd received in the egg deep and dark.

"The dwarves blame you for the crimes of your parents," she whispered. "They've been hunting a very wicked pair, a bronze and his mate, who've betrayed and stolen from the dwarves. Dwarves will move mountains to reclaim their own, if you don't know."

She looked at her companion, off on the other side of the tunnel talking to the dwarves. One leaned on one of the iron rods they'd used to beat him. Another, more potbellied than the rest, pulled at his dim-glowing beard as the man spoke, making noncommittal *hmpf* sounds at the pauses. The tall man unrolled some kind of map, and the potbellied dwarf sneezed.

"I don't hold with blaming offspring for the crimes of their parents, do you?"

He hesitated a moment before answering. Was it wise to talk to a . . . a . . . leaf-hair? *Elf!* So satisfied was he that he had finally summoned the name that he croaked, "No."

The elf showed her teeth when he answered, even though the word was muffled by the binding about his snout.

The tall man came over and talked to the other in their unknown barking tongue. Casually, while he spoke, he brought his heel down on the Copper's tail. The agony made him whimper and writhe, and the elf finally pushed him away.

She yelled at the others until they shrank away from her fury. If only Mother had been this protective of her own hatchling.

Then she knelt beside him again. "Little one, I'm here hunting hatchlings. The dwarves have a buyer willing to pay a princely sum for healthy males or females. That was your sire's bargain with the dwarves, a set of eggs in exchange for much gold and silver. But they reneged and fled.

"I know dragons. I suspect you were driven out of the nest by the stronger male. Let me capture your brother and sisters, if any, and I'll see to it you get enough copper—silver even—to stuff yourself for a year."

She reached into a bag on her belt and extracted some coins and let him sniff. Even in his shattered and weakened state, the smell turned his mouth slick.

She put the coins back, looked at the others. The man approached, drawing a long sword, an evil carved blade extending from the wide-open jaws of a dragon.

"Some king and queen of dragons, this hatchling's sires," the man said. "If my babe disappeared from his home, I'd drag the sky down into the deepest corners of the earth to find him."

The elf snarled something to him in their tongue.

He ignored her. "Just what you'd expect from dragons, leaving their hatchling in the hands of some vengeful dwarves. I'll take his *griff* as a trophy and the dwarves can finish him."

Another dwarf picked up an iron rod.

"No!" the elf protested in Drakine. The Copper would wonder, much later, how and where she learned the tongue. Even hate himself for not being suspicious at their use of Drakine in their arguments. "I can make a bargain with him. Even the dwarves will accept a bargain."

She turned to him, caressed him under the chin. "Little one, you must let me help you. Show me to the egg shelf. We'll take your brother and siblings. They'll be well treated and prized by their eventual owner, and the feud between your parents and the dwarves will be over. You'll have the egg shelf."

The Copper didn't care what they did with his brother. Or the chatterer—they could drag them both off, for all he cared. But Jizara . . .

"I have two sisters," he said. "One goes. One stays. Her name is Jizara; she's got the longer neck and tail. She stays."

The elf's eye widened and he saw her teeth again. She barked at the others. The potbellied dwarf lowered his face and stamped, then grunted something in return.

"Bargain!" she said, and untied his jaws.

The Copper felt better than he had since the first iron-rod blow to his tail. In all likelihood Mother and Father would kill these wretched, torturing dwarves. Even if they didn't, the Gray Rat would be dragged off and have his snout tied. As for the chatterer, she could do with a bit of enforced quiet. He almost smiled at the thought.

Mother told me to overcome. She left out any details of how to do it.

After he told her how to find the home cave, she gave him a purse full of silver pieces to seal the bargain.

Chapter 5

Their plan had the virtue of simplicity. The dwarves would storm the egg shelf, restrain Mother with holding poles, and bind up his siblings.

They showed him the straps and poles and snout cage that would be used on Mother, yet worms of regret were wiggling at the back of his mind. But they gave him no chance to escape, keeping chains on him from the point where he swam through the underwater tunnel with a guideline for the dwarves to the moment tunnelers arrived to widen the cracks.

The dwarves lit their way with hissing firework torches that burned bright blue even underwater and created a minichamber from a polished shell as big as a dragon's head. They cleverly fed the air bubble within the shell with a pair of leather hoses worked by bellows back at the scullery, constantly substituting good air for bad.

The trick, as the Copper saw it, was to have the dwarves make off with Auron and Wistala the chatterbox. If a few of the rod-carrying *poghti* got burned in the process, so much the better.

He thought he knew how.

All three of the other hatchlings explored and hunted within the egg cavern. Auron always scurried around over a wide range, Wistala had a few predictable perches where slugs were likely to pass, and Jizara kept closer to Mother and the garbage pile.

He could take care of Auron. Thanks to the dwarves' meals and generous amounts of metal, his new scales were coming in thick and fast. He could tell the dwarves where to find Wistala, then immobilize Auron somewhere far from the egg shelf—but not too far to be heard—and scare him into trumpeting a warning. The dwarves would not be so foolish as to attack an alerted dragon, and at the first sign of alarm Wistala would certainly hide by Mother.

So pleased was he with the plan, he found himself giving off a slight *prrum*.

The day finally came. They timed it with Father leaving on a hunt.

He met the dwarves and the missing-eyed elf in the now dry chamber behind the waterfall. The dwarves had cleverly diverted the water into a metal tube that carried it off down the cavern of the scullery, save for a little leaking that dropped into a bubbling pool.

Tunnel dwarves were marking the wall behind the waterfall with chalk, muttering quietly to others who carried spikes and hammers.

Behind them warrior dwarves gathered with their holding poles and lines and straps, the potbellied dwarf at the front. Eye Patch, looking tired and smelling of wood smoke from the Upper World, stood off to one side, armed only with a small knife at her belt.

The Copper was rather relieved that the big, cruel man who liked to step on his broken tail was absent. There'd been some talk, he was told, about having a guard outside the cavern in the event Father returned unexpectedly. Perhaps he was in the Upper World. *The farther off, the better*. Once the bargain was struck, the dwarves had become elaborately polite to him, always bowing and tossing him greasy half-eaten joints of lamb or broken old bits of metal. But that man . . . Every time he stared

31

down into the Copper's eyes with those cold, unfeeling round eyes, his *griff* fluttered nervously.

The man meant to kill him. What was holding him back? He doubted even Eye Patch or the dwarves could stop him—even if they wanted to.

And he smelled like dogs. Dog smell awoke an ancient fear in the Copper. In any case, it was time for a few last words. He'd have the egg shelf and his sister at last, or be dead.

"I keep my bargain. Two hatchlings," he said, using a re-hearsed speech in the Dwarvish that Eye Patch—for he never learned her name—had taught him.

The potbellied dwarf started at that. Eye Patch chuckled to herself and said some lilting words to the dwarf, who grumbled into his beard.

"He says no good's ever come from teaching others Dwarvish," Eye Patch said in her bad Drakine.

"Tell him I'm going into the cavern now. I'll come back in a moment."

Eye Patch translated: "He says you'd better, or he'll skin you personally."

He squeezed out through the cracks—just—and swam across the pool. The egg cavern seemed vast now, a great ex-panse filled with comforting smells but doubtful shadows and the echoes of the waterfall. He returned to the dwarves and gave them that strange up-and-down waggle of the head that homi-nids used.

The dwarves began to tap at their chalk marks, timing their strikes to the splashes outside. The work went fast, as it always did when the dwarves had a plan to follow. They spent a good deal of time before and after each job arguing amongst them-selves in their glottal tongue, but when in action together they were swift and efficient.

He slipped back out through the crack and felt his hearts

hammering. He found a patch of dark well away from the now thriving cave moss and waited, every nerve alert.

Auron passed soon enough, sniffing as he hunted. The Copper fell in behind his rival, stopping when he stopped, moving when he moved. Auron paused for a taste of water at the waterfall pool and cocked his head in that odd way of his, listening. He slipped into the water. He'd heard the dwarves tapping!

Clever, my brother.

But not as clever as I.

Auron would head for the egg shelf; he was sure of it. He positioned himself on a low ridge of stalagmites at an alley the Gray Rat would use. . . .

The cave wall fell away, almost silently, toppling inward into netting the dwarves had ready to receive it. Auron hurried from the pool, swimming like an arrow toward Mother.

He mustn't reach the egg shelf or things would go ill. The Copper would terrify Auron into screaming his unprotected lungs out!

The Copper jumped, landing full-weight on his brother's scaleless back. Mother's green gleam could just be seen in the distance.

"Got you! Death has come for you, softling," he hissed in Auron's ear.

The Gray Rat protested, clawed uselessly at the Copper's scales as he whined about intruders. The Copper bit him in the soft tissue behind the *griff* to shut him up. He gave the rehearsed speech, but couldn't help pouring a little extra resentment into it:

"I've lived in hunger and hiding since the day I came out of the shell, thanks to you. So you'll die now, as you should have died out of the egg. Two brothers, both stronger, and you ended up with the nest. It's time to right a great wrong. Nearly time, that is. First you get to watch Mother and the chatterer skinned.

Stop writhing, you lizard—you're worse than a snake! Too bad you won't see me gorge myself on Father's gold."

He let the Gray Rat have a good look at Mother. He'd call out a warning and—

Blinding pain flashed up from his snout, and his vision burned white. He lurched away from the pain and Auron wriggled free. He bit at where he sensed his brother stood and got only air, and when he could see again, he and Auron were snapping at each other.

Why wasn't the fool screaming out a warning to Mother? The dwarves would be on him any moment! What did he have to say to get the Gray Rat to shriek out a warning? He heard a splashing and a clatter behind—the dwarves were gathering.

Auron wasted more time in speech making: "You live this day if you trouble me no further. Though when I tell Father of this, he may feel differently. He'll pull the mountains down to find such as you, who'd lead assassins to the egg shelf."

The words hurt almost as much as the tail-crack. Auron spun and hurried off toward the egg shelf at a dash, finally sounding a warning. A thrown net just missing as his brother ran.

Well, the dwarves would have to deal with that. He'd smelled his sister around somewhere; if he could find her he could hold her down until the dwarves could get a loop around her snout.

He turned and saw the dwarves advancing, widely spaced across the egg cavern.

Behind them he saw a gleaming helmet, two upraised wings, and polished black scale—dragonscale!—about the shoulders. The huge man was down here after all, carrying a spear that glowed and sparked like a log in the concentrated heat of a dwarf hearth.

What was this? The dwarves weren't carrying restraining poles and ropes. Instead they bore great bowed machines balanced across their broad backs, two carrying the bulk with another lifting the fletched end. Others had climbing ladders and spears, spears, and more spears, each with a thick crossbar to keep a pinioned dragon from pulling itself down the shaft toward the wielder.

He marked Wistala climbing toward a hole in the cavern roof above the egg shelf. Mother flung Auron up after her, then nosed at Jizara.

But Jizara stared out across the cavern, met his eyes.

Brother! Look out for the dwarves! We must escape!

The dwarves ignored him as they charged—later he thought it would have been kinder if one had split his skull with one of the broadaxes they carried across their backs—and he searched for Eye Patch. Where was she? He saw the potbellied dwarf, hanging on to the top of a stalagmite, giving orders and pointing with a gnarled bit of polished wood.

The Copper ran up to him, flung himself down.

"Spare the one on the shelf. My sister! My sister!"

The dwarf stepped on his neck. "Hmpf. You don't want to see this."

Ka-thun! Ka-thun!—the metal-and-wood contraptions of the dwarves launched their missiles, exploding into motion and dying a moment later, purpose served.

The dwarves yelled as they stormed toward the egg shelf in a rattle of metal—chain shirts rustling, shields banging, helm flanges rattling on shoulder plates, metal-spiked boots striking the cavern floor, and above all the *kuu-kuuu-kuuuu!* of the dwavrish war cries.

It sounded like the end of the world.

The big man went forward in a series of leaps, springing from prominence to prominence and jumping over formations the Copper had to climb. A flood of dogs led him, and more warriors of his kind followed behind, aiming thick arrows notched in curved bows like half-folded dragon wings.

The Copper smelled the brassy, hot-oil smell of dragonfire, heard the roar of flame devouring air. The shadows of the cave began to dance.

"In there under it, my lads. That's the style!" the dwarf-lord grunted. At least, that was what it seemed to the Copper he was saying, though how he caught the meaning without knowing the words he could not say.

The Copper heard his mother roar, and the sound made him tremble.

"Spare my sister!" the Copper squeaked.

The dwarf looked down. "Poor wretch. We'll not bleed her a drop. She's worth a lot to us. Now what passes? Dogluk, hold him."

The potbellied dwarf hurried toward the egg shelf, and the Copper scrambled up a stalagmite.

Mother lay on her side, chest heaving, neck and chest pierced by great shafts that showed feathers at one bleeding hole and gory barbed heads at the other. Her head still moved weakly, one golden eye rolling this way and that, bathed in fire leaking from her breastbone.

"You have won this battle, Gobold," she said to the dwarf. "But I keep a last trick. The war is not over. My young live. And they are free. Free!"

The potbellied dwarf walked over to her, laughing. "Your young? One of them led us to you. Don't look to your young. Greedy and selfish, like all dragons." The one she'd called Gobold struck her across the mouth with first one fist, then the other.

Mother spit out a broken tooth.

"They will avenge this day!"

The potbellied dwarf laughed and, still laughing, swung his ax and struck her in the neck. By the third blow his boots were awash in blood, his stout helm, beard, and arms splotched red.

The Copper's hearts ceased beating for a moment and he swooned.

A mass of dwarves, men, and dogs crowded on the egg shelf, embracing one another and letting blood from Mother's wounds run into their helmets, which they then passed around and drank. Dogs, wild with excitement, chased from wound to wound, sniffing, biting her where she still twitched.

Men stood, holding nets over Jizara with heavy boot heels. His sister lay frozen in terror, eye whites bright in the cave's gloom. The Copper wanted to fling himself down atop her, protect her, but the smell of dragonblood in the air had him clinging tight-bellied to the cave floor.

The big man came forward, his dragon-jaw blade out and ready. He stepped up to Jizara, glanced over his shoulder at the dwarves dancing and stamping about Mother's corpse.

"Mercy," Jizara gasped.

The big man laughed. "Nits make lice," he said in his rough Drakine.

He pushed his blade slowly into her throat, twisting it this way and that, and, whimpering, Jizara died.

Fiends!

A dwarf dragged him back by his battered tail, but the pain was nothing to the insensate anger flooding his hearts. A howl broke from his throat, every agony he'd suffered since the moment of his hatching gathered into a single scream.

Fiends!

A dwarf stood on his neck. The dwarf called another over, and they bound him in the leather strapping they used to bear their war machines.

The dwarves took up a chant. The Copper heard thwacks and chunks as they employed their axes, and then he heard a strange, high-pitched sound as some blew air through tubes.

Then the singing dwarves marched back out of the cavern,

bearing their wounded and trophies wrapped in salty-smelling fabric on litters made of their spears. He smelled dragonblood everywhere.

One of the men pointed and there was some talk, but Gobold broke away from the others and grabbed the Copper by the crest and lifted his head. The Copper shut his eyes at what was coming. . . .

But instead Gobold spoke, and again, strangely, he understood: "No. This feud started over bargains not being kept. Let none say Gobold—"

The dwarves called out at that; others clapped and stamped their feet or rattled their knives in their sheaths. The Copper struggled against his bonds, wanting to sink his claws into the dwarf's fleshy gut.

"Well, Fangbreaker, then. Let none say Fangbreaker is not true to his word. Or his threats."

Gobold the Fangbreaker let go of his crest. "Besides, he's worthless in trade. That foreleg's useless, and his tail's shattered. The cavern and its treasures are yours, O prince of dragons!" He laughed and slapped his belly. "The honor and glory of this day is yours." He bowed. "Enjoy."

The dwarf hurried off to join the others in their march.

Next the men left, leading their dogs—dried dragonblood made the curs' hair pointy—with the big man in his black armor carrying his spear across his shoulder, a bloody dragon ear dangling from each end.

The big man paused the march by the bound hatchling. He stared down at him, the gruesome flat face working obscenely as he thought.

The Copper felt his fire bladder pulse. He managed to spew a little yellow stream of sulfurous saliva across the dragonscale-covered boot.

The man chuckled. "That's more like it," he said in his

rough, uninflected Drakine. "I'm your enemy. You may as well know my name. I'm called the Dragonblade. Know that I did all this—with your help."

Why didn't the man end the misery? Strike off his head, obliterate each bloody memory, the horror of what he had done . . .

"If you're my enemy, why don't you kill me as well?"

Perhaps the man sensed his torment, decided to leave him with the pain, alone in a cavern with the stripped bodies of his family. He just adjusted the burden across his broad back and called something out to his companions.

"Will you not kill me?" Some little flicker within him still wanted to live, then, for he waited for an answer.

The man expelled a long breath. "You should be wiped out. Bestial. Craven. Look at you. You sold your birthright for a mouthful of silver. The sooner the last remnants of the tyrant-wings are gone, the better for the world.

"Besides, I slay only dragons." He set down his spear and drew his long sword. The Copper shut his eyes again, and he felt a sharp tap along his back. Then a throbbing agony flared, worse with each beat of his synchronized hearts.

"Farewell, worm."

The Copper opened his eyes and saw a jagged rent next to his spine. Exposed meat and bone gleamed among torn scale. It hurt worse than the battering his tail had taken. He took a cautious breath—his lungs were still intact, though it hurt to breathe. The man had crippled his dormant left wing!

Chapter 6

He panted in his binding, pain plaguing both body and spirit. He lay there for a long time, thinking slow, dark, wounded thoughts as his blood thickened across his back.

Mother had told him once to overcome difficulties. How did one overcome oneself? Self-destruction?

Hunger saved him, hunger and the sound of squeaking rats. He heard them moving toward the egg shelf.

He wiggled his head around and began to chew at his bindings. He bent as he reached for the straps on his *saa* and incautiously brushed his back wound against the cave floor, white-hot agony leaving him quivering for a moment, and when he came out of the hurt his brain took a moment to remember where he was. He forced his head between his *sii* and tore through the back bindings.

That done, he lay for a moment, too weak to do anything but breathe.

He crawled toward the egg shelf and saw a ghastly heap atop it, the end of a severed neck dangling off the egg shelf, cave moss in a tiny splash of light where the blood had pooled. Rats, fat on dragonflesh, crept along the cave wall, stupid and weakened by gorging.

He tore into them, biting and flinging them hard against the cave wall, and they dove for their cracks. One was too fat to fit back into his shelter, and the Copper solved his problem for him by biting him in half.

He didn't dare climb the egg shelf. If he got up there and saw what remained of his mother and sister, he'd go mad.

He found a riven helm and nibbled off some chain links. The metal tasted better even than rat. With that he remembered Father's hoard cave.

Father! What would happen when he returned to this?

Time passed, sliding by unmarked as he staggered around the cave. He couldn't drink from the pool, evil memories of the dwarves keeping him far from the familiar waterfall. He couldn't drink from the trickle; he'd spotted more gore and slaughter atop the moss-thick heap of dragon waste; the shadows of the cave held lurking recriminations; the stalactites and stalagmites were spears. . . .

What sort of world was it where dragons were slaughtered in their own homes? He knew almost nothing of the history of his kind, but had a vague sense of the majesty and grandeur that once was theirs, passed down from egg to egg. He'd committed a crime against every drop of blood in his body, every glittering scale passed down from some ancestor.

A hard world, that was certain. Cast out by his own family. Betrayed by dwarves. Of course, he forgot his own intent to betray in his wretchedness, explaining to himself that the dwarves didn't know his plan. Any betrayal on their part carried the full weight of its own sin, not tainted by his own intent.

Then he went a little mad.

He may have even frothed at the mouth. He vaguely remembered thirst-thick saliva crusting on his snout when he came out of it, a good deal thinner and with claws worn down to dull nubs.

When he woke as though from a sleep-terror he found himself bleeding from a cracked scale at the base of his crest and between his eyes—he'd been bashing his head against a sharp projection shaped like a dragonhorn.

What had brought him out of it?

A familiar sound, a dragon roar.

"Irelia! Auron! Wistala! Jizara!" Father called. "Spirits, it cannot be! Not *all*! Curse the Wheel of Fire to flame and ash!"

Why did Father not list him with the others? Was he not part of *all*?

He tried to answer, but his dry throat was capable of only emitting a small squeak: "Fazer!"

Father didn't call for him because he had no name. He needed a name if he were to be called for.

He hurried toward the bellows but found himself stumbling on his crippled forelimb. He caught one quick glimpse of bronze tail-scale disappearing through the shaft that led up and out. Only Father's harsh, angry smell remained.

He found some deer that Father had dropped and nibbled a little, but had no appetite. He should save them for Father when he got back. Father would also need metals; he would return from his great battle with the dwarves needing them. He'd show Father that he hadn't eaten a single coin of the hoard, and in gratitude Father would share some with him again.

Thinking of the hoard . . .

He went to the shaft covered by the great rock. It had been moved aside and smelled of dwarf. He shut his nostrils so as not to be overwhelmed by the smell and descended into the cavern. . . .

The cavern lay almost empty. A few pieces of copper had been left, and a bit of silver glinted toward the back where it had rolled under a projection, but all that remained was the lingering smell of dwarf. There wasn't a full mouthful left for him, never mind Father's vast jaws.

Father would give him some fine names. Thief.

Traitor.

Outcast.

He flung himself down and keened.

Later, he climbed out of the hoard cave and went to the much-reduced pool. The dwarves had rerouted the water so it emptied into some deeper cavern to facilitate their works and crossing into the cavern. It bubbled and belched up from a whirlpool. As he drank he could feel the current.

He heard a wailing Drakine scream from the direction of the egg shelf.

Did one of his family still live? Perhaps Zara had played dead so the dwarves would leave her alone. The smaller body he'd glimpsed was a cruel trick of the Dragonblade's. He hobbled as quickly as he could to the egg shelf.

It was Zara, green and alive and rubbing her fringe against a sharp spur of rock next to a great growth of thriving moss at the base of the trickle where the dragon-waste lay. He could just see the fringe on her back and the side of her head, but it was certainly her, gloriously alive and moving. . . .

"Sizter!" he said, happy beyond words. She must need comforting, with Wistala lying dead next to her; the pair had been closer than stalactite and stalagmite run together.

"They killed her, Jiz . . ." he tried to get out, but the words came only with difficulty.

The green hatchling rounded on him, burning anger in her golden eyes. "I'm Wistala."

Confusion . . . certainty. He missed the rest of her words, or perhaps shut his ears to the accusations he knew to be true. It was Wistala; she'd returned, and she knew exactly what had happened and who was responsible.

Auron wasn't with her. He hadn't made it. Perhaps the Copper could reason with her, confess and beg for a chance at redemption.

"They lied," he said. He needed her to know the whys and wherefores. "A bloody cave, no hoard—"

She leaped at him, tripping in her fury. He fell on her, tried to keep her from biting him. If she'd only listen for a moment, he'd make it up to her somehow. "We need to overcome this, put it behind. Unite. The past can't be changed, but we can make sure—"

She wasn't listening; she was struggling. She threw him off; healthy, well-fed muscle with a good deal of strength in her stout frame forced him backward, over—

"It can be avenged," she said, biting and clawing for his underbelly, fighting as though in a duel to the death, not a hatchling wrestling match. Blinding pain struck as her claws found soft flesh at his eye. He fought madly, broke her grip, turned his good set of backscale toward her, and hit her with his broken and stiff tail. He scrambled away.

Alone again.

Wistala knew what he'd done, the enormity of it, bigger than the cavern, bigger than the mountains he'd never seen save in vague dreams. Somehow that was worse than the pangs of his own conscience. Wistala would carry this knowledge with her for the rest of her life and hate him forever.

How could he overcome her hatred? Or was it not her hatred, but his own, shared in some lesser portion by her?

Yes, he would overcome her hatred, his guilt, the horror that had engulfed their home. He staggered toward the pool, flung himself in, and let the whirlpool carry him away from his lonely and broken life.

Chapter 7

Later he tried to remember how long he was in the water. The darkness made it a fearful journey. He slipped down through the whirlpool, went limp, and waited to become wedged in a crack or hole and asphyxiate.

Instead he had the sensation of bouncing off a rock, and then feeling air all around his body before he struck moving water again with a slap. Something about the smell and temperature in the water told him he'd joined an entirely different watercourse.

Oddly, the interest in that fact sustained him for a moment, long enough for him to right himself and realize he was in a fast-moving current in a tunnel.

The rushing current and the cold were enemies to be fought, and his body responded automatically. He turned to keep his nostrils above water, angled his frame so he rode the current with little effort.

At intervals he passed glowing dots, little clusters of eyes and wagging tongues. They flashed up and by so rapidly he never could make sense of them. In his experience anything regular indicated dwarves, though he couldn't imagine why they should wish to mark a tunnel of freezing water in the dark of the Lower World.

So when he fetched up against a stout chain hanging into

the water, fully as thick as his neck, it was the easiest thing in the world to hang on and look around.

He recognized more marks, similar to the ones in the tunnel behind, differing only in profusion in their verticals and horizontals. Three caves were scarred with signs of mining. Cave moss, a good deal brighter than the kind he knew from the home cave, extended from the water from the common landing.

He reached out with his neck and found a grip, then let the rest of his body follow in easy stages, finally releasing the helpful, wide-looped chain with his *saa*.

He lay a long time and slept next to the rushing water.

Voices came to him in a dream full of dark rocks rushing by.

"Don't m'tell that m'knowing not the smell of blood. Fresh blood."

"Faaaa!" another voice bawled back.

He opened an eye.

"Here e'is. Traveler. A bit of washup from the river."

A horridly upturned face, all ears, black eyes, and nostrils, regarded him from the cavern wall. The thing had leathery wings, with a gripping digit not unlike a dragon's wing-spur. It was a bat, fully three times the size of the ones he'd seen in the home cave. And he'd never understood a word of their high-pitched chatter.

"E'breathing!" a second, smaller but wider one behind said.

"Cave lizard, m'think," the larger said, hanging from his tiny rear legs for a better look. "Strange sort. Hurt."

The larger extended his arms and flapped his leathery wings vigorously. They were thinner than dragonwings, almost translucent. The Copper could see blue veins in the skin.

Under the fanning and the light touches of the wing tips the Copper twitched. They tickled! He twitched.

He tried to give a greeting, but it came out as an unintelligible cough. He shook his head and righted himself.

"E'having a set of scale. A'wait! . . . E'be a dragon!"

"Faaaa!" the other said again, staying away from the Copper and just peeking out into the cave.

The hanging one rubbed his face up and down with his wings, licking his grip-digit and rearranging the face-fur, though there was only so much that could be done with such ugliness. "M'name's Thernadad, an e'be m'mated, Mamedi. A'begging your pardon, sir. Y'be hurt. W'can attend that for you."

The brightness in the creature's black eyes disturbed him a little.

"You're right, I am a dragon," the Copper said. "I do seem to be bleeding." His back wound had opened up again, and it hurt abominably.

"M'told you!" the hanging one said to his companion.

"Once!" the other said to no one in particular. "Once in a three-season turn e'be right, and now m'hearing it until m'let loose for the drop." But she licked her lips, and the Copper saw sharp white teeth.

"If y'will just shift closer to the wall, sir, we work best right-side down. Unless y'want us clinging to your scale, but m'knowing not the extent of your injuries. . . ."

The Copper rolled and the bat shifted. It started licking at the wound on his back, and he felt a slight tingle that transformed into a pleasant numbness. He looked back, and the bat had worked his odd, jutting jaw into the wound and was tearing away ragged bits of flesh and lapping up blood with a blurring tongue that flicked in and out faster than he'd ever seen anything move in his life.

The bat lifted a blood-smeared snout. "See to sir's face, dear, with that soft touch of yours."

The other came forward a good deal more cautiously, eyeing the Copper warily. Finally she hung over him, but kept all her four limbs attached to the cavern ceiling, ready for a quick getaway. She dropped down and went to work in the region around his right eye. He noticed some blurring there, as though the eye regarded the world through a half-closed lid.

"Bit of a mess, here, sir. Just a'going to numb it down a bit." She began to lick about the eye, and he felt that same tingling followed by numbness.

"Y'carrying a set of tunnel nits, tight up against that scale. A'lurking in the moss a'waiting on a tasty bit of juicy skin, like always. May I?"

"Of course."

The Copper felt a tug and heard a crunch. Followed by another and another.

"Finished here," the female said. She touched him with a wing. "Excuses, sir. Y'permit some body work?"

"Certainly," the Copper said, enjoying the warmth beneath the numbness.

He felt the female climb onto his back, gripping at his scale, lifting and digging out insects with more tugs and crunches, moving slowly front to back. "That's kindness! That's generosity. So rare these days. E'be a gentle sort, e'be."

"Y'hearing m'disagree? M'found him, you thick cow!"

"Faaaa! Luck's the only thing y'got in this life, you great squirt."

The Copper fell into a pleasant half sleep, and heard little gassy emissions from the pair. "That's what m'call a feed. Indeed," the male—Thernadad, the Copper corrected himself—said.

"Y'wanting to get away from the river, sir," Mamedi added. "A trunk full of dwarves could pass at any time. Might a'spot your skin and throw out a hook."

The Copper dragged himself around the corner of the cave, ready for sleep.

"Watch out for snakes. Cave snakes in here," Thernadad said.

"E'be too big for all but King Gan himself," Mamedi said.

"Don't y'worry, sir. We'll be right above." Thernadad said more, but the Copper didn't hear it.

He had vague dreams of the bats clinging to him, swelling like great ticks, but woke to find his wounds crusted over with healthy-smelling scab, though they itched a little. His right eye bothered him more than anything; he could see through it as if through a mist, but everything went a little fuzzy and indistinct when he closed his left eye and looked only through the right.

He judged himself to be in a cave, vaster but lower than the home cave, branching off in every direction but up. Always there were the little channels of cave moss—in some places stopped up, glowing bright where the water still flowed. There were a good many small holes driven into the ground, as though something had been fixed there with spikes, like the dwarves had used for their water-diversion apparatus, but the work had long since been abandoned and the metal taken up. While nosing around he found a broken bit of spike and swallowed it.

He heard a flutter off in a corner and saw the big blood-drinking bats yeeking in voices pitched so high he could hardly hear them, and flapping their wings in each other's faces as they hung from the cavern roof. It seemed more of a squabble than a fight, so he ignored the commotion.

The odd thing was that he felt relieved when he saw them. It was nice to have someone speak pleasantly to you, praise you, even if it was only for the number of nits clinging to your scale-roots. And their chatter distracted him from the griefs circling in his mind.

He walked over to the pair, trying to strut like a proud young dragon, but feeling a little off balance, thanks to his stiff tail.

"You, there. Excuse me."

The bats left off spitting at each other. Both licked their gripping digits and straightened up the fur on their ears and chins.

"Sir a'needing something?" Thernadad said, rubbing his gripping digits together under his chin.

"What is this place?"

"Dwarf mine, long and longer abandoned," Thernadad said. "In my oldfather's time, there was a'feasting on draft horses and goats, but now there's nothing but mushroom-fed rats and moss-crawlies. And the snakes, of course, who a'eating our poor young."

"What were you fighting about?"

"Nothing of import to sir."

"Faaaa! E'be a heartless brute, to a'be telling the truth," Mamedi said. "E'leaving my sister to starve! Ooo, ooo, ooo!"

"Sir doesn't want to be a'hearing our troubles."

"Why will she starve?"

"The dwarves just closed off the old air shaft to a stock paddock and she's—"

"Shut it, you," Thernadad made a swipe at her ears, but she ducked over it.

"M'answering the nice young dragon's question! So now e'be starving and yeee-eyee-yeee . . ." Her story trailed off into high-pitched wailing.

"Oh, you should just bring her to this cavern. I'm going exploring. Maybe I'll pick up another set of cave nits."

Mamedi left off crying. "Oh, sir—"

Thernadad snapped his teeth at his mate. "Mind the snakes," he called.

He left them yeeking and boxing again, though Thernadad flapped his wings halfheartedly, as a veteran campaigner who knew a battle lost when he saw one.

This cavern was very different from the home cave. The dwarves had carved it almost wholly from rock, smoothed the floors, and laid the *saa*-width water channels where the mosses still thrived and offered some amount of light.

Deep pocks like spear wounds—no, like rat holes—could be found in profusion around rougher areas where they'd extracted their minerals. He sniffed one and smelled rat. There were damps and trickles, and these supported more colonies of cave moss and mushrooms, which in turn supported rats and mice. When backtracking to the bat cave and river outlet, he found a few soil beds where the mushrooms grew more thickly—the dwarves must have cultivated something in the soil other than mushrooms, for there were stakes and wire lines, but nothing but a few dead, tough vines remained of their crop.

He smelled more rat here and began to hunt by nose. He caught a flash of white skin and bit quickly and instinctively, cutting it in unequal halves. Legless—a snake! The back end had a big bulge—it had obviously just eaten a rat and couldn't creep away as he approached. It took a moment for the front end to twitch out.

He carried both halves back to the bats. Mamedi was away getting her sister, so he climbed up and hung the front end up where Thernadad could easily reach it, and swallowed the back half in one long inhale—with a little gulp at the thickening where the half-digested rat lay.

Thernadad nibbled and sucked. "Not to be a'criticizing, sir, but if y'leaves 'em whole, there's more to lap. Just give 'em a good shake and a crack against a rock, is how an experienced snake killer goes about it. They stay juicier that way."

"I wasn't hunting with you in mind."

"Oh, no, no, no. Of course not." He nipped out one of the snake's eyeballs and gulped it down. "M'sees your wounds are healing up nicely. Glad we got to you in time, sir, so's y'didn't bleed to death crawling out of the river."

The Copper looked over his many scabs and felt a little

ashamed. He should have brought Thernadad and his wife back a whole snake, at that.

"Hope y'didn't chomp one of King Gan's favorites. E'be a mean one. E'doesn't like anyone a'meddlin' w'his snakes. Except hisself, of course. E'eats his own kind."

"King Gan eats his own snakes? Why would they keep such a king?"

"The others not be having much choice in the matter. E'says: 'They can hate as hard as they like, as long as they fear.' It's a necessity, like. There's precious little to fill an appetite such as his.

"A cave snake, sir, twice your length and more besides. The White Lightning. By the time y'knows he struck y'be dead. He's strong enough to swim upstream in the river if he likes. Lost my own poor father to him, and an uncle besides."

"Any area I should stay away from?"

"There's a swampy bit over there." Thernadad pointed with a vein-stitched wing. "Beyond that, a real honeycomb it is, where the dwarves struck gold. There's an air shaft to the surface e'using in summer. Y'be keeping away and not getting ideas, m'hoping."

"Of course," the Copper said. He squeezed into a crevice welled in shadow. "I'm for a nap. Wake me if King Gan goes for a swim."

Thernadad licked his grasping digits and cleaned all around his eyes. "Nowt a'gets past me, sir. Why, m'be having eyes that can spot a rat-tail twitch on the far side of the cavern, and ears that echo off a pinched mouse turd before it hits. M'begging the sir's pardon for the coarse language; m'be forgetting myself. Right! Ears down and all, on duty, quick's the wing and sharp's the tooth . . ."

Thernadad's chatter went on, but the Copper slept through the rest.

———

The Copper woke briefly at a slight smelly *sploit* of bat guano dropping. He rolled an eye upward and saw Thernadad hanging there, wings well over his face, making rasping noises in his sleep.

"There, e'be waking," Mamedi said.

Another, even wider than her and with two little bats clinging trembling to its back, also looked down at him.

Mamedi rubbed her grasping digits together. "Sir, not to be bothering sir, but it's been a long trip and me sister, e'be perishing hungry, and her brood a'be so hungry they barely a'clinging to her back. Just the tiniest of nips out of your tail; won't feel but a pinch, an' a little blood loss heals a big wound, good for the circulation an' all. . . ."

"Just this once," he said, shifting so he could extend his tail.

Mamedi crept down first, found a scale nit, and crunched it down. "Oh, they a'be the very buggers. There's another. Sir, what y'been doing that y'picked up so many so quick?"

He craned his neck a little so he could look behind and saw Mamedi's sister and her children lapping at a slight, pleasantly tingling wound. Another bat crept out of the shadows and joined in the flowing feast.

"Wait, who's that?"

Mamedi lifted her snout from his scale-roots. "Her mate, of course. E's supposed to leave the father of her children behind when she moves into a new cave?"

"I imagine not."

"There's a lesson in generosity for you, nephews!" Mamedi said. "Remember it. Y'don't often see the like these days. E'be a very special gentle sort. It's a rare one that doesn't forge a favor and returns kindness with kindness, Thernie and me saving his life and all."

Her sister and family cooed and yeeked agreeable noises as they lapped.

———

The Copper dozed. He'd hunted again, keeping well away from the set of pools Therenadad had called "the swampy bit."

He wondered if the events in the home cave had been some terrible dream, brought on by exploring the pool, diving, and being injured when he fell into the river. He'd fallen in and out of consciousness often enough, or been half drowned when pulled by undertow. Could all the detail—the dwarves with their faint-glowing beards and the big man with the glowing spear—be the product of frightful, dying-hatchling dreams?

He told himself his family was alive and well. Not missing him a bit, of course, but such was his lot as an odd male—what had Father called him? *Outcast*. They were probably gathered around Mother on the egg shelf now, feasting on some thick-muscled oxen brought back by Father, and Jizara was singing after the feast.

"M'excuse, sir. Sir?" Thernadad said, climbing down the cave wall next to him.

"Yes?"

"The mate an m'talked, and since her sister's come to stay, we thought one more or less wouldn't make a difference." He went into a paroxysm of fur smoothing.

"Why are you telling me?"

"It's me old mum, sir. E'can't make it to the surface anymore, or survive the dangers out there besides. Pitiful shape she's in. If e'could just have a lick or two, e'doesn't have any appetite at all no more, hardly."

The Copper saw a half-white bat, small and frail, above.

"Oh, very well. I suppose her sister's somewhere behind, also starving."

"Oh, no, no. My brother. A great, well-traveled bat e'is; been down every hole in these mountains. Thousand and one stories. Now e'takes care of old Mum. E'pulled her up, again and again, to the cave roof on the trip so she could drop for another glide. E'perishing with exhaustion, e'is."

"So he needs some blood down his throat, too." The Copper felt his *griff* flutter.

"Sir, don't be a'taking me wrong," he said as the tiny old bat crawled down his back. "What you've done for us poor hangers more than makes up for your life being saved by quick thinking an' skill and charity. Wonderful thing, charity. Never know how it a'gets paid back in this life or the next. Here, y'be excusing me, her old teeth, you know."

Thernadad licked him a couple times, and the Copper felt the nook in his *saa* go numb. With a quick bite Thernadad opened a cut and the old bat began to lap.

Thernadad wiped the corner of his eyes again and again as he licked a smear of blood from his limbs. "Oh, sir. Me poor old mum. You've made me so happy. M'won't forget this kindness till the day I drop. No, sir."

"Rich good blood, this dragon," Thernadad's mother said.

"Oh, dragon," a great heavy bat said. He'd shifted to directly above the Copper with surprising stealth. "Haven't tasted that since I flew the whole way 'round the Lavadome. What a place. Thick with dragons. Not as kind as this one, no, nearly got my wings bit off. Y'be falling into the Nor'flow by accident and get carried all this way, m'lord?"

Thick with dragons? "Tell me more," the Copper said.

"Glad to, m'lord. It's only my throat, a'be drying up from the exertions."

"I suppose I can spare a little more."

The big bat dropped down to his flank.

"Ooooo, is there a party?" Mamedi said, crawling across the cave roof with her sister and brood behind. A couple more bats seemed to have joined the family.

"E's flowing nicely," Thernadad's mother said. "Great strong young dragon."

Thernadad's wide-bodied brother shoved his mother out of

the way and pushed his nose in and drank. When he came up for air, he wiped his snout with his wing and dragged himself up the Copper's neck, where he threw a companionable wing around and gave him a bloody leer. "Dragons a'loving treasure stories. Ever heard of CuTar? How about the great glowing stone of NooMoahk? In old Uldam, it is, like a bit of the sun itself dropped into the earth—"

"I'd rather hear about this Lavadome. Where is it, exactly?"

"Oh, an awful journey y'had, to get so lost and confused. To get back y'be having to make it to the Antiope for the southward flow, and there's no good road, in the sun or in the dark, not hereabouts. M'taking another pull and think on it. Hey! Y'be getting out of it, you greedy beggars!"

Mamedi and her relations fought for a place in a wing-jostling heap at the cut in his tail. One of the bigger ones, more enterprising than the rest, had opened another wound in his tail.

"This is a bit much," the Copper said. He dragged his tail away from the greedy mouths.

"Y'be molesting our good host," Thernadad yelled from above.

"Faaaa!" Mamedi answered back.

"Off me mum, you!" Thernadad dropped down on one of his mate's relations who'd shoved his frail mother aside—less vigorously than her own son, it seemed to the Copper, but he was learning that the insult wasn't as important as who offered it. A full-out bat brawl started.

He curled his slit tail around himself—it bent in a funny and uneven manner, with bends more like a dwarf tunnel, thanks to the rod injuries to it, and alternately licked and blew on the cuts until the bleeding stopped, as the bats lashed one another with leather wings and tried to bite off oversize hairy ears.

He woke feeling tired and hungry. He checked his cuts and discovered a new wound in the soft spot just behind his shoulder.

Though bat bites did heal clean and fast, and he could hardly feel the injuries. His head hurt, and he walked down to the river for a drink.

He sucked cold water, and his head began to feel better almost immediately.

Thernadad swooped by. "Sir, y'be wanting to get away from the river!"

Bing-bing. Bing-bing . . . Bing-bing! The metallic clatter was regular, and therefore alarming. He saw a light up the tunnel from upstream, reflected on the flowing water.

"Hurry!" Thernadad urged.

BING-BING!

He scrambled backward and set himself against the cave wall.

A long wooden trunk, a clattering bell anchored at the front and swaying lanterns hung in reflective hollows in its sides, rushed down the river, pushed along by the fast-flowing water. Through long, narrow slits he saw dwarves within, sweating backs rising and falling as they worked at some mystery on their craft. He caught one glimpse of a dwarf at the tail, hanging off a flange and working some kind of apparatus that descended into the water from the safety of a metal cage, and it was gone, moving as fast as a quick-walking dragon.

BING-bing . . . Bing-bing . . . Bing . . . Bing.

Thernadad alighted and smoothed his face fur. "Careful at the river now, sir."

"What was that?"

"The dwarves. They get about on those things here in the Lower World."

"It came from the same direction I did, with the current."

"Of course e'did, sir. Always a'coming from that direction."

"Then how do they get back?"

"Mother! Mother!" Thernadad called back, but not in answer to his question. The Copper heard air move above, and saw the old white-flecked bat turning tight circles low over the underground river.

"M'knew it," she screeched as she flapped back into the cave and rested. "Flies be riding with the dwarves. Snapped up two while y'be working your jaw."

The Copper's appetite had woken with a vengeance, and he began to sniff around the bank of the river. Perhaps fish lived within the fast-flowing current.

"Y'flying days be over, m'thinking!" Thernadad said. "Enjor, e'be saying you could hardly glide nomores."

She alighted next to the channel bearing a trickle into the cave interior and took in water with her quick, darting tongue.

She smacked her thin lips. "Oh, Thernie, just woke up hale this morning, m'did. Full of guano and ginger. M'wanting a bit of air under me wing." She brushed the fur forward on her face and dug in an ear and gobbled down whatever she found within. "This young dragon—yeeek!"

A translucent tongue shot up from where it rested next to the channel. It was segmented, with countless legs a blur, its body like living, mottled eyejelly. To the bat, thicker around than she and many times her length, it was a mortal danger, pincers at the front opening for her. . . .

To the Copper it was breakfast.

He scrambled after it and extended his neck, bit down on the back half, and yanked it skyward. Legs tickling at his throat, he gulped it down.

He looked down to see Thernadad flapping his wings in the face of his mother, who blinked awake. She climbed onto his back and he scuttled back up, in that elbows-out fashion of bats, to the cavern roof.

"Twice grateful, sir," Thernadad said, panting a little.

"Any blood flowing this fine night?" Mamedi said, creeping forward.

"Out of it!" Thernadad bawled. She was out of reach, so he battled the air in her direction with his wings.

"Just thinking of refreshing meself. Like a new-mated bat you were last sunrise. M'be hardly able to keep a grip."

"Oh, son, m'be pershishing of that scare," Thernadad's mother croaked. "Just a wee drop; perhaps y'be persuading our kindly young prince now?"

The Copper saw other eyes shining in the darkness. How many bats had gathered in this cave?

"Sir—" Thernadad said.

"Leave me alone, would you?" the Copper said. He stalked into the cave, leaving the cluster of bats.

"Greedy sots!" Thernadad yelled, and soon the Copper heard the wing-flapping, tooth-snapping sound of a full-out bat brawl.

The Copper found a dark corner and rested. The seemingly still-twitching centipede wasn't agreeing with him.

He wondered about this Lavadome and the dragons there. It must be a wonderful place, with plenty to eat, for dragons to be gathered there. He didn't know much about dragon society, but he knew that Father had to fly far and wide so he wouldn't over-hunt an area—or so that snatched livestock were only a nuisance, and not a regular threat. Would they look kindly on the arrival of a distant relative, hurt by weary dragonlengths of travel?

And they wouldn't know his secrets.

He let off a burp, and the centipede finally ceased its attempts to escape his stomach.

The Lavadome sounded a long way off, and he couldn't fly like a bat.

But he could follow one. . . .

The Copper lunged forward without really knowing why. A heavy force struck the ground behind and all he could think was, *Curse that Gray Rat!*—having instinctively avoided another

59

of his brother's pounces. But he felt the weight of the thing in the air behind, in the tremor that ran through the solid rock when it hit.

He turned.

A huge, pale gray mass writhed over and around itself behind. A head that could probably suck him down as easily as he'd swallowed the centipede lifted itself from the mass, pointing its nose this way and that until it fixed on him.

"You picked the wrong cave, hatchling," it whispered at him.

The Copper didn't know of the old rivalry between snakes and dragons, the contempt in which the serpents held the winged and legged. Young dragons hunted the same game the great snakes did, so perhaps the old enmity was akin to that of lions and cheetahs in other parts of the world, competitors who struck each other's young. He certainly never heard the tale of the deaths of AuZath and Nubiel, dragons of Ydar. They were murdered by a serpent who injected his poison into apples, which were eaten by grazing horses, which died and were naturally devoured in turn by the dragons.

The Copper just knew he was afraid.

"You must be King Gan," he managed to say, though the words sounded a little croaky. Some instinct flared within; he hated the legless, writhing form. But fear froze him. *They can hate as hard as they like, as long as they fear....*

He'd never seen such black eyes. The way they fixed on him, so exactly aligned, it was as if the entire earth were a little off-kilter, as measured by the level of those eyes.

"I am. And all within sight, sound, hearing, and heat is mine. You are mine."

The snake flowed toward him. The Copper couldn't break off; all he could do was watch the eyes approach, twin balls rushing toward him, perfectly level....

Something boxed him about the eyes and crest. "Don't be looking him in the eyes!" Thernadad screeched, darting up and out of the way of the snake.

The snake lunged at him, suddenly transformed into pure energy. Its body seemed to vaporize into a white blur rushing toward him.

He ducked, hugging his belly to safe rock.

King Gan, forced by the bat's intervention to strike a switchback before he was ready, struck the Copper at the head instead of the base of the neck. His fangs, out and forward, folded against the Copper's young crest above his eyes.

The Copper felt hot liquid run down either side of his head as the snake became a snake again, and coiled back.

Fear flowed up from his belly, tightened against his breastbone. He seized up, stuck out his own neck, and vomited, fire bladder emptying toward the snake.

A spray of yellowish liquid, vaguely sulfurous, struck King Gan across the nose.

The great snake went mad. He whipped his head back and forth, writhed, coiled, uncoiled, knotted, until the Copper couldn't tell head from tail but could only run lest he be crushed as the snake rolled and whipped.

A dragonlength away he paused to glance over his shoulder. King Gan flowed toward his swamp as fast as coils would carry him, where he plunged headfirst into the shallow water of the moss-thick mire.

"Right in the pits y'be hitting him. Never saw the like— a'taking the venom out of ol' King Gan that way."

"The pits?"

"Everything here in the dark has a way of a'hunting that don't rely on light," Thernadad said. "Bats be having our ears, that lousy legpincher feels vibrations, and the snakes feel the heat of us poor warm-blood rodents. M'hearing dragons sniff for that what doesn't smell as bad as they do, but y'be free to correct me, cousin."

"Cousin?"

"Your life. Saved three times now. That be making us family, the way bats see it. Speaking of which, m'be working up a powerful thirst saving your life. How about a nip out of the old tail, real quiet, before a whole skytrail of the hungry beggars show up?"

Later, feeling a bit drained, and not just because of the blood Thernadad lapped out of his tail, the Copper rested. He perched high—hopefully out of King Gan's reach—and watched the mire. He heard an occasional bubbling hiss and a splash, as King Gan soaked the heat pits on his nose.

Some piece of him was the tiniest bit grateful to Auron for all the sudden pounces out of the darkness. Without the torments of his brother, he'd never have avoided the snake's first strike.

He began to cry.

Chapter 8

The Copper slept but couldn't rest. He ate but didn't enjoy. He eliminated but felt no relief. More often than not he perched near the river tunnel, losing himself in its steady echo.

Auron and Wistala would come hunting for him. Wistala had already probed the home cave, looking for him, and both knew he used the pool. They'd never felt the pain of iron rods, or soft, promising whispers and kind touches that left one's head in a muddle.

King Gan still lurked in the moss-ringed cavern pools, according to the bats, and his snakes were more aggressive than ever—at least as far as the bats were concerned. One got some cousin of Thernadad's.

Which was just as well. The Copper had lost count of the number of bats gathered in the cave, each with a sad story, each begging for just a lap or two from a nipped-open vein. He'd be about to say no, and then Thernadad or Mamedi would dig at an earhole or push stray chin whiskers back into place and remind him of his escapes from death.

He dipped his stiff, dwarf-broken tail in the river, watched the cut it made in the current, the arrowhead pointing in the direction of the flow . . .

"Water Spirit, you brought me here for a reason. Give me your wisdom."

If he still lived, it meant the spirits weren't willing to take him back just yet. Scarred, lamed, and probably never able to fly thanks to the wound from the big man, he would be denied a normal dragon's existence. What female would take a mating flight that could last no longer than a leap from a rock top?

According to Thernadad's brother, Enjor, there were dragons somewhere upriver of him. That arrowhead in the current pointed toward them.

Did he even want to find more dragons?

He remembered Auron's stalking and pouncing, Father's indifference, Mother's shunning. Anger bubbled in his fire bladder.

Sometimes their deaths didn't seem such a crime.

He saw a six-legged scuttling thing crawling along just under the surface of the water, making the smallest of waves in the current. He plunged his snout in, grabbed it, flipped it out, and cracked its shell with a quick stomp of his *saa* before it could right itself. He tongued out the whitish, rather tasteless meat within and crunched down the legs and limbs. A little grit helped the digestion and was a pleasant change from the dirty, hairy taste of rat. If only he had Jizara to join him in the hunt. One could swim and toss the crabs out of the river; then the other could smash them before they could retreat back to the water.

Jizara's death was a crime. A betrayal piled on a betrayal.

He could almost hear her singing beside the river.

He hurried away, back to the holes in the cavern ceiling where the bats liked to roost.

He listened for a particular pair of squeaky voices.

"Oh, shove off! Y'nose be dripping all over."

"Faaaa!"

"Thernadad, you up there?"

The bats quieted. Thernadad climbed out of his hole and

worked the back of his head with his gripping claw. "Sir be wanting something?"

"I need to speak to your brother."

Thernadad clawed his way across the cavern roof, poking his head into holes, climbing over sleeping bats, throwing an occasional elbow and getting swatted in return.

"What be going on. Party?"

"Oooh! Watch it, cousin."

"Enjor! Rouse yourself, y'fat tick. Sir wants to speak to you."

The brothers' mother popped out of her hole, moving with a younger bat's energy despite her aging frame. "Is a feed on?"

"What do you want, m'lord?" Enjor said.

"How do I get back to my people? The dragons of this Lavadome?"

"Eh? Y'be knowing that best, m'lord."

It took him several tries to get across that he couldn't get back to his own kind without help—help from the bats. Their little mammalian brains took a while to get around the idea that they could travel together. While bats understood sharing living space, the idea of traveling together didn't come easily.

"All roads in the lower world lead to the Lavadome, if y'follow them long enough," Enjor offered, after much thought. "Don't dragons have homing sense an' all that?"

"Mine doesn't seem to be working," the Copper said.

Enjor scratched his tailvent and sniffed at the residue before continuing: "The best route would be the rivers. Only problem is the Sou'flow be a weary and uncertain trip from here. You might have to go the wrong direction a'ways, then cut across, though that would take you near more dwarves and their works a'following the river."

"And then what?" The Copper felt a weight on his tail, found the white-flecked bat at her usual spot, lapping up blood.

65

"Old caves full of nothing but dark and bad air."

"So good y'be to us, sir," Thernadad said as the Copper's teeth ground against one another.

"Perhaps I could engage you as a guide," the Copper said to Enjor.

"Oh, m'be too old for such a fearful journey. Besides, there's old Mum."

Bats fluttered down from the roof.

"Oooo! A party!"

"There, open him up just under the knee; e'flows so nicely there—"

"I'll feed you along the way," the Copper said. "You and your mother both."

Enjor's eyes brightened. "That's a generous offer, m'lord."

"Faaaa! E's our host!" Mamedi said, leaping on Enjor's back.

"Off me, y'daft sot!"

But just as Thernadad shouldered his way into what was working up into a fifty-bat brawl, a bat let out a terrified death screech. A snake had reared up, biting a low-flying bat heading for the Copper's tail and dragging it to the ground.

"Sons o' Gan!" Thernadad shouted.

The Copper hugged rock, protecting his belly, and heard a pained squeak.

The cavern came alive with white shapes, pink tongues flicking as they rushed forward, coiled, struck, and rushed forward again. The greedier bats, stuck on the floor by the Copper's open wounds, fell first.

The Copper found himself eyeball-to-eyeball with a great white snake, almost a rival to King Gan himself. He felt his *griff* lower and rattle, and the snake pulled back, gathering itself for a strike.

It would flash like lightning when it hit, so the Copper preempted the fangs with an openmouthed rush of his own. The snake, for all its size, wasn't used to a dragon dash and seemed to slide in all directions in panic. The Copper bit for the neck—anywhere else on the snake would mean a counterstrike of venomous fangs.

The snake whipped its head sideways and the Copper went with it, clinging with claws and teeth. He struck the cavern wall, saw stars at the impact.

Blindly, he bit down hard, pulling with teeth and pushing with *sii*. The snake rolled and rolled again. The Copper found himself ensnared in coils. But they didn't crush; they just twitched.

He dropped the dead snake's neck and pushed away from the still-writhing body.

"Kill that one! The burning lizard!" the Copper heard. He turned his good eye to the sound and saw the great snake with a black-flecked face. King Gan's smooth nose was peeled and cracked.

Snakes dropped dead bats and crawled for him.

The Copper doubted he had the strength left to fight another such snake, let alone several, or King Gan himself. He ran for the river. A snake slipped sideways to intercept. He jumped over it before it could do more than snap at his legs.

He looked up. The surviving bats were fighting to get into holes too small for snake heads.

"I'm leaving! Enjor?"

"Good idea, m'lord."

"Leave the cave?" a bat squeaked.

"Who be a'needing it?" Thernadad barked. "Snakes and misery and too many bats lately." He glared at his mate.

"E'be our host! W'be coming along," Mamedi said, fluttering toward the river.

"Mum! Mum!" Thernadad shouted. He alighted on the

chain hanging by the river mouth, then turned to search the tunnel and cavern beyond. "W'mustn't leave without m'mum!"

"Past her time, anyway," Enjor said, turning circles over the river.

"Mum!"

" 'Ere me be!" a tiny voice squeaked. "M'been clinging for life to this fool dragon."

A trio of snakes followed as quickly as coils could carry them.

"Unless you want to swim, madam . . ." the Copper said.

Thernadad flapped down and alighted on the Copper's back. "Here, Mum, climb on."

She launched herself into the air. "M'be all right for a bit."

The Copper slid into the river, hugged his limbs to his side, and let his tail rather stiffly propel him through the water. He found that if he took a full breath of air, he could sink and let just his head ride above the waterline.

He gave a glance back and saw a snake plunge into the water, but its fellows clustered at the bank.

With a bend, a dropped shoulder, and a wave of his tail, the Copper rounded on his pursuer, and the snake fled upstream.

The bats fluttered overhead. For all the elbow throwing and head butting they did when clinging to the rock ceiling, they maneuvered in the air expertly, avoiding outcroppings of rock, the river surface—and a hatchling's tiny crest.

They left the brighter mosses of the tunnel for a dim line of growth that existed at the edge of the river, clinging to the rough-hewn tunnel. Every now and then the tunnel widened and the lines fell away before coming together again where toolwork scarred the rock.

At one "lake," Enjor swooped down and guided him toward an outflow. Colored lights glimmered across the lake, reds and blues and oranges, but he had no desire to investigate and risk another encounter with dwarves or whatever else lived down there.

Swimming was tiring—his bad leg dragged on the current, and he had to turn and push to compensate—so he preferred to float, keeping his lungs inflated and just waving his tail enough to stay afloat.

He became used to the cold of the water so quickly he feared he might be going numb and freezing to death. He struck out for the side of the cavern and tried a short climb and found all his limbs still able to function, though his hearts were pounding from the slight effort.

"M'be needing a rest, anyway," Thernadad said, landing. His mother clung to his back, a tiny white-flecked thing atop his bulk. Her spurt of energy must have given out.

The others soon landed.

"M'be perishing," Mamedi said. "Just a tiny drop of blood, sir."

"I need my strength," the Copper countered.

"Faaaaa!" she said. "You're just floating there. Us on wing be doing all the work."

"M'mind be muddled with exertion and shock of seeing cousins slain right and left, m'lord." Enjor coughed. "A fork be coming up in the river. Unless I have my wits w'be going wrong."

The Copper was tempted to tell him to return to the cave and deal with King Gan.

"Oops, you'd better be climbing higher, sir," some young relation of Mamedi said. "Another dwarf boat a'coming!"

The Copper saw its light before he heard the faint ring of the approaching bell.

From what he could remember of the craft, the only dwarf who could see out the front was in a cage at the back of the boat.

"I'm tired of swimming," the Copper said—though he'd been floating, there was no reason for the bats not to think him as tired as they were; otherwise they'd each clamor for blood. "Let's ride with the dwarves."

"Muh?" the bats chorused.

"You cling to rock well enough. Hang on to the front of the boat."

"With all that racket?" Thernadad said. "A'deafened by that bell? Can't echo with all that noise."

"Leave the steering to the dwarves. Anyway, I'm going to ride for a while. Try to keep up."

"The lordship's right!" Enjor said. "M'be for it. The dwarves know their business."

The Copper slipped back into the water.

Bing-bing. Bing-bing . . . Bing-bing.

It filled the tunnel like an angry dragon, light and clanging and churning as it cut through the water.

The Copper reached for it, but the front had been smoothed where it met the water. He slipped beneath its prow and felt the pull of current toward the bubbling stern, clawed frantically, and finally got a grip on a sort of rail running the underside of the vessel. He locked *sii* and *saa* on the projection and used it to climb back to the nose end.

He rode for a moment between front point and bow wave, catching his breath. Using the power in his *saa* and his good *sii* to grip, he managed to round the nose and found the bats huddled unhappily, their gripping digits white with terror. Worked metal in regular spiral shapes had been driven into the bow. Whether it was decor or functional he couldn't say, but it did offer a grip.

He wrapped himself around the bow as comfortably as he could.

"M'feel like a bit o' flushed dwarf-waste," Thernadad said. His face was wet from being splashed.

"Ooo, ooo, ooo, such a tragedy," Mamedi blubbered; some cousin of hers had slipped and fallen into the water.

Some of the bats climbed on the Copper, as his scales offered better grips than the smoothed wood.

"Sir, m'be losing strength," Thernadad's mother said. "Just a quiet nip and none be wiser."

"Oh, very well."

The bat dug around in the soft tissue behind his ear and he felt the usual tingling numbness as she licked the area before biting. He couldn't move his head without squashing her, but he rolled an eye down and saw the other bats feeding.

Irked that they didn't ask permission, he was tempted to eat one in the hope that it would teach the others some manners. But Mamedi had finally left off her blubbing.

The river wasn't always flowing and channeled. Three times the boat plunged into rushing, frothing water, thoroughly drenching them as it nosed into walls of water. Bats and one exsanguinated dragon hung on until the bat claws hurt him more than the teeth. At these moments the dwarves shouted to one another and beat a drum, and the Copper heard a clanging within as they worked their machinery.

Other times the boat stopped at steel doors in the water and waited until the dwarves finished turning wheels and clanging, then passed through to another chamber shut by another set of steel doors, sometimes raising the boat and sometimes lowering it. During this process the Copper and the bats hid under the nose of the ship. The dwarves emerged from the boat's interior and stretched on the flat top of the craft, or fouled the water with their waste.

These water chambers were thick with rats, but the Copper didn't dare leave to hunt. The bats were under no such compunction, and whipped through the chamber, clearing it of insects.

Thernadad returned, cleaning his teeth and gum line with a darting tongue-tip.

"Wherever dwarves go, rats go. Wherever rats go, bugs go. Wherever bugs go, bats hunt."

"Maybe you should live here, then."

"Oh, sir, w'be sticking to you. Be a heartbreak to leave you after all w've been through."

Water bubbled all around the craft as the chamber filled, and the dwarves shouted to one another. The Copper, splashed and cramped from clinging to the underside of the boat, felt a nip at a sore spot behind his *saa* joint.

He lashed out and down, heard a brief squeak as he crushed a bat in his jaws. He swallowed it.

The other bats yeeked in terror.

"Stupid sot," Thernadad said. "That'll teach 'em some manners."

Mamedi set to yeeking with a group of bats. "Cruelty, cruelty, a poor starving bat . . ."

The Copper felt rather better for the snack. "Did you see who it was?"

"Me cousin twice removed by mating. Too dumb to dodge a cave wall. W'be better off without him. If sir's in the mood for afters, Mamedi's sister wouldn't much be a'missed. By me, anyway." He threw a companionable wing around the Copper's shoulder. "Let that be a lesson to the rest of you," he yeeked.

"They're getting set to open the doors again," the Copper said. He heard the dwarves tramping back into the center of the vessel and going to their positions.

He looked back at the huddled bats, eyes wide and glinting at him in terror, and felt better than he had since he spit in King Gan's eye.

Chapter 9

The Copper longed to sleep, but Enjor insisted that the tunnel they needed to get to was "just a bit ahead."

They'd had to leave their first boat at another lake and swim to a different river mouth before coming upon a new vessel, smaller and more beat-up than the first, worked by a trio of dwarves.

Twice their own boat idled, hugging the side while larger vessels going the other way passed. One was wide and had heaps of black rock piled within, and crawled along only a slug's pace faster than the current.

The other almost flew down the tunnel, a long, narrow craft with dwarves sitting in the front and rear at some kind of apparatus that reminded the Copper of the foul machines they'd used to attack Mother in the cave. Instead of a bell, this one sounded a horn at intervals. Its lights, throwing tight beams from curved copper lanterns, almost blinded him as they searched the water's surface.

At last they came to another landing, where the dwarves reached up and snagged hanging chains and yelled back and forth as a pair of dwarves laden with bags hanging from wooden poles joined the boat.

"M'lord," Enjor whispered in his ear. "This passage be getting us to the other river."

The Copper nodded, and Enjor roused Thernadad. The Copper waited until the vessel got under way again and slipped off the nose with hardly a splash. He floated for a moment until the dinging bell receded, then dragged himself up into the chamber.

They passed into another cavern. The floor was littered with broken bits of masonry, and cave moss in several colors—red, blue, and green—still thrived where water was dripping. The Copper looked at characters scrawled on a wall in a reflective color, like liquid dragonscale, though someone had clawed through it.

"What is this place?" he asked Enjor on one of his swoops.

"Old dwarf settlement, m'lord. Abandoned in the wars with the demen."

"Demen?"

"Deep Men. Filthy bunch. Not above throwing a net over a bat and a'sticking a skewer through him for roasting."

"Demen?" Thernadad's mother cried. "They snip off bat wings and roll up their awful moss paste in it."

"Faaaa!" Mamedi said. "They bite our heads off before singing a battle song. M'be going no farther."

The Copper hopped up a set of stairs and peered through a broken portal. He smelled rats and damp wood rot.

Enjor hung upside down and picked at his tailvent. "Only other road to the south river is right through the heart of the Wheel of Fire city. A black bat in full cave-dark couldn't make it. I'm resting where I can hear them coming."

"Wake me if you do," the Copper said, too tired and cold to fear dwarves or demen. He found a pile of smashed wood and rotten fabric and went to sleep.

He heard rats scrabbling around in the dark and shifted position. The noises faded as the rats fled, but they returned. They always did, drawn by the smell of dragon-waste.

He followed the sounds and smells, then spit out the thin contents of his fire bladder. While it wasn't ready yet to burst into flame, it could blind or wound. He jumped after the pained squeaks and trapped two rats under his good *sii*, then swallowed them before his prey knew what had happened.

Feeling a little better with rat in him, he went back to sleep.

Enjor led them up a winding, rough tunnel, claiming that it went all the way to the surface, with a fair prospect off a mountainside if you followed it long enough.

Thernadad's mother rode his back the whole way. The tunnel smelled decidedly dwarvish. It made the Copper nervous.

"Sir, I can fly a bit if y'be just generous enough to give me a small lap."

"The last time your family left me light-headed. I need my wits."

They took a crack and descended some rough rock to a cavern filled with a confusing array of smaller chambers. Enjor flew off to be sure of the path. The Copper sniffed out a discarded iron-soled boot and carried it in his mouth until they took a rest break, where he thoughtfully chewed it down. Tearing and devouring the mixture of leather and metal was most satisfying, even if the dwarf-foot smell could poison a cave slug.

"Oh, m'be perishing, sir. Perishing!" Thernadad's mother lamented.

"Just a little, then," the Copper said, feeling generous with a belly full of heel and hobnail. "But be quiet about it."

She opened him up just under his bad *sii*. He couldn't feel much of anything in that limb anyway.

Enjor flapped back, gasping. He shoved his mother out of the way and took a hearty drink of dragonblood.

"What's all this?" the Copper said.

"Better and better still," Thernadad's mother said. "I feel a maiden bat again," she called, flapping off into the cavern. "Up and at 'em, y'slugs. Darkness a'wasting!"

"Careful, Mum!" Enjor called. "Not that way!"

He flapped heavily into the air, shouting, and in a few moments his mother returned, flying in irregular loops. She didn't so much land as nose into the cave floor.

"What's the matter? Drunk on dragonblood?"

"Bad air," Enjor said.

"Eeeeee, that's a funny color moonlight," the old white-flecked bat said. She rolled her eyes this way and that, coughed, and was still.

"Mum! Mum!" Thernadad said, flying down from the ceiling.

"She went down the wrong tunnel," Enjor said. "Bad air."

Thenadad landed next to her and head-butted her hard in the stomach. The body didn't so much as twitch. "Mum!" He rounded on his brother. "Why didn't you watch her?"

"Me only just made it out myself!"

Thernadad snapped at his brother's ear.

"Stop it," the Copper said. "She's dead."

The other bats crept across the ceiling, yeeking at one another in the shadows.

"That's three lost. How many more?" Mamedi's sister said. "This dragon's not such a lucky strike after all."

"No one asked you all to come," Thernadad said. He made to fly up, but the Copper put a *sii* claw on his wing.

"Let's keep moving."

"Once a bat drops . . ." Enjor said, flapping back up to the ceiling. "M'lordship's right."

"And just be leaving her here?" Thernadad asked. "Bats should be living above the bones of their elders."

"I'll carry her, if you like," the Copper said. He picked up the cooling little body and swallowed it whole.

"Awwwww, sir," Thernadad said. "That was unkind."

"She had enough meals from me. One in return seems just. You'd rather the rats and slugs got her?"

"Y'see another gone," Mamedi's sister whispered. "Who's next?"

"The Lavadome's worth a few odds 'n sods droppin'. Like outside, underground."

"Long way yet," Enjor said, whipping back. "Little to eat until w'be reaching the river."

Enjor hurried the party past another shaft plunging down—the source of the bad air—and they entered some naturally formed caves. The moss here was the natural variety, faint blue and green threads that vanished whenever the eye moved. White things with waving antennae slipped into cracks as they approached, and insects with bodies like glass froze against the striped cave walls.

The older bats grew tired and clung to the Copper as he walked, and only Enjor, tireless for all his bulk, and some of the first-year bats had energy to flit around.

A bat squeaked.

"What's that?" the Copper asked.

"Boktemi found something," Mamedi said.

A brighter patch lay ahead. The Copper smelled rot and metal on the air.

The source of the odor was two figures sitting back-to-back, dead for a day or two at most.

"Ahhh, that be more like it. There's some juice there still, down in the lower quarters," Mamedi said. She crawled off the Copper and began to scratch around at an outthrust leg. Tendrils of blue cave moss had found the bodies as well, and climbed toward wounds on the bodies.

The Copper examined the faces. These were no dwarves

or men; they were thicker-skinned than either, pebbled like a dragon's stomach and with thick ridges of horn making fearsome flanges at the skull and jawline. A row of spines, thin as straw, grew from their backbones.

They wore helms, though not in the dwarvish fashion. These helms were open, a series of reinforcing rods that capped the natural ridges on their skulls, and had a fearsome spike on the top. One's spike still bore a bit of dried gristle.

"Are these—"

"Demen," Enjor said. "Ech. The blood's gone bad."

"M'be calling the eyeballs," Thernadad said.

"A'taking more than your fair share!" Mamedi protested.

"Says who?"

"Faaaaaa!"

She jumped up on one of the creature's shoulders, bristling for a fight.

"Easy, now," the Copper said. "I'm trying to read this."

"Who be a'caring how they got here?" Enjor said, shoving a younger bat away from some slow-seeping fluid.

"Blast these thick skins," another bat commented from the darkness. "Wish these were dwarves."

The Copper tried to ignore the bats. The two demen bore grievous injuries, yet no dead lay around them. So they must have fought elsewhere before sitting down to succumb to their wounds. But why back-to-back? And why hadn't their fellows carried them to safety?

He suspected that the answer to both questions was a lost battle. They were either on guard against the victorious dwarves—or whomever—or something deadlier lurked in the darkness.

Threats in these caverns or no, he needed his strength. He chewed down a mouthful or two of the rotting flesh and the metal tip of a scabbard, then crept off to sleep scales-out in a protective nook.

———

He woke and found two new brown-stained wounds on his tail.

The greedy bats had taken advantage of his sleep.

"Thernadad!" he roared.

The bat flapped over, and the Copper waved his tail in front of his upturned nose.

Thernadad combed his ears. "Sir, m'be telling them to take only a lap or two each. There be so much energy in dragonblood, and w'be all bone-weary from the journey. Only a few drops out of your great body, nothing to you, but a lifesaver—"

"I was tired enough as it is. Now I'm drained. Who am I going to ride on when I get tired?"

"They be a rotten bunch of sots, yes; m'won't let it happen again."

"You've got only three songs, Thernadad, but you sing them well."

He stalked back toward the bodies of the demen. "Tell them to keep clear. I'm having my breakfast and I'm tempted to juice a bat to wash it down."

"Told you his lordship—" Enjor said.

"Faaaaa!" Mamedi screamed, backhanding her mate's brother with a wing tip. "Y'be the one saying he wouldn't miss—"

He ignored the fighting and nosed around in the corpses. Their vital organs were a putrefying mass—he settled for a bit of thick shoulder. The blood had drained down from the upper half of the bodies, and the shank had tenderized a little as it aged.

A clattering—a pile of dry bones falling was how it struck the Copper's ear—made him look up, still attached by an un-severed hunk of tendon to the corpse of the deman.

He couldn't say what appeared out of the dim light, for the cave moss lit only the lower underside of its body, only that it was frightfully spindly, standing on many legs, with two long, pincer-tipped claws on its front limbs, a cluster of eyes, and a long rise up from the tail, curling around.

He'd seen a scorpion or two in the home cave. They liked the dark and the cool, and if you flipped them and gave them a good smash at the leg joints with your tail they had tastier meat than a slug, though a good deal less. But those were compact little creatures.

The bat brawl stopped.

Odd how the bats looked up to him. It was only a lucky splatter that allowed him to escape King Gan. And this armored monstrosity . . . it would stick him with that barb and lift his slight body up in those great claws and drag him off to some dark hole.

He backed up, wanting the bodies of the demen between him and the scorpion. The tendon running from his mouth to the corpse tightened, and the body lurched.

A blur, and then a *thwak* sound—the spindly scorpion struck the deman's corpse. The force of the blow knocked it over and its wiry helmet fell off. The Copper hugged the cave floor and the helmet rolled, its arc limited by the spikes, up against his nose.

The scorpion rushed forward and took up the corpse in its claws, and the deman's companion, now with nothing to lean against, slowly sagged a claw's breadth at a time. The scorpion rounded on the motion, wary, and struck again with its tail. It pulled its prize in a little closer and guarded it with the other pincer, as though the second body meant to challenge it for the meal.

The Copper ever so slowly tongued the snared tendon out from his teeth and took the deman's helmet in his jaws, trying to think his way through a fog of terror that kept his *sii* and *saa* from obeying. Maybe he could ward off a blow, the way dwarves did with a shield. . . .

The vast creature, for all its size, was a slave to its senses. No doubt it would take the corpse it had acquired back to whatever hole would accommodate those long, thin, segmented limbs, and eat in peace. But how long would it be until it grew hungry again? Would the short, regular steps of a dragon hatchling draw it after them?

Summoning his courage, he pressed his tail against the leaning corpse and gave it a shove so it spilled over toward the scorpion.

The insect let out a shocked, whistling breath and struck with its tail again.

The Copper dragon-dashed forward through two of the impossibly thin legs, got under the thing, and struck upward with the spiked helmet, right at the joining of its eight limbs.

He pulled back down just in time to feel himself stepped on as the beast sprang sideways, crashing heedlessly into the cavern wall. It tipped, fought to right itself, claw arms and tail waving this way and that.

The Copper didn't wait to see whether it would die or not.

"Enjor—which way?"

"Oook."

He threw the helmet at the bats. "Lead the way, curse you!"

The bat flapped off and the others followed. The Copper kept up, and as the fright seeped out of their bodies they collected themselves in a cramped corner, where he could press up against the ceiling with the bats, catching his breath.

He listened for that bone-rattle sound of the thing's feet, but heard only his own hearts pounding.

"You killed a cave scorpion," some young nephew of Mamedi's—Uthaned, he thought the creature's name was—said.

"The dead men did the fighting for me," the Copper replied.

"What be that to us? Bug juice is poor in vitality," Mamedi said. "Besides, w'be leaving the body behind."

"Ooo, m'be famished, how about—" one of Mamedi's relations began.

"None of that, now," Thernadad said. "Our host has done enough. Suck air and saliva for a bit."

The Copper hardly heard them. He wished he hadn't thrown away that helmet in a fit of temper. If nothing else, he could poke the more annoying bats with it.

"Good news, m'lord," Enjor said.

"Almost any change could be good news." Food, freshwater, an end to all these twists and turns. Even a change in light level. He was tired of groping through the dark, led on by bat yeeks from patch of dim moss to patch of dim moss.

"W'be at the river."

The Copper had been walking for the last thousand paces or so with just one eye open, trying to sleep as he slid his three good legs forward and hopped over his bad.

"How far?"

"Y'be smelling it just over this next incline."

The bats flew wearily ahead. He climbed up a rocky tunnel. Someone had cleared a path of loose boulders.

"All I smell is dwarf."

"Must be a'fighting with the demen again," Thernadad said.

They passed over a makeshift wall in the tunnel, the source of all the loose boulders, and descended. The Copper smelled wood: Splintered shields lay all about, some with arrows growing out of them. He extracted a few arrowheads and swallowed them. What had made this dark pocket of emptiness worth fighting over?

"M'perishing," Thernadad gasped.

"We'll rest."

The Copper hoped he could find fish in the river. His appetite had progressed from tickle to gnaw to worry two marches ago. He curled up. Past the "wall" the tunnel turned into another series of chambers leading off in various directions, mostly down.

"Lights. Lights!"

It took the Copper a moment to realize that he'd been asleep. He shook his head, clearing cobwebs some industrious spider had woven on his ear. He scanned the downslope with his good eye, marked the beams of light waving around, probing corners.

Behind the beams of light he saw the outlines of glowing beards and thick curves of light-frosted helmets. Dwarves.

"A'searching the cavern," Thernadad said. "Better run, sir."

"I don't think I'm up to it," the Copper said. "Here, all of you gather 'round; let's go down this incline. Oh, never mind the damp . . . I've got an idea."

The Copper clung to the cavern roof in the downslope, hidden by a series of serrations not very different from the ones on the roof of his mouth. The dwarves had broken up into smaller groups to better search all the chambers and shafts of the system behind the wall.

A dragonlength below and up the slope from him, the bats lay on the floor, as relaxed as he could make them, save for Mamedi's sister, who cowered in a crack for fear of being stepped on by a dwarf.

The dwarves probed the darkness with their lights and began to descend into the chamber. This had better work, or he had nowhere to run. . . .

A dwarvish lantern flicked across a length of stiff bat wing, and the Copper got a momentary glimpse of the delicate finger bones and veining in their remarkable construction.

"They're going to step on us," Enjor yeeked.

"Faaaa!" Mamedi said. "Keep your ears down."

The dwarves froze in their tracks and grumbled to one another. One made a loud sniffing sound.

The young bat, Uthaned, gave a twitch.

The dwarves hurried back up toward their fellows, shouting warnings.

"Good work, you all," the Copper said. "Everyone gets a lick of blood for that. Except you," he said to Mamedi's sister. "No risk, no reward."

The dwarves passed over to the other side of the wall, leaving only a group of sentries standing at the gap. As soon as the others moved on, the sentries stacked their arms and started a low fire. Soon the smell of sizzling meat cooking had the Copper's mouth gushing.

If there had been just two dwarves he might have become reckless and attacked them for their food. Luckily they left four behind, so the hatchling wasn't even tempted to rashness. The only alternative to listening to his empty stomach groan as the dwarves ate was a quick escape, so he roused the bats—most of them reenergized by a quick nip from his tail—and crept away. The only sentry the dwarves left watched the long incline on the other side of the way, not the warren of caves the dwarves had already searched.

And so they came to the southbound river—the Sou'flow, as Enjor styled it.

And were checked again. One of the dwarvish hollow-log riverboats rested in the current, in what seemed the dazzling brightness of cave moss and numerous lanterns at front and back. The craft waited, hooked to chains hanging down from the ceiling and occupied by a dwarvish crew.

The Copper evaluated his chances from the shadows. With the amount of light in the cave, he felt as though one of the dwarves focused lanterns right on him, but told himself it was only the long trip in the dark that had oversensitized him.

He heard a strong breeze moving with the current. Between the wind and the sound of water in the tunnel breaking against the swinging chains and the back of the dwarf boat, they wouldn't hear him slip into the water or swim past.

The dwarves seemed glad of a chance to escape their vessel, and lounged ashore, sleeping or tending to their beards or gathering around a flat bit of cavern floor where they spun coins at one another, stamping and barking their satisfaction or disgust with the course of the game.

Enjor flapped off to hunt for insects on the water, and the Copper saw a dwarf comment and point at the bat's darting black form.

"I need a diversion," he told the bats. "Thernadad, Mamedi . . . could you fly up to those chains hanging from the ceiling? Start a fight, as noisy as you can."

"Us? Fight?" Thernadad said. "A more unnatural act m'can't imagine! W'be as close as ever two bats—"

"M'willing," Mamedi's sister said. "M'making enough noise, if sir will let me have a nip first."

"After."

"I'll go too, Mum," Uthaned said. His speech inflections had grown almost dragonish, but then, he was a young bat with more brains than the common run of them.

The bats flitted off and alighted on the chains. There they commenced yeeking and swatting. The dwarves noticed the commotion and turned to watch.

The Copper had considered creeping across the cave wall or ceiling—the dwarves would be less likely to look there—but he opted for speed instead of concealment. He shot from his hiding spot at the dragon dash—though his was a little strange in that he used his front limbs only to land; his *saa* did all the work because of his withered *sii*.

One of the dwarves bent to pick up a loose rock. The Copper couldn't say what made him shift course—later he decided it was both dislike of dwarves and a worry about the bats losing heart to go on if they lost still another—but it wasn't a conscious decision at the time.

He caught the dwarf in the back of his stubby knees as he threw, and felt a weight come crashing down across his back.

Dwarvish yells of alarm—none louder than from the dwarf unexpectedly finding himself atop the hatchling's back, riding it like a child attempting to make a pony out of too small a dog—followed him right into the water, where he kept running along the river bottom, weighed down by the dwarf.

He lost the dwarf to buoyancy and surfaced in the current and hazarded a look back, expecting to see the dwarves running to their weapons or the ship to give chase.

Instead he saw one bedraggled dwarf scooting out of the water as quickly as limbs and backside could carry him, and the other sailors bent over, laughing so hard their glowing beards dripped light.

Chapter 10

The journey south took a good deal more time, both because of the greater distance they traveled and the infrequency of tunnel boats. Most of the craft on this part of the river were warships thick with well-armed dwarves and throw-lamps. He didn't dare ride any of those, for dwarves rode in the front, with a good view of the prow of the ship, sometimes tossing lines to probe the water depth.

He even encountered one being laboriously drawn back up against the current by dwarves using poles and hooks, sweating and grunting and chanting as they worked.

They clung and splashed to another vast lake, and Enjor advised them to make for the other side. It was easy enough for the bats to fly, but the Copper had to fight his way through a waterfield of spongy pads anchored to the bottom by long roots. A black slime thick with biting water mites infested the underside of each pad. The slime caught in his scales, and he began to itch immediately.

All the Copper could do was curse the bats for their ability to fly, and his curses were all the more venomous thanks to the foreknowledge that he would never fly, even if he lived to see his wings uncase.

They lingered at the edge of the lake for a day or two in a warren of half-submerged rocks and sand and muck. He had no way of telling time other than his body's natural rhythm, as he tried to scrub out the nits with sand and freshwater, scratching himself until he was raw and bleeding. In this case the bats were a positive blessing; their saliva took away the itch as they worked over every sore spot.

But the nits always rallied and returned. Each time he woke, fresh masses had gathered.

He'd never forget the fish of that deep, vast lake. They were bony, and had thick hides with horny dimples running the back and side, with long shovel noses. But the softest, tastiest flesh he'd ever sampled ran from just behind the jawline and along the underside down the long tail. If he dipped his tail in the lake and poked at the bottom, overturning rocks, the fish would often come, drawn to whatever creatures were stirred up by his probe. And more often than not he could get his jaws on one before it could flee, though he once was taken on a wild underwater ride by a specimen three times his own length.

He came back bloody-mouthed, having lost a pair of hatchling teeth.

He feasted on fish and the bats feasted on him and the nits feasted on both—though the bats were better at digging the creatures out of their fur. Scale had its disadvantages.

But after a period of rest and feasting on fish he felt the urge to move on. The bats took some convincing, for there was good insect hunting, especially over those awful pads in the middle of the lake, but after one of their number was eaten by some swooping thing that was all mouth and wing, they saw the wisdom in moving on.

Just when he thought it was time to strike off downriver again, they were delayed by one of the younger bats giving birth to a trio of young. The bats had a strange system of feeding their young in which the newborns lapped fluid from their mother. It struck the Copper as being wasteful; to his mind the sooner young learned to feed themselves the more likely they were to survive. But considering the utter helplessness of a pink newborn bat, their system had been literally born of necessity.

Thernadad cadged twice-daily feedings of dragonblood for the nursing mother. The Copper agreed, mostly because Thernadad said a well-fed mother would mean well-fed young, and well-fed young would soon be able to cling to their mother as she clung to the dragon, and thus they'd be able to get going downriver all the sooner.

It meant more fishing, and as fish were growing scarce at that end of the lake, the Copper explored its edges. He found a few old dwarvish camps and exploratory tunnels filled with little but mold and slime.

During one of these trips, swimming back with half of one of the bony fish floating along in his mouth, he came across the wreck.

He'd missed it during his climb across the rocky edge of the lake because it was more than half-submerged. It was a strange sort of vessel, hardly large enough for more than three dwarves, only a quarter the width of the other vessels, and entirely lacking in machinery. Parts of it were charred, and the wood that was in contact with the water had rotted.

The Copper found a few tasty metal pegs made out of a greenish heavy metal. They smelled hearty, and he extracted one with his teeth. Finding it palatable, he pulled out a second one, and the vessel parted from its lower half and rolled over, breaking into two pieces, one of which was dry and still floated.

What dwarves could do, he could. He hopped into it and, after a moment of precarious rocking, found that it supported him. It was curved, and about half of it went under the water. He found that if he lay between the two raised arms he could be mostly out of the water.

He pushed off and paddled with his *saa*, alternating with

tail swipes when his legs grew tired. With this, he didn't need a dwarf boat. It wasn't quite swimming, nor could it be called riding, but it would do.

He paddled it back to the rocks where the bats waited, clinging to the cavern ceiling, and showed off his prize. The bats were more interested in the fish than the find.

The Copper had gotten better at pounding ideas into minuscule bat skulls. Or perhaps the bats had grown used to following his orders. "This way you don't need to fly all the time. You can rest on the wood edges, there."

"Ooo, m'be not liking that," Mamedi said. "Bit of dwarf craft. It'll go wrong and end up on top of me in the water!"

"Then cling to my back. I won't roll over. Here, try."

She stayed where she was on the rock until Thernadad gave her a shove. Then she fluttered down and settled on his head.

"You're blocking my good eye with your wing."

"M'regrets, sir," Mamedi said.

He pushed out and swam in a slow circle. He wondered how the piece of wreckage would handle in the stronger current of the river tunnel. But even if he bumped his whole way to the Lavadome, it would be easier, and warmer, than swimming. The dwarves, for all their faults, knew how to get from one bit of cavern to another with as little discomfort as possible.

Another advantage of the Copper's discovery was that it allowed the young mother bat to travel with her young.

Looking back on matters later, he counted the final leg of the journey as one of the key turning points in his life. A thousand tiny circumstances might have caused him to miss the camping demen and their egg. Had he ridden lazily in the piece of wreckage instead of paddling, had he not passed up likely landing places because of dwarf-smell and pushed the bats, had it been another season when the river flowed more slowly, or more quickly . . .

The strange chain of events started when he saw a distant shape in the dim light of the tunnel. A brighter patch of light that marked a tunnel mouth revealed it as three hominid shapes rowing in a little shell of a boat not much larger than his own bit of wood.

He reached out a *saa* and arrested his drift.

Three demen struck the tunnel mouth. Two dragged their boat out of the current while a third scouted, spiny projections on his back bristling. The two began to take baggage out of their craft.

"Kuu! Kuu! Kuuuuu!" a chorus of voices shouted.

The demen shoved their boat back into the river.

The Copper heard a scream, and he saw one of the demen fall toward the boat, sprouting new quills in the chest and leg where none had been before. He dropped some light-colored orb into the water as he fell. His companion shoved their craft into the water and fell on board.

The Copper saw sparks fly as missiles struck the tunnel wall.

A group of dwarves charged into view, striking at the deman who'd gone ahead to scout. He fought like a mad thing, lashing out with blades in each hand, head-butting dwarves with his spiked helmet, but fell when an ax caught him across the horned spine. The dwarves didn't stop to celebrate, but threw wide, flat-bottomed craft of their own into the water and pursued the wounded deman and his companion.

The Copper waited with the bats, who filled the time by complaining of exhaustion and hatred of the river and travel. He ignored the chatter. The only bat he couldn't afford to lose was Enjor.

"Keep out of sight," he told the bats. "If I jump off the craft, just drift with it for a while."

He approached the tunnel mouth. He caught the smell of

burning flesh —heard the dwarves chattering as they burned the body of the slain deman.

A pale white object just beneath the river's surface caught his eye. He arrested his silent drift and retrieved it by pinching it between his good *sii* and the crippled limb. The dwarf watching the river stiffened and took a step toward the bank.

It was an egg. Smaller than a dragon egg and wider at one end than the other, it had a faint, clean smell that reminded him of wet sand.

He released his grip and let his raft continue downstream. The dwarf looked out onto the river, unsure of his own eyes, but by the time he called his fellows over the Copper was rounding a riverbend.

He heard a distant hammering sound. Not long later they came upon the dwarf boat, anchored just beneath a series of cracks in the cavern wall that led to another hole in the cavern roof. He smelled demen here, and a little dwarf.

The dwarves had anchored their craft with an arrowlike piece of metal driven into one of the cracks. The Copper bumped up against the dwarf boat.

He dug his teeth into the line holding the boat. A quick grind of his teeth and the boat commenced drifting. He tossed the egg into some canvas at the bottom of the boat, hopped in after it, and sniffed around the bottom. He found some bread and dried meat wrapped up in waxy cloth, ignored the bread, and swallowed the meat.

As he ate he sniffed the boat. It was a clever thing, with canvas sides held up by wooden slats. It leaked a little through the hinge at the bottom. He guessed the dwarves folded the boat up to carry it through the tunnels.

He smelled a slightly sweet fluid and looked at the egg. It was cracked, either when the deman dropped it or in his clumsy retrieval—perhaps even when he'd tossed it into the boat.

He tasted the fluid. Delicious! He widened the crack and began to lap at the fluid within, and found it so tasty he greedily shoved his nose in and sucked the yolk down. He felt like a new dragon afterward.

The bats, always sensitive to a meal being served, joined him. They licked up bits of egg that had dripped or pooled in the cracked shell.

He smacked his jaws open and shut and ran his tongue around the edges of his mouth. It was the best meal he'd ever had. If he were ever king of his own land like the dragon-lords of old, he'd eat one just like it every day.

He crunched down the shell. Then he left the dwarf boat. No one would ever mistake it for a bit of flotsam. And if the dwarves needed it back . . . well, war was a series of misfortunes, wasn't it?

"Who lays eggs like that underground?" he asked Enjor.

"No idea, m'lord. No birds be a'living down here. At least, no birds y'be wanting to meet."

The river drained off into a mire filled with giant mushrooms. The less said about this portion of the trip, the better—the Copper remembered only having muck and filth between every scale, every tooth, even working its way into his eyes.

The only ones happy about it were the bats, for insects flew so thickly here they made mistlike clouds. The bats ate their fill and then some—except for the young of Mamedi's relative: They had hair now and an unslakable thirst for dragonblood.

Luckily they were so small they took only a few drops each.

He came out of the mire a bedraggled dragon, sick of filtering mouthfuls of filthy water through his teeth to eat the worms that wiggled through the mire bottom. He assuaged his appetite by tearing off mouthfuls of fungus.

At the other side of the mire they passed through another series of tunnels, these sided with a hard, shiny surface that offered cave moss no purchase. He had to be led through the blackest patches by the bats, who probably drained him each time he slept.

"Almost there now," Enjor said, so often that Thernadad took up the refrain. "Almost there now."

"What's almost?"

"One more river to cross, the river of slaves. It flows in a circle around the Lavadome. Then the passage up."

After one of his "scouts," Enjor returned in excitement. "W'be there. You'll get a good view if the sun is right."

They reached the river, its current so slow that it was hard to distinguish from a lake. This river cavern made the dwarf-boat tunnels seem little more than chutes.

It had a high ceiling, sheer walls climbing to a dark roof cracked in places where true sunshine fell through. Shafts of light, one or two angled just right so the sunlight fell in neatly edged beams of gold, illuminated the gray-green river surface, tendrils of mist hovering above it in zephyrs of air. Titanic granite boulders rose from the waterline like teeth guarding the far edge.

"One more swim, m'lord," Enjor said.

He saw a winged shape cross through one of the shafts of light.

"What are those?"

"Nothing y'be wanting to meet," Enjor said. "That's the *griffaran*—the dragon-guard."

"Who are they?"

"Bat eaters," Enjor and Thernadad said together.

"Hunt by?"

"Sight, m'lord."

"Let's cross once the sunlight goes, then."

He rested on the riverbank and saw a long, thin boat with

a line of hominids on board, crossing the water, beetle-sized in the distance. One of the flyers, a black shadow with vast wings, hovered overhead.

He waited until the beams lifted and vanished, disappearing into a faint glow from the sky. The shadowy wings still flew over the river, though. He nosed around the riverbank as the light faded, but found only a tasteless snail or two. He wedged himself into a crack—more to prevent the bats from feeding on him in his sleep than because he feared discovery—good eye on his vulnerable side.

But he couldn't sleep, so excited was he to be this near to the Lavadome. He three-quarters shut his good eye. But why weren't there dragons whirling above the river? Surely such a vast body of water had those long, bony, shovel-nosed fishes living within?

He felt a cautious nip at his leg. He reached out with a *saa* and heard a bat squeak.

"Thernadad! You!"

"Sir! Didn't think you'd miss—"

He squeezed.

"You're wrong there. Listen, Thernadad, or I'll squeeze every bit of my blood back. I'm putting you in charge of my body. I wake up with any more slits, nips, or cuts, no matter how well concealed, I'll assume you did it and squeeze you."

"Yeek!"

"I can't hear your voice at that pitch."

"Y'be very generous, sir," Thernadad grunted.

"Spread the word."

"M'don't suppose, as a gesture to our new understanding . . ."

"No. Once we're across the river and I'm in the Lavadome. Not before."

The cavern was eerie in the way the lighting changed into full dark. He understood light changing from cavern to cavern, but the idea of the amount of light over the lake altering over a single digestive cycle was new to him.

He set off into the water, the three thriving young bats riding upon his crest. The water was a good deal warmer than that of the underground tunnels, warmer than the rock or air, thus the low mist that hung over the water.

"Stay low," he suggested to the bats on wing. "The, umm—"

"*Griffaran*," Uthaned said, turning a tight circle over the Copper's nostrils.

"—*griffaran* shouldn't be able to pick you out through these mists."

Something else was using the mists to hide. A boat, a version of the deman craft he'd encountered on the river, rowed across the water as fast as paddles and demen hands could move it. It held three demen, two rowing and a third in the center.

The deman in the middle of the boat lifted up a round, white object—an egg! and wrapped it in a cloth before placing it in a basket. He wore colorful feathers tucked through each ear piercing, set so they covered his shoulders.

The Copper's stomach rumbled. An egg or two would be just what he'd need to get him the rest of the way to the Lavadome.

He swam alongside the boat, matching its direction and speed. The boat neared the far bank. The rowing demen jumped out, and the other climbed out, then extracted his basket. The rowers lifted the boat.

Appetite helped him make up his mind.

"You'd better be old enough to fly," he told the young bats.

He dove and swam for the basket-carrying deman. It became more of a wet scuttle as he neared the shore.

"*Jt tht aleet*," a deman shouted as the Copper pushed past a leg.

He spun, using his tail to take the deman's legs out from under him. The hominid fell into the shallow water with a splash.

The Copper didn't want to fight the demen so much as cause confusion and make off with an egg. He nosed into the basket and extracted an egg and—

Urk!

His head was jerked out of the water. The jerk originated from his neck, and his neck was attached to a line, and the line was in the hands in one of the demen rowers.

It took two of them to drag him, fighting madly and still clutching an egg to his breast in his good *sii*, and haul him out of the water.

Another deman got a line about his *saa*.

The Copper fought on pure instinct, determined to either die or be freed of the lines. He'd never be bound and tortured again, and if that meant his hearts' blood pouring into this underground lake and his last breath rising up through those far-off cracks, he'd overcome even the fear of death.

He fought to bite through the line on his *saa*, but the line on his neck pulling in the other direction restrained his reach. Every time he tried to reach up to dig his claws into the line on his neck, they pulled again to straighten out his body so he couldn't reach.

All he could do was hiss, gurgle, and fling his tail this way and that.

The demen, pulling him first one way and then another, dragged him out of the water and toward the cavern, shouting to each other in their rattling language. The third got his basket of eggs and ran into the rough-cut, low-hanging tunnels.

He returned with a short tube. He made a gasping sound, and his obscenely short throat expanded. He put the tube to his mouth.

A bat struck him between the eyes. The dart that flashed by the Copper's ear missed. The other two young bats who'd been nursing on his blood were flitting back and forth between the demen with their lines.

If the Copper hadn't been otherwise occupied by being choked and dragged, he would have gaped in astonishment. Bats, shy and fearful as any whisker-quivering rodent, attacking creatures a thousand times their own size! What had gotten into them?

The deman with the tube hissed and extracted a strange sort of a weapon, a long, wide-ended blade. He didn't raise it like a dwarf, but reversed it so the blade was shielded under its elbow. It whistled through pointed teeth and came forward.

The Copper tried to right himself, but his bad *sii* slipped on slimy stone. He went down on his side. The deman at his *saa* ran forward and looped the line around his free limb and tied them at the joints, avoiding the Copper's claws.

The blade flashed down and then up, and the Copper saw his own blood fly into the air, splattering the deman.

Anger, hurt, fear—his breastbone convulsed, and a wide gout of flame shot out of his chest.

The deman had only a moment to regret his inexperience in dragon fighting before the liquid fire consumed his face, chest, and shoulders. He lit up like a dwarf's oiled torch. The deman with the line at his neck caught a little of the spray on his arm.

Pain struck—hard. Harder than the blade, or the tail-breaking iron bars of the dwarves.

The strain at his legs vanished as the deman groped for the fallen blade of his companion. The Copper wiggled toward the water. And here was the dropped egg!

He tucked it under his arm and saw a pair of stout, thick-skinned, horn-jointed legs next to him. He looked up to see the remaining deman ready to chop his head off.

A pair of black-taloned claws opened above the deman, took him up by the shoulders, and the Copper felt a wave of wind flow across him at the beat of feathered wings.

The Copper turned his head so he could watch the flier with his good eye. It was a strange sort of creature, a half dragon with twin tails, hardly any neck at all capped by a tall, arching head with a hooked snout, and feathered wings. It rose and turned, screeching, and another almost identical flier passed, flying in the opposite direction. The other reached out a claw and grabbed the kicking legs of the deman, and with only the briefest of jerks the deman parted messily.

Another flier came down and plucked him out of the water, its talons closing around his chest. Yet another approached, and the Copper wondered what it would feel like to be torn in twain and for how long he could watch his back half being carried off, but the second bird-creature flew under, eyeing him before alighting at the riverbank and poking around in the deman's boat.

The feathered avian carried him up, across some of the tall towers of rock, and to a splinter of stone that made a convenient ledge. It dropped him and turned its leathery-skinned head almost completely around to watch him, a fierce cast in its eyes thanks to streaks of yellow and blue eyelid decorating the round black orbs.

It didn't have a tooth-filled mouth, but a beak with a pink-white tongue inside. He saw it as it opened his mouth to cluck at him. What he took to be twin tails were in fact only feathers, like the heavy-ended blades he'd seen in the demen's hands, only longer.

"*Tlock*—the fire was you?" it asked in good Drakine. The Copper noticed that it had a silver ring set into the fore-edge of a wing bone near the shoulder.

The Copper could only pant, the wound in his chest burning.

He shut his eyes, and opened them again only when he heard high bat yeeks. The great bird-creature had left as silently as it had dropped on the demen. Thernadad, Mamedi, Enjor, and one or two of the other bats clung to a crack in the rock.

Real greenstuff grew on these pillars of stone. Enough light must come down through the cracks to support true plants rather than the mosses and lichens and slimes of the Lower World.

The bats nibbled and lapped at his wound, but as they seemed to be doing more good than harm, he left them to it. The pain faded to an ache. Awful, but tolerable. Scales, stuck together with blood, closed over the wound.

Suddenly they scattered. The fliers returned, bearing the woven basket.

One of the bird-creatures—*griffaran*, he reminded himself—climbed down the rock face from above, using its two limbs and beak.

Another placed the basket on the shelf beside him as it alighted.

"Egg thief!" one croaked.

"Egg thief! Death to all egg thieves!" others called, drifting on air currents.

Another landed and turned its head so it looked at him, first with one eye, then the other.

The Copper gulped. With so many gathered around would they each take some piece of him in those hooked beaks and yank him apart?

A vast *griffaran*, its beak battle-scarred, one eye socket dry and empty, and two digits missing from its right foot, landed. It wore a pair of golden rings, one in each arm, with fabric like bits of woven sunlight looped through and knotted.

"*Gak!* Any other prisoners?" it asked in Drakine.

"No, none. They've run again."

"Curse the thieves," one of the watching creatures called. Others squawked in agreement.

The one with the gold bands looked into the empty basket. "We will see justice done, drake. Prepare yourself."

It reached out with a spread-taloned claw. . . .

BOOK TWO

Drake

"FOOLS AND THRALLS TALK OF GOOD AND EVIL.
THEIR MASTERS THINK IN TERMS OF TIME AND PLACE."

—*Tighlia*

Chapter 11

The gold-shouldered *griffaran*, with two silver-winged companions soaring beside, flew to the far side of the water. The Copper rode, clenched in maimed talons, protecting his chest wound with his bad *sii*.

The Copper was more than a little surprised they didn't tear him to shreds, or eat him, or drop him to break and die against the rocks below.

The *griffaran* sailed into line and entered a tunnel. He heard wing tips brush the chiseled sides. He looked ahead and saw the tunnel's end, but the *griffaran* didn't slow. They dropped, picking up speed, as though to dash themselves against the wall.

They beat their wings powerfully, and turned up, and rose through a hole in the cave ceiling, and suddenly there was open air and light all around.

The Copper looked around in wonder, wishing both his eyes worked so he could take it all in properly.

He couldn't see much overhead, thanks to the commanding *griffaran*, just a vague sense of an oddly regular dome shape rising above, like a vast hollow mountain, and a glowing light source at the apex of the dome. Was that the sun? It was high in the sky and bright enough, but it hardly dazzled, and it seemed held in place with no blue about anywhere, so unlike the vague mind-pictures passed down from his parents that he decided it must be some imitation.

Below he saw a vast blue-green plain, with little rises of red rock, some needle-shaped, others leaning, a few formed like toadstools, and many more low hummocks scattered about. Mosses thrived in the wet crevices; ferns dripped from the edges of pools and streams.

At the center of the Lavadome stood a black carbuncle, like the pupil in the middle of an eye.

The fliers were making for the black rock.

As they flew closer and turned above it, he saw that the rock, unevenly shaped on all sides and resembling a kidney, had been sculpted, added to, cut and galleried and tunneled, enlarging what had been irregular holes scattered around the minimountain like the eyes of a potato he'd once seen a dwarf eating.

The fliers dropped toward a long garden filled with flower-covered vines set atop one of the rises in the rock. A sculpted river flowed through it, complete with waterfall. Statues of dragons—rampant, reclining, rearing, crossing necks, even dipping their noses into pools of water—surrounded the greenery. It smelled like earth and green growing things.

His captors swooped down and landed gently.

Hairy, broad-backed hominids dropped jugs and tools and scattered as the avians alighted. A rise of black rock overlooked the garden.

The *griffaran* fluffed their wings and let out loud calls.

A dragon—a real dragon, huge and silver with black tips at his *griff* and crest and tail-line—stirred from where he'd been resting atop a small rock.

"High Captain, what brings you to the Imperial Resort without invitation?"

"I have a wounded young drake. He was involved in an egg raid. I'll speak to the Tyr."

Dragon snouts emerged from the rock. A head or two rose from holes. The Copper saw golden, and red, and pink, and even purple eyes looking at him. He heard whispered dragon voices.

"The Tyr rests."

"*Yark!* He has always trusted my judgment in waking him."

The silver dragon inclined his head sideways—rather like Auron when puzzled—but there seemed to be lassitude to the gesture, and disappeared into the rise. The Copper noted that it was the tallest prominence on the black rock; even the garden was above much of the rest of the top.

The others looked and sniffed at him with interest, not contempt. The smell of dragons, the odd sense of the vast space around while still being underground, the faint throb of so many heartbeats and breathing bodies and shifting claws and scales—it overwhelmed him, and he felt his throat go thick and his good eye blur.

The Copper's eyes roved in wonder around the dome. What he'd taken to be the sun was just a glowing patch of light at the top of the dome. He suspected it was in fact sunlight being filtered through translucent material. But that wasn't the only glow. Jagged streaks of orange light, brightening and fading and pulsing, flowed down the sides, adding a red-orange cast to the brighter light above.

A smallish, wide-bodied dragon, with scales that seemed deep red or purple depending on how the light struck, carrying seventeen, eighteen, nineteen ... twenty-one horn-tips atop his crest, emerged from the rock. The horns grew up, sideways, down, as though interested in what was happening all around the dragon's head. But for all the creature's evident pride in the number of horns, patches of bare skin showed around his eyes, mouth, and the edges of his crest where scale had fallen away.

A pair of wide-shouldered, stooped-over hominids wearing white loincloths trailed behind, with brushes, scoops, and a basket.

"It's you, Yarrick. They just said a *griff* captain or I would have hurried. It is the hour of white?"

Yarrick stepped in front of the Copper, cutting off his view of the Tyr.

"But one. We thought it best to let you sleep, Tyr," the silver dragon said.

"Oh, bash it. I like getting to work early. You should have roused me. But I'm forgetting our visitors. What news from the water ring, brave Yarrick?"

"Another egg raid, Tyr. Well organized. They distracted us, poisoned the nest guardians. Sixteen eggs this time—it would have been the worst loss we've ever suffered. And then there's this."

He sidestepped from the Copper. The Copper felt the gaze of two slightly cloudy eyes the color of aging gold coin. He stared back defiantly. If this dragon was going to watch his own kind torn to bits for nest raiding without singeing so much as a feather—

"Really? That's terrible," the Tyr said.

Yarrick fluffed his wings. "This drake—still with egg-wet behind the *griff*, if I'm still fit to judge dragons—almost lost his gizzard to the demen while rescuing our eggs. But there were guts to spare in that one."

Rescue?

It took the Copper a moment to get over the shock. He felt doubly fortunate that the fight with the demen turned out the way it did, even at the price of a stab in the firebladder. What if the *griffaran* had found him eating from a broken egg?

"What is he, some young relative of yours eager to prove himself, my Tyr? He shows the old FeHazathant spirit."

"NoSohoth," Tyr said, "is this some relative of mine? Why

hasn't he been presented to me? Such old scars on a young drake, too. He's taken honors from three bitter fights, and I'm just looking at the front end of him."

The silver dragon with the black *griff* tips lowered his head and looked at the Copper closely. "He's no hatchling from the Imperial Resort, Tyr."

Tyr glowered. "Hmmmm. Yes. Why does that not surprise me?"

"Let us sing of glories proudly won," a golden drake said from one of the flower beds. The Copper saw a couple of bats flit under an overhanging rock behind him.

"Let's keep our fool's mouth shut for a change," NoSohoth muttered.

"Let the drake sing, old fellow," Tyr said. "At least he's got an appreciation for the old virtues and deeds."

"Sir, I've no time for songs," Yarrick said. "I'm here to see that justice gets done to this brave little fellow. He saved six eggs."

"Did he? Did I doze off and miss part of the story? Well, if you say so. What's your name, lad?"

The Copper opened his mouth, but couldn't find words.

"Perhaps he's in awe to be in the Imperial presence," NoSohoth said. "You've nothing to fear, drake. Glorious Tyr is grandsire to all of us, a part of our lifesong whatever our parentage. Just answer honestly and no harm will befall you."

"Nice to see daring young drakes plunging in among enemies instead of crying for help. Not enough about. Not enough," the Tyr said. He settled down over his *sii* and *saa*, perhaps to be less threatening.

"I . . . I've no name, sir. I'm . . . my sire and dam . . . dead."

"What? Who?" Tyr said. "NoSohoth, what's this? Are you keeping ill news from me again?"

"No, Tyr," NoSohoth said. He turned to the Copper.

107

"There've been no attacks in the Lavadome in two generations. Are you from one of the Upper Provinces?"

"I'm not sure. Perhaps. I came down the river. I've been traveling for ages . . . ages, it seems." The Copper wished his voice hadn't sounded so squeaky. He wondered if he could even be heard over the *surr-whooosh* of the Tyr's breathing.

"Yarrick, where did you find him?"

The avian straightened up. "The lake circle."

"The lake circle, Tyr," NoSohoth corrected.

"Oh, never mind that," Tyr said. "We're old friends, and this is a friendly visit."

"Of course, Tyr," Yarrick said. "On the far bank, to the north. Downstream from the thrall crossing."

"Who were your parents?"

The Copper wondered if the truth would be a mistake. Something about the friendly stare of Tyr made him tell the truth. "AuRel and Irelia, sir."

The dragons looked at each other. "Irelia? That's no staion-name. AuRel . . . hmmm, what line?"

"I . . . I don't know."

"I don't know, Tyr," NoSohoth corrected again.

"I don't know, Tyr," the Copper repeated.

"He's lying. He's an outcast; I'll put my fringe on it," a hard-edged voice said. A beautiful green dragon joined the others in the garden. She was rather fleshless about the hips, more so than Mother at her hungriest, and had startling violet eyes.

The dragons and avians dipped their heads at her approach, save for the Tyr, who tickled her under the chin with his tail. The golden drake in the garden bowed especially low.

"Now, Tighlia, how could you know that?" the Tyr said. "Do you know his parentage?"

"No. If I had, I'd order them to have such a cripple drowned."

"Then do be quiet. I let you have your way with the drakka, don't I? Let me see to this drake."

He looked back at the Copper. "You found your way here through the Lower World? Down a river thick with dwarf trunks and demen boats?"

"Yes, Tyr."

"You're a drake of singular purpose," Tyr said. "What did you expect to find here? Safety?"

The Copper wanted to tell the Tyr all about his dreams of protecting his kind from lying, torturing assassins, but when surrounded by all these great dragons, it seemed a silly hatchling fantasy.

"Have you had anything to eat this morning, my love?" Tighlia asked.

"Hot watered fat and a fresh sow's head."

"And your kern?"

"Haruuummm . . ."

Her claws rattled the river-smoothed rocks in the walkway between the door and a garden pool. "I'll roast your cook. What you need is an elf, not that blighter."

"But he can braise an ox so that it melts—"

"You'd sleep better if you'd just listen. And there'd be less groaning at your eliminations."

"Tyr, I must get back to my command," Yarrick said. "I won't rest until I see the drake here settled here in the Imperial Resort."

"What? A half-starved, bedraggled stray here?" Tighlia said. "The bones of my grandsire will crumble."

The Copper wondered at her hostility. Did she know more of his deeds than she would admit? Why would she not tell the truth, if she knew it, as she was so clearly against him?

"Why, I think that's a fine idea. We could use some new blood on the Rock."

"Quite right, Grandsire," the golden drake said. He crinkled up the corners of his mouth at the Copper, who started, fearing a bite.

"Perhaps we could discuss it later, at feast," NoSohoth said.

"Delay, delay. You always counsel delay," the Tyr said. "No, I like the idea. I'll have him."

"CuRassathath over by Wind Tunnel and his mate are barren," Tighlia said. "He could go and live with them. They've a lovely hole."

"There was a time when brave deeds merited a place in the Imperial Resort," the Tyr said. "I'd like to restore the tradition."

"You're always cross and impulsive when you haven't eaten properly," Tighlia said.

"I've not been cross in years. Cry settled, for I've made a decision. NoSohoth, get it inscribed at once. This lad . . . Oh, dear, what was that name . . . ?"

"I've no name, Tyr." His wound throbbed, but he did his best to stand straight, neck up and head alert.

"I told you. An outcast," Tighlia said. "And you wanted to settle him in the Black Rock."

"Now, lad, take heart. You're not as forlorn as you'd think; it's happened several times in my lifetime. Why, I could tell you stories—outcasts tend to be lucky, for a start, and I'll take a lucky dragon over the quickest tongue or the stoutest scale. You rate a name for your deeds this day, and a good one." He looked around. "What shall we call him?"

"Cripple," Tighlia said. "Half-wit. Both highly appropriate names. Look at that eye and tell me he wasn't cursed in the egg."

"How about MiKalmedes," the golden drake said. "He was a copper, wasn't he?"

"Insolence!" Tighlia spit. "You flakescale. My own grandsire and one of the founding—"

The golden drake scratched himself behind his *griff*. Loose skin and bits of scale-edge wafted toward Tighlia.

"Stop quarreling," the Tyr said, and the others fell silent in an instant. "He'll be Rugaard."

"Tyr, your own grandsire by the female?" NoSohoth objected.

"He was wounded at hatching, and he turned out all right. His jaw never grew quite right, of course. Not much in the way of wits, but a fierce fighter, and he gave the demen what-for. I think it suits him. How do you like that name, hatch—er, drake?"

The Copper's hearts swelled. Not just a name, but a name from an illustrious line! "Thank you, Tyr." He wanted nothing more that instant than to devote himself to this great dragon's will and prove himself worthy of the compliment.

"Grandsire, lad. Grandsire from now on. You're the Tyr's ward now. Be worthy of your new heritage."

"Grandsire," the Copper said. The golden drake was turning up the corners of his mouth at him again.

"See that he's given a lair," the Tyr said. "Not in the nursery, now—a battle-scarred dragon deserves a real chamber of his own. I know—have him join the Drakwatch. Give him a chance to prove himself to you doubters. Attend to it, won't you, NoSohoth?"

The female checked a loosened scale on the Tyr's haunch and shot a look at NoSohoth as he bowed to the Tyr.

"A fine addition to the family," the golden drake said, rolling so he came up with flower petals caught in his scales. "We won't want for entertainment as long as he's around. I can't wait to see him limp his way through a court dance."

Chapter 12

NoSohoth led the Copper through what seemed a maze of tunnels, beautifully sculpted, with dragonscale patterns on the rises and drops to help the claws find purchase. The rock inside was shiny and black, with veins of white where it had been left natural, but in many places, like projections and corners, it had been coated with metals or ceramics in intricate designs. The floor wasn't quite smooth, the better to give dragonclaws places to grip, but it was polished. Splashes of water from drinking trickles looked like blood.

Turns, drops, and climbs were marked by burning fat-lamps.

"Don't you use moss?" the Copper asked.

"What is this, a mining camp? You're in the Imperial Resort. Besides, there are other advantages to lamps. Smell."

Some kind of substance had been thrown into the mix to give a pleasing, relaxing aroma.

"What's that burning, sir?" the Copper asked.

"You're a polite hatch—young drake. I haven't heard 'sir' from the Imperial lines in three sets of scale. You've never been in the Upper World?"

"No. I've seen shafts of sunlight; that's all."

"The smell's hardy pine. It has an oil that's useful in a variety of ways, a solvent for a start. We put it in the fat-lamps. Some mint and rosemary are added to the oil. Eucalyptus is even better, but hard to come by these days. Otherwise the dragon-smell can get thick in here. Drakes get aggressive, and the drakka play up too much, and dragons who should know better get to dueling. We dragons are thralls to none but our noses."

The Copper had no idea what "eucalyptus" was, but had more important questions on his mind. "I like the smell of dragons all around. I keep fearing I'll wake up and be alone again."

"I wouldn't mind a year or two alone, myself. Now, let's see, plenty of empty space on this level, as it doesn't have much in the way of egress. Everyone in the Black Rock thinks they're born deserving a gallery with its own trickle."

The Copper gave up counting passages and turns by the time they descended a third time.

"You'll learn your way around soon enough," NoSohoth said. "If you get lost, just remember always to go from smaller to larger. That'll get you to the Central Spiral."

"That big downshaft with the columns?"

"Yes, where we first descended. Just ask a thrall; they all speak Drakine. More or less. They'll put you right. If they don't, you're free to eat them."

The passage rose and then fell away to a wider, lower tunnel. There wasn't so much frill and decor along the passages now. Hominid skulls lined the wall here, grouped in threes and sixes and nines, grinning at him from beneath a coating of bronze or pewter.

"This is the old Drakwatch level. When I was your age, we had an elvish sorcerer who could make these skulls talk. The stories they told! Plenty of room here; there's just old NeStirrath and some orphans from the provinces adopted into the Rock. Here, this one's got its own passage, which is nice. Can't stand sleeping with air on more than two sides, myself. And room for growth."

"How might I learn more about this RuGaard, sir?"

NoSohoth stopped for a moment, raised his head up, and spit into a wrought cup connected to a larger pot. The flame lit the passage. The skull of a creature with four horns projecting from the temples and two shorter ones out of the jaw decorated the entrance.

"A young drake should look to his duties."

"Isn't my first duty to learn about the heritage I'm charged with defending?" He was rather proud of that little speech.

"Hmmm. That eye is deceiving. You have some wit about you."

The Copper thought it better not to reply beyond a "Thank you, sir."

"Listen to the storytellers, then. If you've a taste for the exotic, you could read some of those old scrolls and things the archivists keep. The Anklenes keep their traditions, as undragonish as they are. They live in the Marble Slope, just on the other side of the Gardens."

He led the Copper to a climbing wall. "There's a shelf on top. How do you like it? I hope that's not too difficult a climb."

The rock reflected just enough light for him to see the interior. Though the entrance was cramped, the cave opened up nicely. No air moved, and the dragons' thickening odor made him nervous. He felt very small among the echoes of their shifting scale.

"It's quiet. Is there a trickle?"

"There're downspouts with water in the common pool. Let me show you."

NoSohoth backed out into the passage, turned, and led him down another length or two to a graveled chamber. Four burning lamps illuminated a pool fed by a spiral of sculpture that reminded him of . . . of trees, yes, that was what they were.

His guide loosed a strange, whistling cry. "He must have

the drakes out on a circuit." What the Copper guessed to be a a blighter and a human with one hand were cleaning the gravel with strange implements and a tub of water. They scrubbed harder.

"Ka! You there. Man!" NoSohoth said.

The man, a rather hairy and stooped-over specimen, looked at the blighter and came forward. Trembling, he held out his tool, a stick with what looked like straw bundled on it. The straw smelled rotten.

"Please? Need fix," the man said, in rather wretched Drakine. He shut his eyes as he spoke.

"Never mind that," NoSohoth said. "Thrall, you've just been promoted. You're this dragon's servant now."

The man opened his eyes and bobbed.

"Do you know the duties of a servant?" NoSohoth asked.

"Get food. Get water. Get ingot. Clean scale. Clean teeth. Very good, I clean the all," the man said. At least the gibberish seemed that way to the Copper.

"What's your name?" NoSohoth asked.

"Harf," the man said.

"He belongs to you now," NoSohoth told the Copper. He took a chain out of his ear and hung it around Harf's neck. A piece of dragonscale edged in bronze hung from it. The man examined it, openmouthed. "And, Harf, do something about those bats, will you? They keep getting in here."

Harf let the piece of scale go. "Clean bats. Yes."

"Vermin." NoSohoth snorted. "Good man. Young Rugaard, just obey NeStirrath and no harm will come to you. Understand? My apologies, of course you do. If you need anything, just ask your thrall."

"Thank you for Harf, sir."

"You'll get on together, I hope. Try to be forgiving with humans; they're intelligent enough, but terribly lazy."

"Why did you choose him instead of the . . . the blighter, sir?"

"You've both got a bad limb. Honor and glory, young Rugaard."

"Thank you, sir."

NoSohoth turned and stalked out, sniffing the air around a crevice concealing the bats. The blighter looked at Harf and made a chopping motion at his neck. Harf showed a mouthful of brown teeth and patted his belly.

"My prince want food?" Harf asked, holding up his neck marker so the Copper could see it.

"Yes. And be quick."

Harf disappeared in the lurching, two-legged run of his kind. The Copper wondered how he didn't fall over. Humans struck him as half-finished—and the completed half wasn't much to look at. Badly balanced, thin-skinned, just the odd patch of hair on their heads that seemed to do nothing but get in the way of their eyes, nostrils, ears, and mouths, and they smelled like wet bats. The Air Spirit must have had his mind on other things as he created them.

After a refreshing sleep he explored his new home caves. The wound over his firebladder wept a little clear fluid, and felt tender but not painful. A projection of rock, like a long limb, reached out from the wall and almost to the pool. It smelled strongly of male dragon.

A bat flitted past his eye. "The others be frightened, m'lord," said Uthaned, the active young bat. "They want to know where to go."

Harf made a move to swing at the bat with his scrubbing stick, but the Copper gave him a sharp, "No!" He sniffed at Uthaned; the bat smelled exhausted. "That cave with the big horned skull will do for now."

"Mamedi is ready to drop, and the three young aren't used to so much flying. Might we have a taste of generosity?"

The bats had gotten him here, and food was on the way. "Oh, why not. But let's go somewhere private. Back to my cave."

The bats opened him up front and rear. He did a quick count: only eight left. He couldn't even remember how many had been with him when he jumped in the Nor'flow, but it was a lot more than eight. Of course, rodents were made for dying.

"Did y'be seeing those herds of cattle below?" Thernadad said as he sat on Mamedi, keeping her from a trickle of blood leaking from the Copper's armpit.

"M'smelling fresh air wafting up from below. We've got an entrance near," Enjor agreed. "Water, too."

"Faaaa!" Mamedi said, pushing her bulky mate off and getting a few quick tonguefuls of blood. "Dragon reek so bad in here, m'eyes be watering."

"W'be in the happy flapping land," another bat said.

"Sharply now," a deep voice from the outer passage echoed. "Krthonius, what can you say for yourself?"

Whoever Krthonius was, he didn't have anything to say right away, so the deep voice bellowed, "Aubalagrave?"

"Strange smell in the cave, your honor."

"That's more like it," the deep voice said. "Just because you're home doesn't mean you're safe. Remember that. Many's the wing-sore dragon who's lost because he returns to his cave already half-asleep."

"There haven't been assassins in the Lavadome in—" a rather lisping voice said.

"Thrall revolts. Leadership battles. Cave claim jumping. I've seen dragons die in all of them. Any of you lot able to identify the strange smell?"

"Ummm. Bat?"

"Yes."

"Here's a hamcart," the lisping voice said.

"Get up to the ceiling and hide yourselves," the Copper told the bats. With a mixture of burps and flaps, they took off for the deep shadows above.

The Copper climbed off his shelf and walked out into the light of the passage. He saw a vast, ruby-red twelve-horned dragon. The Red had been maimed, with nothing but a stumplike projection from each side of his spine where his wings should be. Three young drakes, one a dazzling white, the other two blacks, narrowed golden eyes at him.

"Excuse me, are you NeStirr—"

"Rough-and-tumble, lads. Here's our intruder. Give him what-for, but don't bleed him."

The drakes dragon-dashed forward. The attack came so suddenly the Copper's brain froze, and he could do nothing but hug the floor of the passage before they were on him, each bigger than he.

The white reached him first. The white had an ugly wound on one side of his face, exposing teeth and gum line. He head-butted the Copper in the snout, then threw himself across the Copper's neck, pinning his head. The others wedged their noses under his side and flipped him, exposing his belly. They scrabbled at his skin with sheathed *sii* claws.

The Copper smelled blood in his nostrils. The larger, heavier drakes squatted atop him; he was as helpless as a lamb in a dragon's jaws.

"That's the style," NeStirrath roared. "We'll teach this scat to poke his nose into our home cave. And the Imperial shelf. Bite a toe off, Krthonius. That'll be a memento."

"I was given that cave," the Copper squealed. He felt a hard squeeze on his left *saa*.

"Vent-drippings!" The old dragon snorted.

"NoSohoth told me!"

"Your honor, look at the hamcart," the white drake said. He lisped thanks to his words leaking out of the lipless side of his mouth.

"I don't have to look; I can smell it. Oh! Let him up, you fools. Let him up!"

"He's in the Imperial Family," one of the blacks said. The other spit out the Copper's severed toe.

"Cry settled! Cry settled!" the deep voice of NeStirrath shouted.

The pressure vanished, and the Copper rose and saw the black drakes backing away wearily. One had a bit of bloody flesh hanging out of his mouth. The Copper looked down and saw that a toe was missing. Oddly enough, it didn't really hurt; he just felt a warm, tingling sensation.

The Copper looked at the widening of the passage. Harf stood there beside a two-wheeled cart. Fragrant sides of meat swung from hooks on a wooden frame.

"Finally, something other than guts, hides, and hooves," one of the black drakes said.

Harf was doing his bobbing thing again, holding up the dragonscale on the chain around his neck.

"An Imperial Family thrall," NeStirrath said, as Harf waved his icon at the drakes, bobbing and bringing the cart forward a wheel spoke at a time. NeStirrath made a wretching noise: *Grf grf.*

"Well, we've landed in it, lads. What are you doing down in the Drakwatch caves, sir?"

"I was told I should learn from you. I've just arrived."

"That's a good way to get your guts spilled, showing up un-announced. We might have had a tragedy here."

"NoSohoth couldn't wait," the Copper said.

"Accept our apologies, sir," the white drake said.

The Copper bristled. His toe was starting to really hurt, and the drakes were lowering their heads and exchanging wary glances. But he was going to live here, and if he got too high-handed, what was stopping them from gutting him and going to NoSohoth with a tragic tale?

E. E. KNIGHT

Besides, he didn't really know what being in the Imperial Family meant.

"No one's fault but NoSohoth's, I'd say. I came down the river from the north, and the *griffaran* found me. The Tyr gave me the name Rugaard and put me under your eye. Your honor, if I'm to join the Drakwatch, maybe we could all have a fast feast and begin afresh."

NeStirrath licked drool from his lips, and his wing stumps relaxed against his sides. "That's a kindness, sir, that is. Better put a mesh of cobwebbing on that toe, sir. I'll show you where you can find—"

"Rugaard will do, your honor. I can take care of it myself."

He rather enjoyed the generosity of the gesture. The dragons each tenderly lifted a joint off of the cart's hooks and tore into the meat. NeStirrath took the smallest of the joints and sucked at it for a long time, as though relishing the taste, before swallowing it. "Smoke and flame, lads, we'll be eating well with an Imperial scion among us. Tails up and heads down for Rugaard, newest member of the Drakwatch!"

The Copper learned his duties, and learned them well.

From the first, he learned that every drake of the Drakwatch wanted honor in his lifetime, and a glorious memory after death—a name proudly sung to a line of future hatchlings and would-be mates.

Word came down from the Tyr himself that the Copper was to be treated the same as any other member of the Drakwatch. With permission to unsheath his *sii*, so to speak, their leader saw to it that the Copper was treated as roughly as any of the others, in fact more roughly, for he was the junior, and so the others considered it their duty to pummel him for the slightest error. NeStirrath liked aggressive young drakes, and almost any question, from order of line at mealtimes to order of march out in the

Lavadome, was settled by pairing off into duels or all-out brawls. Claws sheathed and teeth only for gripping, of course.

The Copper took his first blows learning that there were separate pools for drinking and bathing, and that his fellow drakes would knock him about the ears and *griff* if he forgot to use the right one.

Then he learned about the honorable, glorious history of the Drakwatch and how it was organized. There were perhaps six or seven claw-score of drakes in dragon watch—provided you were counting with a full set of twelve true-claws, that is. The Drakwatch was charged with patrolling the area of the Lavadome itself in search of hominid thieves and assassins. They could also be called on by the leaders of the various hills to present a show of force to troublesome thralls.

What the drakes of the Drakwatch liked best of all was the chance to compete against the Firemaidens. The young females performed similar duties to the males, if not quite so wide-ranging, placed at important posts to guard and inspect and supervise.

Some of the more aggressive of the Drakwatch, and a few wild-*griff*ed and claw-loose Firemaidens, would explore far beyond the underground river that circled the Lavadome, looking for signs of dwarf, blighter, or demen activity. There was great honor to be found in that sort of territorial assertiveness. Only a victorious battle with the hominids themselves could bring more glory, and with it the chance of a fine cave, thralls, and flocks to supervise upon reaching dragonhood.

When they needed physical rest they got lectures. NeStirrath made them recite proverbs and learn about battles won and lost—but mostly won.

NoSohoth gave them a lecture that seemed to stretch on through the day and into the night about the importance of honor. One dragon being able to rely on another to keep his word was the solid ground into which the lasting cave of civilization was dug. He went on and on about this point, until the Copper wondered if he was simply rearranging the same words into every variation possible.

The Copper's favorite days and darks in the Drakwatch were spent wandering from horizon to horizon in the enormous Lavadome, looking in on the thrall hovels, or counting cattle and swineherds, or running sorties to check the alertness of the Firemaidens on watch at the various tunnel entrances. The Firemaidens had their own set of teachers and taskmasters in the form of the Firemaids, the unmated and oathed-never-to-mate dragonelle guardians of the Lavadome.

NeStirrath drove his drakes hard, delivered bites and bashes as they climbed or jumped or dashed or swam, lobbed bruising stones into mock battles at any dragon who lagged or paused too long in evolutions. They learned to ignore pain and blood until the objective was achieved, be it a bit of tattered banner on a sharp pile of lava rock or a pumpkin-headed scarecrow with a tin crown. If they could keep the drakes off the scarecrow-king for a set time, heavily padded blighters armed with hatchling tooth–studded clubs could win a cask of the malty beverage they adored, with a leg of beef thrown in for any who managed to draw drakeblood.

They learned to take turns volleying flame in groups as they advanced or retreated, though the Copper's stream came out thinner and more liquid than the others' and seemed to take forever to light properly. They hunted boars goaded to savagery by cruel wires twisted into them by blighter herders. To keep things fair NeStirrath applied similar painful wires to the hunting drake's *sii* or *saa*.

It was a toughter, tested bunch that passed out of the first-year caves.

There were losses. Sometimes adventuring drakes would

simply disappear. Others were crippled permanently in duels or skirmishes. Fallen drakes would be replaced by younger drakes from NeStirrath's little enclave of "yearling" trainees in the Black Rock.

The Copper didn't quite feel the equal of the three other trainees. Though they bashed him and joked about it afterward, they seemed to think his joining their ranks was sort of a stunt, a bit of preening from a member of the Imperial line destined for a high cave in the resort. Though NeStirrath ordered him around and cajoled him much like the others, he never got water spit at him the way the others did around the pool, or received a playful nip as they hurried toward the hamcart at mealtimes, and while halfhearted duels were fought every other day between the other three over who should have the honor of leading the next patrol or running a message from one *sissa* of the Drakwatch to another, no one ever challenged him when he asked for a chance at the honor of leading an ore raid on the caves of the Firmaidens.

So once again, it seemed he wasn't to fit in, a stranger in his own cave.

It took a full season before the Copper could walk the inside of the Lavadome without standing and gaping upward.

When the sun was down and the shining oval at the peak was dark, it was at its most spectacular. Glowing rivers of fire rose or fell along its sides, sometimes brighter, sometimes darker.

"What holds the world up?" he asked NeStirrath as they rested on one of their "*saa*-hardeners": a pile of volcanic rock, the slag heap of an old tunnel leading down to the water ring.

"The Air Spirit must have made it," Krthonius said. "Some battle with the Earth Spirit."

"The Anklenes say it was a mighty scale that fell from the sun," NeStirrath said. "It plunged deep into the Lower World and expelled a ball of gas."

"The way you do when in the washing pool, Aubalagrave," Nivom, the white drake with the slashed-off lip, said.

"Give me a whole pig for dinner and I'll produce one as big as what made the Lavadome," Aubalagrave said.

"May you choke on your next mouthful of pig, boaster," Krthonius said, and he and Aubalagrave wrestled for a moment, scattering sharp lava rocks and ending it bleeding from a wound or two.

"Who are these Anklenes?"

They all looked at him.

"Half-a-drake strikes again," Nivom muttered to the others.

"Remember, he didn't hatch here," NeStirrath said. "The story goes that the Lavadome was found long ago by a wizard named Anklamere. He was a grasping, conniving sort of fellow, like most hominids, and had it in mind to control everyone and everything: dragon, hominid, beast, even the worms in the earth, I expect. NooMoahk, Black Glory of Legend and Eternal Guardian of the Sun-Shard, finally got rid of him, but not before he enthralled some dragons and set them up here. They're a spiritless sort of cringers, and they fiddle around with scrolls and books and whatnot. Always blending melting metals or heating stones or poking around in the bodies of dragons who should be decomposing honorably under a lava-stone cairn. The dragons of the lines of Wyrr and Skotl put them in their holes when we moved in."

The Copper knew little more about the lines of Wyrr or Skotl, but after asking about the Anklenes he decided not to press his ignorance. Besides, Krthonius was getting twitchy. He had the honor of leading this patrol and wanted to set a taxing pace.

They returned to the towering black overhang of the Imperial Rock sore of claw and thirsty. The others hung back, arguing and snapping, until the Copper drank, then jostled one another and splashed and slurped up their thirst. The Copper's good front limb felt as though it were going to fall off, and he dragged his tail on the way back to his shelf.

NeStirrath entered and took a nostrilful of air.

"Whew. Smells of bats in here. What, are you keeping them as pets, Rugaard?"

"Habit from my travels," the Copper said. "I . . . I used them to mask my odor. I got to kind of like having them around."

NeStirrath wrinkled his nostrils. "They call you 'Batty' when your crest is turned, you know."

"I've heard them," the Copper said. He knew NeStirrath thought him soft. "They're a good ward against starvation too. Food's hard to find when you're traveling underground."

"I'd have to be starving to eat a bat. But I wanted to have a talk with you, lad. You might be in charge of a whole *sissa* of young drakes someday. You need to scrap it up a bit. More of the rough-and-tumble, or they'll never accept you or respect you."

The Copper felt his stomach sink. "I don't like fighting. They're all older and bigger than me. I always seem to come out of one worse off. Like my toe."

The missing digit itched as though solid with scale mites, a sensation made all the more disagreeable by the fact that it wasn't there anymore and he couldn't scratch it.

"You've got to be willing to be the first to jump into a fight if you're to win respect from this lot. Even if you lose a tooth or two, stick up for yourself, lad. It's not the size of the drake that wins the fight; it's the size of the fight in the drake. Let your father know he hatched a dragon."

Mention of Father just made him miserable.

"Don't look glum," NeStirrath growled. "Doesn't matter where you came from, or what you know or don't know. You're in the Imperial line now. Cor, someday you could be the Tyr himself. Keep your thoughts behind your eyes; don't wear them on your face—and above all, let them know a set of dragon hearts beat behind your scale."

"Yes, your honor," the Copper said.

NeStirrath loved to pit his drakes against one another in contests and challenges and games, when they weren't having the weak points of ax-dwarves or fighting-shield demen pounded into their heads, that is.

He ran dragon dashes (the Copper came in last), jumping contests (the Copper fell short of the mark Krthonius set, even the time Krthonius stumbled before the vault mark), and tried to whack a barrel full of sand off a dragon's nose with his tail (the barrel easily avoided the Copper's stiff tail).

They looked at one another in triumph. He knew what was going through his fellow drakes' minds: *Another rodentlike performance from Batty, lowest of the Imperial line. They probably sent him to the Drakwatch so they wouldn't have to look at his odd eye and listen to him limp about the upper chambers.*

At each failure he shook off the dirt and dust and tried to keep his face from showing his disappointment. Krthonius found all the athletic events so easy, but he held his tongue and didn't bark out his triumph. Unlike Aubalagrave, who sometimes could outjump his black-scaled comrade and let the whole Lavadome know it when he did. Nivom also rarely won anything, and it put him in a foul mood.

It was after a particularly gruesome humiliation in which the drakes had to climb up a sheer wall with the drake behind gripping at the tail, a deadweight to be hauled (the Copper's two-toed *saa* gave way at the last and he and Nivom fell three full lengths to a mud pit) that Nivom pushed past the Copper on the way to the bathing pool.

Harf and a couple other thralls hurried to get hot water and pumice to scrub the dragonscales.

"Filthiest last, or you'll dirty the water for the rest of us," Nivom said.

The Copper, still smarting in his tail from Nivom's hatchling-sharp teeth, let out a squawk that everyone later said sounded more like a startled chicken than a drake's battle cry. He threw himself on Nivom and thumped him in the snout with the joint of his crippled arm.

Snarling and growling, the Copper thumped him again every time Nivom tried to shrug him off.

"Batty's tearing Nivom a new tailvent," Krthonius cried out to Aubalagrave.

"Rugaard!" the Copper snarled, *griff* rattling all on their own as though they wanted in on the contest. He left Nivom and dashed at Krthonius, head low and down so Krthonius couldn't get under his guard and flip him.

Some of the hominids shouted in excitement.

Krthonius turned sideways, as he always did in a brawl, so he could strike with head or tail, off-side up against a cave wall with a line of bronzed skulls just where a mature dragon's wings usually brushed the walls. The Copper split the distance and jumped up between tooth and tail-tip, pushed off the wall, and fell, rather awkwardly, on Krthonius's back. He wrapped his neck around Krthonius's and began to pull scales with his teeth.

"Yeow! Yeoow!" Krthonius shouted, bashing the Copper with his tail.

Aubalagrave joined the brawl, defending his friend's honor—and scales. The Copper found himself sandwiched between two larger drakes, and much beaten about the head and hindquarters. All he could do was try to make Krthonius or Aubalagrave miss, thus striking each other when they were trying to hit the Copper.

"Keep the claws in, you," he heard NeStirrath shout.

He didn't have much success. Aubalagrave gave him a *saa* swipe across the snout, and he saw brilliant fields of flowers.

"I'll finish it," Nivom shouted, forcing his way through the others.

The Copper wanted to flee, but instead he flung himself on Nivom again. They went up on their hind legs, boxing each other with *sii* and exchanging bites about the snout and *griff*. Nivom stood tall on his hindquarters and rattled his *griff*.

"Tail swipe," one of the thralls shouted. Despite the urging, the Copper's tail refused to reach. Krthonius yanked on it and he fell, belly-up, under Nivom.

"Cry settled!" Nivom urged.

The Copper got both *saa* under Nivom and launched him into the bathing pool. He could hardly see out of his good eye, thanks to the blood, but he could make out Krthonius well enough, and charged at him again.

He felt tail strikes and a weight above his *saa*—Aubalagrave was atop him, hammering him with kicks while he clung with his *sii*—but he still pushed forward for Krthonius and grappled. Krthonius easily pushed his nose into the bed of rocks lining the floor.

"Cry settled," Krthonius grunted.

The Copper managed to poke him under the chin with his crippled forelimb. Krthonius backed off, making retching sounds and coughing. Aubalagrave sank his teeth into both sides of his head behind the crest.

"Kah ettehld!" Aubalagrave said.

The Copper rolled, rolled again, at great pain to the tender skin at the back of his head, and managed to plunge both of them into the bathing pool. He got Aubalagrave's head underwater and pushed for all he was worth. Aubalagrave refused to yield and go limp.

Something hauled both of them out of the water—NeStirrath, trying to keep Aubalagrave from breathing too much water. The Copper gave him a tail strike for his interference and was dropped atop Nivom and Krthonius. Cheering from the thralls—or maybe the pained roaring of a tender-gummed old dragon—sounded in his ears.

They rolled, a three-colored mass of fury letting out battle cries in high-pitched drake voices. The Copper got his teeth into Nivom's shoulder and forced him down, pushing for all he was worth, keeping Krthonius's head pinned with his in the crook of his crippled limb.

Aubalagrave and Krthonius boxed him about the head, trying to get him to let go. He grabbed Aubalagrave at what felt like a *sii* digit, twisted.

"Cry settled! Cry settled! Cry—" the three chorused. But their voices seemed far away and receding. The smooth rocks of the flooring gave way to the soft, mossy pads of the river-lake, only there was no itchy slime or biting water mites this time. . . .

He woke, his face wet. His eye rolled this way and that, but his vision was misty.

"Give him another," NeStirrath said.

Krthonius spit another cheekful of water on him. Thralls were huddled all around, and Harf was counting knocked-out hatchling teeth from hand to hand.

"Did I cry settled?" the Copper croaked.

"No, we did," Nivom said. "You'd gone dark and wouldn't let go of Aubalagrave's dragonhood."

"Hope his mate can fall sideways on the wedding flight," Krthonius said.

Aubalagrave sat with his hindquarters in the coolest part of the pool, his face contorted.

"Good fight, Rugaard," Aubalagrave said between quick breaths. "Good fight."

———

The bats had their fill of blood for once, that night. Even Thernadad finally gave up, crawled a length or two away from the Copper, too swollen to fly, and went to sleep. Harf made to swat him with a waste scoop, but the Copper threw a protective *sii* over the bat.

The next day he could hardly see. He looked at himself in the polished black rock just beneath the lamp and a frightful, swollen face looked back out of the reflection-world, every scale out of place. He was excused all duties, given an extra ration of meat and ore, and as the other three had bites and bruises enough for a whole *sissa* of Drakwatch, NeStirrath called for a lesson day.

To NeStirrath's considerable vexation, the Tyr decided to pay a visit.

A pair of broad-shouldered blighter thralls led the way, with dragon-headed incense burners letting out of trails of rich-smelling smoke, equal parts spice and oil. The Copper smelled it a long way off and felt better disposed to the world and his aching body. He managed to climb off his shelf and join the others in the common room by the drinking and bathing pools.

NoSohoth led the way, and immediately went to NeStirrath's side and led him in a bow to the Tyr. The Imperial retinue flowed into the common room, and attendant thralls shrank into the corners.

NeStirrath pointed his charges into a line behind him.

"Always good to smell drakes again," the Tyr said. "There's too much drakka scent about the upper levels. I grow tired of the eternal bloom of females. Drakes and blood . . . well, what's this?"

Behind the Tyr the Copper saw a forest of legs. The sleek young golden drake was there, and another, sort of a reddish-purplish color that reminded the Copper of the radishes the thralls chewed to wash the dragon-smell out of their mouths at the end of a long day.

"And I thought it was just thralls making stories up, as usual," the Tyr said. "There was a fine old fight down here, wasn't there?"

The golden drake walked the perimeter of the Drakwatch caves, peering into the eyes of the skulls and fighting yawns all the way.

The Tyr shifted so he could make room for the dragon behind. "You should know what's going on in your own caves, SiDrakkon. I know you've got other titles, but as my mate's brother you're also in charge of the Drakwatch."

The radish-colored dragon just glowered.

"Simevolant, stop idling and come have a look at these drakes."

"Yes, Grandsire." Simevolant, the golden drake, approached the line of bruised and bashed drakes. "Impressive specimens. A credit to the Drakwatch. But glory does bring out the ugly, doesn't it?"

The Tyr looked sharply at NoSohoth. "I'd like a little more ferocity on the Rock; a dragon should fight with tooth and claw, not tongue. Too much of that. What's this, old friend? Is that a lump on your jaw? Don't tell me you were involved in the fracas." The old dragon chuckled.

"I was pulling them apart and your young ward there loosened my teeth for my trouble."

"Is that . . . er . . ." the Tyr said, looking at the Copper.

"You decided to call him Rugaard, Grandsire," the bright young Simevolant reminded the Tyr.

"Rugaard, yes. I'd hardly recognize you. You're beginning to fill out a little."

"It's the swelling, I think," Simevolant said. "Most hatchlings are ugly, but they get better proportioned as they age. I do believe you're getting worse, Rugaard. Someone should take some studies of you for posterity."

The Tyr ignored the byplay and tapped radish-colored SiDrakkon with his tail.

SiDrakkon sniffed all the drakes. "There's an opening for a messenger in Deep Tunnel. Which drake of these is your fastest?"

"Krthonius, with the big haunches, there," NeStirrath said.

"Good of the Empire, now, think for the good of the Empire," the Tyr muttered.

"Why won't you let me make a decision? It's my responsibility!" SiDrakkon sputtered.

"Imperial messengers do a lot more than just memorize reports and run," Tyr said.

"I should know. I was one," SiDrakkon said.

The Tyr's jaw tightened; then he relaxed. "And a fine one, too. So you know that sometimes they are asked for an independent opinion of the situation in some distant, tight corner, or even to assume command if there's been an unexpected death. That requires sound judgment."

"Nivom's very bright, Tyr," NeStirrath said. "Best memory of the bunch. Aubalagrave is strong and clever in a fight."

"Who's in charge of the Drakwatch?" SiDrakkon roared.

"Bearers, more oliban there; fire bladders are starting to throb," Simevolant said.

The thralls with the smoking dragon heads extracted some milky chips from pouches at their waist and dumped a small handful each into the dangling brazier. The rich, aromatic smell filled the cavern, and one of the blighter thralls sniffled.

"Honored friend," the Tyr said to NeStirrath. "Let's say we were at Three Tunnels again, with the blighters hip-deep all around and battle horns blowing. Which of the three would you want with us? Good of the Empire, mind."

"Little Rugaard, there. Kept his teeth dug in, even when he went unconscious. He's no duelist; he fights as though his neck were on the line."

"Does that help, SiDrakkon?" the Tyr asked.

"Why do you even drag me along if you're just going to have your way anyway?" SiDrakkon said.

"The decision is yours."

"I'll have Nivom. A mixed message can lose a battle."

Nivom straightened, and his pink eyes shone. The Copper felt his joy and gave a little *prrum* for him.

"As I said, the choice is yours," Tyr said. "I'm sure you've made a good one."

He turned to the bruised drakes. "Don't worry, you others; there'll be for you glory enough in your turn. It's always the ones that you'd never expect who become legends."

Chapter 13

The Copper remained longer in NeStirrath's part of the Drakwatch caves than most. Krthonius joined an Upper World *sissa* who patrolled the plateau on the rocky slopes covering the Lavadome. Aubalagrave served on the river beneath the wings of the *griffaran*, as part of a new aquatic *sissa* protecting their nests from raiders.

Drakes came and went. They usually had only one or two others, and never more than six. Each time a review was held, SiDrakkon or one of the wingless Drakwatch leaders walked up and down in front of the drakes, and each time a drake left. Once, after a bloody battle with a company of elvish mercenaries that resulted in the destruction of a *sissa* before help from the *griffaran* could arrive, they took every drake out of the training caves—except for the Copper.

He practiced leadership of his drakes under NeStirrath's tutelage. He learned to praise in public and reprimand any first offense in private. He rewarded group efforts with group pleasures: After particularly successful brawling raids on the ore bins of the Firemaidens, he'd let his drakes have a "sun day" on the water ring. Of course, the same went for punishments. When his drakes woke to find their own ore supply emptied in a stealthy Firemaiden·raid in return, a taunting note reminding them that a drakka named Nilrasha had left a noisome present in the washing pool, he gave the Drakwatch thralls a rest day and set his drakes to work cleaning out the thrall pens, washing and airing bedding. His bats got their fill of bedbugs.

After the drake who'd fallen asleep on watch fished out the turd with his lips, of course.

The bats thrived, and grew to know Imperial Rock better than the Copper did, for they flew around the upper levels, hunting insects, or flitted out into the Lavadome in search of tied livestock.

The adult bats aged quickly, in the manner of rodents. Mamedi dropped eventually. Thernadad grew old, almost blind and deaf, but his appetite, and that of his brother's, never flagged.

The trio of young bats—the Copper called them Big Ear, Spike Hair, and Wide Nose for their most prominent features— grew into truly colossal bats, bigger than Thernadad and his brother put together. The Copper suspected they sneaked dragonblood when they could.

NeStirrath had him apply his energy to the drakes as a sort of assistant, saving the old dragon's *saa* wear on the longer hikes and expeditions.

The Copper made the best of his time, plaguing NeStirrath with questions about the Lavadome, draconic history, even how he came to lose his wings.

"It was in the civil wars, of course. Dragon family against dragon family, a terrible business. It was an aerial duel. A Skotl-clan dragon named AgMemdius tore into my back. Most dragons would be satisfied with just crippling a wing, but he wanted me to fall to my death. The Tyr himself pulled me out of my fall, and we splashed into a lake together. In the end we reconciled only when the blighters rose."

"How did the Tyr come to lead the dragons here?"

"Strange you should ask that. Rethothanna is creating something she calls a history—it's like a lifesong, only you sing it about someone else—and she's on me like a leech. Seems a waste. If you're so wretched you don't have any deeds to sing of, better to die trying for a few lines of your own than reciting someone else's *laudi*. Anklenes," he finished with a growl.

"What does she want from you?"

"The lines of my lifesong about the war between the Skotl and the Wyrr and the Anklenes. I hardly know her, and here I'm supposed to spew out my lifesong as though she were my poor Esthea? Just seems wrong."

NeStirrath always darkened at the mention of his mate. The Copper didn't know the circumstances, only that she was dead.

"Tell them to me, your honor. I'll go over there and deliver it for you, and bring back any questions. I've been curious about their hill; I'd be glad of the errand."

"Dragons set too much on appearances. Why not? You're practically a son to me. We'd have been proud to hatch you. You're a quality drake. I feel much better now, having one I can trust. Among dragons trust is more seldom shared than even gold."

The Copper gulped. Usually NeStirrath was finding fault with the sharpness of his *saa*, or telling him to always poke his head over a ridge's crestline and examine the other side closely before crossing, lest game be scared away or enemies forewarned, or barking at him to take brief naps when in the field and save real sleep for safe, well-guarded caves.

"I'm not much for wordplay—that's an Anklene pastime—but here are the parts:

> *When CuTar's sons in battle met*
> *One perch but we nine who sought*
> *Two-score dragons fell to earth.*
> *In Rednight's reckoning fought*
> *Three lines at war for power's pride*

Black murder just a tool
AgMemdius struck, my hatchlings died
A bloody cave I found
An anguished roar, a wish for death
I sought my bloodstained foe
And over Kog's hill, trading breath
We perished, each aflame . . .

It went on for quite some time, about how the dragons fought to rule the great cave. Meanwhile an alliance of dwarves, demen, and blighter thralls took advantage and struck, attempting to recapture the Lavadome. But a dragon named FeHazathant rallied them, made peace between the lines, and organized the dragons according to their abilities.

Old RaHurath, unable to fly without first dropping from a height, called on his old friends the *griffaran*, who helped turn the tide when the dwarves attacked Imperial Rock. FeHazathant himself, hiding a grievous spear wound, flew from point to point, rallying dragons and convincing them to abandon their caves and treasures for a last stand atop Black Rock. A beautiful dragonelle named Tighlia went bravely into the blighter camp, ostensibly to negotiate, but instead sowed discord between the blighter army and their allies, so they quit the battle with cries of "betrayal" when they suffered a reverse. EmLar, a slender, scaled gray born an Anklene thrall and a grandsire of Nivom, was put in charge of the drakes. He had them bury themselves in the gravel of the lower passages. The drakes trapped the demen's storming column, collapsing a wall that trapped half the demen forces inside the rock, and took turns volleying flame at any others who tried to get in to reinforce them.

"They died in these chambers. That's where we got many of these skulls."

The Copper repeated back the song. NeStirrath corrected

him, and he repeated it back again almost perfectly. The first few lines still intrigued him.

"You wanted to be Tyr?" he asked.

"I was young. I wouldn't take it now if it came with a river of gold. Dragons are always quarreling, and no matter how wisely the Tyr settles matters, both parties grumble and blame his judgment."

The Copper had never been in the strange, smooth hill of the Anklenes before. He and the Drakwatch had seen it from every angle on the ground, and once he'd looked down on it from the Imperial Resort on a botanical tour of the gardens, but he'd never walked past the twin statues of robed hominids, one holding a lamp and the other a quill and scroll, and up to its entrance.

He paused there and let Harf catch up.

Flat spaces yawned at the base of the statues. According to NeStirrath, there'd once been statues of dragons crouched beneath the figures on their pillars, but the dragons found the arrangement vaguely offensive—hominids towering above dragons? The statues were moved to more illustrious accommodations on the Imperial Resort. Now they looked down on the Anklene hill.

The base of the Anklene hill—if *hill* was the right word, for it was too regular to be a natural formation of the cavern and seemed too big for anyone to have constructed it—was exactly square. It sloped away from its base, at first very slowly, but then the angle increased until the four sides met at the peak. Viewed from the entrance, the peak seemed very high and far-off.

The hill was coated with pink-white stone, lined and divided like good plump meat. The Copper passed under the statues on their columns and approached the entrance, a portal that mimicked the peak shape of the entrance. He saw—and smelled—lights burning within.

A human hurried toward the entrance, adjusting his thrall-wrap. He had the potbelly of a thrall who wasn't worked hard enough, or who perhaps filched food. The Copper gave NeStirrath and Rethothanna's names, and the thrall led him inside.

The passages were low and wide within, carved out of a more natural-looking brown stone, reinforced in spots with steel or scale-chipped wood. They'd been smoothed and coated with a paste the color of a hatchling's belly to make the most of the lights. A similar sort of surface covered the floor, only tiny rounded pebbles had been thrown into the mix. Two dragons could just slip past each other, if they adjusted their stance and didn't lock wings. The place also had that disgusting wet-bat smell of humans.

The thrall led him on a zigzagging course like a snake's trail. It seemed there was only one main tunnel in here, winding upward in a series of turns, opening out on galleries and larger rooms that extended to the hillside. Greenish light filled the rooms that didn't have lamps in use, and the copper recognized baskets dripping with cave moss hanging from the ceilings. There were thralls, naked from the waist up, who did nothing but carry yokes and buckets of filthy-smelling water. They'd hook a ladder to some eyebolts in the ceiling and climb up, endlessly watering the thriving moss.

The thrall fell to his knees at a wide gallery. A female stood within, her heavy haunches to him. She examined a series of pieces of matched paper hanging on a line, with writing scrawled on them.

"Very well. Put the new page nine in," the dragon told another thrall. This one was elvish, a female with hair like dead cave moss.

The prostrate thrall glubbed something out into the set pebbles of the hallway pavement, raising dust.

"Who? I don't know a Rugaard-nester." She turned, showing

eyes that struck him as bulging and a little oversize, though her nostrils had an elegant upward curve that reminded him a little of Mother.

"Rugaard. Sent by NeStirrath," the Copper said. "I have some lines from his lifesong—"

"You're too late," she said, settling down with forelimbs crossed. "That old fool. This is just like him, making difficulty just when I'd given up. My history's complete. It's to be presented tonight; the Tyr himself wants to hear it at the Imperial banquet."

"We could present the Tyr with a revised edition later," the elvish thrall said, in remarkably good Drakine. "You'll recite tonight personally, won't you? He'd like a few lines about NeStirrath; they are old friends."

The dragonelle ignored her. She swung her neck sideways, another unsettling gesture, for it reminded him of a snake, and looked at Harf and shut her nostrils. She returned her wide-eyed stare to the Copper. "What did you say your name was again?"

"Rugaard."

"I'm Rethothanna. Wait, you're the one who was adopted into the line three years ago?"

"Yes." The Copper wasn't sure if she deserved some sort of honorific or not. He started to recite the poem while it was still fresh in his head.

She interrupted him after six lines. "Look at your scale. What's that servant of yours been doing with his time, the one-handed hominid pastime? The banquet's in three hours!"

"I'm . . . I don't know about a banquet."

Rethothanna's overlarge eyes widened, and the Copper wondered if they'd pop out. "You're of the line. It's an Imperial banquet. You must be at your place."

"Er . . ."

"Don't pollute your locution! Say something worthwhile or be silent."

The Copper settled on silence, so fixed was he on the vast whites of her eyes as she looked him over.

"But not looking like that. Yam, go get every scale polisher and claw shaper in the hill. Open your mouth, drake. Well! Those teeth aren't bad. There's many a drake who'd be proud of a set like that. A little oil and they'll gleam admirably; maybe they'll divert attention from that eye. Eyegrit, are those bat bites? Where *do* you live?" He heard Harf take a few steps back. The shifting head turned on him. "Yes, you, thrall, you'd better cower. I've half a mind to eat you. Who taught you to use scouring salt on a dragon's scale?"

"All scale clean! All them clean!" Harf said, covering his head with his forelimbs.

"Yam, have you died and rooted?"

The elf hurried off into the passage.

"Now, let's have what passes for poetry from NeStirrath again. While they're getting you cleaned up I'll see if I can't make something of his word butchery. His stanzas might be ranked enemies, the way he scatters them. . . ."

Rethothanna kept Yam busy filling gaps in her scale with similarly colored green scales, which required much working with wire, attaching them to their neighbors so they'd stay in place.

The Copper had a thrall at each quarter, and one rather young, small, deft-handed female human working his face and teeth. First she trimmed the edged of his face scale with shears, then a file; then she went to work with a brush and something that smelled a little like paint. She poured dust though a straw into the crevices in his scale, then dusted his face with a glittery mixture that smelled of metals.

"Don't skimp on the oliban and bay leaf," Rethothanna said as a thrall painted the trailing corners of her nostrils, making them look even longer and more elegant. Red powder around her eyes set the deep green of her face off admirably, and gave her eyes life and fire.

The girl nodded and bent for a long, heavy wooden box topped by a broad handle. She came up with a pair of silver bottles with golden tops, and applied fragrant oils to his crest.

"Dragon-ward behind his *griff*. If he rattles them, I want the dragons to know it."

The girl nodded and dabbed something into the folds of the skin behind his *griff*. It smelled like hot iron and blood to the Copper.

"His teeth now," Rethothanna said.

The girl smeared a clear oil on his teeth. The Copper didn't like the taste and pulled back his lips a little to keep it from getting in his mouth.

"Exactly," Rethothanna said. He'd never heard her use such a satisfied tone before. "Your mother taught you well, girl."

The girl tipped her head down a little.

"Bring a mirror-plate. Our young drake finally looks worthy of the Imperial line."

Two thralls held up a polished sheet of bronze. He looked into it. The odd sense of depth to the reflection gave him a moment of dizziness, soon overcome as he adjusted to the idea of his reflection. It was like seeing your image in the water, but tinted with the colors of a coal fire.

His scale had a depth and polish and glitter. She'd shaped the displaced scale at the gouged side of his face so as to minimize the scarring, and added a pewter-colored powder to the crevices in his crest that emphasized the strong, smooth ridges.

So it was a proud young drake who followed Rethothanna over to the Black Rock and up to the Tyr's Gardens.

The Copper had never seen such a gathering, or imagined there could be anything so splendid. It must have been dark outside, for the peak of the dome was a plate of midnight. This, however, made the fiery streams of lava running along the exterior of the dome all the brighter and more colorful.

Female dragons with fringes painted and smooth ribbons wound about their necks in fascinating knotwork, males with vivid red or blue lines painted on their wings—Rethothanna said it was a form of display of *laudi*, recognized by the Tyr himself and worn for all to see—drakes and drakka playing and singing and mirroring.

At the middle of the Gardens an open oval free of plants served as the center of the party. A little lower than much of the terraced garden, it was paved with shields and helmets and breastplates, trophies taken in battle and presented to the Tyr. At the center of the open area was a long masonry trench shaped like a drawn bow. At the notch of the bow lay the Tyr and his mate, on a low rise of wood and cushioning that gave them a commanding view. Where bow would give way to string, stairways led down to the kitchens. The most splendid of the dragons reclined at the bow. The string was reserved for the younger drakes and drakka.

For a moment the Copper's eyes were tricked, and he thought platters of food slid by magic from dragon to dragon. He spotted thralls bearing vast platters on their heads. They rose heavy-laden from the stairs and circulated, always in the same direction to avoid collisions in the narrow trench. The roast chunks of meat went around the circuit, and emptied as the dragons reached down with jaws and plucked the tidbits. Sometimes instead of platters they bore a long pole in a sort of harness-and-cup, and from cross-braces at the top of the pole dangled whole roasted joints from hooks. These seldom even made it to the drakes and drakka.

At the very center of the dining plaza was a sandy pit. According to Rethothanna, new hatchlings of the Imperial line would be exhibited there so all could see them, but there were none at the moment.

"Any guests the Tyr wishes to particularly honor get seated to his left, so they have first choice of the dishes," Rethothanna explained.

Rethothanna didn't mix—she wasn't of the Imperial line— but instead waited to be called by NoSohoth, in his usual role of organizer. His gleaming silver shone especially bright tonight.

A scream and a clatter. The Copper's attention went to the far end of the bow, near where the thralls entered and exited the kitchen.

"Drop him, Simevolant," the Tyr said across the sandpit.

The golden drake ceased dragging a thrall up out of the trench. "But his platter was empty and I'm *hungry*."

"An empty platter's not his fault. A thrall's a thrall, but you can't eat them for no reason at all. Let him go, now."

Simevolant released the man. The thrall was so frightened he scuttled for the exit without picking up his platter. The other food bearers continued circling. He noticed they quickened their step at Simevolant's end, sometimes bumping into one another.

"That's done it, worm," Tighlia said, looking pointedly at Simevolant. "Their tiny brains can't hold more than one thought, and now they're more concerned with being eaten than keeping step."

"Let's have some drumming," the Tyr said. "Where are those clever blighters with the kettledrums?"

NoSohoth extended a black-tipped wing toward a grove, and a trio of blighters came forward, two bearing pairs of vast, leather-topped drums and a third with a hollow polished log. They went to work on their instruments, filling the gardens with rhythmic pounding. The Copper liked the sound so much he couldn't help swaying and stamping his feet.

"Mind the step, now, fellows; no one's been eaten," the Tyr said to the thralls passing under his nose. "That's more like it.

Steady on and I'll order a barrel of sweet ferments up for you after the meal."

SiDrakkon, sitting to his sister's right, hardly ate at all, and worked at the edge of an embedded shield with his claws, prying up the rim.

"SiDrakkon looks unhappy," the Copper said to Rethothanna.

"He's always in a temper. Pay him no mind. Stuck between the ambitions of his sister and the directions of her mate. He's the Tyr's eyes and voice in the Lavadome, and he's not an energetic dragon. Doesn't like parties, either. Speaking of which, how is your first Imperial banquet?"

The Copper looked around. "It's the most splendid thing I've ever seen."

"It occurs to me that I'll have to hear your lifesong at some point. You're the first outsider to seek the Lavadome in . . . oh, a generation's time. Of course, we don't advertise our presence. Even with such allies as we have on the surface, we have to keep our home secret."

The Copper would have liked to hear more from her, for he was curious about the Upper World and its dangers, but the drummers had exhausted themselves, and NoSohoth waved her over.

"My turn. May the Air Spirit carry my voice well," she said. She stepped forward, and all eyes turned in their direction as NoSohoth announced: "Cry hear and hear, for we'll have poetry now. A new work on the late feuds of the founders of the Lavadome by Imperial memoriam. Hear Rethothanna."

Simevolant scanned the crowd, found the Copper. "I say, cousin, what are you doing there, lurking in the blade-bushes? Come and find your place at the banquet."

The Copper stepped forward, and Simevolant made room for him, nudging a drakka aside.

"Hear me, Spirits; hear me, Ages; hear me, dragons great and small, for I tell a tale of the founding of a new Silverhigh. . . ."

145

Simevolant ignored her preamble and snatched a plump sausage linked into the shape of a curly-tailed dog off a platter. "Now, how are things in the lower levels? I so seldom get down your way. Is the strength of the Drakwatch still keeping the Imperial Resort from falling?"

The drakka around Simevolant fluttered their eyelids and *griff* at his joke.

"Little has changed since your last visit," the Copper said. He'd rather listen to Rethothanna than chatter and joke.

"I've traveled with the Drakwatch. Muddy, tiring business. Wars and body pieces. Have you made it out of the training caverns yet?"

"No," the Copper said.

"You won't lack for learning. But nothing teaches like experience. Even up here, you'd be amazed at what a young drake can experience." He tapped the drakka next to him on the nose.

The Copper tried to close an ear to his yammering, but Simevolant kept asking questions. How many thralls were being brought across the river, the size of the herds driven underground from the surface provinces, improvements to dwelling space in the Skotl Hill . . .

The Copper caught only bits of Rethothanna's performance. It dealt with the Tyr's vision for a new Silverhigh here in this deep fastness, and told how he rose to preeminence after a series of duels and feuds between Skotl, Anklene, and Wyrr lines that divided the dragons of the Lavadome, uniting them through a rigid hierarchy where even the lowest dragons at least commanded numerous thralls. Thus, "Each dragon a lord, each dragonelle a queen."

The Copper wondered what it was like to be one of even the lesser lords around the banquet, so important that your deeds were sung by others. They must be proud dragons indeed. And what dragonelle would not be pleased to be a queen?

But there were queens and there were Queens. Rethothanna dropped in a few lines of praise for Tighlia's beauty, "a flower of the Skotl line, plucked and placed as high as any Wyrr for all to admire."

Simevolant brought up a fragrant quantity of gas at that, loudly enough that Rethothanna had to pause until he was finished.

"I do beg your pardon," Simevolant said. "Go on. I'm a dragon turned to stone by the power of your words."

During kern, a thick, yellowish paste full of smashed vegetables that aided the digestion, Rethothanna finished with Fe-Hazathant's victory at the duel of Black Rock, after which the "iron-willed, steel-limbed" dragon assumed the old Anklene title of Tyr, borne by the dragon who ruled and commanded his fellows in the old, half-forgotten Age of the Sorcerer, when Anklemere ruled.

"They wallow too much in the past, that generation," Simevolant said. "Refighting old wars. What's going to come after the Tyr dies? That's what concerns me. I've no ambition whatsoever, but there are plenty who do. Dragons can be ruthless in getting what they want."

The dragons spat *torf*-sized gobs of flame into the water troughs placed here and there among them, and Rethothanna bowed to the crackle and hiss of water turned instantly to steam.

"Excellent," Tyr said, casting flame into the sandpit at the center of the banquet. "So polished, and all the grim business of bodies and broken eggs left out. I don't like brave deeds tarnished, you know. Come, Rethothanna, take first position there and eat your fill."

A dragon, wings thick with red *laudi*, moved over, and with some shoving and squashing the dragons rearranged themselves around the banquet.

The Tyr thumped his tail. "Now I have an announcement.

Our Uphold in Bant has suffered some serious reverses of late. The humans and blighter tribes there are set upon and need our assistance. I'm sending a dragon up to set things right."

"Bant. Oh, how tiresome," Simevolant said. "Humans. They can't stand to see the moon change without starting some new feud."

The Copper would have liked to ask what the moon was, but he kept his tongue.

"I don't need to tell anyone at this table how important Bant is to our food supply. I've decided that SiDrakkon shall go and help our Upholder in Bant, ummm—"

"NiThonius," Tighlia supplied.

SiDrakkon glowered, going even more purple about the cheeks. He reared his head back, but the Copper saw his sister quickly put her head across his neck and whisper something in his ear.

"He's not even of the Imperial line, Tyr," Tighlia said. "My brother is only to 'help' him?"

"NiThonius is a wise dragon. The Bant are a raucous crowd, argumentative as crows and headstrong as boars. He knows how to handle them."

"I wonder who is handling whom. Two more like him in the Upholds and we'll be skeletons down here. Food is short enough."

The Copper wondered at that, with thralls sweating and groaning under the weight of the platters that flowed around the banquet. But perhaps exceptions were made for banquets.

"I want full powers," SiDrakkon said. "As the Tyr's representative. Three good, battle-tested dragons. And three *sissa* of the Drakwatch to support."

"I don't want another surface war," Tyr said. "The hominids lose ten thousand and we lose ten, and they have a fresh ten thousand before ten eggs are even laid."

"Let me manage things or find another dragon," SiDrakkon roared. The whole table went quiet.

Tyr stood.

Thralls hurried to throw more sticks of incense in the braziers, and a thick, sweet odor fell over the banquet.

The Tyr glared at his mate's brother. "Fair enough," he said in a steady voice. "Best to speak softly, with a fearsome host behind the words. You pick the dragons. As to the Drakwatch, I want Nivom leading the three *siisa*. He's impressed me. I understand he's quite driven the demen away from the caves bordering the far shores."

Tighlia looked sharply at her mate as soon as he mentioned Nivom.

The Tyr got a faraway look in his eyes. "I'll give him a stripe for that when he gets his wings. Blue will look well against that white of his."

He blinked, and looked around the banquet table. "We'll need an Imperial messenger to report progress. Simevolant, you haven't been off Black Rock these three years."

Simevolant tucked his head against his shoulder for a moment. "Tyr, I'm touched, really, with this expression of the Imperial confidence. But I've got a notion—send Rugaard, here. He's never even been to the Upholds. The experience will do him good."

"Rugaard?" Tyr said, looking at the Copper as though he'd never seen him before. "Wasn't he killed at . . . Oh, yes, of course. The egg saver."

Simevolant offered one of those smiles that made the Copper's scale bristle. "Yes, the eternally budding flower of the Drakwatch training caves. Is he not a marvelous young drake? Stand, Rugaard, for you are looking fine tonight, and let the assembly see the future of the Imperial line, adopted by the Tyr himself. I don't believe he's attended a banquet before, and he needs an introduction anyway."

The Copper rose, shifted uncomfortably, and did his best to open his bad eye. He didn't want to be exhibited thus, but Simevolant had such a musical way of putting things, you followed his words this way and that the way you did a good blood trail.

"The Drakwatch calls him 'Batty,' I understand," SiDrakkon said. "He keeps bats as pets."

The drakka twitched their noses and fluttered their eyelids. They were laughing at him. No matter how polished his scale, or even his edging—

"Burn it, Sime; you're always wriggling out of things," the Tyr said. "You chatter your way through life like a drakka. I won't have it."

"Stand up for yourself, cousin," Simevolant said out of the side of his mouth. "You want to stay in those drippy holes forever?"

The Copper found his voice. "I'd be grateful for the opportunity, Tyr."

"That's a norther's vocalization if I've ever heard one," a dragon opposite the Copper at the banquet said. "How did he ever come to the dome?"

Tyr's tail tapped in thought. "Never been to the Upper World?"

"No, Tyr."

"Well, Bant's as good a place as any to get sunstruck. NoSohoth, get his shoulder line painted, won't you?"

"Congratulations, Rugaard," Simevolant said. "Keep out of the way of most of the arrows. Remember to put a little dwarf's-beard on your wounds."

The rest of the banquet passed in a blur. He met the dragons and dragonelles, drakes and drakka of the Imperial line. A trio of drakka, who he later found out were directly granddaughtered to Tyr, twitched their noses as they greeted him and perfunctorily laid their necks across his, pressed on by their mother, a rather pinched-looking, tight-scaled creature named Ibidio. Two were sleek, beautiful specimens, the third rather thin and sickly, but they were polite enough under the urging of their mother. Her mate, AgGriffopse, the champion of the Tyr's first—and only—clutch before he lost his first mate, had been badly wounded fighting dwarves and died of his injuries within a year. Many sad tales were sung of AgGriffopse, and the Copper was glad of a chance to meet some of his titular relations at last. AgGriffopse and Ibidio's daughters were gracious enough to greet him as a brother, and his hearts beat hard at their touch as they crossed necks.

The only one of the three who really spoke to him was the sickly one, Halaflora, conversing between tiny mouthfuls of food. Perhaps that was why she was sickly. She was interested in details of life in the Drakwatch. Ayafeeia and her sister Imfamnia spent most of their time discussing how they would have organized the banquet.

"No, no. Make the dishes stationary. That way the society has to circulate," Ayafeeia said.

"Look at Tighlia up there, queen of all she surveys. How I envy her," Imfamnia said.

"Envy's nothing to brag of, daughter," Ibidio said, raised scale in her voice.

Tighlia's relations of the Skotl line, on the other hand, didn't mix much with those from the Tyr's Wyrr side. They didn't have quite the decor of scale and elegance of manner the Tyr's side possessed. He spoke with only one, a grim, battle-scarred dragon with still-healing wounds on his uncased wings—SiDrakkon's son, SiBayereth. He glistened, a deep red oily color, like blood spilled in shadow, but was polite enough to tip his head as he congratulated the Copper.

"Heartstrong of you to jump forward, cousin. Don't let them frighten you about the Upper World," he said in the growling accent of his Skotl clan. "Our family's just so used to being guarded down here, they swoon at the thought of risk."

The Copper swelled with pride, willing to hurl himself against a wave of spears at such praise. A guard! And of these splendid, noble, glamorous, glittering dragons—his . . . his *family*.

Chapter 14

The Copper walked around the caverns of the Drakwatch trainees one last time. The rather brackish pool, the loose skull that one of the thralls had jammed back into place upside down, the boiled kern and fatty joints, the smoky smell of the fat-lamps and drakes—each bore a memory.

He limped around saying good-bye to his trainee companions. He knew they told jokes behind his back, because of his age. But they didn't dare snicker when his eye was on them. He towered over them, thanks to years of Imperial hams and chucks.

"You'll need a good travel thrall," NeStirrath said. He looked into the Copper's cave, where Harf scrubbed the decorated archway in his usual halfhearted manner. "Strong and road-wise. That fool can feed your bats until you come back." Harf scratched his paunch and edged out of the way. "I'll give you one of mine, Fourfang. He's mostly blighter, strong as a dragon, for his size."

"I've come to wish the drake honor and glory as well," a drag-onelle's voice called. Rethothanna didn't bother to announce herself as a stranger to the Drakwatch caves or wait for an invitation, but the drakes would hesitate to attack a full-grown female.

She closed her nostrils. "Fee-fie-foe-*foul*, when was the last time these holes were washed out?"

"There's a sluice from the upper levels that backs up," Ne-Stirrath said. "But do not tell the Imperial Family that their waste stinks; they'd never believe it. What are you doing bringing your refined nostrils to these caves, female?"

"As I said, to wish young Rugaard safe horizons. I give him a gift, as well."

The girl thrall who'd worked his face stood just behind, a heavy quilted coat around her and a woven basket tied to her back.

NeStirrath dug around behind his *griff* and extracted some loose scale. "For an egg-dripping drake you make the journey, but you couldn't be bothered to come wait on me for your blasted song?"

"Even the oldest of trees needs to bend now and then. I wanted the advantage of home ground to hear your song, lest my hearts melt and I lose all my concentration in your glory."

"Don't jest with me."

"You old, stump-winged fool. I've wanted you beside me for years. You're the best dragon in the dome, and yes, I include the Tyr himself in that assessment. But we can talk later. It's youth that needs the benefit of our years now." She swung her ox-eyed head around to the Copper. "To glory bid, eh, drake? I've brought you a gift. Come forward, Rhea."

The girl stepped up to the base of the dragonelle's neck, her flat face hidden behind her straw-colored hair. Harf put down his brush and made an ooking noise.

"You remember Rhea; she arranged you for the banquet. You need a proper body thrall, and she needs some time in the sun, or she'll grow up all bent and spindly, no matter how many fish she eats. Bant's sunny enough."

Rhea shivered despite her quilted coat.

"She's worried about Black Rock. Thralls get eaten in here," Rethothanna said.

"Not in my caves," NeStirrath said. He pointed his tail toward Harf. "That idle-fingers is still intact, as you can see."

"Can she make a journey?" the Copper asked. The slight girl didn't seem up to a climb to the gardens.

"She's young. She'll harden to the road," Rethothanna said.

NeStirrath brought Fourfang over. The blighter had shoulders fully as broad as the girl was high, and legs like a dragon. He offered a long list of instructions, both to Fourfang and the Copper, as Rethothanna inspected the skulls decorating the passages. "Above all, remember your lessons and keep a dragon's virtues. You can't go far wrong."

The Copper thought it funny that the same advice went to a blighter as well as a dragon. What would a blighter do with learning? It would pass through him like water, clear going in and smelly and tainted coming out.

"And keep off that poor girl," he finished.

That must have been directed at the blighter. Fourfang grinned, showing his sharpened teeth.

"What can you tell me about Bant?" the Copper asked Rethothanna.

She fluttered a *griff* at NeStirrath. "You mean what kind of food is to be had?"

"No. Our allies in the Uphold. What are they like? How do we keep the peace with them? What's the nature of this problem SiDrakkon needs to solve? But if there's some delicacy to be had . . . well, I'd hate to miss a new feast."

"He is a promising young thing," she said to NeStirrath. "Interested in the essentials. Very well. I'll give you the essential for Bant: water. Bant's either dry or rainy, depending on the time of year; the rainy season starts right around the summer solstice, usually a little before. It's made up of rocky, rather dry plains that go lush during the rains and tinder-dry the rest of the year. There are three rivers, all flowing west to

155

the Ocean of the Summer Sun, and it's control of the rivers that's everything, for there are rich forests full of trade goods and spices along the rivers. Very good land for herding on the plains, as long as the herds can get to water holes or the rivers in the dry season.

"The elves lived there first, along the rivers, but tribes of blighters came and dispersed them, though they didn't quite get rid of them. A few still live on in the deeper woods or around the better-watered rock piles. A dwarf or two pass through, usually engaged in trade or craft with the ivory and hardwoods. Some tribes of men as well, distant relations to the Ironriders of the north, I believe, as fierce as the blighters when fighting on horseback."

"So it's hard to keep the peace between the groups?" the Copper asked.

"Well, yes, they'll go to the dragon to settle disputes, when neither side thinks it can gain an advantage. But this case is difficult. The Ghi-men, the stone shapers, are pushing south and taking over the rivers, from what I understand of the messages the Tyr has shared with me. They're well organized—their armies will put up a fight against even dragons in the field—but their real skill is in digging and roofing and wall building. When they're behind their battlements they're as tough as a scale digger."

NeStirrath's wing stubs dipped. "If SiDrakkon thinks he'll throw his main strength against one of their fortress towns, we'll be singing laments from Imperial Resort again."

"You do travel light," SiDrakkon said three days later, as they assembled at the northeast riverbank. "Only two thralls?"

"You said it was a six-day journey."

"Barring delays."

"I've gone hungry before."

"That's why I bring extra thralls. Once you've consumed the baggage, there's no need for baggage carriers."

Nivom had two *sissa* of Drakwatch and a *sissa* of Firemaidens. He wore a golden ring in his ear, a mark of a Drakwatch full commander, a rare honor for a wingless drake. Beside the Tyr's brother-by-mate and and Nivom, the Copper also noted three battle-scarred dragons, two blacks and a red, with purplish tones shading their coloring.

"The worst of the Skotl clan," Nivom said quietly. "Duelists."

The Copper hadn't seen a duel yet, though his bats had witnessed one while hunting. The Tyr discouraged the custom for the dragons in the Imperial Resort, and absolutely forbade it among the Imperial line. But on some of the other hills, dragons settled their differences in combat. For the wealthier dragons who didn't want to risk losing an eye or something even more vital, challenges could be settled by means of a duel-by-proxy.

"What do you have against duelists?" the Copper asked.

"A rich dragon can hire professionals, and then start a squabble with a poor one to take what little he has." His *griff* rattled, though he kept them sheathed.

The three-score drakes and drakka under Nivom snorted and whispered: "They've finally let Batty out; Spirits help us."

SiDrakkon walked back up the line of dragons, flocks, baggage, and thralls at the northeast tunnel mouth. They'd go down for a short distance, to the water ring, then start the underground journey to Bant. He paused again by the Copper and took a long sniff at Rhea.

"She's just maturing. Ahh, but that's a smell," SiDrakkon said.

The Copper found her aroma pleasing, rather soft and mammalian, but not nearly as interesting as forge-fresh steel or a fat joint sputtering in an iron pan. But there was no point in being disagreeable.

"Yes," he said. "The blighter could use a daily wash, as she does."

SiDrakkon glanced back at the distant wart of Black Rock. "I'd have a garden of such women, rather than the Tyr's wretched ferns and darkblooms, if I had my way. But duty calls. Which reminds me—Nivom, where's that old courier ring of yours?"

Nivom nosed around in his baggage, and approached with a bronzed token on a chain.

SiDrakkon took it in his *sii* and held it up. "Your first *laudi*." It was a pair of equal-sized bronzed bones, joined and wired at the center so crossed as a dragon might cross his *sii* before settling down to sleep.

"The crossed man-bones of the Tyr. This shows you to be a courier of the Imperial Resort." He opened the length of chain, and the Copper bowed so he might slip it down his neck.

The links rattled down his scale and finally stopped.

"Of course. It doesn't fit. You're wide across the neck base, drake. We'll have to find some smithy and get it adjusted." SiDrakkon smelled hot and angry, like Father.

"My . . . my line was thwick-bodied," the Copper said.

"Watch that lisp. What's wrong with you? You sound like a hatchling. Nivom there speaks better, and half his lip is torn off."

The Copper averted his eyes and swallowed.

"Well?" SiDrakkon growled.

Some of the Firemaidens were whispering among themselves.

"Sow—sorry."

"Be careful with that necklace in battle," Nivom said. "It gives foemen a good aiming point."

The lounging drakes chuckled, and even SiDrakkon deflated a little. "Confound it, we were supposed to have more baskets of chickens. Where are they now?" He swung around and stalked back up the line.

Nivom edged closer. "What do you mean, your line *was* thick-bodied? You still live, so your line does."

"Bad wing. I'll never be able to mate." At least the words came out with a dragonly inflection. He felt comfortable around Nivom.

"Nobody cares about those back-mountain rituals anymore. Well, almost nobody."

SiDrakkon, satisfied at last with the preparations, set the column in motion. They left the Lavadome, with the tunnel guardians of the Drakwatch and the Firemaids raising their necks and trumpeting.

The families of the thralls in the baggage train who'd made the trip to the assembly camp added their own wails. Bits of wood and bone on string were passed from fathers to sons, or between mates. The Copper had been told a dragon could spend a lifetime describing the different good-luck charms and fetishes of the hominid races.

SiDrakkon placed him behind the thralls of the column, with the rear duelist dragon and the *sissa* of the Drakwatch. They came to the encircling river and he again took in the wonder of the high-walled cavern, with sunlight falling through the cracks and landing in golden slivers upon the fetid water. A group of hatchlings sunbathed under the watchful eyes of their mother, and two young dragons swam. *Probably newly mated*, the Copper thought with a pang.

There were boats drawn up for the thralls and provisions. The dragons all swam.

"You'll need to ride in a boat, I expect," SiDrakkon said as he watched the thralls load the last boat.

"No, sir. I'm a strong swimmer," the Copper said, plunging into the water.

"Don't come crying halfway across. Maybe one of the bodyguards will let you ride on their back, but I won't carry you."

"Of cowse not sir."

"And stop that flapping lisping!"

"Y-yes."

The Copper clasped limbs to body and swam off after the *sissa*.

At the other side of river—two bonfires marked the wade-out—the Copper was able to lose his shame again in the fascinating activity of loading and manning the rut-carts.

Here by the river ample cave moss lit the scene. A wide tunnel, with two shining bands of metal running off into its darkening length, left sun-shafted beachfront and disappeared back into the depths of the Lower World. The Copper was so used to the pool of yellow light coming down from the top of the Lavadome or the orange flicker of fat-lamps that the faint green glow of the moss seemed strange again.

Wheeled contraptions rested on the bands of metal. Some had sides; some were just flat platforms, but all ran on four or, rarely, six wheels. The wheels were small things, with lips along the inside that kept them in place on the iron bars. Specialized thralls, barefoot with thick leather belts and wrist braces, minded the oily-smelling joints and laid out and checked pulling lines.

They were dwarvish contraptions, of course.

"I've seen these lines in tunnels before," the Copper said to Nivom.

"They're rut-carts. Have you ever seen a road?"

"No."

Nivom never minded showing off his knowledge. "In the

Upper World hominids use these chariots and wheeled carts and such, and they eventually dig furrows in the ground. This is the same principle, only instead of furrows the wheels sit in the iron furrows. They're a little noisy, but you can pull a heavy load quite easily. The dwarves use them for mining, or for transport when there's no underground canal about."

The Copper blinked for a moment as he tried to absorb what Nivom had said. Nivom was a clever drake, but didn't make allowance for those not as bright as he.

"So the cart . . . floats on the rails. Like the dwarf boats on a river."

"Yes, you'll see."

The thralls went to ropes attached to one end of the carts. SiDrakkon barked out an order, and Nivom distributed his drakes to the heads of the lines, putting their necks through harnesses made for draft animals.

Some of the drakes grumbled at doing beast work.

The Copper put Rhea on one of the flat carts with some of the other female thralls, who cooked or toasted a grainy paste on metal bracking rods for the males.

"Exercise won't do any of you harm," SiDrakkon said. "Toughen you up before you get to the Upper World."

The Copper, though frightened enough of SiDrakkon to keep well out of his way lest he be barked at again, had to grant him this: He kept the column working and moving. The thralls didn't have time to worry about being eaten, and the drakes were so busy they couldn't get into squabbles.

"I'll take a line," the Copper said.

"You're a courier. You needn't—"

The Copper stiffened, extending his neck as though getting ready to issue a challenge.

"If you want the fatigue, have it. I'm riding in a cart, as befits a commander."

The men went to knotted lines and threw loops across their shoulders, padding them with bunched clothing. The Copper let the sweat-stained leather ring—it smelled deliciously of equine—fall about his shoulders. It fit better than the Tyr's emblem.

"Set . . . step . . . off!" SiDrakkon shouted.

"Take the strain. The start's the worst," Nivom shouted.

The carts set up a chorus of metallic screeching, and the chickens clucked in alarm and the sheep hurried out of the way, but the procession lurched into motion.

"Sorry, lads, it's mostly uphill to Bant," SiDrakkon said as he lowered his head to watch the wheels on their iron ruts.

The Copper liked the challenge of the pull; you could lose yourself in the effort. He did most of the work with his *saa*, just hopping forward on his bad leg during a strain.

When a thrall slipped and fell so that he lay dangerously facedown across the rail, the Copper quickly hooked him under the arm with his tail and helped lift him to his feet again before the grinding wheels could take off a leg. The thrall looked at him wide-eyed from behind his shaggy hair.

Fourfang clapped the thrall upon the back and grunted out a few hominid words, pointing at the Copper. The Copper had earned little enough honor among Drakwatch and Firemaidens, but even the respect of his thralls counted for something.

They took their first rest at a cave spring. The thralls instantly fouled the tunnel with their waste; the grains and roots they ate resulted in enormous quantities of excrement that rivaled bat guano in its unwholesomeness.

Nivom came to check on him.

"Ride for the next quarter."

"I'm well enough."

"I don't want the Tyr's courier dropping of heart seizure. Water or blood?"

"Blood." He thirsted for the salty taste. Fourfang made a nuisance of himself, pulling up his *saa* and applying some kind of ointment that smelled like sheep fat.

"There's a pan. SiDrakkon's already shared a pair of sheep with his duelists. Better hurry, or your fellow line drakes will have had it all."

He walked while the pullers were changed, but as soon as they took another break, went back to the traces.

"No. Drake ride. Fourfang pull," Fourfang protested.

"I like it," the Copper said, settling into the collar.

"Only unimportant drake pull," Fourfang said. "Unimportant drake have unimportant thrall."

"Is that so?" the Copper said. It hadn't occurred to him that the thralls had some kind of clan system of their own.

"Pride of place."

"Oh, all right. I'll walk beside. If you get tired, let me know."

The blighter planted his short, bandy legs. The column squealed into motion again.

"These carts need tinkering," Nivom said, looking at the wheels of a particularly noisy contraption in front of the Copper. "If only dwarves didn't starve themselves so quickly when enthralled. Get some fat drippings over here. That helps."

At a widening of the tunnel SiDrakkon had found a rock pile to rest upon and watch the column as it passed. "That's it, Rugaard. Work 'em hard and they're too tired to make trouble. True for scales as well as hair."

They had to leave the carts on the fourth "day"—as measured by sleep periods—and go on foot.

They lost only two thralls on the trip to Bant, one to sickness and one to a badly broken leg when he fell under a cart and seemed unlikely to recover. In both cases they had their heads quickly bitten off by the big duelist dragons as they slept. The others accepted the deaths fatalistically, though they turned their backs when the bodies were shared out and eaten, except for some of the younger thralls, who watched the process with a sort of dread fascination.

At last they saw golden light at the tunnel mouth again. A female dragon, with dust caked thickly in her scales turning her almost white, guarded the entrance from a pallet of wood and straw.

SiDrakkon had them rest in the cave until the sun had lowered so they wouldn't emerge into full daylight.

The Copper took his first step into the Upper World at sunset, blinded and blinking for a full hundred heartbeats. When he finally looked about, squinting, he saw a dizzyingly vast landscape, bronze-colored and dotted here and there by taller green lacework that Nivom identified as trees. An orange sun, so perfectly round it seemed an eerie visitor as strange to the landscape as dragons, rested on the horizon, illuminating a distant rise.

"That's the Sunshard Plateau," Nivom said, pointing with his nose to the distant break in the horizon. "The Lavadome lies beneath. We've come all this way. It fills the sky when you're nearer."

The mouth of the cave had bones scattered all around the looser gravel below the cave gap. "My warning to trespassers." The Firemaid chuckled.

SiDrakkon flew into a rage when he saw the tiny, tired collection of animals gathered at the watering hole at the base of the mouth-mount, watched by a few sandled herders in thin white robes who threw themselves on their bellies when they saw the dragons.

"Courier! Come here!"

The Copper approached, trembling.

SiDrakkon had turned quite purple. Or maybe it was the

color-shifting light of the setting sun. "Your first duty is to hurry back with a message for the glorious Tyr. Tell him I'm relieving that fool NiThonius, friend of his or no. We'll come to the Mud City half-starved, thanks to him. Eat one of these pathetic, scrawny sheep and go!"

It appeared his visit to the Upper World would be as brief as it was dazzling.

Chapter 15

As it turned out, the Copper didn't return to the Lavadome that day. Nivom hurried up to SiDrakkon and convinced him that ill news would be better received by the Tyr if it were mixed with good.

SiDrakkon sputtered some more, but when Nivom pointed out that the Tyr might just appoint SiDrakkon as replacement governor of the Uphold, and SiDrakkon would spend a goodly stretch of years in Bant, the dragon finally retracted his *griff* and claws and cried settled.

The next morning the Copper looked more closely at the Bant hominids as they washed. Their skin was a similar tone to his own scale, though a good deal less shiny, and he decided it made them look healthier and more intelligent than the paler thralls from the Lavadome.

Two tiresome marches later, guided by another dusty dragonelle who could easily converse with the locals, they came to the Mud City.

The Copper got a chance to study a depiction of the lands on an animal skin, with inked squiggles representing rivers, ranges of hills, stone outcroppings, and water holes. Once one got used to maps they made sense. The Mud City was a collection of dwellings and workshops and markets on the southernmost of Bant's three great rivers. Downstream the riverbanks teemed with life, according to SiDrakkon, with the assorted kinds of trees growing so tall above they blocked the sun, rendering the Upper World much like the Lower, though better lit, at least in daytime.

The Copper discovered that while dirty, the Upper World had its compensations. For one thing, all the light sharpened his eyesight. He picked up detail at a distance. In the muted light of the Lower World colors faded and shadows muddied edges. Up here the Spirits' wonders and labors in shaping all between blue sky and black earth stood under brilliant light as though it were a statue on display in the Anklene hill.

The Mud City stood on both banks of the river, surrounded by green, well-watered hills and walls of various age. The buildings were all a white or sandy color, sprouting wood supports or a plot of gardening here and there. The dwellings looked cracked and dry, like Fourfang's sunburned skin.

He expected to see flocks and herds on the surrounding hills, but there were few animals on the heights grazing, and what there were kept close to town.

The dragons camped in a vale between two hills overlooking the town, with good cliffs to one side and a steep slope on the other.

"The Ghi men's horsemen have not yet raided south of the river," their Firemaid guide said.

"I don't put anything past men. They always show up where you don't expect 'em," SiDrakkon said.

"And don't let your thralls cut wood from these trees; these belong to the local chieftain. Wood pilfering will create a grudge."

"Of course."

The Firemaid departed, and SiDrakkon immediately ordered the thralls to gather wood for cooking fires—but only dead branches and deadfalls.

Rhea spent weary hours cleaning dust out of the Copper's scale, while Fourfang made some kind of gruel in a pot as he was toasting a spitted lamb. Fourfang and Rhea licked the spit clean of grease when the Copper was through eating.

The Copper hoped the provisioning would improve soon; already the thralls were pushing and shoving over food allotments.

The next morning NiThonius arrived, and the whole camp stirred at the news.

He was an odd-looking dragon, rather bony and the color of a rusty shield, and had strips of cloth running from his crest and twelve horns, all tied to an ivory tusk piercing his nostrils, creating a sort of fabric shield for his eyes and nose.

Alongside him rode a fine figure of a man with a long, forked beard wrapped in gold cording. More gold cording held a sun cloth to his head, and his robes had glittering strands woven into the lapels.

SiDrakkon lined up the drakes and Firemaidens to meet him, with his bodyguard just behind him. "Let's wait downwind; we'll be able to hear better," Nivom said.

"Eminent of the Bant Uphold, I bring you the Tyr's greetings," SiDrakkon said.

"Mate-brother to the Tyr, I long regret the Tyr's absence from my hearth and hoard. Will you cry ally?"

"I do cry ally."

They both made a perfunctory clucking noise at the sky.

"I welcome your coming," NiThonius said. "Let me introduce King Onato of the Rains and Winds and the Three River Savanna. You met his father, I believe."

"A great warrior and friend to the Lavadome," SiDrakkon said. He gurgled out a few words in a tongue the Copper did not understand.

"Did you catch that?" the Copper asked.

"I can't make snout nor tail of their yammering. But I expect I'll learn if we're here long."

Some of the king's retainers unrolled white material and tied it between the branches of two spreading trees. The king sat beneath atop a folding wooden sort of post-seat, and NiThonius settled down beside. SiDrakkon dismissed the welcoming party and joined the repose, calling Nivom forward. The Copper followed behind.

"A Drakwatch commander and an Imperial Courier. I'm impressed you've come so well arrayed," NiThonius said.

"I was not impressed with your welcoming banquet when we emerged from the Lower World."

NiThonius pulled back his head a little. "I did not expect so many. I'd asked my old friend the Tyr for a cunning dragon or two to help me cope with the Ghi."

"And what could be accomplished against fortresses by a dragon or two?"

"I would rather attack them where they are vulnerable, rather than behind scale or stone."

"Where are they vulnerable?"

"Where their archers can't stand behind battlements and their war machines throw javelin, rock, and fire. I'm a little old to be flitting about, laying waste to flocks and herds. The men of Ghi, the Stonemen, would probably be induced to quit most of the lands they've grabbed if we make the lands unprofitable. They are keen calculators, not prideful. Also, they have some salt mines and clayworks and lumber camps. Burn them and kill the workers, swim up under their trade boats, scatter their herds, and burn their crops in the night. A war of stealth and surprise will weary them before too many years pass. That's why I asked for an active young dragon or two. And that is what our allies gathered provision for."

SiDrakkon tore up the ground with his claws, and the king and his retainers scooted back on their hindquarters, perhaps fearing their new ally would lash out. "I've no patience for that kind of warfare. The Lavadome needs Bant's herds, not tales of a burned crop or shepherd's lodge."

"A salt mine is no shepherd's cot. Without salt, men do not last here."

"A war of many small cuts doesn't answer our need."

"It is the only kind of warfare left to us, at least in Bant."

"How is that?"

NiThonius said a few words to his human ally. "The king has lost many of his finest warriors in fruitless assaults. Those who remain are discouraged and scattered."

"You say that as though the fault lay at another's *sii*."

"Perhaps I delayed too long. The northern half of the country was under the protection of my clutchwinner. After he and his mate were killed, the collapse came so quickly—now the Stonemen build a new strongpoint at a watering spring just north of the Green Dancer that flows below."

"Build?" SiDrakkon said. "It's unfinished?"

"They have a stout wooden palisade. The stoneworks rise day by day."

"There is where we'll strike, then. They won't expect a hard blow after having won so much, and I wish to move before word of our arrival may spread. Nivom, tell your *sissa*, rouse the Firemaidens—we fly at once! We'll give them a taste of dragon fury that'll put hearts back into these spiritless whelps."

After the longest, hardest march of his life, the Copper stayed far to the rear of the attack, watching events from the top of a rock pile.

He didn't feel the least bit tired, not with the night full of the fire of battle. If it weren't for SiDrakkon's forcibly expressed orders . . .

The plains beyond the rivers had these rocky, windswept piles of stones like river-smoothed rocks grown to dragon proportion and heaped. The Copper had become almost as acquainted with the wildlife of the rocks as he had with the grasslands. The rock piles were thick with hopping, naked tailed rodents that the Firemaidens flushed with a quick blast of flame. As he watched the battle, he probed his gum line with his tongue for the remains of the rat he'd just eaten.

He watched carefully as SiDrakkon's orders were executed, remembering details for a report to the Tyr.

His orders had the virtue of simplicity. First the Firemaidens, the most skilled huntresses of their number at the fore, would attack whatever sentries stood on the outskirts of the water hole. One had been killed on the rock pile where the Copper now stood, and his blood still scented the air.

When Nivom gave the signal that the sentries and outwatchers had been cleared, the Drakwatch went forward.

Then SiDrakkon swooped overhead, low enough to smell the bubbling fire bladders (the dragons chewed an irritating pepper called green fury to fill their bladders), his three duelists in line behind to lessen the chance of their being spotted.

The aerial dragons struck and struck hard, setting alight the nests of wooden spikes that warded off horsemen, then picking the flaming bundles up in their *saa* or knocking them around with their tails.

The men rallied to the circle of stone, firing their bows and setting their spears against a descent when the Drakwatch struck, all loosing their flame at a roar from Nivom. The Drakwatch swarmed over the unfinished ramparts, scale glittering in the firelight, and the Copper wished more than anything to be with them.

The Stonemen broke and fled for their lives, and the Firemaidens had much sport hunting down stragglers in the grass.

At last a Firemaiden called to the Copper and told him that SiDrakkon bade that he join in the feast and survey the night's work.

One of the Drakwatch had been killed in the fighting. Apart from bloodless arrow wounds to the wing tissue, SiDrakkon and the duelists had not been scratched.

They devoured some of the beasts of burden killed in the action and made presents of the rest to King Onato of the Rains and Wind and other titles. Such heads as didn't disappear down dragon or drake gullets were lined up on the unfinished ramparts as a warning to the Ghi.

"That's how you do it, Rugaard. A fast, heavy blow. Smash 'em up, and they'll break and scatter," SiDrakkon said. "When these human and blighter tribesmen see this work, they'll rally to the king's banner again. Especially if the banner's carried by a victorious dragon."

"Four victorious dragons," one of the bodyguards said with a belch, as he nosed up a silver-hilted knife from the dirt, broke off the blade, and swallowed it.

"Forget not the drakes!" a pair from Nivom's first *sissa* chorused, where they rooted among the burned bodies for coin to eat.

"The Firemaidens took their share of honors," a dazzling, golden-eyed drakka said as another licked the wounds about her *sii* and *griff*.

SiDrakkon stood and roared a victorious bellow that no doubt sent the rock-racks digging even deeper into the sand. "Now, Rugaard, now you may return to the Lavadome. Tell the mighty Tyr what has been accomplished in his name this night. But hurry back, for the feasting will be even greater when we strike their fortress from the depths of the very river they so arrogantly claim!"

No one but the departing Copper noticed NiThonius, who'd stayed back from the attack as well. He remained at the edge of the celebration, using his nose to help the Bant tribesmen gather spent arrows and dropped swords. He simply sighed quietly.

SiDrakkon roared after him: "Give your report to the Tyr, and tell my sister to keep her advice. Her snout's in too many caves as it is."

Chapter 16

The road back to the Lavadome was wearisome in several respects.

For a start, the king awarded them, through SiDrakkon, a rather broken-down and dismal donkey, who complained, in the simple words of the beast tongue, that he would be eaten as soon as the Copper grew hungry. For a while Rhea rode him, but he staggered and bellowed, so they left him with just carrying grain and dragon-smoked meat.

Rhea performed her scale-cleaning duties until her fingers bled from beneath her nails. She slept rather close to him. Fourfang, however, continually disappeared while they passed back south through Bant, especially when the Copper smelled tribal blighters around. He'd slip off quietly in the night, and come back smelling of scented oil.

"Where do you go nights, Fourfang?" the Copper asked one morning.

In response, the blighter made a motion of such obvious obscenity that the Copper almost scorched him from the waist down. The Copper wondered how many prominently toothed blighter litters would be born next season.

On their last day of travel the rains began. Blue-bottomed clouds boiled up out of the east and gathered, and water fell from the sky, first in a drizzle and then in such torrents it was pointless to seek shelter, so they simply squelched on through the mud to the next soggy camp.

The donkey complained that not only was he to be eaten, but he was going to be eaten wet and uncomfortable.

"The rains, at last," the Firemaid guarding the underground entrance said. "You leave us so soon?" The rain had washed and brightened her scale.

"I'll return with messages, I expect. I'll offer you a gift of this donkey to remember me. I suggest you eat him; it's the only way you'll ever have any peace and quiet."

The Firemaids kept a goodly supply of meat, gained hunting on the plains, and there was even a little fish pulled out of a stream that morning, for with the rain the fish were hurrying to mate and lay their eggs. The Copper ate the fish as soon as it was offered. If his time in the Lavadome lacked anything, it was a good piece of fish now and again.

The trek down the tunnel was long—fortunately there were few places one could get lost, and when in doubt the Copper simply smelled for the leavings of the flocks driven downtunnel. Once they met up with the dwarvish iron ruts it was simply a matter of following the lines down. Their trek had little to remember, save that Fourfang slept soundly each night with his head pillowed upon the Copper's rump, and Rhea, lacking the warm sty provided by her fellow thralls, huddled against his leathery stomach. So they came again to the Lavadome with little doubt or danger. The deman boatman who carried them across was a gruesome specimen, and fondled Rhea's sun-colored hair as they climbed in.

"Enough, you," the Copper growled. The demen were useful enough in keeping order among the thralls, but he still found them loathsome. "Keep to your end of the boat."

The deman and Fourfang exchanged looks. Fourfang licked his lips and showed his teeth.

The deman's spines rose. "No brawling," the Copper said, placing his tail between them.

The pens and dragon-holes of the Lavadome's hills felt shrunken in scale now, after the horizon-stretching space and light of the Upper World. They had to rest only once, crossing easily on common paths, and instead of blue infinity overhead, they enjoyed the intricate beauty of the fire-streaked dome. He left Fourfang and Rhea on the lower entrance to the Imperial Resort. He would have liked to see how things were getting on in the training caves—though he'd been gone only two-score and five days it felt like years—but Tyr would need to hear about events in Bant.

He hurried up one of the steep, narrow back step-passages used by the thralls. He was still small enough to fit, and he could avoid some of the transverses leading to the garden level.

Thralls worked the Tyr's Gardens, diverting trickles from the central pool and splashing water on the ferns and vines. One had a dirty joint shoved in his waistband, probably cast aside during a banquet and found in the underbrush, and guiltily dropped it.

Well, let him enjoy his find. "I'd boil it well if I were you. A joint can go a long way, made into soups," he said. The thrall just blinked. "Go on; pick it up. You found it; you enjoy it."

He met NoSohoth in the plaza before the Tyr's outer entrance, eating a dish made of meat shredded into thin, stringlike strips and swimming in gravy, as a thrall poked around behind his crest, cleaning dirt and dead skin with a rag-wrapped stick. Saliva flooded the Copper's mouth at the smell of the dragon's breakfast.

"I'll say this for you, Rugaard: You're easy to identify at a distance. Your hop-walk is distinctive."

"I bring news for the Tyr."

NoSohoth took another tongueful of gravy. "I'd be surprised if you didn't. SiDrakkon calls for three more dragons, I suppose."

"My mate is sleeping," Tighlia said, emerging from the Tyr's cave. She moved rather stiffly.

Thralls exploded out of the corners of the plaza like a flight of startled birds, converging on the Tyr's mate.

"Yes, some breakfast, just a little kern," she said, looking from thrall to thrall. "No, no bath. Just some ointment for my joints. My shoulders again. Leafdrip's formula and none other, now. Oh, leave off; the scale's still lined from sleeping. It'll smooth on its own."

She shrugged off her attendants and took a long drink from Tyr's trickle basin.

"Restless night again, glorious Queen?"

"Not a good turn to be had, NoSohoth." She looked at the Copper. "What on earth are you doing here?"

"Our newest courier has returned with news from Bant," NoSohoth said.

"My mate's lame little indulgence. Well, out with it."

"I bring news for the Tyr himself," the Copper said.

"Be off with all of you," she said to the thralls. "You too, NoSohoth. See what's keeping my kern." She sidestepped toward the trickle spilling into the basin.

The Copper regretted to see the shredded meat in gravy go, but the hard eye of Tighlia made him forget his appetite.

"We can talk here, you. No one will overhear. Come closer; I've never bitten a drake in my life and I won't start this morning. What news?"

"I'm the Tyr's courier," the Copper protested. He wondered if he should relay her brother's exact words.

"Don't question me; it's not your place. FeHazathant needs twice the sleep that he gets. I'm eager to hear every detail of my brother, and you have my promise that the Tyr will hear your report."

"I'm under instructions—"

She interrupted in a quiet voice. "You would be wise to obey me. I've given my word: Tyr will hear your message. Will you offer insult to me by disbelief? There is no shortage of champions who will duel to defend my honor."

"Yes, great Queen. Our journey—"

"Stomp the journey. How go things in Bant?"

"They are hard-pressed by the Ghi men. Two of their river valleys are lost. Their forces have been defeated, scattered, and discouraged."

"What has my brother done to retrieve the situation, or is the Uphold lost?"

"SiDrakkon won a victory against the Ghi men. He destroyed a fortification before it could be completed, with small loss."

"Ninny! You should have been shouting that from the moment you passed into the dome. A victory! FeHazathant must hear of this." She rounded on a kitchen thrall hurrying up with a steaming bowl of milky, yellow kern. "You there! Let's have a skewer of steaks for the Tyr's breakfast, and if they're not still sputtering from the fire you'll be turning on the next spit."

Within a dwarf-hour the court was roused and the Tyr came into the plaza to hear the story. When the Copper repeated his news and told of the battle, all the Imperial line began to twitter.

"Well, that is good news," NoSohoth said when Tighlia nudged him. "A roar for SiDrakkon."

The dragons roared, but to the Copper it sounded half-lunged.

The Tyr nodded. "Well, if it's begun, at least it's begun well. But open war . . . the Ghi men are strong and numerous and craft-wise. What's the spirit of the warriors in Bant?"

The Copper chose his words carefully. "NiThonius says

they're in poor spirits. They've been broken by defeats. SiDrakkon believes this victory will bring them round."

"What do you think?"

"I, Tyr?"

"Yes, you've been up there recently and I haven't. What do you think? Can Bant win a war?"

The Copper remained silent for a moment. "I . . . I can't form an opinion. I haven't even seen them fight."

The dragons chuckled at that. "Don't overtax my poor cousin's abilities, Grandfather," Simevolant called.

"SiDrakkon seems confident they can win," the Copper said.

"And why not?" Tighlia said. "Hominids are always braver behind a dragon than in front."

The Tyr stared off to the northeast, as though trying to pierce crystal, lava, and rock with his eyes. "Rest for three days, Rugaard: You look worn. Then return to SiDrakkon and give him my congratulations. Tell him that if there is to be a war, let it be a short one, and seek concessions from the Ghi men rather than battles. Do you understand?"

"Yes, Tyr."

As it turned out, he didn't return to his familiar shelf in the training caves. NoSohoth arranged a cave midrock in the better-lit south quarter, among some of the wealthier dragons who stored their hoards in the Imperial Resort and wanted caves near their coin. He even had a nice crack in the wall where he could look out and take the air—though he suspected his head would be too large to fit out the hole anymore as his horns began to come in—and was near a cascade of only occasionally tainted water.

Tyr sent him a gift of a small bag of coins. He ate just a few and stuck the rest on a little shelf by a corner the bats were exploring for grips. He was a growing dragon and should think about establishing a hoard.

Harf, Rhea, and Fourfang even had their own room just off his, with a thick curtain so it was warm and cozy. Naturally they set to squabbling when Harf started pawing at Rhea and trying to mate with her. The Copper sent Rhea to see about some fresh clothing for herself and Fourfang, for the journey had tattered their simple tunics, and put Harf to work scrubbing a noisome corner the previous tenant had left. Why couldn't dragons be bothered to use the waste pits?

"Fourfang, you know about these things. If she's not ready to mate, she shouldn't, right?"

Fourfang probed his ears, perhaps prodding his brains into activity. "Not know humans of many. Not want babies for sell?"

"I'm not sure she's even mature enough for that. Don't they get those suckle points when they're ready for children? Bigger is better, no?"

Fourfang thought that funny.

"Well, if he starts pawing at her again, stop him. Or tell her she can sleep in here, but there's a draft from that crack, I'm afraid."

The bats were happy to probe his scales for juicy ticks and fleas that had come along for the journey, and they told him of what they saw and heard while he was gone. Uninteresting bat gossip, mostly involving the movement of herds or sickly, deep-sleeping dragons. Old Thernadad, blinder than ever but still with some hearing, relayed some details of a good fight in the Drakwatch caves. The Copper decided that when he returned to the surface he'd take a few bats along, just to keep the vermin out of his hide.

The bats stirred at some motion in the outer passage. The Copper smelled rich perfumed oils.

"So you do keep bats," Tighlia said, thrusting her head in.

The bats flapped back up into their holes.

She sniffed at the bat crack and clamped her nostrils. "I thought it was just gossip. Scale and tail, as my granddam used to say, it's cramped in here, and the bats are making my eyes water. I want to talk to you, Rugaard. I don't believe I can fit without squashing you. Perhaps you'd better come out into the passage."

The coins rolling around in his innards had left him in a contented mood, and he followed her fleshless hips out into the tunnel. She looked around, and though there was nothing but a sleeping thrall on a mat in front of a passage, waiting for her dragon to return, Tighlia still followed the sound of falling water to the cascade. She made a pretense of wetting her face.

"Now, my ill-favored little adoptive granddrake, I thought we should have a talk before you returned to Bant."

"Yes, Granddam. I'm honored by—"

"Of course. That's the only thing I can stand about you. You're polite rather than wheedling or sycophantic or challenging. For all your faults, it seems you have a good memory. I want you to send my compliments to my brother. Can you manage that?"

"Yes, Granddam."

"With one piece of advice. This is imperative. If he's going to win a war in Bant, he needs to inspire the hominids. They're not thralls; he can't just threaten and bluster and drive to get what he wants. He has to handle them. Make them want the war."

She paused, so the Copper guessed she expected a reply. "Handle them so they want the war."

"Yes. Aren't you wondering how?"

"Doesn't he know?"

"You've no intellectual curiosity at all, have you? Don't answer; you're tiresome enough when silent. My brother's much the same. The trick to getting hominids worked up for a war is to fixate them."

"Fixate them, Granddam?" the Copper said.

"Yes. Find some old wrong the Ghi men have done to them and get them talking of nothing else. Make sure it's something long enough ago so the memory's clouded about exactly what happened. Then tell them all their difficulties spring from that source, like a salted well slowly poisoning the land around. Fixate! If their sheep are dying, it's because of the Ghi men. If the rain causes a mudslide, it's because the Ghi men cut down their trees. That kind of thing. Their brains can't hold more than three ideas at once, and my brother must make sure at least one of the ideas is useful to him."

If the hominids are so dull, why must we hide from them in the Lower World?

"Fixate them so they blame the Ghi men for everything. Yes."

"He should call an assembly of their king and shamans or witch doctors or whatever they have and put the idea into their heads."

"Thank you, Granddam."

"For what?"

"For bending your thoughts to the crisis. The Lavadome is lucky to have such wisdom."

She let out what in another dragon might have been a *prrum*, but it was strangled deep in her throat and emerged as just a sort of gargle. "You're almost a credit to my mate's wisdom, Rugaard. Now get back to my brother, before he flings his dragons against towers and war machines. The Bant think it's their country; they should be the ones dying for it."

As it turned out, he didn't return to SiDrakkon in time. After reluctantly pressing Harf into service as a food carrier, he, the bats riding in a two-layer basket, and his thralls made the surface two days sooner than it had taken on the trip with the main force, thanks to a quick passage on the rails. The Copper drove the cart day and night, sleeping uncomfortably on the noisy rails when he wasn't pulling.

The rains had turned the countryside green in the interval, and there were herds everywhere, following the water and growth. Dry washes now ran with water, and armies of frogs had appeared as though by magic.

The bats had good hunting at night, for the waters had awakened all manner of insect life as well.

Harf disappeared one rain-filled night, and Fourfang guessed he'd run away. The Copper toyed with the idea of sending the bats to find him, but was in fact relieved to be rid of him, and wished him well. Fourfang prophesied: "Day and day at most before lions eat him."

They reached the Mud City, and the Copper simply waited in an open square, watching some half-grown humans practice throwing spears, until NiThonius showed up. He'd taken the laundry off his horns with the rains, but he still looked haggard.

"I'm relieved to find you here," the Copper said. "I really must learn a few words of this tongue. I can't even ask those children playing there where to find you."

"Children playing? That's part of the king's guard, now. Every family in Bant has had to send a fresh warrior, and rather than give up strong men they're sending the old and the young."

SiDrakkon had taken his war, and what of the king's forces he could scrape together, all the way to the Black River. Nithonius gave him three blighter guides, who took him across the savanna, hunting as they traveled. They also taught him several words for the local flora and fauna, though he made little progress with the language beyond that.

So within two-score days' time of leaving the Lavadome he found himself on a bluff overlooking a green river valley, and a battle being lost.

It was a strange transition. One moment the Copper was walking up a long, grassy slope still wet with morning dew. A spotty-hided feline watched them from a dead tree limb, the silence so perfect he heard each grass-parting footstep from the guides in front and Fourfang and Rhea behind.

Then they crossed the hillcrest into chaos.

The river broke into pieces here, lined with sandbars, some with trees up past their roots in floodwaters. On the far bank stood a fortress of the Ghi men: a rounded hill, crowded with stone housing and surrounded by a wide, stout wall and marshy ground. The fortress stood next to taller hills cut open and butchered for the stone they contained.

A dead dragon lay on the riverbank, below a raised path that led up to the fortress gate. The path itself was littered with what looked like colorful bundles, and it was only after a moment's reflection that he realized they were bodies.

Another of the duelists lay, apparently unconscious, panting, bleeding, while a couple of blighters pulled gingerly at spear shafts sticking out of his underside. The Copper left Fourfang and Rhea with some gibbets of drying game and dead Ghi men and approached the wounded dragon. It was HeBellereth, the red.

The Copper looked downriver and saw confused motion at the bank of some eddies in the river. Bant men and blighters were riding or wading across the thigh-deep water, retreating from the far bank.

"One more flight, NoTannadon. Just one more flight," SiDrakkon was saying. "You must keep them off the Drakwatch and what's left of the blighters. Otherwise they'll never get back across the river. They're out of range of the war machines now."

The duelist dug in his throat with his *saa* and extracted a piece of an arrow. "And end up like HeBellereth, or the corpse across the river? Go yourself."

Several deep *thwack* noises rose even to the hilltop, and the Copper saw the arms of war machines whipping up from thick hedges of concealing brush. They threw masses of stones high in the air, dark clouds that dispersed as they fell on the river crossing. Warriors threw cowhide shields up over their heads for protection, but they had no more effect than a mist. Blighters fell by the score.

"Curse them!" SiDrakkon roared, and flapped into the air. He swooped down over the river crossing and loosed his flame upon the bushes and war machines.

He turned a tight circle over the river valley and plunged among the burning machines, throwing men and their constructs this way and that in his fury.

The Copper saw a group of Drakwatch clustered around Nivom—he was easy to see at a distance, a white vesper with head rising again and again to call to the drakes. Nivom loosed his flame into a mass of rock and washed-up timber on the riverbank, and was rewarded by the sight of tin-helmeted Ghi men running, throwing aside their weapons. Nivom dashed through the inferno and came back with something in his mouth. He dropped it long enough to call to the last few Drakwatch on the north bank of the river, and as they plunged into the current he retrieved his prize and followed.

The blighters staggered back up the hill, some throwing themselves into the first piece of cover to pant or tend one another's wounds. The proud Drakwatch had an easier climb, being four-legged, save for the wounded. Nivom stalked right past his injured drakes and started up the hill.

The Copper looked from blighter to drake and back again. Dragons were a superior species in every physical respect. Their scale kept out arrows that felled the blighters, their crests could deflect a fall of stones such as rained down on the blighters at the ford, and their fire terrified even if it did not kill.

But the blighters would not abandon an injured fellow warrior to his fate.

Nivom threw down his captured weapon, a contraption of wood and metal, in some respects similar to a bow. "Curse them. They're using dwarvish crossbows."

A bleeding drake just made it to the top of the hill and collapsed. The Copper approached to see to his wounds, but the drake just snarled a warning: "Keep off!"

The wounded drake curled into a ball.

SiDrakkon flapped across the river and landed on the hilltop, somewhat bloodied about the *griff* and gums. A blighter ran up and tugged at an arrow projecting from his *saa*, and the dragon growled and struck him down.

On the other side of the river, the Ghi men sallied out of their fortress, teams of spearmen hunting about the riverbank. They flushed a wounded drake and put an end to him. Wounded blighters they beheaded, digging into the ground the warriors' short stabbing spears and setting the taken heads atop, grisly flowers lining the road leading to the Ghi men's fortress.

"Come, NoTannadon," SiDrakkon said. If he noticed that the Copper had returned he gave no sign of it. "We'll return to the Lavadome and there ask for more dragons to redeem this. Nivom, go back to the Mud City as best as you can. I'll return with two-score dragons ready for war!"

With that he flapped into the air, the remaining duelist trailing behind.

"Rest a moment," Nivom said to some of the Drakwatch who rose to begin the long journey south. "The Ghi men aren't crossing the river just yet. Might as well eat the hanging meat; Spirits know when we'll have full bellies again."

He looked at the receding dots of the dragons flying south. The wounded duelist gave a groan.

"Two-score dragons," Nivom said. "Three will come over footsore and give up before they're out of the Lower World. Two will get into a duel, killing one and leaving the other too wounded to go on. Six will see all the game on the savanna here and decide to spend the season hunting instead of in warfare. One will see a village in the distance, immediately attack, and it will turn out that he just burned out some headman of the king's and will have to be sent back in disgrace. Four will argue with SiDrakkon about the orders he gives, and return to the Lavadome rather than serve under one they consider inferior to themselves. Two more will quit the first time an arrow goes home; for having shed blood honorably, they will consider their bit in the war over. Of the half-score remaining one will always be too ill to fight, another too cowardly, and a third will fly into a rage and die atop the first tower he sees. Leaving SiDrakkon with three reliable dragons again."

"You should have a mouthful yourself," the Copper said. He'd never heard Nivom so discouraged. "Just as many lengths for you as the rest."

"What I'd like is some wine. Have you ever had wine, Rugaard?"

"What about HeBellereth? And the wounded on the hill-side?" the Copper asked.

"You think this is a training march? I won't bleed victorious dragons looking after losers."

"The blighters don't feel that way."

"Blighters!"

The Copper stared off across the river. Trails of smoke rose from the town.

"It's that cursed wall that did it," Nivom said. "See how the causeway runs along it? They could fire down on us, throw

187

rocks. Rothor and NiHerrstrath tried climbing it, but they were picked off from the towers."

Some of the Ghi men had ventured out beyond the broken gate and were crowded around the corpse of the dragon, cutting trophies of their victory.

The Copper suddenly noticed something about the wounded and the survivors. "What happened to the Firemaidens?"

"SiDrakkon grew desperate. After the first rush against the gate was thrown back, he sent the Firemaidens to lead the blighters. Some fell under the towers. I think that's Agania there, being lifted by those rats."

The Copper approached HeBellereth. The blighters had managed to get the horrible, hooked spear out, and the dragon lay on his side, panting. He rolled an anguished eye at the Copper.

Nivom shut his nostrils and walked over to the hanging meat.

"Can you walk, sir?" the Copper asked.

The dragon managed to right himself. He got his hindquarters up, but managed only a short, shaky rise on his *sii* before collapsing again. "No. I'm vanquished."

"I've been vanquished too," the Copper said.

"Yet . . ." the dragon said, "you wear *laudi*."

The Copper inflated his lungs, looked down at the wounded drakes struggling up the slope. He couldn't say who was talking or where the words were coming from, only that he was angry about the sacrifice of the Firemaidens, and the wretched humans across the river, pulling teeth and claws from the corpse of the dead dragon. "Not yet! Drakwatch of the Lavadome, you're hurt but you're not dead. Not yet!"

A drake pulled himself out from the rocks at the bank of the river.

"Up. Up, drakes," the Copper said, rearing onto his hind

legs, a strange clarity in his mind. "Climb. On three legs if you have to." He waved his shriveled limb to emphasize his point.

One drake made it only a few paces before collapsing.

The Copper scrambled down the hill. The drake, a coppery color not much different from his own, was bled out, his gums and eye sockets almost white.

"Vanquished," the drake said. "Cry vanquished for me. To what little glory I've earned I depart this——"

"Not yet! Climb on my back. I'll get you up the hill. You'll heal and get another chance at them."

Six or seven blighter warriors were gathered nearby, resting and chewing on some kind of leaf. Some no longer had their spears or shields.

"Up the hill," the Copper said.

They looked at him blankly as the drake climbed on his back. Luckily he was slender-framed. The Copper gestured with his snout. "To the top. Top."

The Copper appreciated the hill's difficulty more on the way up than on the trip down. Especially with the weight of a drake supported by only three limbs. The Ghi men would have a hard time coming up it, at least from the riverside.

The wounded drake's claws relaxed and he slipped off. The drake's tongue hung out as he breathed.

"Can you grip my tail?"

The drake didn't answer; he just closed his teeth around the Copper's tail, then shut his eyes. The climb was harder, not to mention painful, with the deadweight of the drake pulling at his tail, but he made it to the others.

The wounded drake breathed no more. The Copper pried the jaws loose.

He thought furiously. The drakes would lose heart, staring at that cooling body.

"I don't know this drake. What was his name?"

"Nirolf," another said.

"This is Nirolf's hill, then. Let's put him in those rocks, there, where he'll have a good view of the fight."

"Why name a hill after one who was vanquished?" a drake asked.

The Copper didn't have an answer, so he just snarled and rattled his *griff* until the drake backed away.

Nivom returned to him, chewing, negotiating a course through the wounded drakes as though wishing to avoid droppings.

"What's this about you remaining behind?" he asked.

"I'm not so sure this battle is over."

"I am. I felt the rocks fall. I felt a dragon crash to the ground. Those stone houses of the Ghi men do not burn like some blighter village."

"There's still a fight in these drakes. The Ghi men will learn that if they try to come up this hill."

"Your honor," a drake said. "If there're still fighting claws dug into this ground, I don't want to leave it." He sniffed at one of his wounded fellows with a scabby snout missing a few scales.

Nivom looked around. Enough of the unbled drakes had crept up to listen to the conversation, while still keeping their distance from the wounded, so he had an audience in two rings. The duelist dragon licking at the wound in his chest formed a little hill all his own.

"How do you propose this battle be fought? No wings, no mobility, and no hominid levees."

The Copper lowered his head. "I'll follow any order you wish to give, Commander. As long as it doesn't involve my leaving this hill and the wounded."

"You mean the vanquished."

HeBellereth lifted his massive scarred head. "Not yet, drake."

The Copper felt a thought break loose in his mind. "Yes! That's the spirit. Not yet. That will be our battle cry. *Not yet*."

Nivom took a deep breath. "It'll be dark soon. We'll post wind sentries on the adjoining hills. If we get everyone out of sight they might think we've left. Then I'll slip back with a *siisa* to the ford. . . ."

The Copper could almost feel the heat from the gathered and the filling fire bladders. He looked across the river. "Not yet, you milksops. Not yet."

Chapter 17

A scent Nivom called "jasmine" hung in the night air. The flowing moonlit waters beckoned below, seeming to tickle the base of the hill with silver fingers. Night birds warbled amid the flooded trees, their soft calls denying the existence of blood-caked spears and war machines that sent rocks hurtling from the skies.

Even the fortress town on the opposite bank slumbered in peace, a few slivers of light showing from shuttered windows.

The night passed quietly. The remaining blighters, no more than a few score, clustered nervously behind the wounded He-Bellereth. The Copper suspected they were too frightened to venture anywhere else.

A rather long-haired blighter with unusually large eyes closed the wound in HeBellereth, using bits of sharp wooden peg and leather to close the gash.

As the sun went down the Copper asked Fourfang to go among the blighters and see if they'd be willing to send messengers to seek help from the nearby tribes. He'd seen enough burned villages while following the guides to the river to suspect that the local blighters would be more willing to fight the Ghi men than would those from farther south. He dispatched his own guides back to the king to report that there'd been fighting but it was "inconclusive," and that they were camped within sight of the Ghi men's walls.

Then he loosed his trio of bats on HeBellereth to do what they could to soothe his wounds. HeBellereth protested. Being tended to by savage, unenthralled blighters was bad enough, but he didn't want "vermin" nosing about his wound—until the first licks and the numbing tingle the bat saliva brought made his eyes widen in amazement.

"Those are the biggest bats I've ever seen. They're like hunting dogs," Nivom said.

"They were raised on dragonblood," the Copper said. "Almost from birth. It appears to agree with them."

"They'll get their fill this night."

Nivom told him what had transpired between his trip back to the Lavadome and his return. SiDrakkon sent NiThonius to the Mud City to press on the king the need for more forces—men or blighter—then he and his dragons caught a large force of Ghi cavalry in the open and scattered them. SiDrakkon concluded that with their main strength gone, it was time to strike at their largest settlement in Bant, the quarry city on the Black River.

But the Ghi men had prepared against the coming of the dragons. Poor iron spears, tin axes, and cowhide shields were met by steel broadswords, chain armor, and far-flying dwarvish crossbow bolts. As for the dragons, the war machines of the men struck as the dragons turned and dived, and every issue of flame was fought by bucketfuls of sand.

Leading to the debacle the Copper had partly witnessed.

"They'll come in the morning to finish the wounded off," Nivom predicted.

"They'll have to cross the river to do that," the Copper said. "Humans can't swim like drakes. Not with their false-scale."

"My father told me once that the best place to strike an upright is in the crotch, when they take a long step forward."

"Wise dragon. Does he still live?"

"No. A Wyrr was he, like the Tyr himself, and distantly related. He lost his hill and his life to a Skotl-clan duelist. My mother, an Anklene, took her own in her despair."

The Copper thought it best to switch subjects, as Nivom could become gloomy, and he wanted his old cavemate alert and active. Every time talk turned to clan friction it left him non-plussed. Had not dragons enemies enough? "So that's where you get your cleverness. The Anklenes."

"I shouldn't be surprised if you had some Anklene blood in you too. Your eye ridge is like theirs, though that odd eye spoils the effect. You spout strange ideas. Why all the concern over a vanquished drake?"

"I'm not sure I can put it into words. How are you with mind-pictures?"

"Baby stories? I'm a drake, and you're not my mother. Or some dragonelle angling to be flattered."

"In my travels I came across the bodies of two demen sitting back-to-back in a cave, as though they were guarding each other as they died of their wounds. When I smelled the bodies, it was just two more bodies; I'd seen plenty before. But that . . . that . . . comradeship . . ."

"Did you just say comradeship? That's a queer word. I think it's taken from a hominid tongue."

"Dragons could use a little of that, instead of always working out who's above whom and adding to their own store of glory and gold."

"You're not one of these foamers who wants everyone to have the same rank and offer up metals to those who can't be bothered to get it on their own, are you?"

"What do you mean?"

"We've had a sun-struck dragon or two before. Do your dreaming while you're asleep."

The Copper thought it best to change the course of the conversation. "So what do you propose to do about catching them in the crotch?"

"I'll take a *sissa* of the healthy drakes to the river. Can you handle matters here on the hillside, with the better of the wounded?"

"Yes. I was thinking that trick they played, with their war machines hiding in the brush, could be played on them too. You grab them at the crotch and I'll bite their arms off."

"By the Earth Spirit, yes! Rugaard, I'd be proud to cry havoc with you at my side."

"I was thinking. Some cooperation from the blighters might help. How are you with their tongue?"

"I know a little."

The Copper thought. "I have a thrall who has a way of making himself agreeable. Maybe he can fill in the gaps."

A very unlikely reinforcement arrived after a short rain squall— the weather at this time of year seemed to mandate a rain in the early afternoon and a second in the long hours of the night before dawn—a bashed and mud-splattered Firemaiden named Nilrasha.

According to Fourfang, the blighters now named her Ora, a word that in their tongue referred to some hunting season festival or other, during which one of every kind of game animal was sacrificed to their capricious deities. But the blighter shaman always chose one sacrifice at random—the Ora—to be released back into the wild to let the rest of the game know that though the herds might be thinned and a few jaguars brought down, enough would be left to ensure future hunting. According to Fourfang, Ora either meant *lucky* or *redeemed*, as the rather fatalistic dragon-tongue didn't have many words for those blessed and guarded by the gods.

The Copper found her sucking rainwater off of leaves and

eating some of the hung meat, and told her Fourfang's tale. While he did this a pair of blighters toasted meat on sticks and gave the bits to her.

"So that's why every muddy blighter on this hill's been patting me," Nilrasha said.

She had a lot of mud on her, and blades of grass caught in her scale. Drakka who joined the Firemaidens didn't shirk from dirt and muck, but they were usually cleaner than the drakes. This one either didn't give a flame for her appearance or was too tired to care for herself. "What happened at the gate?"

"It was so quick. I just remember a hail of projectiles: Some were stones; some were those infernal crossbow bolts. Mivonia in front of me, four struck her, two in the neck, or I wouldn't be speaking to you now. There was flame, and some of the blighters rushed into this sort of open space at the center of town. Then one of the dragons overhead was hit; I didn't see it, but I heard his cry as he fell. Everything went wrong after that."

"The blighters didn't run, then?"

"No. Not the ones with us, by my maidenoath, though I can't speak for those behind. But the dragons overhead vanished and the men lost their fear. They poured down their walls and out of their towers.

"Some of the Firemaidens loosed their flame to drive the humans away with heat and smoke, and I chased some through a burning building. Then a wall or a roof fell on me, and I was senseless for a time, though—this is very odd—I heard my mother singing. I distinctly remember it. When the singing stopped it was night, and I moved and some rubble shifted, and then I found myself in their town. I sneaked out through a drain hole that goes under the wall. I think there was meant to be water in it all the time, for the walls and ceiling were covered with dead shell creatures, but something must have gone wrong with the flow, for it was dry everywhere but the floor. It let out by the river, so I just swam across and smelled my way back to the hill. And so you see me."

"We're going to see if we can't avenge your dead sisters tomorrow," the Copper said.

Nilrasha looked across the river. "I should like that. By my maidenoath, I should like that very much."

"You've had enough honors. Stay back with HeBellereth, please. That route into the Ghi men's town may prove useful. I'd like your head to stay on your neck."

She rose, and some bits of hardened mud rained off.

"Who are you to give orders, Batt—Rugaard? You're just a courier."

"I'm also the Tyr's eyes and ears wherever I go. I can be his voice as well, if *griff* meet teeth. But I'd much rather ask than order. So I ask again, please stay back behind HeBellereth. If matters go as badly as they did yesterday, I expect you'll have another chance to fight."

The blighters lit a few cooking fires, but just a few, on the hillside, allowing them to go out as the warm night passed. HeBellereth agreed to act as bait, and morning found him stretched out on the hill, head lolling, looking like one of those savanna rock piles of red scale.

The Ghi men were no fools, however. They marched their archers to the ford in the river and sent scouts across. The blighters threw spears, hiding from the archers behind the trees with their roots in the floodwaters. The blighters ran as soon as the men in glimmering armor went forward, arms linked at the elbows as they fought the current, crossing like some fantastic serpent.

The blighters got into the spirit of the game, gathering here and there on the hillside to scream insults at the men, sometimes tossing a rock that would go bouncing down the hill and land well short of their foes. Each rock was answered by a hail of arrows once the archers came across and the blighters retreated uphill.

The Ghi-men scouts, clad only in light tunics and sandals with a brace of javelins across their backs, hurried to high vantage points and blew signal horns. The archers crossed from behind. Men with long spears and tall shields had come across, and a group of heavily armored men with great helms and wide blades tied across their backs began to venture into the current.

The Copper watched all this from thick grass halfway up the hill, with strips of thick green sod dripping with ants and beetles laid across this back, his scale rubbed with dirt—Rhea had misunderstood his orders at first, and braided some flowering bramble around his crest and tucked flowers into his spinal ridge. Once she understood that he wanted to be grubbed up, she put a thick paste of mud on every scale.

The Ghi-men scouts found the body of Nirolf lain atop a pile of rocks sticking up above the grasses of the hill, and went to work with their knives.

The drake near him, who'd wormed his way into the center of a thick succulent-leafed bush, growled.

"Still," the Copper ordered. But he liked the sound of their anger; it meant they'd got their spirit back.

More scouts hurried up toward HeBellereth. One pointed to the spot on his belly where partially digested coins could be found, and two set down their javelins and drew blades while a third kept watch, signal horn in one hand, javelin in the other.

The spearmen came up the hill in a rather ragged line, some falling behind thanks to rougher terrain, others forgetting themselves and hurrying toward the fallen dragon, eager for a chance at a trophy.

"Still," the Copper said again as the spearmen approached,

but kept his good roving eye on HeBellereth. The duelist had unusually steady nerves to let a pair of men approach his leathery belly. Or had he slipped into unconsciousness?

HeBellereth suddenly rolled, putting the two men under his massive weight.

The third scout's mouth dropped open, and he reached for his horn, brought it up toward his lips—

A flash of green scale exploded out of the hillside as Nilrasha leaped on the scout. The Copper's brain made sense of it only once it was over, so improbable was her sudden appearance, as though she were conjured up out of the blades of grass that could never conceal a creature of her size. The precision of her leap matched her stealth. She struck high, wrapping herself around her foe like a constricting snake, digging in with her claws, and the struggling pair toppled into the grass. The horn spun in the air and fell.

Why didn't Nivom start the contest? What was he waiting for? The lines of spearmen were almost to the dead tree that marked the widely spaced hiding holes of the wounded drakes. . . .

A warning horn on the hillside sounded. A scout, somewhere he couldn't see, must have seen HeBellereth move. The spearmen looked to their companions and stepped sideways to close. . . .

"Cry havoc!" the Copper roared—well, trumpeted—and if some sentry far down the river valley thought he heard a goose being strangled, it was because the Copper didn't have much of a roar yet.

Showers of dirt flew in the air as the drakes rose. Bright gouts of flame erupted on the hillside, spreading and falling as it rained on the warriors. Screams of pain competed with the signal horns and bellows of the Ghi-men chieftains.

The Copper dragon-dashed forward, threw himself on a

hastily upflung shield, and brought both shield and man down. He gouged, kicked out a *saa*ful of belly organs as he'd done on practice bullocks, and moved on to the next target, a warrior running forward, spear set to skewer him.

His head whipped up and back and his chest muscles tightened. He spit—what was this? A thin stream of liquid hit the man across the shield and shoulders, but no flame. The warrior danced for a second as though he were on fire, and then the Copper and the man locked eyes as they each realized what had happened. The Ghi man raised his spear for a throw, but a green flash flew over the Copper's head.

"What are you waiting for?" Nilrasha said, spitting out a mouthful of tendon and blood vessel from the warrior's gaping neck. "They're running!"

So they were. What was left of the spearmen hurried down the hill, using their spears as a third leg, holding their shields across their backs against further flame.

The Copper marked oily smoke rising from the riverside foliage. A body of swordsmen in a rough triangular formation let the archers pass through and take shelter behind their blades and shields. Little puffs flew from the formation into the trees on either side of the ford. The Copper realized he was seeing the bright feathering on the archers' arrows rather than the arrows themselves.

A drake dashed forward, hurled himself onto the swords and shields, and disappeared into the mass of men. A cheer rose from the Ghi men.

"HeBellereth," the Copper called. "We need a shield wall broken. Can you move?"

"Out of my way, drakes!" HeBellereth roared. "I've hot blood to cool in that river. Try to take my gold-gizzard now, you dogs!"

The dragon pushed off with his back legs and began to slide

down the hillside on his belly. He tore through brush, snapped and flattened small trees, and a wounded drake only just limped out of the way before he pushed past, tail swinging as he tried to keep balance.

And failed. He hit a steeper slope as he neared the river and one of his back legs slipped under his hindquarters. The great red dragon upended and fell sideways, rolling down the hill like a felled tree.

But he was too close for it to make a difference. What the men thought in those last heartbeats could only be imagined. Some of the archers fired, but the arrows had all the effect of pebbles hurled into floodwaters. The triangle dissolved, spreading to each side.

HeBellereth righted himself in the center of the warriors, biting and thrashing. The battle turned into a rout. Pieces of armor and pieces of swordsmen flew in all directions.

What was left of the swordsmen nearest the river ran for the ford. Spearmen, finding their line of retreat blocked by the raging red-scale, waded into the trees, only to be pulled under by drakes—or a crocodile or two that smelled blood in the river and decided to take an easy meal courtesy of warfare.

The Copper spotted men and beasts pulling war machines that looked like oversize crossbows toward the bank of the river and hurried toward HeBellereth. But Nivom anticipated him and called for his drakes, and the mighty dragon, to take cover behind the trees at the riverbank. HeBellereth, his blood flaming in the heat of battle, even found the strength to fly a few dragon-lengths to reach a thicker section of trees.

The catapults on the other side of the river sent a rain of stones, but they fell somewhat short of the bank. A drake or two waded into the river to roar defiance at the retreating men.

"We gutted them," a drake said, looking at the bodies scattered on the hillside.

"This is news our Tyr will wish to hear," Nivom said. Blood ran from both nostrils, but his eyes were bright with triumph.

"We've just given them a shock," the Copper said. "Now it's time to complete the victory and burn that city. Our good Firemaiden Nilrasha knows a way in—"

"Ghioz is strong. They'll send armies to avenge their dead."

Nilrasha appeared at his side with her usual stealth. "The bigger the army the better," she said. "More mouths to feed. Let them sit behind their burned-out walls and starve; we'll cut off their flocks and take their wagons."

The Copper half expected Nivom to roar and snap, for some captains didn't like arguments. Nivom just said, "We've traded blood for blood; it's time to send in the king's headmen and arrange a peace. They may be inclined to agree to stay on the north side of the river from now on."

"Our Tyr won't like the sound of that. A fight, a win, and a peace will please him," Nilrasha said. "Honors all around."

Nivom, for all his brains, had little experience with hominids. The Copper knew what bargaining with hominids brought. They designed deals only to get what they wanted for a moment, and the instant their need was met, the deal was forgotten. They had to be made to shake in fear of ever giving offense to dragonhood, and tuck their squalling broods in at night with tales of fiery vengeance falling from the skies if the scaled gods were offended.

"You won't get a lasting peace unless you're negotiating from a position of strength," the Copper said. Nilrasha chirped agreement, sniffing him now that his blood was up.

" 'Settle terms only once your claws are pressing their neck to the ground,' " Nilrasha quoted, using one of NoSohoth's briefer maxims.

"The Upholder would just as soon end this war quickly," Nivom said. "In his Uphold, NiThonius speaks with the Tyr's voice."

The Copper tried to count the warriors left in the towers, his blood cooling and the wisdom of Nivom's words settling his scale. "A few days behind those stone walls and they'll mourn their dead and get over their fear. They'd give in fast enough if there were nothing between them and the blighter tribes but a pile of rubble. If only we could bring them down somehow."

"Yes, the walls are an enemy as strong as the Ghi men. But I saw fire slide off the stones like rain," Nilrasha said.

"War machines would help," the Copper said. "Couldn't the blighters build some?"

Nivom sighed. "Not to match the Ghi men's. They're cleverer when it comes to such contraptions, and they have better steel and wood than the bleached-out timber under this sun around here. Their projectiles can always fly higher and farther. . . ."

Nivom gave a little choke, and the Copper wondered if he was having an attack of some kind. Had a poisoned arrow pierced him somewhere unsuspected?

"Air Spirit, Rugaard! I think we can do it. Yes, I'm sure we can!"

Over the next day the two sides gathered, each on their own bank of the river. According to the blighters some of the smaller farming settlements and posts had been abandoned as Ghi men sought safety for their families behind the thick stone walls of the town. Boats soon crowded the riverside below the town, and herds sheltered at night beneath the city walls.

The blighters gathered too, but some of them, seeing no fight at the moment, little food, and no plunder, grew bored and wandered away. Even the king himself came, with NiThonius and such forces as could be spared from guarding the river crossings, which set the blighters all to groveling and celebrating as they heaped the few remaining captured weapons at his feet.

Meanwhile, Nivom worked with HeBellereth. The dragon

recovered from his wounds quickly, eating rainy-season-fat Bant cattle and gazelles, though he sometimes winced when he had to walk far. The king watched HeBellereth's endless flights and practice drops with the stones, and then ordered his people to assist the dragons with their strong backs.

Each day the Copper took Rhea to the riverbank for water and bathing. He liked to check on the men's boats in any case, to see if it looked as though any had been loaded. There were two-score or more small, narrow vessels and they could get a substantial force over the river if they so desired. Once satisfied that another day had passed with the two armies glowering at each other from their opposite points, they went to an island-sheltered bank and he'd let Rhea bathe him, and herself. He ventured out into the pool first to check for crocodiles; then she went in and scrubbed him over with rushes. Sometimes he would roll over and she'd tickle his belly.

Fourfang didn't think much of bathing, but he took a captured Ghi-man spear into knee-deep water and came back with a fish or two, sucker-mouthed bottom-feeders that he would fry on an old shield, bathed in herbs.

While they dried, Rhea would sometimes skip stones at Fourfang and spoil his fishing. She took perverse pleasure in making the blighter splash around and curse her. At times she laughed, and the Copper found the sound so pleasing that he prevented Fourfang from thrashing her with cattail stalks.

Nivom joined them one evening.

"I wonder if this will work after all," Nivom said. "Should we even attempt it if it might fail? Another failure before their walls will just encourage the Ghi men. The king sent a messenger across, letting the Ghi men know he was present, but they sent forth no emissary to plead for peace."

"Is he having trouble dropping the stones?"

"If he releases them too high, he misses the target marker. If he releases them low enough so they're sure to hit, he'll pass over the town belly-down. Their war machines will get a chance at him then, and it will probably take many stones to collapse the wall. He still wants to try. It's a terrible thing to have a vision and not be able to see it through."

The Copper didn't know what to say. If Nivom wasn't smart enough to figure out how the walls might be brought down, the Copper certainly couldn't improve on his plans and practices.

Out in the pool Fourfang speared a fish and bent over to retrieve it. The Copper nosed a river-smoothed rock toward Rhea.

She cackled and picked up the stone, then flung it with her arm out sideways so it skipped across the water and hit Fourfang square in that odd assortment of reproductive apparatus male mammals displayed.

Fourfang howled as he clutched his fish and his loincloth.

Nivom took a startled breath. "Of course! Of course! Why didn't it occur to me? Speed—speed's the thing, and he can get all he wants far from the walls. That's it, Rugaard; your little human did it!"

He hurried off up the hill without any more explanation.

Chapter 18

SiDrakkon returned before Nivom's attempt against the walls could be put into effect. He seemed rather surprised to find the drakes and HeBellereth still camped on that hilltop, with some of the signs of an intact army at war: herds of cattle and goats, blighters making charcoal, members of the Drakwatch on the adjoining hills and keeping watch from stone piles on the savanna.

With him were two young dragons with wings freshly uncased, and another veteran duelist, a one-eyed, rather fat dragon who collapsed to the ground as soon as they alighted and roared for food to be brought to him.

"Cursed ill luck," SiDrakkon said, looking south at the rolling cloud banks portending the afternoon's rain. "I set out from the Lavadome with a full score, but everyone had to get a turn of hunting in when they weren't arguing. I've brought what I can; the rest will catch up or deal with my wrath on their return."

Nivom and the Copper exchanged a soft snort.

SiDrakkon looked from the working blighters, using drag ropes to bring a boulder up the hill, to Nilrasha teaching some of the Drakwatch how to stalk in tall grass, to the temporary huts and corrals that had been built for the Bant king and his retinue.

"What transpires here?" SiDrakkon asked.

"We're preparing for an attack on the walls," Nivom said.

"With what forces?"

"HeBellereth."

"He lives? Good. But one dragon would be wasted. Now, with all five of us, we've got a good chance of clearing those towers of war machines."

"They've built more, many more, on every rooftop in the town," Nivom said. "You can see them from our hilltop."

"Delay always allows the enemy time to prepare," SiDrakkon said. "Still, enough fire should make them abandon their machines. It may take several days, but I've seen it done."

"Your honor, Nivom has a plan to bring down the walls," the Copper said.

"Sacrifice every blighter here to the Earth Spirit; it still won't bring an earthquake."

"No, sir. With rocks. Dropped by HeBellereth."

"Ahh, youth," SiDrakkon said, softening his tone a little. "Always thinking they can reinvent warfare. It's been tried in other places. Never works—not one stone out of scores of scores goes true. No, I've got the experience."

"You don't understand," Nivom said. "It's a matter of force and momentum. He's been knocking down trees for days now—"

SiDrakkon's *griff* dropped and rattled. "Trees don't shoot back. No, we'll start this very night. No, not another word out of either of you! It seems I got here just in time before you all got yourselves killed. Fire and terror are the way to go with humans; believe me. They're not dwarves, after all. Fire and terror, drakes. Fire and terror. Now, we've got to hurry. According to the *griffaran* there's an army of Ghi men on the march, big enough to sweep this collection and two more besides off these hills."

———

SiDrakkon's second assault on the city walls was an improvement on the first only in its brevity. His duelist, enraged by javelins fired into his wings and belly, plunged into the city, and managed to make a good deal of noise roaring and smashing before he was silenced. The two young dragons, fast friends since their days in the Drakwatch, according to Nivom, died together when one was brought down in front of the gate tower and the other flew to fight beside him.

HeBellereth had the sense to empty his fire bladder in one long pass over the city and returned, setting the blighters to work fastening shut the holes in his wings with bits of leather and wooden pegs.

"They're ready for dragons, all right," HeBellereth said, wincing as a bone needle passed through his wing skin.

SiDrakkon alighted and the blighters ran from his growlings. He knocked over a tree with his tail and tore apart a meat-smoking hut.

"With four more dragons I could have done it," he raged. "Three to go in and draw fire, and the rest to attack the war machines before they could be reloaded. Only four more!"

Nivom had a few words with HeBellereth and approached SiDrakkon. "Your honor, we can still try the rocks. HeBellereth is willing, and he wasn't injured."

"I should think not, the way he dropped his flame and flapped away. Yes. Send him back over there. I'd like to see that."

Nivom set the blighters to work at the rock pile. There was a good deal of cheering and horn blowing from the other side of the river, and the men ventured from their gates to swarm over the corpses of the young dragons like hungry ants on a bit of dropped fruit.

HeBellereth waddled over to the steepest part of the hill, and the blighters, who'd rolled a more or less round boulder into position at the edge of the cliff, jostled for positions to watch.

"No. He'll never get off the ground with that. It's too big," SiDrakkon said.

HeBellereth clutched the boulder against his chest, wrapping his front limbs about it, spread his wings, and launched himself off the cliff.

SiDrakkon, who hadn't seen the stunt, stood with mouth agape as HeBellereth picked up speed down the steep hill. Then he leveled off, shooting down the river.

"He's going downstream," SiDrakkon said.

"Just watch, your honor," Nivom said. "He just needs a long, straight run. We're going to try for that ramp leading up to the main gate."

HeBellereth shrank to a hard-to-see shadow against the night sky, banked, then rose a little using his momentum, and for a moment the Copper could see him framed against the low-hanging moon.

The dragon adjusted his course, rose with a few strong flaps, and then extended his wings as wide as he could and began a long glide toward the city.

"His idea, the glide," Nivom said. "Oh, I can't wait until I get my wings, can you, Rugaard?"

The Copper didn't say anything. There was a chance, he supposed, that his wings would come in properly. The injury from that foul human seemed so long ago now.

Then HeBellereth was over the ground. Several arrow-flights away from the city walls, he released his boulder and soared off across the river, skimming the surface low enough that his wing tips broke the surface as they beat.

His stone bounced twice up the causeway. The first time its trajectory was almost flat; the second it must have caught on some projection, because it flew almost straight up. It struck hard just over the gate.

"Well, that didn't seem to do much."

"The angle was wrong," Nivom said, sounding a little doubt-ful. "It took a bad bounce."

HeBellereth came up and rested for a few minutes. Nivom helped the blighters select another stone and roll it into position.

"You're wasting your time, I think. But if it amuses you . . ."

"Not an arrow struck home," HeBellereth said. "Attack-ing a town is hatchling play if you can keep your scale to the wretches."

"I found a rounder one," Nivom said, returning with the blighters rolling the stone to the edge of the bluff. "If only we had some dwarvish stonecutters. Rounded stones would fly truer."

HeBellereth repeated his performance, falling, then turning downstream and banking once again for the drop. Nivom held his breath as the stone was loosed. The Copper noticed Fourfang and Rhea crouching in the underbrush, clear of SiDrakkon's eye, watching as well.

This time the boulder stayed low as it bounced. It hit the tower next to the gate, and they heard a series of shouts and crashes from the buildings in town.

"Did it! Did it!" Nivom said. "It punched straight through; did you hear?"

SiDrakkon resettled his wings. "So you made a peephole in the wall. Much good it does us."

"Let me take that big, diamond-shaped one," HeBellereth said, panting a little. "Just let me rest for a moment. They're shooting at me as I pass the wall, not as I approach. I think I can release it closer."

"If you think you can do it," Nivom said.

This boulder was a little larger than the others, and the watchers heard tree limbs snap as HeBellereth passed over them. On this flight, rather than releasing it low over the causeway, he altered his wings so he rose, and released the boulder on the upswing. HeBellereth executed an elegant turn, keeping his belly away from the city walls.

The boulder transcribed a short arc and struck the wall with a crack the Copper felt all the way across the river. The gate tower shuddered, then toppled backward with a long, groaning crash, sending up a cloud of dust.

"I'll be gutted," SiDrakkon said.

The gate crumbled next; then a piece of wall where the tower had been attached fell away. A huge, crescent-shaped gap opened up.

The Copper roused Fourfang with a poke of his tail and sent the blighter to give a message to the king.

HeBellereth returned, a big chunk of his wing flapping as he landed. "Stitchers!" he roared. "They punched a hole in me with a rock of their own," he said as the blighters went to work.

"You've done enough for now. Rest," Nivom said.

"I'm getting the wind under me now," HeBellereth said. "I'll bring down another section of wall before you can recite Ryu-Var's *Tally of Drakine Virtues*—if I can get this wing fixed."

"Can you teach me how to do this, Nivom?" SiDrakkon asked.

"It takes practice. Some days of work," HeBellereth said.

"The cheering and horn blowing have stopped over there, I notice," the Copper said.

HeBellereth put in a long night, making two-score or more runs. Some simply missed, or the boulder bounced wrong, or it did no apparent damage. But by the time dawn came up the town looked very different. The smooth stone wall had been opened in three wide sections, the entire gate area lay in ruins, and the southernmost tower had collapsed, leaving a whole quarter of the city undefended.

The humans were frantically arranging the rubble to form an improvised wall.

But the real blow to the Ghi men came at dawn. The sun came up to reveal the king's army camped south of the city, the hillsides thick with squatting blighters that made them look like vast melon fields. The tribes howled and clashed their spears against their leather shields, setting up a steady, doom-laden thrumming that echoed from bluff to bluff in the river valley. The Copper wondered if any human in those closely packed streets counted on still drawing breath by the next sunset.

Rhea stood and watched through the night, trembling and crying, and refused any food or comfort.

In the end, the king sent forth a messenger once again, announcing his presence and leaving it to the Ghi men to decide. They met on a hilltop thick with fuzzy fruit the blighters called "sweetdrops," and the Peace of the Sweetdrop was announced.

The Copper, though cynical about such arrangements, had to admit that the terms were very advantageous to Bant. NiThonius himself advised the king on the whys and wherefores.

- No Ghi man would come south of the Black River without seeking the king's permission.
- The Ghi men would keep their mines and saltworks, but pay over the worth of one burden out of ten extracted from Bant in the form of coin, goods, or thralls. Value of goods or thralls would be determined by the king's representatives at the mines. New mines and works would be opened only with Bant's permission.
- As a sop to the Ghi men, the Black River would be considered open to commercial traffic to the sea, and trading posts would be kept, along with sufficient garrisons to defend them from bandits.

The Copper wasn't sure that there could be a permanent peace with hominids—either abject submission into thralldom or the peace of a corpse was the only practical alternative—but even the historian Rethothanna chuckled when he said so on his return to the Lavadome. Though she knew the evidence flanking his arguments better than any, she said, "We must make do with fortune when it favors us."

The mighty—and now newly victorious, thanks to the events in Bant—Tyr heard the report in the shadowy gardens of the Imperial Resort atop Black Rock, with accompanying songs and stories of the returned Drakwatch, the lone Firemaiden Nilra-sha (whom the blighters, even in the Lower World, forever after called Ora), and his mate-brother.

The march back had been one of the most pleasant experiences of the Copper's life. The blighters sacrificed bullocks to the dragons all along the way, and held bonfires in their honor, where the tribal youths and maidens danced until they dropped in exhaustion. The king's praise-singers wore out even their iron throats describing the victory, and the Firemaids at the entrance to the lower world bowed at head and tail as their contingent passed.

Even SiDrakkon was in a good mood for once. He let Rhea, easily the most comely of all the thralls in their party, ride on a strapped-down cushion at the high ridge of his back and wave at the garland-throwing crowds.

Though the Copper asked several dragons, none could tell him anything about his strange failure of flame. He could bring up tiny wads from his fire bladder, which when spit would flare after a moment. As an experiment he brought up every drop he could squeeze out. It just splattered and gave off a sulfurous, oily smell.

He finally realized he had one more crippling injury to add to the others. At least this one wasn't visible. No dragonelle would flutter her eyes in amusement.

Even wise old NeStirrath could only guess that it had something to do with the injury to his fire bladder, from the fight with the demen over the *griffaran* eggs. NeStirrath had a thrall touch a torch to his spew, and it burned brightly enough, but wouldn't ignite on its own if he brought it up in any quantity.

To celebrate the victory in Bant, the Tyr commanded a garden-filling banquet, inviting not only the dragons of the Imperial line but the chief dragons of the other hills of the Lavadome.

The Copper made no effort to color his scale; he just had Rhea make it as clean and even as possible. She tried covering his bad eye with a bit of red silk she'd taken off one of the Ghi-men bodies, but the result made him look like he was flaunting an injury, so he told her to keep it.

This banquet was more splendid than the last. The great dragons brought their own thralls to help attend them, and offered up whole bullocks and hogs and bone-crusted river fish as long as a drake and wine aged in artisan glass to the Tyr to add to the gorging and merriment.

The Copper kept to the edges of the banquet this time, in no mood for gorging himself as Simevolant made jokes about the walls of a Ghi-men city being brought down by HeBellereth's tailventings rather than stones.

Fools! Just because they happen to be safe and well fed now, that does not mean things will always be so comfortable. The bones of four dragons are being nibbled at by those tasty fish of the Black River, and all they can do is laugh over jokes about bodily functions.

He passed the time with Rethothanna. She questioned him closely about conditions in Bant, and especially about the weight and composition of the stones.

"They were reddish, some sparkle to them. I can't say more," he answered. "The Ghi men made use of them in building their walls, homes, and the ford, by the look of it. There were cuts in the hillsides to extract it."

"Iron balls would be better. I've heard of the dwarves using them in warfare against dragons. They attach them to harpoons and then bring the dragons down with their weight."

NoSohoth approached and gave the briefest of bows to Rethothanna. "Famed historian, beloved of the Tyr for her wisdom. May I tear Rugaard from you for a moment? A small question has come up regarding events in Bant."

Rethothanna bowed deeply, not so much to NoSohoth but to the command of the Tyr. "Off you go then, Rugaard. Though personally I'd rather be dropped into a dueling pit."

The Copper approached the great dragons, perched on benches above the banquet pit, braziers all around burning oliban. The Tyr and his mate, with SiDrakkon on one side and Nivom on his other, clustered about with the three granddaughters of the Tyr. The Copper limped up and made a greeting bow.

The Tyr looked from one wingside to the other. "Ahh, er, Rugaard, we've run into something of a question that I was hoping you'd help us with."

"Of course, Tyr."

"I won't have lies spread about my brother, whatever the source," Tighlia said. "This half-wit can't tell vermin from *griffaran*."

The Copper felt a quick flush. How good it would be to attend a banquet like this with Zara. Her eyes would burn like the sun, as Tighlia's did, when others made jokes. He didn't care what Tighlia thought of him; he rather admired her for her defense of her brother.

The silence, threatening from SiDrakkon, cautious from Nivom, put Rugaard on edge.

"Please be quiet, my love," Tyr said. "Rugaard. It seems negotiations were made possible only by a good deal of damage to the walls of that stone city on the Black River. Can you enlighten us as to how that came about?"

The Copper wondered if he could be challenged to a duel over his answer. "I believe so. HeBellereth knocked them down by dropping stones."

"Bravely done, yes," the Tyr said. "But how did all that come about?"

"The idea was Nivom's. He and HeBellereth worked on it for days, practicing, and he put the blighters to work finding the right kinds of boulders and gathering them. The night of the battle SiDrakkon ordered the actual attack, and of course he was in command at the time."

"Ha! See, the victory is mine," SiDrakkon thundered.

The Tyr flapped a wing. "Quiet now; don't intimidate this drake. Now, Rugaard, correct me if I'm wrong, but the stones were used only after an attack had failed. An attack that cost the lives of three dragons. Am I wrong in any detail?"

"The last thing I'd wish to do is correct my grandsire," the Copper said.

The Tyr snorted. "Yes or no, do I have it right?"

"Yes, great Tyr."

Nivom seemed to swell. SiDrakkon's tail knocked over two braziers, and thralls rushed forward to right them and pour water on the smoldering coals and incense.

"Is that all, Grandsire?" the Copper asked.

"Tyr, this fool had a thrall run away on him, I believe," SiDrakkon said. "Escaped into Bant. A man named, er, Harb."

"Harf," the Copper corrected, wondering how SiDrakkon knew that.

"Don't bother me with trivia," the Tyr said. "I know your games, SiDrakkon. I want to know the truth about events in Bant, not the comings and goings of dropping scrapers."

"I'm sorry for his escape, Tyr," the Copper said. "Should I have chased him down?"

"Never mind that. There's one other question. It seems after my mate's brother lost two dragons on the first assault on the fortress, he gave orders for a retreat south. Why weren't those orders followed?"

"We were in a strong position, Tyr, and the Ghi men had lost much of their cavalry."

Tyr cocked his head. "According to some, everyone was ready to quit the hill until you said you'd stay by the wounded. He-Bellereth insists that it was you who wanted to stick and fight."

"HeBellereth was badly hurt at that point. I helped look after his wounds, so that could be why he remembers me. Nivom was in command, Tyr. The glory and honor of the victory the next day belong to him—and HeBellereth, of course—for breaking the shield wall with his own body."

"Someone really must make a song about all this," Tyr said. "NoSohoth, call for silence. I want the banquet to hear something."

NoSohoth raised his wings, which had little chimes looped into the trailing edge. He flapped them, and at the ringing the company turned their attention to him. "Our glorious Tyr asks for silence."

The Copper slunk out of the way so he wouldn't obstruct anyone's view.

"Answer my thoughts, for a change!" Tighlia hissed into her mate's ear. "Let us retire and discuss before you make any announcements."

The Tyr ignored her. "Free dragons of the Lavadome and hope of our united lines. Twice now this honored drake at my right side, Nivom, has done great service to all of us.

"First, let it be known that I'm adopting him into the Imperial line. As a son, mind you, to replace AgGriffopse in position if not in our hearts."

That set the banquet to talking. NoSohoth had to sound his wing chimes again to give them time to settle down.

"Second, I'm getting older and don't have the attention to detail I once possessed. Nivom will take a few of the lesser responsibilities from my wings, that I might be able to pay more attention to the greater.

"Finally and most pleasantly, he'll soon be sprouting his wings, and it will be time for him to be mated. I offer any of the daughters of AgGriffopse, the champion of my only clutch, to him, so that we might be joined by more than duty and respect. He can look forward to some pleasant years choosing among my beauties, for their wings are just beginning to bulge."

The assembly at the banquet liked the sound of that and thumped their tails. Thralls danced out of the way to avoid being struck.

The Tyr's young granddaughters fluttered their eyes and *griffs*, save for the sickly one, who shrank behind her longer, stronger, better-fleshed sisters.

"I hope he's not expecting a blushing maiden," Simevolant said, staring at them.

The Copper glanced back at his own spine. Two ridges ran down it, parallel to his vertebrae. His were some years off too, but it made him feel better to know that horns and wings were growing.

SiDrakkon left the banquet almost immediately. The Copper grabbed a dropped mouthful or two but kept away from the throngs. They dragons either asked idiotic questions about whether arrow wounds stung much or joked about his bats.

"You, there," a cold voice said. "Rugaard. Come and have a word with me."

It was Tighlia, and her scales were up and out as though she were expecting battle. She led him to a prominence looking out over the south end of the Lavadome, where fewer orange streams lit the crystalline surface.

"Hurry along now and sit beside me. Yes, close to the edge, so you have a good view. Oh, don't blanch; I've never pushed anyone to his death, and I'm not about to start tonight.

"I like this view. There was never the fighting at the south end of the Lavadome that there was at the north. Just a few thrall hills and livestock pens and mushroom fields. No memories of where friends died."

"Was this what you wanted to speak to me about?"

"No, outcast. My time is too valuable. I expect my mate will have you in for a little chat shortly. You might want to tell him that this Nivom fellow isn't all he appears."

"What makes you think so?"

She scowled. "I know a calculator when I smell one. He weighs everything by his own ambitions. I fear for what will happen if the Tyrancy passes to a Wyrr-Anklene mix. There's already resentment in many Skotl caves. They will have their turn at the Tyrancy one way or another. Civil war could break out again."

"Why do you tell me this?"

"Because, oddly enough, I think you've got the simpleton's faith. The same as my mate has. You're duller—and uglier, certainly—but I believe you think of dragonkind first and yourself second. My mate has that quality too."

"He has all a dragon's virtues—"

"Oh, rot all that tripe. Virtues? What's the first of them?"

The Copper thought for a moment, remembering his lessons. "Destiny. The gifts of the four Spirits in shaping—"

"Mythological balderdash that lets dragons with nothing to offer the world get puffed up about themselves. Next!"

"But everyone knows—"

"No, they don't. That's the problem. Let's have another; your tongue's slow as your wit."

The Copper stiffened. "Courage to—"

"Courage? Exhibitions of courage have killed more dragons

than spears. Give me a dragon who sneaks in when the warriors are otherwise engaged and visits the cribs of the hominids; they put up as much of a fight as squalling babes. Next."

The Copper found her aroma warm, comforting, pleasant. Almost motherly. She was obviously enjoying this. "You can't have anything against fidelity to mate, kith and kin. Every dragon in the Lavadome admires your devotion to our Tyr. You and your brother—"

"You're not old enough to know better. We'll talk again when your mating flight was four scale-ages ago, and your precious clutch champion has breathed fire into your face as he drives you away from your hoard. When some bright young thing spreads her wings for you and promises better times, we'll speak again. Come, come, I'm eager for more."

"Serenity."

"Now, there you may have something. It's the dragon who can control his emotions, wait instead of rage, take an insult or a setback with a song—that's a dragon to be feared. Never let your thoughts past your tongue; never let a competitor know what you really think of him."

"Then why do you tell me what you think of me?" the Copper asked.

"Because you're the sorry, sawed-off tail-tip of the Imperial line, not a competitor. Go on now; you've scored a hit. Press home."

The Copper thought it over. Tighlia was mistress of a thousand details in the Imperial Resort, from arranging matings to seeing after the quality of her mate's kern. "Diligence. It's attention to detail in the routines of—"

"Oh, and now you've gagged on it. Strained at a bat and swallowed a warthog. I'm devoted to idleness. Adore it. Gives one time to think. You'd be amazed how few dragons sit down and just think these days. Don't look cross; I'm giving you medicine that tastes bad, but it'll do you good if you have the sense to repeat the dosage." She tapped her claws on the shining black stone of the rock. "I'm waiting."

"I was going to say charity to those in your thrall, but I expect you'd answer that the more you task them, and the greater they fear you, the better the results."

"Now you're learning. Maybe you're not hopeless after all. There's only one left, so I'll save you the breath. Strength. Strength I believe in. But I'm not talking about roaring and stomping and being able to knock down trees with your tail. That just brings the foemen. Intellectual strength to form a plan, physical strength to carry it out, and moral strength to see it through—those are virtues indeed. That alone will take you farther than the rest of your Drakwatch ideals put together."

"Why do you tell me all this, Granddam?"

She winced as though struck. "Tomorrow a messenger will come for you, asking for a private interview with my mate. He's going to give you a new position as a reward. An important one. I don't want you buggering it up and making slippery bat droppings out of it. Husband your strength and display serenity, and you'll do well enough."

"Thank you, Granddam."

"That's not all. My mate may ask you about SiDrakkon and matters in Bant. Praise him and you'll find me grateful. Those who are good to me make no complaints about my kindnesses in return. But guard your tongue against any slanders, if you know what's good for you."

"I have no slanders to offer, Granddam."

"That's a clever answer, drake. Be equally clever when you talk to my mate tomorrow."

He spent a restless night in his cave, listening to the bats go in and out. Two new litters of hungry young bats suckled at a vein on his inner *saa*, leaving him rather dreamy.

He rose early and had a hearty chicken-and-kern breakfast brought by Fourfang, who burped and vented all while arranging the platters, proof that he had filched a hearty portion for himself.

"Let me smell your fingers, Fourfang."

The blighter shrank away. The Copper clacked his teeth together. "Your fingers or your head. Which will it be?"

Trembling, the blighter held out his hairy hands. The Copper sniffed them.

"I thought so. Don't go digging around in my dishes before I've eaten, or I'll bite few fingers off next time. Wait until after I've finished, like Rhea. Don't I always leave generous portions?"

"Yes, your honor."

"You're not the cleanest with your hands, Fourfang. Your always either digging in some orifice or scratching scabs. In either case I don't like the residue in my food. Just the other night I was offered an elf to take your place." Which wasn't true, but Fourfang couldn't know that.

"I hope to see some improvement in the future, or I'll have to make changes. But I hate unpleasant talk at the beginning of the day. Draw some water and take care of these bat droppings, won't you?"

Fourfang showed admirable energy in getting a bucket and a bristle. The Copper watched the blighter work while Rhea cleaned and filed his claws. Fourfang scrubbed his hands in the bucket after finishing the floor.

"Much better. Now go down and get yourself a dried apple. One for Rhea, too; I think she's exhausted from all the travel."

The quick elf messenger came from the Tyr before Fourfang returned from the stores. The Copper followed the messenger up the winding air shaft and through the Gardens, where Simevolant was lounging, eating honeyed beetles.

"Come over here, Rugaard. The shadebells are blooming.

You must see them. You don't posses any beauty, but you have an eye for it. Oh! What did I say. An eye? I beg your pardon."

The Copper wasn't in the mood for Simevolant's jokes. "I'm on my way to the Tyr. He summoned me."

"Oh, he's arguing with SiDrakkon; you've time to spare. Speaking of which, look at the purples; doesn't it rather remind you of SiDrakkon when he's angry?"

"A striking color," the Copper said.

"I've been staring at these flowers all morning. You know, no two are alike? Why do flowers differentiate? The petals are just going to drop in a little while anyway, and unless you get right up under them, it's hard to tell. I wonder why they bother."

The elf cleared his throat.

"Don't make noise, you," Simevolant said. "You're wilting my flowers. Look, that one's gone all sad. I'll have your hair plucked out by its roots for that." The golden drake stood up.

"I can't keep our Tyr waiting," the Copper said, putting himself between the drake and the elf. "I must be off, cousin."

The elf led him past the Tyr's outer chamber, where messengers, many either bearing gifts themselves or with thralls to carry the load, waited. Curtains blocked the far end, and the elf slipped through them.

A few moments later the Copper heard a heavy tread, and before the curtains could even be opened SiDrakkon stormed out, glaring. The Copper shrank against some baskets of metal rings to clear his way, but SiDrakkon was staring at something only he could see.

The elf gestured for the Copper to come in.

He passed through a door of stone and steel that turned on a central pivot, and two blighters rushed in with braziers burning incense to clean away the angry smell within.

The Tyr's audience chamber was roughly oval, with the door at one end and a shelf at the other. A cascade of gold coins and two waterfalls of silver made it look as though the Tyr reclined upon a mountain of gold. The walls were stacked with glittering, polished samples from the Imperial horde, the metallic art of a thousand or more years, coin, cup, statue, and frieze. Curtains hung thickly about the back of his shelf, and pleasing aromatic fragrances emanated from behind them.

Polished wooden shafts like ribs ran up either side of the chamber, joining at a peak in the top. Captured banners, some tattered and stained, hung here. Above the banners were four members of the *griffaran*, with polished metal talon extenders on their formidable feet. They sat on perches in the shadows above, vigilant as hawks. They looked strong enough to tear him into quarters of twitching dragon meat.

One of the *griffaran* let out a friendly click from the side of its mouth, and its fellows looked down at him.

"Ah, Rugaard, don't let the bodyguards worry you. Come forward, and we'll talk."

The Copper smelled NoSohoth somewhere, perhaps behind the heavy curtains surrounding the Tyr's shelf.

"What service can I do you, your honor?"

"I should be asking you that, drake. Take a mouthful of gold. No, don't pretend; just enjoy. I've more than I could ever eat if I live to be another thousand."

The Copper swallowed a mouthful of coin. The heavy yet soft metallic taste made him feel pleasantly fierce, ready to take on anything the Tyr asked of him.

Which, he supposed, was the point.

"I wanted a quick chat with you without a dozen ears listening to every word."

"Yes, Tyr?"

"According to Nivom, you're one of the better drakes in the Drakwatch, yet you always get overlooked because of your . . . well, let's be frank about it, your injuries."

The Tyr stood on his shelf and turned, as though finding a more comfortable spot from which to speak. The Copper marked heavy scarring, as from a burn, on the inside of one *saa*. He'd never seen the injury before, but then, the Tyr always rested so it was hidden against his underside.

"It is a wickedness that dragons count so much on appearances. That's the way of the world, and there are some things that just can't be changed. But you've got nice teeth and some impressive horns coming in. Hopefully they'll draw attention from the rest as you grow into your wings.

"I'll tell you this, Rugaard: It's something that impressed me about you from the very first. You get around very well, considering that *sii*. There are dragons who'd play it up to inspire pity, and tell their tale of woe at every pause in the conversation. But now my hunt's lost the game trail. Oh, yes. Obviously, you've done well as a courier, my eyes and ears and all that, and you've shown good judgment, which is worth a whole set of limbs."

"Thank you, Tyr."

"Do you know anything about our Uphold in Anaea?"

"We . . . the kern comes from there, does it not?"

"Do you like kern?"

"Not much. It fills one up, I suppose."

"That's how I feel as well. There are two varieties, yellow and orange, as you've probably seen when it's mashed. The orange variety is rarer. But there's something in kern—it keeps dragons who live long underground healthy. Without kern, scale doesn't grow right, the teeth loosen, eyesight fades. Why, I've even seen an old darkwhittled dragon or two missing claws and teeth. These days it's often overlooked, because we either eat it directly as mash or get it through livestock, but in my own grandsire's generation darkwhittle was a very plague."

"I'll be sure to pay more attention to my ration," the Copper said.

"And it's quite cleansing. I think half SiDrakkon's problem is that he doesn't eat his unless it's in a chicken's stomach, and he's always blocked up. So the pressure builds and he explodes out the other end."

"I know it's a long road to Anaea. Will I have a guide?"

"Yes, the Drakwatch is in charge of patrolling the road, and there are Firemaidens at a couple of key points as well. We'll get you a guide."

"What am I to do there? I hope the supply isn't threatened."

"Oh, no, no, nothing like that. It's just that old FeLissarath and his mate deserve more help than they get, and I'd like to relieve some of their burdens. They've done their bit. Responsibility wears after a while. And they are cut off from society at the end of that long, dark road. They deserve to start taking an honored place in society here if they wish."

The Copper bowed. "I'll do my best, Tyr. Nothing shall threaten the supply of kern."

"Then my mind shall be at ease. Let me tell you one more thing, Rugaard. I just said this to Nivom, by the way, so I apologize if it sounds practiced. The great dragons . . . well, they're fine warriors and all that, but it's the dragon that can handle the problems of peace that keeps an empire going. The greatest warrior fights least and all that. Do you understand?"

"I'm not sure that I do."

"You will. In time. Now, no hurry about your departure. You have a good rest. Another mouthful of silver and gold before you leave this room, as well. Can't be too careful where your scale is concerned. If you have any needs for thralls or anything, just see NoSohoth; he'll attend to it."

"Thank you, Tyr."

"Oh, one other question. About the fighting in Bant. How much did you see of it?"

"I was there for the attack on the tower under construction.

I missed much of the first attack on the city on the Black River, but I was there for the rest of it."

"You know, it's odd. SiDrakkon was in the thick of battle, from his reports—battle that cost the lives of four dragons. Yet there's not a scar on him. Three engagements with heavy fighting would leave most dragons' wings in tatters, yet he's hardly holed. Did he lead his dragons against the Ghi men the whole time?"

The Copper wondered just how he could shade the truth. "He struck fast and hard. His attack on the first tower was brilliant. I saw him personally burn war machines on the first attempt to take the fortress. Even though we were thrown back, the campaign ended successfully. He deserves his share of the glory."

"I don't like dragons taking credit for the courage of others, you know. Don't like it at all. Anything to add? Just between the two of us. If you're worried about my mate, I don't tell her everything, you know." He winked.

"No, Tyr, nothing to add."

"I won't press you. Visit anytime, officially or unofficially. I enjoy the presence of virtuous young drakes. We need more of your sort."

The Copper left and saw NoSohoth in the outer room, organizing the visitors to the Tyr.

As he descended into the rock, he became lost in his thoughts. He should pay a visit to the Anklenes and learn about the conditions on the road to Anaea. Find out what he could about the kern trade. He had a vague idea that it came in on pack animals. It wouldn't hurt to ask a little of the history of Anaea as well—he wondered how somewhere so far away even became an Uphold.

Fourfang was waiting at the outer entrance to his cave. The blighter almost danced with anxiety.

"Bad! Bad news! Drakwatch came, took Rhea! Took Rhea to SiDrakkon, your honor. I think he eat her!"

227

Chapter 19

The Copper had been to the outer chambers of SiDrakkon's cave only a few times to deliver routine messages concerning the younger Drakwatch trainees. He occupied one of the highest levels, practically a whole sublevel of his own, on the well-watered eastern spur of the Imperial Resort.

SiDrakkon's doorwarden thrall, a rather fleshy human with a shaved skull, begged him to wait and disappeared inside.

SiDrakkon's mate, an almost gruesomely thin dame with tired golden eyes, greeted him. "I cry welcome. You'll find my mate in his wet grotto. He's in one of his moods." The Copper had no idea what her name was, so he simply bowed.

"I'd be grateful to be shown where that is, honored dame."

"Just follow the sound of water."

He could hear splashing, and the babble of human voices, and a plucking sound of some musical contraption or other that grew more distinct as he passed a burning brazier or two throwing off expensive smelling scents. SiDrakkon's mate dropped some fragrant leaves on the flames and took a deep lungful.

A curtain blocked further progress.

"Your honor," he called. "It's Rugaard. Your mate admitted me. I wish to speak to you."

"Go away, drake."

The Copper sniffed at the moist air around the curtain.

He smelled humans, along with wine and the vaguely sickly smell of fruit.

"I want my thrall back. The girl, Rhea."

"I sent you a replacement. Didn't she arrive?"

"I don't care if you sent a calf of solid gold. I want my thrall back."

"Well, come in, then. Let's talk. You should appreciate the air in here."

The Copper pushed through the double layer of tanned hides on the door. The air was moist, warm and a little steamy. A pool of water filled almost half the chamber, and in an alcove on a woven matt SiDrakkon reclined, reading something written on metal plates laid out under his nose.

The place was crawling with human females sweating in the heat. Some polished his scale, one stood with a barrow containing more metal plates, one played an instrument with strings that made those annoying twanging sounds, and several more just lounged around, drinking or eating or bathing. Only a few bothered to wear even the lightest kind of wrap.

"Take a breath of nepenthe, Rugaard, and relax. Here you can let the cares and responsibilities fall away."

The thick human musk made the Copper hungry, if anything. He looked around for Rhea and didn't— Wait, was that her, huddled with an elder of her sex in a corner? So hard to tell without the coloration. She looked shocking with all her hair shorn off.

He noticed that none of the females had very long hair.

"Why did you shear her?"

"All my cushions are stuffed with human hair. Adds a pleasant air to the room, and they still bring a good price once they lose the smell. What do you need that one for? She's just a thrall, or does she do something special for you? She's only just ripening now. The next few years are going to be exquisite. I won't eat her for years, I promise."

229

He sniffed at one of the wine-sipping females. She giggled something to a companion. The Copper guessed none of them spoke much Drakine.

Rhea looked at him, a silent plea in her eyes. A muscular blighter came in bearing a stone the size of a dragon egg in iron tongs, and dropped it into a smaller pool connected to the main one. It hissed and steamed as it struck.

"I'm fond of her, and she's quiet. I'd like her back. I don't care about the hair. In fact, every time she gets a new coat, I'll have it shorn and sent to you."

"You've made enough trouble for me, showing me up on the Black River. You're lucky I've calmed down or I'd be challenging you."

"My memory of events on the Black River isn't clear at all. You'd better hope it doesn't come back, or I'll remember how you hung back while you sent dragons to their deaths."

He rolled and straightened. "You whelp. Nivom's bitten out one heart, and you're after another. Do that and I'll challenge you to a duel of honor."

"Challenge away. It won't keep me from telling the Tyr all I know. Kill me and I'll swear to its truth as I'm dying."

Griff flickered on each of them.

"I can't stay angry in my grotto. Take your silly little girl and snuffle away."

The Copper switched to the rather slower form of Drakine used for the thralls: "Rhea, come away from there, if you like. Back to my cave." The girl threw a wrap around herself and hurried to his side.

"I can get a dozen just like her in here tomorrow, you know," SiDrakkon said.

The last sounded like more of a promise to himself than a parting blast at the Copper.

"Thank you, your honor," the Copper said. He held the curtain open for Rhea and together they escaped the steaming grotto.

Sure enough, a "replacement" for Rhea arrived the next day, a craggy-faced female with a basket of her own scale-shaping tools. The Copper had no use for her, so he gave her as a parting gift to NeStirrath, who was kindly to his thralls. NeStirrath didn't bother much about his appearance, and sometimes looked quite deranged about the ears and *griff*.

He also received a small flower from Tighlia's own garden, with a message wishing him fortune in his assignment.

As this was no simple journey to the surface and back, the Copper had to decide what to do with the bats. He released them to go where they would, though any who wanted to come with him were welcome, but he warned them that they'd have to make themselves useful.

Thernadad was too old to fend for himself, too blind to find himself food, and too bloated to be of much use to anyone, so the Copper allowed him to drink himself into insensibility on drake-blood, then had Fourfang break his neck with a quick twist as he slept.

"What do with body?" Fourfang asked.

"I don't care. Burn him and use his ashes for cleansing paste. Or make a stew out of him; he's fatty enough."

And so passed the strange, greedy bat who almost accidentally saved the Copper's life.

Over the next few sleeps Rhea made frightened, whimpering noises. Not knowing what else to do, the Copper woke her each time, and she'd sleep soundly afterward.

As the day for departure grew closer, Nivom visited him twice. Nivom now spent much of his day accompanying the Tyr in his duties, both in the audience chamber and in brief visits to the other hills. At the end of the day they would sometimes eat, or be groomed together by thralls, and his adoptive father, as Nivom called him, would talk the day's decisions over with him and explain why he overruled a dragon's punishment of a thrall, or granted a petition, or refused a gift.

"The Lavadome obeys him because he's loved. I wonder what would happen if a dragon who wasn't so universally admired took his place atop the Rock."

"Fighting, I expect," the Copper said.

"It's . . . it's like a giant game of mirroring to them, with the object being 'please the Tyr' so they get what they want. These court dragons in the line, and the leaders of the six hills, they're just carrion birds and jackals waiting for his death. All playing different games where no one's quite sure of the rules, so everyone cheats as best as he can."

"I'm glad of my place at the tail end of the Imperial line. You've got the end with the teeth."

"If the head gets chopped off, the tail dies too."

"Oh, now you're being as gloomy as SiDrakkon. Why so downcast? I heard you were cheered as you crossed Wyrram Ridge the other day."

"And had waste kicked up as I passed between the greater and lesser Skotl hills, let's not forget."

"Oh, probably just drakes. Forget it. It would take a mighty turd to slay a dragon."

"I'd almost rather be back in a war in Bant," Nivom said. "Well, I must be off. A good journey and success in Anaea. Honor and glory, Rugaard."

"Honor and glory, Nivom."

On the day he told NoSohoth he would depart, he met his guide: the Firemaiden Nilrasha. She awaited him at the western exit ramp from Black Rock. He had two long, narrow cave carts, each pulled by a plodding ox waiting for him, one filled with food and supplies for him and his thralls, and the other with grain for the oxen. The Copper bore nothing but his small hoard loaded into a hollowed log, all traded into gold so it would carry more easily, and an introductory message from Tyr to FeLissarath.

"This is a happy chance," the Copper said.

"No chance to it at all. I bribed NoSohoth with every silver piece in the Tyr's victory bequest."

The Copper wondered at that. Why would she throw away the beginnings of a hoard? From what he had learned, Anaea was a quiet Uphold with little fighting chance at combat honors. "You know the Anaean Trail?"

"I served my time at its mouth."

"Good enough for me. Let's be off. I want to be at the river by dark."

Several good trails led westward. The western quarters of the Lavadome were rougher, with growth only in patches of soil trapped between the rocks. Rather scraggly-looking goats roamed here under blighter herdsmen. Fourfang went forward with a switch to clear the way of both the animals and the lesser blighters.

They rested at the riverbank and waited their turn at a flatboat, and the Copper worked up the nerve to ask a question of Nilrasha:

"Why so eager to get to Anaea?"

"I get bored with duty in the dome. All anyone talks about are the banquets atop the Imperial Resort, and it's like having a feast described when you're starving. That or who's on top of which hill, six little Tyrs under one big one. They say the trail to Anaea is the most magnificent of all the lower roads."

"They say? I thought you knew the route."

"Oh, of course. There's the Long Fall, then the Lake of Echoes, and then Tooth Cavern—"

"All of which are listed on several maps. I've looked at them too."

"Don't send me away! I have been on the trail. I was second in the endurance march in the tests to pass into the Firemaidens." She swallowed. "I just haven't been the whole length. But it's easier after the Tooth Cavern; there are no major underroads off the trail. I've been that far."

The Copper chuckled. "Oh, I wouldn't send you away, not for half of the Tyr's gold." In fairness, though, no one was making the offer.

"Why's that?" she asked, glancing at him from lowered eyes.

"You're lucky. NeStirrath always said he'd choose the lucky drake over the toughest or the most skilled. I imagine the rule applies to drakka as well."

"I've never thought myself lucky."

"It's in that name the blighters gave you, Ora."

"Some would use the word *cowardly*. I lived because I hid."

"Besides, you saved my life. I'm not forgetful when it comes to things like that."

Their journey to Anaea was lengthy but fascinating. They passed through several different strata on the Long Fall, and the Copper saw geologic formations he'd never viewed before: rocks like eggs with crystals inside, gardens of colored stone that some indigent blighters kept polished and shaped and exhibited to travelers for gifts of food or coin, even veins of iron and copper they could lick to get the pleasant taste of heavy metals and cleanse their mouths.

In the tunnels after the Long Fall they caught up to a mule train bearing bags of shed dragonscale to Anaea for trade. Shaggy humans handled the mules under the supervision of a thick-hided deman and a drake apprenticed to one of the Lavadome's trading houses, very simplified versions of the roving markets the dwarves had perfected. The drake's conversation was boring, and he continually pointed out that the Copper was giving his draft animals and thralls too much to eat to ever make a profitable run.

By the end of the trip the Copper was loosing his bats to feed on the unpleasant drake every other night. Fatigue shut him up about the weight of grain given to his oxen when they were unhitched.

The Lake of Echoes required that they take a flatboat. They poled on its broad back across the water. The vast cavern was low and dripping, divided in places into chambers by walls of old rock that hinted at masonry, some underground settlement drowned long ago by a shift in water drainage. The ceiling of the cavern was covered with slimy creatures that lived in shells, like snails with many tiny legs. Translucent insects gathered around the flatboat's sole lamp, which they took turns spitting fire into to keep it lit, at the request of the dwarven ferrymen. They were an odd bunch, outcasts from better dwarf societies, the Copper suspected, and sharp dealers who would take only gold. The dwarves tried to sell them grain and dried fish, and Nilrasha advised him to purchase the first but avoid the second. But they took them across and on the other side picked up a two-score mule train bearing bags of kern.

The bats feasted on the insects, and the dwarves muttered among themselves. One held out his hands as though estimating the wingspan of the bats, and another pulled at a scraggly, unlit beard.

They came to the Tooth Cavern, and even Rhea stopped and stared with mouth open. Far in the distance to the north it was open to the sun, but here it was just a wide chasm with hanging or rising formations carved by wind whipping through the cavern. The road here leaped from massive stalactite to massive stalagmite, most slightly bent and sharpened like dragon teeth.

A garrison of Firemaidens greeted them here, including two *sii*-sore young almost-hatchlings at the end of an endurance march, and the Copper saw a nest of *griffaran* on a high ledge.

The bridges were strange patchwork contraptions of metal, wood, stone, wire, even thick rope, an odd quilt that showed evidence of all manner of different builders' hands. There were even carved poles of wood that he suspected had been decorated by elves, for they bore faces. Skulls dangled from the bottom of the spans and overhangs, trophies of fights on, below, or around the bridge.

"During the last siege on the Lavadome, the demen threw a whole army into this cavern," Nilrasha said.

"But that was ages ago, Nilrasha," the Firemaidens of the garrison said. "All we have to worry about these days are bandits."

"Which does not mean it can't happen again," Nilrasha said.

"You've been visiting those sour-bellied historians. Spirits! When I get back to the Lavadome, I'm joining swimming parties on Sunshaft Beach, not listening to Anklenes recite their epics."

They picked up an escort of Drakwatch at the other side of the canyon. The tunnel here was wider, with small cracks and passages that hostile hominids sometimes used, but according to the drakes they fought one another rather than risking the ire of the Lavadome. But desperate demen might be tempted by an unguarded party.

Nilrasha made interesting conversation, but she never chattered for the satisfaction or the noise of it, a failing of some drakka the Copper had observed.

She often steered the conversation to him, which he found a

little unsettling. He wasn't used to drakka asking him anything beyond, "Rugaard, please don't drool on the platters," at banquet. She was even interested in his bats, how he became affiliated with them, and he told her an abridged version of his time in Thernadad's cave.

"I'm not used to talking about my life," he confessed.

"Why not? You're in the Imperial line. You're well thought-of. I've heard the story of you and the *griffaran* eggs, and that alliance is important to us, for they guard the plateau above and the river below and the Tooth Cavern. Being of the line, you'll never want for food or pleasant accommodations."

"I'm a . . . fortunate dragon, in that respect. Why is my situation of interest to you?"

She looked at him a moment before speaking. "I've no intention of ending my years as a Firemaid. You may want a mate someday. A dragon in the Imperial line needs someone clever at his side."

Her honesty was as startling as one of her sudden leaps from the grass.

"I haven't thought of mating."

"Few drakes do, and then they lose their heads to the first flash of green that crosses their path after they crack their wings."

"About that. I . . . I was injured as a hatchling. I may never be able to fly."

He showed her the scar, a little more visible now that his growing wings were rising beneath his skin.

"So you're a little bitten and bled. I get sick of drakes so full of themselves they do nothing but swell and preen."

"Then never having a mating flight doesn't bother you?"

"Well—oh, Spirits take it. I figured out life isn't a song years ago, Rugaard. No, it wouldn't matter. We wouldn't be the first dragons forced to mate under stone rather than above the clouds. But what do you think of me?"

"You're just the sort of drakka I think any drake would want."

"Any drake?"

"Yes. Especially a rather beat-up one."

She touched her neck to his. He felt an electric thrill run up his spine, and something stirred under his skin along his back. "Then I really am a lucky drakka, Rugaard."

The trading drake interrupted the conversation with an opinion, detailed and long-winded, about the advantage of selling him the oxen at the end of the trip, and the Copper tapped the side of the wicker chest housing the bats with a *sii*-claw where the drake couldn't see.

Nilrasha fluttered an eyelid at him flirtatiously.

Chapter 20

The Copper spent his last years of drakehood in diligent service to FeLissarath and his mate. They were both courtly, well-mannered dragons when humans were about, and quite informal when they weren't. The pair had been unable to have a clutch of their own, so they looked on the kern kings of the high Anaean plateau almost as their own progeny.

He learned much of what he needed to know about the humans there his first summer. Their lives were organized around agriculture, growing kern in their high, sunny plateau. Something about the soil and the dry summers, bright sun punctuated by heavy rain at either end of the season, lent itself to their strange-sheathed crop. There were planting festivals and rain ceremonies and harvest celebrations and winter pod picking for their other staple, a rather reddish, bulbous berry that made decent enough wine but tasted eye-crossingly sweet, at least to a dragon.

The kern kings traded dragonscale for kern. The dragonscale they used at human or dwarvish trading houses to buy finery for themselves, or gold. These humans had a lust for gold that matched that of dragons. They wore it, wove it into their hair, girdled themselves in it, decorated their bedchambers with it, ate off it, and even, the Copper suspected, voided their bowels into it if they could afford the pots.

E. E. KNIGHT

The mated dragons, when they weren't talking commerce, talked only of hunting. They were friends with the great condors of the mountains, who kept them abreast of conditions of the herds, and they hunted deer, mountain goats, sheep with vast, twisted horns, elk, even woodland sloths and the taut-bodied big cats that preyed on all the above.

Whenever their presence wasn't required at some kern-king ceremony, they were off after game.

The kern kings had no enemies that could get at them on their mountain-girded plateau, though sometimes their young warriors descended the slopes to raid the fringes of what the Copper learned were the old southern borderlands of the Hypatian Empire, dragging off females and stealing horses, more for sport than bloodlust.

A single, lonely Firemaid guarded the dragon lair and the entrance to the lower world. Her name was Angalia, and she took Nilrasha to be her own long-awaited replacement. She sniffed Nilrasha's back every morning for signs of wing growth.

"The air's too thin up here. I'm not a high-altitude dragon; never was," Angalia complained whenever the Copper visited. Constantly. "My hearts beat so. I'll burst my hearts and be dead within a year. Mark my words!"

But Nilrasha had it worse. She had to live at the entrance to the Lower World with Angalia, risking burst ears at the endless complaints.

He had a nice chamber in the Upholder palace temple, filled with square carvings of grimacing faces of the kern kings. The men had built a sort of temple to their dragon gods on a spur of one of the mountains surrounding their plateau, over the mouth of the gate to the Lower World. Like all the other constructs on the mountain-girded land, it was done in what the FeLissaraths styled the "Anaean Royal." Meaning great, heavy square blocks of limestone, elaborately carved, piled on other great,

240

heavy square blocks. They also liked stone globes, smooth and undecorated as turtle eggs. Sometimes the builders placed them on the great, heavy square blocks. But for some reason, perhaps religious prohibition, they never put great, heavy square blocks atop the globes, unless the globes were holding up a roof. Then it was allowed.

"Hominid frippery," the Copper said to himself, extracting a crunchy beetle from a crevice with his tongue.

So much for the dwelling place of the Anaean royal families' god allies. Almost every morning the Copper arose to cool, fresh air and bright yellow light. When there was no water in the raincatchers he had a short walk to a melting glacier and tasted runoff from ice older than any dragon and most legends he knew.

In his opinion, his rooms here were as fine as the Tyr's in the Lavadome, and a good deal sunnier.

A long, straight flight of many scores of scores of scores of stairs led down the mountainside to the dragon-keepers, special priests of the kern kings who offered up pigs and cattle whenever FeLissarath and his mate didn't have fresh game—a rarity. It was hard to stand at the top of that stone ramp and not feel part of a higher world. He wondered how FeLissarath and his mate seemed such normal, earthy dragons. It would be easy to get delusions of godhood with such a vista.

The Copper made such improvements as he could to the long road back to the Lavadome. After studying how the kern kings sent messages by relay runners carrying hollow, gold-dipped bones with scrolls carried inside, he copied the practice.

He colonized a few caves with bats, and taught the Drakwatch and Firemaids to use them as messengers in return for either draft-animal blood or a taste of dragon vintage. Some of them found the practice creepy, but others enjoyed the tickle of a bat tongue and the euphoric light-headedness and the strangely pleasant dreams that followed. In any case, they reserved drag-onblood for the most intelligent of the messenger bats who could be relied upon to carry either a verbal message or a written one to the right post.

At this remote Uphold, they got their news rarely and in large, sometimes confused batches. SiDrakkon's thin little mate died of a stomach disorder. The incense trade so vital to peace between male dragons continued to leap in price with barbarian attacks on the trade routes in the east, and Nivom had opened his wings and begun instituting contests between the Drakwatch and the Firemaidens, in which they fought mock battles for hills and caves.

So the years passed and the Copper's horns came in and the bulges on his back rose. He looked forward to his wings emerging, just because there was so little going on in the plateau, with its unvarying seasonal routines and cool, sunny weather. Nilra-sha, perhaps a year behind in her own wing growth, would rub fats into the stretched skin to soothe it. They became translucent, and FeLissarath judged them ready to pop.

"You should return to the Lavadome, Rugaard, so that there can be a proper celebration. You're in the Imperial line, you know," FeLissarath said one sunset as the plateau turned to gold and orange.

"Yes, take this winter off and return. Take poor Nilrasha with you," FeLissarath's mate added, looking at Nilrasha, who sometimes went stalking on the mountain slopes with the older dragon-dame, and therefore was frequently invited to dinner. "She's a lively young thing. A great huntress, too. It's a depriva-tion to be up here, away from society."

"I do have friends I'd like to see. But will you be all right on your own?"

"You've learned little these four years to ask a question like that. Nothing ever happens in Anaea."

"All the same, I'd like to stay here. I'm not much of a drake for parties."

Oddly enough, something did happen in Anaea that very night.

It began with being woken by Nilrasha. "Rugaard, there's a wounded dragon come up from the Lower Road. He asks to speak to you in private. He's just ouside."

Rather than being frightened, the Copper was almost delighted to hear it, after the first startle of being prodded from a deep sleep, of course. "Send him in."

A silver-white dragon, his *sii* and *saa* wrapped in rags to enable him to move more quietly on the stones of the palace, mud smeared all over his wings, and his face wrapped in bloody bandaging, stepped in.

He glared at Nilrasha.

"A moment, please, Ora," the Copper said. The visitor's wild eye looked panicked.

NiVom tore off the false bandage covering his torn lip as soon as she left. "The blood is from a donkey," NiVom said.

"NiVom! What in the two worlds—" The Copper at least had wits to pronounce his adult name correctly.

"I'm a fugitive, Rugaard. Hunted. Branded a coward."

The Copper would have sputtered questions until the bats returned, but instead he listened.

"It's all Tighlia's doing, you know. She's room for only one dragon in her heart, her brother. She aims to make him Tyr, and she's destroying any dragon that stands in her way. First AgGriffopse. Then DharSii. Now me."

"Have some wine. Some food." The Copper looked in on Rhea, who had a comfortable anteroom. "Rhea, get the leftovers from last night's dinner. Hurry, but do it quietly." He worked a small cask and poured some wine into a bowl, and NiVom took a deep draft.

"Spirits, that's good," NiVom said. "Oh, Rugaard, I've been such a fool. I was set to be mated to Imfamnia, and now I suspect she's lost to me. I've been blinder than any of your bats in the sun. Imfamnia, gone. As though she'd care; she'll fly with SiDrakkon if its his destiny to be Tyr."

"How did this come about?"

"Let me see. Five, no, seven days ago—can it be only a week?—seven days ago Imfamnia threw herself down before the Tyr and Tighlia, covered with bites and scratches, claiming I'd done it to her during an argument. She's never had so much as a cross word from me! I was brought before the Tyr, and I challenged her word, and Tighlia worked herself up into a fury and named SiDrakkon's son SiBayereth Imfamnia's champion."

"I remember SiBayereth. He seemed a decent sort."

"He's obsessed with dueling ever since his wings came in. He lives for the pit. He's my size and half again my weight, and has a very long neck and tail. I'd never live close."

"So you fled?"

"No, like a fool I took the challenge. My blood was up, you see? The accusations—I couldn't think. Then Tighlia—"

Rhea arrived bearing a platter of meats and kern. NiVom stuffed food into his mouth like a dragon starved.

"Please say there's more, Rugaard," he said.

"Rhea, get Fourfang up and have him help you in the larder. A whole side of beef—raw is fine; it's hung." The girl fled.

"Thank you, Rugaard."

"You were saying something about Tighlia. . . ."

"She accused me of always being a blighted egg. Said I lied about her brother. So . . . oh, what did I do? I challenged her, and anyone else who said I didn't give a correct account of matters at the Black River. So she appointed that old duelist ventlick of SiDrakkon's to defend her word, NoTannadon.

"Oh, I said some very fine words to that. Quite a speech, all about my innocence seeing me to victory. The Spirits themselves would fight on my side—*ha!*" He spit out a chuck-bone. "But that night all I could think about was my poor, lame father—he had a limp a little like yours; did I ever tell you that?—in the dueling pit. How I jumped down atop his body."

NiVom looked away. "I was terrified. I flew, flew across the Lavadome like baying dragonhounds were after me. Rugaard, I'm a coward."

The Copper looked at the blazing, mud-smeared victory insignia painted on his former cavemate's wing-leather. "You're nothing of the kind. Nivo—NiVom, I'm honored that you came to me this night."

The onetime future Tyr gulped. "Honored?"

"That you trusted me. And you can trust me. What can I do to assist you?"

"You've done enough. Keep quiet; there will be hunters after me, I expect."

"News of this is bound to reach the ears of the Upholder and his mate. You must leave before they rise."

"Of course."

"I'll put off the pursuit and confuse the word, if I can. You can't hide in the plateau; the kern kings will wonder at it and report to the Upholder. The condors see much of what happens on the outer slopes. The mountains trail off farther south; you could try there. When Nilrasha gets her wings I'll send her looking."

"What about your own— Oh, of course. Well, so be it. Don't worry, Rugaard; I'll speak to none but you or Nilrasha."

"I think the Tyr means for me to take over this Uphold when I mature. When I do, and they've left, I'll have the roof marbled white. Look for it. That means it's safe to visit."

"Roof marbled white. Very well."

"It shouldn't be long. My wings are almost in. Failing that, visit late at night. The balcony is big enough for you to slip through."

Rhea and Fourfang arrived with the side of beef, bearing it on a pole between them. NiVom tore great gaps in it, belched, and then crept out onto the balcony and spread his wings. He fell into open air and soared off.

Thanks to the clear moonlight the Copper could watch him for a long time as he flew south. He called Nilrasha to him and told her a somewhat expurgated version of events.

"So what now?" she asked.

He almost swore at her in his frustration and grief at NiVom's news. "We're taking that trip back to the Lavadome. I'm going to do what I can to confuse the pursuit. Then I need to see the Tyr."

"Darling, your wings are weeping. I think they'll be in any day now. Must be all the excitement."

He went over to one of the square stone blocks bordering the balcony and tore his back across it. Nilrasha gasped. The pain, and with it hot, sweet-stinking relief, helped his ugly fighting mood. He raised his left wing. Beautiful blue-veined membranes blotted out the moon and the receding dot of NiVom.

He turned. Now for the real test. He opened the right, and pushed out the wing.

He was thankful the pain blotted out some of the disappointment when it wouldn't extend. The main joint at his forespur kept slipping each time he tried to unfold it.

Nilrasha stifled a sob. "I'm sorry, Ru. But it doesn't matter. Your wings are uncased." She began to lick his wounds.

By hooking the wing tip in a crack on the balcony and pulling his bad wing open he was able to let the membrane dry.

"You're a dragon now, my love," she said.

"Good. Because I've got a dragon's work to do."

BOOK THREE

Dragon

"Your true strength is not discovered easily,
or without grief. Like a desert seed it lies dormant,
waiting for the hard rain."

—*Lessons of NeStirrath*

Chapter 21

The Copper paid his respects to the FeLissaraths at the morning meal the next day, showing his wings.

"I've thought about it, and I would like to go back to the Lavadome. Just for a season or so. Nilrasha said she'd welcome the change of scene."

"You deserve to have a party where your dragon-name is cheered, RuGaard," FeLissarath said. His mate nodded. "Too bad about the wing. But there's many a grounded dragon living a long and happy life. That fellow who trains the Drakwatch, for example . . . er . . ."

"NeStirrath," the Copper supplied.

"I had the oddest dream last night," his mate said. "I could have sworn I smelled a strange dragon in the palace. It was almost alarming."

"You talk to the condors too much," her mate said. "They think every far-glimpsed *griffaran* is a dragon."

"I hear there was a herd of elk spotted on a frozen lake on the northern slopes," the Copper said, turning the talk to hunting.

"Yes, we should go," FeLissarath said. "Shouldn't we, dear? The larder's looking rather empty."

"Fattening up for my trip," the Copper said.

"You're a wise young dragon, RuGaard," FeLissarath said.

Though he was almost dancing with anxiety to leave, the Copper delayed another day or two, for a train of kern was assembling, the last of the fall harvest. It would be irresponsible of a future Upholder not to see it through.

Fourfang groaned about having to take care of mules, and Rhea looked glum. She liked the sun and air of FeLissarath's palace, though she still never said a word about any matter, great or small; she just nodded and followed orders and sometimes cried in her sleep.

Putting up a second set of bed curtains cut down on the noise.

On their first day into the cave they came across the pursuit, the noisome NoTannadon and another Skotl dragon searching westward, sniffing at every strange tunnel. Their reek set the mules to bawling, and the blighter mule tenders cursed and shoved them aside, clearing a way in the tunnel.

And the Copper moved up to block it.

"Cry meetings," NoTannadon said.

"Cry meetings, NoTannadon. Haven't seen you since the Black River fight."

"You're . . . you're RuGaard, now, as it looks," NoTannadon said. "Have you seen anything of NiVom? He's visiting the western Upholds and the Tyr has need of him."

"I'd be glad of the visit. But no dragons have passed through the cave mouth, have they, Nilrasha?"

"A dragon? No. We'd have welcomed a new face. Ha! No dragons, I'm afraid."

"I told you the trail went cold at the Tooth Cavern," the other Skotl dragon said. "He flew out there. We should turn around, catch up with the others."

"This drake—er, dragon . . ." NoTannadon said, then fell silent.

"Yes. Both my ears work, duelist. What were you going to say?"

"... Is in the Imperial line. I expect he'd notice if a dragon emerged in the middle of his palace. We should turn around."

"I'll send word back that the Upholder should tell him the Tyr needs him, should he show up for a surprise visit, shall I?" the Copper asked.

"Yes. Yes. That's a fair wind of an idea," NoTannadon said.

The dragons turned around in the rather cramped tunnel and hurried in the other direction.

Their arrival at the Lavadome merited no special reception, as it was simply another load of kern coming in. The trading house saw to its distribution to various wareholes and livestock corrals.

"Where will you go?" the Copper asked Nilrasha.

"Wherever you like, my lord."

"We're not mated yet, dear. Things may go ill for me on the Rock. Perhaps you should go to the Firemaiden quarters on your home hill. Your association with me could be hazardous."

"It's my blood. It flows for you. If you die, it might as well be spilled too."

"Where can I find you?"

"I grew up on Dufu hill. Yes, the milkdrinker's hill, among the thralls. Not much of a home, but the tunnels are clean enough. At least there's little chance of society from the Black Rock visiting."

"I'll come to you in a day or two. Take care of my thralls until then. If anything happens, treat them well; they've earned it. And as for you—if they come for you, just do what they say and feign ignorance."

"The way you feign your lack of ambition. Certainly."

"You may have to do more. Tell them you grew sick to death of the sight of me in Anaea. They'll believe that."

"I shall. But I won't enjoy it."

He wound his neck around hers, squeezed her, then broke it off and looked across and down the river.

"I did enjoy that, however," she said. "I'm told the Anklenes have some scrolls about how dragons can mate in a river, and it's like flying. It seems delightfully perverse."

"We'll have to find out."

They said no more. The Copper told the kern train that he was exhausted and would spend the night on the riverbank, washing and resting and preparing for his return to the Imperial Resort with a bellyful of fish.

And with that he hurried off toward the high rocks of the *griffaran*.

Yarrick's perch looked much the same, though the *griffaran* who flew him up to the high perch grew so exhausted he had to set the Copper down on a ledge and bring the aging grand commander to him.

"You right! *Yark!* It is that lame copper fellow."

The bird-reptile cocked its head so Yarrick's good eye was pointed straight at him. "It good to see you again. We heard about a battle in Bant, let loose victory cries on your behalf."

The Copper wondered what would happen if Yarrick knew the truth of his "rescue" of the eggs. He felt a twinge as he cleared his throat and spoke the words he'd rehearsed in his mind.

"Long ago, Yarrick, you befriended me and flew me to the Imperial Resort. I ask you to fly again, and beg the Tyr to come to me. All this must be done in secrecy."

"Too old for courier flying these days. Molting. Fishing is all I do anymore, and even then I need a long rest before returning to the perch. I'll send a younger set of feathers. The Tyr will come, though he, too, does not care as much for flying as he once did."

———

The Copper waited until the shafts of sunlight falling to the river disappeared. Though he sought it, sleep evaded him. He wondered how he looked after a long tunnel journey. Better than he would have without Rhea's endless cleanings and polishings, he supposed. The girl—no, woman, now—could do wonders with wet ash and a brush.

He saw the Tyr flying, a *griffaran* to either side, turning slow circles in his climb to the perch on the *griffaran*'s rocks. He alighted rather heavily, and the *griffaran* retired.

"It is you, Rugaard. Or, I'm sorry, RuGaard now. Why this strange form of meeting? I know you don't like court ceremony, but this is a little extreme."

"I've seen NiVom, Tyr."

The Tyr's teeth disappeared and his neck straightened. "You have. Come to beg for his pardon, have you?"

"Your honor, it's all lies. He never attacked your granddaughter."

The Tyr sighed. "He's always been a bit of a brawler. You should know. He's welcome to come back and defend or explain himself anytime; he doesn't need to send emissaries."

"NoTannadon and another Skotl were hunting him on the western road. I met them."

"Hunting him? I said there was to be no pursuit! He's disgraced, and a coward to run away from a challenge issued and accepted, but no harm's been done apart from the bites and scratches on Imfamnia. I'd say the only permanent damage to her was to her dignity, but she's a flit young thing and has little enough to hurt." The Tyr rested in thought. "NoTannadon and another, you say?"

"I met them myself, Tyr. I doubt they were seeking him to share some meat and a song."

"He should have stayed and defended himself. The spirits would have seen him safely to his home cave if he's innocent. These things have a way of working out."

"Do they? How did they work out for your son, your clutch-winner? And what of this DharSii? I don't know his story, but NiVom seemed to think he was the victim of treachery. NiVom wouldn't hurt a female—of your line or any other—unless he had been attacked first. He said he had no idea how the marks got on her."

"Imfamnia would never make up such a thing. What has she to gain? She was getting a good mate, in all likelihood the future Tyr, there even if his lip was a bit torn up."

"She would if it meant reigning as queen over the Lavadome."

"She would have had that anyway. They were to be mated!"

"My guess is she doesn't want to wait and leave anything to chance. It's a plot, your honor. It's a game, with the throne as the stakes. Your life may be in danger."

"Yes, danger and I are old friends." The Tyr paused, and his expression went blank. "No! SiDrakkon hardly knows the drag-onelle. I'll swear he's not spoken to her more than three times, all at banquets."

"If you become incapacitated, who rules?" the Copper asked, though he knew the answer.

"With NiVom gone, the title of Tyr passes to my mate's brother, for at the moment I have no heir."

"Would Tighlia be happy to see her brother in your place?"

"Of course. It's only natural. I just have never much liked SiDrakkon. He's too quick to quarrel. You can't hold dragons together if you're going to be the first to start a feud. That and his taste for human females. It's just not done. One can enjoy a discreet sniff now and then, but this habit of his, wallowing in it, it's revolting. I need a new regent. As it is, if I dismiss SiDrak-kon the throne would fall to SiMevolant, now that he's matured. Physically, at least. He's still a tailgazer."

"You must hurry and appoint a new heir, then."

"Perhaps. No. No! They couldn't be so deceptive."

"I think they've wronged you worse than you can imagine, Tyr. Certainly one heir can be lost to accident. Twice might be a coincidence. But three times? That's the work of an enemy."

"I'll question Imfamnia again in the presence of her mother. Ibidio thought highly of NiVom, and a mother can sometimes get the truth out of the toughest dragon."

"Don't tell your mate or SiDrakkon any of this, Tyr, until you've learned the truth."

"You're a sly one, RuGaard."

"You must know I have no ambitions, Tyr. I speak only on behalf of my friend."

"If all this comes to pass you'll move several places up in the line. Perhaps I should be suspicious of you."

"I'm content to go back to Anaea for the rest of my years, Tyr. Get to the truth of this matter with NiVom. You might ask some questions about the others, as well. I don't know enough about those dragons."

"I will ask some questions. Starting with Tighlia."

"Tyr, no. Avoid her. Don't let her influence you."

"You've not been mated yet, have you? When you're older you'll understand these things. I can handle my own mate, dragon. Don't worry; your name will not pass my lips or waft across in thought."

"Go to Ibidio first, Tyr. I beg you."

"I'm not without resources, RuGaard. Where can I contact you?"

"I'll let the *griffaran* know where I am. I won't be far from these rocks."

"RuGaard, thank you for coming to me with this. Bravely done, if it's the truth. If this is all some scheme of your own . . . well, bravely done for that, too. I'll forgive you personally. But as Tyr, matters will go hard with you."

"I ask only that you try to find the truth, your honor."

The Tyr raised his wings, nodded to the *griffaran* escort, and dropped off the towering rock. He caught an air current and disappeared into shadow, entering the tunnel through which the Copper had been carried years ago.

Even the fresh fish the *griffaran* brought him soured in his mouth. He picked at rocks with his claws and wondered about Nilrasha. Finally the Copper could sleep, though it was a fitful one. His mouth had gone dry from the tension.

Yarrick himself woke him the next day with news that the glorious Tyr was dead.

Chapter 22

The Copper stood before the massive Black Rock in the center of the Lavadome; it was dozens of dragonlengths high, heavy and black and forbidding.

He'd always thought it looked everlasting, a guarantee of dragonkind's survival. Now it seemed a marker in a vast, empty, crystal-topped tomb.

He could return to the Uphold and act as though nothing had happened. Perhaps he'd just been escorting the final bounty of the year's harvest to the Lavadome, ensuring its prompt arrival intact.

In the end, he decided he had to play his part in the tragedy, for good or ill. He walked up the path leading to the lower caves, the smaller one the Drakwatch used. There were dragons idling about the more elaborate main entrance, waiting for news, and more clustered at the servants' door, pestering thralls running errands.

The Rock seemed deadly quiet, as though expecting another outburst of battle. The Copper took the most familiar path, to his old residence in the trainee wing, and saw a good deal of water on the floor. They were fixing the water feed on the upper levels again.

The young drakes were sitting around the pooled water, chatting in low voices. "A visitor," one said.

NeStirrath stuck his aging, tangle-horned head out of his cavern. "That's no visitor; that's one of the Drakwatch, but so long away he's become a stranger. How are you, Rug—RuGaard. Wings up and out at last, I see!"

"Out, anyway. I've not managed up yet."

"You have heard the news, I expect."

"Yes. The Tyr is dead. What do you know of it?"

"It happened in his mate's chambers. I had only a quick word with NoSohoth; he could tell me no more. He advised me to get back down here and ready the Drakwatch, saying those were SiDrakkon's orders. So here I sit, awaiting further orders."

"I'm going up."

"Squeeze up the thrall passages, if you can. The great winding one is blocked by those waiting for news and spreading rumor."

The Copper took his advice and made his way up to the Imperial kitchens, at some cost of scrapes to the poor, thin-skinned humans he had to squeeze by. He fought his way out into the gardens, past dragons, drakes, dragonelles, and drakka thronging the garden.

Some of SiDrakkon's Skotl clan kept them back from the doors, exchanging rather profane insults with the catcalling Wyrr.

"We want NiVom back; he was an honest Wyrr!"

"Anklene, more like," a Skotl roared back.

"Make a breach, you; I'm in the Imperial line," the Copper boomed, a little surprised at how loud his voice sounded. "Let me in to see my family."

"Air Spirit, even Batty's turned up," someone said.

"NoSohoth," the Copper roared at the Tyr's door. "I know you're on the other side of that. Let me in."

"He fought with NiVom at the Black River. Let him pass," someone in the throng shouted.

"He's a no-line half-wit."

"Not even hatched in the Lavadome. What business is it of his?"

The portal opened, but the Copper didn't catch what was said. In any case, the fat Skotl toughs made room for him.

"RuGaard, what a pleasant surprise on this tragic day," NoSo-hoth said. Naturally he was the one dragon who pronounced his new appellation effortlessly, as though it had always passed his lips that way. "Follow me."

Nervous thralls gathered in the shadows. Even the tiniest brazier was aflame, sending out soothing fragrances. At the larger versions blighters worked the fire with bellows.

"Where's Tighlia? I wish to speak to her," the Copper said.

"She's obviously in a delicate condition, shattered by the loss of her mate. It happened in her sleeping chamber, you know. Tyr SiDrakkon is holding court in the Tyr's chamber."

"Why don't you just call him Tyr? Did the Tyr name a new heir?"

"Careful, now. There's the traditional one-year period of mourning."

"Of course. I'm no courtier; I apologize."

The Copper heard SiDrakkon's voice as he passed through into the Tyr's audience chamber. It was smaller than he remembered it, perhaps because of the crowd. *Griffaran* crowded the upper areas, two to a perch, looking agitated.

"We'll speak with one voice. United. I'm Tyr and that's all there is to it," SiDrakkon said. "They'll have to accept it. The succession is legal and according to tradition. The worst thing we can do is divide and argue like this. Blood could be spilled at any moment."

Imfamnia lounged at his side, looking as though she were enjoying the view down on the Imperial line.

"I still say NiVom should have a proper trial," Ibidio said.

She stood just below the shelf. "One Anklene, one Skotl, and one Wyrr judging him."

"Mother, not that again," Imfamnia said. "He's violent. War-worn, I expect."

"He ran from a challenge. He's not going to appear for a trial," SiDrakkon said.

"You seem very sure of that," SiMevolant put in airily. He'd dusted his golden scales with ash for the occasion; otherwise he would have outshone the whole room.

"Are you implying anything?"

"Imply? Me? I come right out and say things. I've no ambition to conceal. I was just wondering if you'd had him killed, is all."

SiDrakkon turned a deeper shade of purple. "Of course not! Shut your snout if you've nothing to offer but blather. Talk! Talk! Talk! Talk! That's all the whole lot of you is good for. We have to act. Let's go out there and tell them something before flame begins to fly."

"Yes, I think that would be for the best," a raspy voice said.

The company hushed, and Tighlia emerged from behind the curtains. Both *griff* were down, and her wings dragged in mourning. She cleared her throat, but could produce only a rather loud whisper: "I won't have all that my mate worked for destroyed. If we go out and present a united line, they'll accept SiDrakkon. Well?"

SiDrakkon glowered down at everyone, and Imfamnia looked warily at her future sister.

"If no one's dragon enough to venture out first, I shall," Tighlia said, moving toward the door down one of the silver waterfalls.

"No, Granddam," the Copper said. "I'll go out first. No faction can do much worse to me than life's already done."

"What a way to begin your reign, Tyr SiDrakkon," SiMevolant said. "A lame half-wit announcing your ascendance."

"And a garrulous bit of rabbit fluff bringing up the rear, no doubt," Tighlia croaked. "Go on, RuGaard; show us what you're made of."

"I'll lead, blast it," SiDrakkon said. "Are you coming, Imfamnia?"

"You must be joking," she said, staying on her shelf. "I had dung thrown at me on the way in. They're like humans."

They began to file out, and the Copper felt a pressure on his *saa*. It came from Ibidio, who maneuvered him into an alcove between half-melted war trophies as the others walked past.

"Ummmm, RuGaard, is it now?" She glanced around to make sure none were listening, not even thralls. Outside, the crowed roared as the doors opened.

"Yes," the Copper said.

"You had the Uphold at the end of the western road. Did NiVom come your way?"

"If he had, I certainly wouldn't give him away. He was a good friend."

"I believe he's being hunted."

The Copper heard SiDrakkon roaring out a few emphatic words. A good deal of noise came back from the crowd.

"The Tyr came to me last night. He said he'd selected a new heir. He told me if anything happened to him, to ask you."

"Ask me what?"

"Did you see him or didn't you?"

"I did. I told him NiVom was innocent, and to ask you for the truth about your daughter. And your mate, and DharSii, whoever that was."

"He was our best air commander. Once."

"Dead?"

"No one knows. It's not important; we have only a moment here. Who is the heir the Tyr mentioned?"

"NiVom, I expect."

"What happened to the Tyr?"

"I was one of the first at my mate-father's side," Ibidio said. "We heard a roar from Tighlia's chamber. I tore down the curtains and rushed in. The Tyr was flat on his side, and there was a terrible smell in there. It made my head swim and brought my meal up. I found Tighlia on the balcony."

"What could have happened?"

The crowd outside was quieting.

"I don't know. She's half deman, that one. But I'll tell you this: Look behind her *griff*. There are claw marks. Deep ones. Someone tried to tear her head off."

"I have to go."

He hurried toward the door, but SiDrakkon was already storming back in, his face spattered. "They'll just have to get used to the idea," he said. "I'll be spending the rest of the day at the bath."

"In all fairness," SiMevolant said, "I don't believe they were throwing *their own* dung at you. It was some animal's. I think that makes a difference."

SiDrakkon ignored him. "The rest of you, go through the Resort, and then to all the hills. Talk to your friends and let them know I'll be Tyr, and there's to be no fighting, no changes in control of the hills. No decisions of the Tyr will be voided, no policies changed, and all are welcome to petition me after a six-day mourning period."

The line dispersed, with SiMevolant sighing. "I was hoping for a banquet. . . ."

Save for Tighlia. She walked, a little stiffly, up to the Copper.

"I see your wings have come in," she rasped. "What's wrong with the odd one?"

"An old injury, Granddam," he replied.

"You call me that just to annoy me, I expect. Well, I'm sorry for you. Come to my outer chambers tomorrow. I have an interesting piece of news for you. Oh, come now. I don't bite, and after all these years I'm not about to start with you."

The Copper spent the night in anxiety in the strangely empty Imperial Gardens, trying to make out figures on the milkdrinker's hill. He wanted to go to Nilrasha, but she couldn't be linked to him so publicly until he learned what Tighlia had in mind.

His imagination offered plenty of possibilities, none of them less than terrifying. She was the most dangerous dragon he'd ever met, and she never even so much as extended her claws. He suspected she intended to entrap him with some giveaway.

He slept but little.

Bone-weary from his journey and the upsets of the previous day, he splashed cool water on himself and ordered a thrall to bring him some toasted meat and a little wine. Fortified, he made his way to her caverns adjoining the Tyr's. Or, now, Tyr SiDrakkon's.

He scraped outside the curtains.

"Come," she rasped.

It was gloomy in her reception chamber. On a happier day there would be light bouncing off the glasswork mosaics worked into her walls and floors. He was rather surprised at how cheery the room could be, if it were better lit.

"RuGaard. I'm glad you made it early." Her voice sounded a little stronger today. "I hate it when I invite someone over and they either don't show up at all or spend the whole day getting ready for the visit. Wastes my time."

"How are you feeling, Tighlia?"

"That's better. Dragons never realize how much dragonelles— and yes, dragon-dames—love hearing their names said. It's always 'dear' or 'my love' or 'cloud-dream' or 'tenderness' or something they've heard their fathers use. Just say her name, Ru-

Gaard. You have your faults, but you do speak well. It seems to me when you first came here, you lisped like a hatchling."

"I remember. I hadn't been around dragons much."

"Just bats. Yes. Well, at least you don't smell like them these days."

"How can I be of service, Tighlia?"

"Good news. I've selected a mate for you."

"What?"

"You heard me. Don't act fixated. Whatever else is the matter with you, you can make up your mind and not just stand around gaping. I saw that yesterday."

"I can't imagine my mating or not is of consequence to you."

"I want you a little more firmly in the Imperial line. The *griffaran* think well of you, and as you've no line to call your own, nobody hates you outright, which is more than can be said for most of your relatives."

"I'm surprised you have time to think of such things with your dead mate still cooling. One might wonder—"

"You know, you almost look like a dragon who is working himself up to asking me if I've murdered my mate. And that would lead to a horrible scream from me, and a challenge, and then probably a duel, unless you have brains enough to flee for your scale, like NiVom."

"Thank you for your thoughtfulness, Tighlia."

"Everyone has the wrong idea of me. I want peace and quiet and beauty. Nothing more. No screaming dragons, no burning hills, no eggs tailswiped off their shelves to smash against uncaring, unknowing rock. Order, RuGaard. Simple order. You can help preserve that order."

"I had other plans—"

"Well, forget them. Here's my dilemma. Halaflora, my beloved mate's oldest granddaughter through AgGriffopse and Ibidio—you remember her?"

"The sickly one."

"You're one to talk, but I like your honesty. Halaflora is from AgGriffopse's first clutch. SiMevolant was the champion. Those eggs were laid under an evil star; that much is certain. Imfamnia and Ayafeeia came later. None of the males survived the hatching contest. Whatever's the matter? She's not that ugly."

"Nothing. Go on," the Copper said.

"Of course, Imfamnia—silly's not the word for that brainless bit of fluff—has been dreaming about being mated with every breath her whole life, and now she's got her wish. An Imperial mating, no less. It will be the celebration of a tri-score year."

"What has Halaflora's mating to do with this?"

"I was getting to that, if you'd tuck in your *griff*. Ayafeeia is taking formal vows to go into the Firemaids. Sensible girl—if I had to do it over again . . . Well, it doesn't matter. But Halaflora. Poor little dear. She's not as dumb as Imfamnia, but just as dreamy, and not as idealistic as Ayafeeia, but just as devoted. She wants nothing more than a mating flight, and those wings of hers aren't even strong enough to get her off the ground. Poor dear. I'm not going to draw breath and have a titular granddaughter of mine sobbing her eyes out as her sister is mated. And I want some good news in this family for once! It's like the last act of some bitter elvish tragedy. And fresh, hungry blood never hurts, if we're to raise a new generation of dragons and not lounging, scaled felines. You need some new males now and then or you get more glittering piles of dung like SiMevolant. A mating between you and Halaflora is just the thing."

"I've met a dragonelle already. Well, a drakka. She'll have her wings in a year."

Tighlia's eyes narrowed. "Who?"

"I'm not sure I want to jeopardize her health by giving you the name."

"I suspect it's Nilrasha."

This time the Copper was dumbstruck.

"Of course, you could do worse," Tighlia said. "Do you forget that I've got the management of the Firemaidens? A word of advice, RuGaard. She's from a bad family on a worse hill. She's out for a position in the Imperial line and a lookout from this rock, nothing more."

"What would an old viper like you—"

"So young. So young." She pushed open a curtain, and light came into the room through tinted panels of some thin-shaved crystal, or perhaps glass. As the Copper suspected, the colors were bright and cheery. She tore a bit of fabric off a polished piece of brass.

"I'm not as vain as I once was, but I'm vain enough that I can't stand what I see in this anymore. Look into this, RuGaard. Look into the mirror. A beautiful, vital young dragonelle is going to want that?"

He looked at himself. The half-closed eye, the sloping stance, thanks to his bad *sii*, the broken-jointed wing that wouldn't close . . .

"Lame and twisted, that's you, RuGaard. Another hatching under an evil star. She's after your line, not your scale."

"We neither of us much like what we see in that mirror," he said. "Perhaps you should give it to Imfamnia as a mating gift."

"You can live in the world and accept it, or you can pretend the hatchling songs and stories are true. Which will it be, dragon?"

"At the moment, a quiet life in Anaea seems enough of a dream."

"Easiest thing in the world. Simply mate with Halaflora and you can be back on the western road the next day. You'll forget your little Firemaiden soon enough, roasting ceremonial kern."

"What if her love is some pleasant dream of mine? What's

wrong with dreams? I've seen enough of the world to prefer them."

She took a deep breath. "Oh, you are a prize fool, boy. I try and I try to help you. And this is what I get. Ingratitude. Ah, well, you'll get no more help from me. Or my brother. I'll see to that.

"Go to your precious Firemaiden, RuGaard. Someday you'll learn what dreams are made of."

He sought out Nilrasha on the milkdrinker's hill. The place was a warren of aboveground dwellings housing mostly human thralls, with blighters in huts on the other side of a filthy stream running in twin channels with a wall between that held washing.

He remembered NeStirrath on one of the hikes telling him that the humans wouldn't drink or wash in the blighter water, and the blighters wouldn't drink or wash in the human water, yet both were indistinguishable in their foulness.

There were dragon-holes on the hill too; in fact, the whole area was sort of one vast catacomb, with little ledges and chambers off the main passage, so that few had what could really be called a place of their own, and mother dragons had to shelter their eggs with the weight of their bodies to keep them from being disturbed, if not accidentally crushed.

"Our day for visitors," a mud-speckled Anklene said, looking at the painted stripes curling back from his shoulders.

"I'm looking for the Firemaiden quarter. I was told it was down here somewhere."

"Down it is, and then some; they're well below. Bottom of the air shaft to the left, your Imperial grace."

He had to climb slowly, thanks to his *sii*, but he made it to the bottom of the shaft. A few of the Firemaidens made jokes or hooted about an invasion of Drakwatch.

He searched for Nilrasha but could learn nothing more than

that an Imperial messenger had come for her. He managed to find Fourfang, and told him to make ready for a journey back to Anaea.

He hurried on the path back to Black Rock, scrambling up every prominence and kern mill to look over the grounds for Nilrasha. He hoped it was just some matter of business with the Firemaidens, or that she'd gone to visit friends.

He marked a lone female sitting on a wall next to a mushroom field, and hurried toward her. With each step he became more certain it was Nilrasha.

He limp-trotted up to her. "Nilrasha! I've been looking for you for hours."

Her tail flicked up, but she kept watching the mushrooms. "So you've found me. I understand you're to be mated to the late Tyr's own granddaughter. Well-done."

"No, you misunderstood. I refused her."

She turned and looked at him. "Refused *her*, or refused Tighlia? That was a foolish thing to do. Such a strong connection to AgGriffopse's line would be to your advantage."

"I'm not looking for an advantage, just a chance at what . . . what my parents had."

And who took that away? Not Tighlia.

She looked away again, flicked out her tongue, and consumed a black beetle climbing the stones. "I've changed my mind about mating. I'm taking vows as a Firemaid."

"Have they threatened you?"

"No, they've not threatened me. I'm a poor drakka from a lowly line. What could they possibly take away that I cherish?" She blinked, and the Copper saw a wetness in her eyes; then she took a cleansing breath. "Our eldest was thrilled to hear me decide to take the vows. Offered me any guard post I wished."

"No. Come back to Anaea with me. There's nothing to stop us from mating."

"Nothing but the fact that I don't love you. I was just using words, words used by mated dragons for ages, and they worked their magic. But the Skotl clan is on the rise now, and they'll never let go of Black Rock. I had hopes for you."

"I thought—"

"I made you think, you mean. Yes, just as Tighlia said. I was after your lineage, your position, not some comedy of a mating."

"How do you know what Tighlia said?"

She looked uncertain for the first time since he'd come upon her, resting on the wall. "I can guess. She's a venomer, thanks to that tongue of hers. Go. Mate with that sickly little thing."

She jumped off the wall and ran, making a retching sound, leaving the Copper feeling as though his body were dissolving, flowing into the rocky soil of the Lavadome.

Nothing to overcome now. The course of his life was set. Perhaps he'd take up hunting.

Their mating was done, and done quickly.

A goodly crowd turned up to watch them leave the Imperial Resort. According to NeStirrath, Halaflora had fond memories attached to her, for she used to ride atop her father as he went from hill to hill. AgGriffopse thought air and travel might improve her weak constitution, and his mate had no interest in leaving the Gardens atop the rock. So she was associated in the dragons' minds to AgGriffopse more than to Ibidio.

Almost everyone of the Imperial line trooped out behind them, even SiMevolant, who disliked the dirt and rough stones. Thralls walked to either side with pieces of soft cloth at the ends of sticks, wiping dust kicked up by the mating party from his scales.

SiDrakkon led the party, with *griff* extended and a challenging eye, as though daring any of the spectators to throw dung.

269

Imfamnia skipped next to him. Her wings were bulging against translucent skin and soon it would be her turn.

The party halted twice to let Halaflora catch her breath.

They finally came to the shaft everyone called the Wind Tunnel. Some trick of direction and air density ensured that this short tunnel to the slopes of the plateau always had a howling wind passing through it, equal to an uncomfortable mountain-top in a storm.

It was also called the "death tunnel," for sometimes escaped thralls tried to climb out of it, or thieves tried to creep in from above. The winds usually snatched them up at some point and hurled them down the shaft. But no one called it the death tunnel today.

The Copper climbed to the top of a wind-cut rock with Halaflora and sang his song, with all around listening as best as they could in the wind. Rethothanna had helped him with the wording. The Copper felt that as long as the mating was to be done, it might as well be done well, so he sang of rivers, egg-snatching demen—who said a lifesong must be all true?—and wall-smashing boulders skipped across battlefields.

And with that, they spread their wings—SiDrakkon reached up and kindly helped him extend his injured left with a discreet pull—and jumped.

His mating flight lasted what a dwarf would call a full ten seconds. They hung in the wind for a moment, the Air Spirit's untiring voice shrieking in their ears, Halaflora touching his good wing, and slowly glided to earth.

"I think they're laughing at us, my love," Halaflora said.

The Copper looked around at the assembly. Only SiMevolant was outright laughing—"That was worth a walk in the dust!" he seemed to be saying, though with the wind carrying his words away it was impossible to be sure—but most were at least flutter-ing their eyelids in amusement. Even the usually dour SiDrak-kon looked to be enjoying himself for a change.

"I care not. This is the happiest day of my life. If I can share out some proportion of my own joy, all the better."

The expression on his mate's face washed the sting out of whatever wounds this exhibition cost him, and made the lies, if not pleasant, at least palatable enough so they didn't stick in his throat.

Chapter 23

So the Copper and his mate returned—by a journey made in very easy stages, out of regard for his mate's health—to the Uphold in Anaea.

The Copper was relieved to see that Fourfang and Rhea seemed to get along with Halaflora's thralls. His mate took a special liking to Rhea, and soon she was supervising the other body-servant.

He took pleasure in pointing out the sights of Anaea and introducing her to some of "his" bats. Their lines had so intermingled, it was impossible to remember who was descended from Thernadad, or Enjor, or his oversize trio raised on dragonblood. She petted their strange furry skin and marveled at their ears and delicate wings.

At the western mouth everything was just as he remembered it, unexpectedly so. Nilrasha was back in the cave guarding the tunnel mouth, now with the Firemaid's red-painted stripe around her neck, though she still had not uncased her wings.

She kept her eyes downcast as she greeted him. "Welcome, future Upholder."

"We thank you," the Copper said, his mind whirling like a leaf flung down the Wind Tunnel. What madness was this; did she wish to torture him with her presence? "On behalf of my mate and myself."

"You're very lovely," Halaflora said. "You could be a statue in the Imperial Gardens. I hope we'll be good friends."

"Thank you, your honor," Nilrasha said.

The first few feasts with the rather robust Upholder and his mate were a little on the awkward side. Halaflora had difficulty swallowing unless she ate tiny bites, and the tough-fibered game they brought back to the banquet floor was difficult for her to get down without choking.

But within the limitations of ill health, she was a superb mate. She made and arranged cushions for him on all his favorite lookouts, and she explored Anaea with FeLissarath's mate and returned with rich, scented oils that she rubbed on the worn spot on his bad *sii* and the stuck folds of his wings, or fixed lines on his growing horns to make them come in so they matched each other in a slight, attractive curve. She experimented endlessly with their meals, discovering what they both liked—fish, sadly, which was rare save for the small specimens found in some of the mountain lakes—and sang to him at night.

He decided there were many dragons worse mated, and if she didn't make his hearts hammer and his scale stir the way Nilrasha did when she stretched, there were other compensations.

Then there was his work. He tried to learn more about the ins and outs of the scale trade.

"Why is dragonscale so valuable to humans?" he asked FeLissarath.

"Jewelry, I've heard. Tips of sword scabbards, or holding wooden shields together. In some principality or other on the banks of the Inland Ocean, they use it as currency because it's impossible to forge, and dangerous to get hold of. Very wealthy hominids will lay it on their roofs to keep off fire. Some of the larger hominid cities suffer terribly from fires, nothing to do with dragons."

"It might behoove us to have a shortage of it now and then,

especially when there's a particularly large crop of kern. I think we could get more bags in trade for scale."

"We have good relations with the kern kings, and the values were set long ago."

"To their advantage. I've heard one of the kings now has a stairway decorated with golden dragonscale."

"He'll slip and break his neck when it rains." FeLissarath laughed. "Ah, the follies of humans. They don't live long enough to really learn what's important in life. Did I tell you about the bear I got yesterday? Yes, you heard me right, a bear. . . ."

The Copper spent a good deal of time on the western road. Thanks to a bridge collapse at the Tooth Cavern, almost an entire pack-train of kern was lost when inattentive handlers allowed the mules to bunch up on one of the more rickety spans.

They were already making repairs when he arrived to survey the damage—thanks to the bats, he heard about it the same day it happened and left immediately—and a Firemaid was flying back and forth carrying thralls—mostly men, who, if their workmanship wasn't quite as skilled as that of dwarves, at least labored more willingly—and tools from one end of the break to the other.

"Oh, your honor," she said. "There's a thrall been asking every day to speak to the dragon in charge. That would be you."

"A human?"

"Yes. He's got some plan or idea or bargain or something."

The Copper half expected to see Harf again, recaptured, but the young man who came before him wearing the tatters of some very tight weaving just looked at him with clear blue eyes. He was extraordinarily handsome, as far as he could tell hominid standards went.

"What is it you want, man?"

"Great one. This bridge of yours. It's a death trap." He spoke the simplified pidgin Drakine with a thick accent; he hadn't been in the keeping of the Lavadome long, it seemed. As for his observation, that required no great mind to discern, with the bones and bodies of dead animals and handlers scattered all over the floor of the canyon below.

"Do you offer a remedy, or is this just idle conversation?"

"I know how to improve it."

"Do you, now. Have you built many bridges?"

"I've been involved in several construction projects. I was trained by dwarves."

"I didn't know they shared their secrets so readily with outsiders."

"I was a kind of special apprentice, your honor."

"What's your name?"

"Rayg."

The Copper did like the look of him, except for the fact that he didn't appear particularly afraid of dragons. New thralls usually bent and tucked their heads down between their shoulders like frightened turtles.

"I should like to hear your plans."

"I have a condition."

"You forget your place. I could lift you and toss you down to rest with the other bones, and no one would say a word."

The man called Rayg just blinked at him.

The Copper relented, though he wondered if it was a mistake to do so. "What's your condition?"

"My freedom."

"Oh, dear. I can't say that I blame you, but there's a problem. You're not my slave."

"I'm sure I can be traded."

"Let me see your plans. Then we'll talk again."

He widened his stance. "No. Buy me, and then I'll show you the plan. If you like the plan, I'll expect my freedom."

"You'll supervise the construction?"

"Yes. As long as I can get more, much more, of the materials you're using now. And some good stonecutters."

"If I'm satisfied with the bridge you build, I'll grant you your freedom. You seem intelligent enough, so I'll see about buying you."

Negotiating with thralls. The duties of an Upholder, even an Upholder-to-be, had a variety of flavors. Which made him think of the herbs Halaflora added to those big-footed rabbits Fourfang had caught. . . .

He learned from the grunting deman overseer that this Rayg belonged to a general pool of Imperial thralls, to be used for mundane duties like building dams, clearing tunnels, mining for ores necessary to a healthy dragon's diet. As a member of the Imperial line he could make claims on such thralls, so he simply affirmed that the Uphold in Anaea needed him and paid out a small sum to the overseer as a kind of gratuity.

The Copper was very grateful his life couldn't be bought and sold so easily.

He had Rayg transferred to his household and introduced to Fourfang and Rhea with a minimum of squabbling. He set Rayg to work with a chalk tablet used to keep track of rations—it would take time to get paper—and tried to do what he could to retrieve the bags of kern from the fallen animals. Blood or rats had spoiled much of it.

The Firemaid told him of rumors from the Lavadome of some political housekeeping carried out by SiDrakkon. Nothing severe, just a replacement of some staff with his Skotl supporters. There'd been a few duels and deaths. SiDrakkon had also converted the Imperial Gardens to a private topiary and bathing area for himself and his mate-to-be, which was causing some grousing, as a walk in the mushroom fields or past livestock pens couldn't compare with the view from Black Rock.

SiMevolant would have to find new flowers to contemplate. The thought brought him some pleasure.

Rayg presented him with a rough version of the plan, a mixture of tunneling through the stalactite formations and a new platform added to one of the rising rocks, complete with a drawbridge.

"I made it draw up toward the Lavadome," Rayg said. "I believe you are more worried about enemies getting down into the Lower World than threats coming up."

The Copper wondered if Rayg knew more about the jealousies and rivalries and head-hunting going on in the Lavadome than he let on.

"It's wide. Will it hold?"

"I thought you might like to take carts across. Yes, it will hold. The calculations are there, based on the materials I've seen. It's dwarven notation; can you read that?"

"Hmmm. Do it well, and you'll get your reward," the Copper said, dodging the question rather than admitting that a thrall could do something he couldn't, which seemed wrong in an indefinable way. "How long will it take?"

"Two years. Unless you give me more tunnelers and tools. A furnace on site would speed things up as well."

"I'll see what I can do."

It was rather nice to leave all the details and worries in the hands of Rayg. He left instructions to the Drakwatch and the Firemaiden garrison that everything he asked for should be given.

"It will take some time to assemble the materials. Maybe you'd like a little sun?"

Rayg's eyes lit up. "The surface?"

"Yes. Plenty of food, too. It's been a good summer; kern is coming out of our ears."

———

They had to return for SiDrakkon's mating, of course. They traveled light, bringing Rayg back to the works to supervise the first stages. A rickety catwalk replaced the gap in the bridge, and the Copper for once was slower than his mate, hobbled by his bad *sii*.

The Copper quietly warned the Firemaidens to watch Rayg, so that he didn't use his authority to fashion an escape. The project seemed well begun, and Rayg liked his work and got along well with the other thralls, but there was no telling with hominids.

The Copper went so far as to have Rhea decorate him for the mating banquet, as she had for the first time he'd attended a gathering atop Black Rock. NeStirrath helped him prepare by having a pair of blighters paint his war decorations on his good wing.

SiDrakkon reopened the Imperial Gardens to show all the improvements. There were more statues and galleries and plant beds everywhere, and it had been redesigned so a lone dragon could walk the perimeter in something like isolation, at the cost of making the space less functional for multiple dragons to enjoy.

But then, as Imfamnia liked to remind everyone, "It is *our* garden."

Halaflora set herself on some cushions near the banquet trench and spoke to her other sister, now grave in her Firemaid ring.

Their mating flight commenced with a long, expanding flight around Black Rock, then the inner hills, and finally the outer edge of the Lavadome. Thralls had been coached to cheer them from the rooftops and hills, and dragons who knew what was good for them trumpeted their well-wishes.

Imfamnia was in her element at the mating banquet, alternately roaring orders and simpering. The Copper was rather glad for a sickly mate rather than this whirlwind in painted scale. "This? This is nothing," she said. "Wait until we get a new trade route open. I want everyone to shake off every scale they can. There are some new metal-based paints that will drive everyone mad with excitement when they see them. Such vivid colors!"

"Is it wise to send dragonscale directly to the merchant houses?" Rethothanna asked. "Especially for luxuries? I always thought it was wiser to bring scale to market indirectly, so its source would be harder to trace."

"And what of it, if the source is found? We control every road and every river in the Lower World for many marches in every direction," Imfamnia responded. "I've even heard the Wheel of Fire has been smashed in the last year by barbarians. Those dwarves had the only army capable of forcing itself anywhere near here, or so my mate says. Isn't that right, Tyr?"

"Yes, the main threat against us in the Lower World is gone. And as for the Upper, the Ghi men got a lesson," Tyr SiDrakkon said, for in the Copper's heart there would only be one Tyr, and the title choked on its way out his lips. "We'll teach the same to any who dare come against us."

"War, war, war," Ibidio said. "You make it more likely with your foolishness and bragging. There's always risk in war. Always loss."

The Copper suddenly noticed that Tighlia wasn't at the celebration. "Where is my granddam?" he asked. "I would like to pay my respects."

"The old has-been keeps to her room," SiMevolant said. He'd had his claws painted up with gold striping and added black to his tail. The Copper thought he looked like a bumblebee among the coneflowers bordering one of Anaea's kernfields.

"She doesn't like being outdone by our beautiful new queen," SiMevolant continued, bowing to Imfamnia. "Ladies, look to your mates, for no hearts remain true when Imfamnia passes. Beautiful Imfamnia."

"I'm going to go see Tighlia. Will you be all right, darling?" the Copper asked his mate. She smiled up at him from her cushions and nodded.

"When has Halaflora ever been all right?" SiMevolant asked, and everyone waggled their eyebrows.

"You go too far, SiMevolant," the Copper roared in his face. "Cry challenge, and meet me in the pits!"

"RuGaard, you really must have your body-slave look to your teeth and tongue," SiMevolant said, his *griff* not even twitching. Behind him, NoSohoth pushed his way forward, guiding blighters with incense to calm the situation. "Unless you intend to slay with your breath. But soft! I cry submission. I meant no offense; it was only a little jest at my sister. She's known me for years. I mean no harm."

"Thank you, my lord," Halaflora said, ignoring her brother and staring at the Copper. "Thank you for that."

Her sister Ayafeeia looked at him with new eyes. She flicked a *griff* at him, one warrior to another. He turned away.

"Now I know why he walks so oddly," SiMevolant said. But softly. "It's that lance stuck up his tailvent."

He left the party and sought out Tighlia. One of her thralls admitted him.

"No, no more visitors," he heard her cry, followed by a low humming hominid voice. "Oh. Well, I can stand him," she said a little more quietly.

The elderly female thrall brought him into the cheery little room. Now a bronzed tooth and a scale and a claw from, he guessed, her mate stood on a special pedestal in the center of the room. Other than that it was largely unchanged, though perhaps the air was a little heavier, as though she rarely left the room.

"I've come to pay my respects, Tighlia," the Copper said.

"Wine?" she asked, indicating a deep cistern next to her low shelf. She took a tongueful. "It's good. Go ahead! I've never poisoned a guest's wine, and I'm not going to start today."

"A little, thank you." The Copper took a tongueful. "Why aren't you at the mating banquet?"

"Because my brother's going to be there," she said a little thickly. "I suppose you find that odd."

"I grew tired of the banquet myself."

"You know what he's done with the Gardens, I expect."

She's even drunk! All I have to do is make one good leap. I've got enough strength in my good sii *to—* "Made them into a private park for himself and—"

"Yes, that's bad enough," she said, taking such a great slurp of wine a little ran out of the corners of her mouth. The spill somehow disarmed him, and he relaxed. "Oh, how sloppy of me. Yes, bad enough to deny decent dragons the view, but do you know he's stocked it with his precious, plump human females? Brought at great expense, oh, yes, the demen slave traders and ferrymen are happy with him. He's in there all day sniffing around like some wretched dog. Getting himself puffed up for a night with Imfamnia."

"She's an energetic young dragonelle—er, dragon-dame," the Copper said.

"There's something sad about that mating. Of course, there always is with a dragon his age and some bright thing with her wings fresh out. Happened before, just not in the Imperial line. If you must dilly-dally you can at least be discreet about it and not bring the jade-scale into company."

"Manners have never been my specialty."

"He hardly visits me anymore," she said, and paused for a little more wine. "Doesn't care for my advice. You know what he told me, once we had things sorted in the Rock? I brought him a whole bellyful of matters needing attention. He said, 'I'm Tyr now; I can do what I want.' "

She paused.

" 'I can do what I want.' What a child. What an old, foolish child. It's quite the opposite, you know. Perhaps he never really understood what it meant to lead."

"I came to tell you about some improvements I have in mind for the western road," the Copper said. "I was wondering if you had any advice about stonecutters."

"Oh, I've had too much wine for any of that. How is your mate?"

The Copper tried to find the proper words. "I'm . . . I'm content."

"Good for you, RuGaard. I hope you will be able to stay content. As for me . . . oh, I must do some serious thinking. But first, a little more wine. It is the day of my brother's mating, after all. Oh. Stonecutters. Yes, come tomorrow and I'll give you a name. Fat human, smelly as a pig's arse and dripping fleas, but he does good work with his crew."

The stonecutter's name was Hiriyal, and he did excellent work and regulated an efficient crew. With their quick—albeit expensive—help, each day saw the tunneling progress and the slag pile grow. Hiriyal was a "free slave," which sounded like a contradiction, but he made his strange social position work for the benefit of himself and his men.

The Firemaidens had carried out their orders a little too enthusiastically, and he found Rayg chained by the ankle to a heavy boulder. He got around by having a blighter help him lift it into a barrow, and together they could move it to the next site, though negotiating the catwalk was obviously impossible.

The Copper had the chain struck off and set up a temporary household while the most difficult element of the work, the stonecutting, was carried out under Rayg's supervision. After a few arguments about methods with Hiriyal, they made good progress.

The Copper was surveying the first span with Rayg when the young man suggested that he fly below and look at the supports.

"I can't fly."

"Is it that wing? The one that hangs?"

"Yes, useless. Not even good to glide; it's more of a swooping fall, I'm afraid."

Rayg walked around him. "I believe the problem's in that joint. It looks different from the one on the other side, like the two ends are slipped."

"I know the cause," the Copper said.

"I might be able to fix that. It looks like all it needs is a brace to keep the outer edge from sliding and then folding over the inner."

The Copper hardly dared hope. "You can't be serious."

"It's simple . . ." He said a word the Copper didn't understand. "Just a matter of give and take."

"If you do that, I will set you up like a kern king. Once you finish the bridge."

"I'd always heard dragons are terrible. You're better than barbarians."

"I should hope so," the Copper said.

Over the next weeks Rayg worked with two pieces of wood carved into shapes that resembled a crescent moon, thick leather, metal bands, and some studs. Rhea helped him, holding the wing still as he tested model after model. It infuriated the Copper, as each session ended with an "I've got to build another model" that became an inevitability ending the experiments.

He wondered if all this work was just an excuse to divert

his attention from an escape attempt, or some bit of spycraft, but all Rayg seemed to do was spend more and more of his off time with Rhea.

Then one day, after an unusually long session extending and retracting his wing over and over and over again until the Copper's muscles grew weary, with Rayg making chalk marks on the wood, the man said, "This model will work."

"You mean—" the Copper began.

"Oh, I've got to improve it. A little more shaping. But this one folds just enough. It's a little stiff, but better too rigid than something that'll give way when you're in the air."

The bridge, and the wing contraption, both progressed daily. After having his skin rubbed raw extending and retracting his wing, he tried a short glide from one construction platform to another.

His wing stayed open! Hearts beating, he threw his head to the sky and roared, so loudly that the Firemaidens came running, thinking there was a fight.

With that he launched himself off the platform. Rayg shouted something but he didn't catch it; it was lost in the sound of air as he flew. He tried one beat, two, three, gaining altitude with each stroke of his wings. He had never realized how good it would feel to use the muscles on his back properly, how perfect the sensation—

Snap!

The device flew off and he felt the old, faint grinding sensation of his bones folding against each other. His wing collapsed and the world spun around him. No, yes, he managed a turn, leveled out, and then the ground was suddenly beneath him and it struck hard.

He woke smelling his own blood. But he managed to stand, and looked at the skid mark he'd made in the canyon's side. He'd lost a few scales as well.

He picked up the broken contraption and made the long, slow, sore climb back up to the construction site.

"I'm glad you live," Rayg said.

"How thoughtful of you," the Copper responded.

"No, I'm truly glad. The Firemaidens said that if you were dead, they'd throw me off the bridge."

"Ten lengths ago I would have told them to do it. I'm too tired now."

"Didn't you hear me shout? I wanted to take it off and make sure the leather strap was holding. It's meant to be permanently fixed with steel pins."

Rayg worked on his model for a few more days, and was extra diligent at the bridge as well. They went through a few more practice glides, and the Copper flew back and forth and did turns under the bridge—with the harness tied around his limbs and a long, long line leading back to the bridge, just in case.

But in the end, he flew. He knew he didn't fly well; nor could he do any of the fancy maneuvers he'd seen some of the dragons flying over the Imperial Resort perform for the sheer joy of it, but the ability made him feel complete, perhaps for the first time in his life.

And it hurt to know that Halaflora wasn't up to it.

After showing his mate, he demonstrated his wings to Nilrasha. Her wings had come in some months ago, but he'd purposely kept away so he wouldn't have to watch her fly. It didn't help that Halaflora described the occasion in excruciating detail, full of praise for how natural and well formed she looked in the air.

"Oh, it's a miracle, your honor. The Spirits are rewarding you at last."

"You don't have to call me your honor, Rasha. Not when we're alone."

"I like formalities. It's so easy to hide behind them. If you offered to take me up, I'd say yes. You know that."

"Take you up?"

"You know. Mate."

"Nilrasha, my mate is above in the palace."

"Oh, we wouldn't have to fly out together, silly. Go out separately, and meet where she couldn't see."

The Copper felt bar-struck. "I meant a dragon should just have his mate."

"So we are never to . . . I thought you just mated with Halafora to make the line happy."

"Yes, but it doesn't make the mating anything less for that. She's been kind to me."

"And you to her. Too kind. Do you ever—"

"I don't want to talk about that. You've got the wrong idea about me if you think I could—"

"Could? Do you have another injury I'm unaware of?"

He rattled his *griff*. "Would, then. No. Not while Halafora lives. I've pledged myself to her, and that's an end to it."

"But do you still love me, RuGaard?"

He couldn't answer that. If he did, he'd never be able to look at Halafora across a feast again. He turned tail and left the Firemaid's cold, chaste quarters.

Chapter 24

He told FeLissarath and his mate that as soon as the bridge was completed and he could turn his attentions to Anaea, they would be free to leave.

"The odd thing is, I don't think we want to go," FeLissarath said. "The hunting is good, and we have friends here among the humans and condors. Perhaps we'll leave the palace to you and set up somewhere in the mountains. A little cave. Really rough it, like young, wild dragons of the north first mated."

His mate looked at him and she loosed a *prrum*.

Talk turned to politics, as it often did. Rumor had come up through the Drakwatch that SiBayereth, SiDrakkon's first clutchwinner, had been killed, not in a duel, but in his bath. Some were saying he was assassinated in retribution for some of the killings and forced duels that had been taking place with greater frequency since SiDrakkon turned Tyr.

Others said that he'd bodily insulted some maiden dragonelle and she'd taken the traditional revenge of a female wronged and discarded.

The Copper returned to his cushions and his mate, exceptionally happy to be in Anaea and out of the Imperial Resort and its feuds. He slept with his neck across hers in silent appreciation.

So eager were the FeLissaraths to be in their new digs that

they started hunting for caves almost immediately, and turned over all the day-to-day temple duties to him.

Now that he had his wings he hunted for NiVom, searching the mountains to the south, but there was no sign of him. He spent a rather cold night in the mountains—the Upper World made him feel exposed and watched; he didn't like it, even when the unpredictable weather was nice—and flew back in the morning.

It was a brilliant, clear day. The sort of day that wouldn't think about being evil, and instead put off ill tidings until the next overcast.

He saw a distant dot. It was a dragon, male—and therefore not Nilrasha, nor FeLissarath. It was light-colored, reflecting the sun, perhaps white.

He beat his wings hard toward it. He hoped if it was NiVom he'd recognize him rather than think him an assassin, despite the improbability of his being in the air. The dragon turned a little, not running away then, but coming toward him.

They rushed toward each other with frightening speed. The Copper saw that it was a light shade of bronze, though a good deal smaller than Father, at least Father as he remembered him. The dragon gained altitude at the last moment, as though seeking an advantage, and the Copper veered away, fearing a tailstrike on his weak wing and upset by something odd about its lines.

The dragon had a rider!

The implications so upset the Copper that he dropped toward the palace as fast as he dared—Rayg said that he couldn't be certain that the joint wouldn't give way under what he called "extraordinary stress" but refused to further define it.

His wing held as he leveled off, making for the staircase cut into the side of the mountain, topped by the familiar outlines of the dragon palace.

The other dragon—for some reason the term *hag-ridden*

popped into his head, but he couldn't remember the origins; perhaps it was some story mother dragons told their hatchlings to compel them to behave—followed his course, though it made no attempt to catch up.

He came in for a landing at the wide lower entrance hall, and Fourfang trotted up.

"Get my mate and Nilrasha. Danger!"

Fourfang glanced up and turned around, doing a fair attempt at running on all fours to get back inside the palace.

The Copper backed into the entrance to get solid Anaean stone between himself and the stranger—there was that term again, *hag-ridden*.

The man shouted words down at him, but he couldn't comprehend their meaning.

"May I land?" the dragon roared.

"What is it, my lord?" Halaflora said from the entrance.

"Stay back. If a fight begins, use your flame to help me and then run for the Lower World." He stuck his head out. Oh, this was cowardly! He stepped out.

"Cry parley and land away. Beneath me, now."

The dragon turned one more circle and landed well, though it rocked the man in his leather seat a little. The hag-rider wrapped the reins around a curved tooth at the front of his seat and hopped off, though he kept hold of a rope linking him to his leather seat.

The Copper tried not to stare at the elaborate reins linking dragon, head and wing, to the rider. There were copper rings punched through the skin of the dragon to better fix the lines. He wondered if that hurt.

The man glubbed out a few words.

"That's Parl," Halaflora said. "It's a trade tongue here on the surface."

"Can you speak it?"

"Only a few words. I know a greeting."

"Then say it."

She coughed something out that sounded like the mindless yapping of a dog.

The man took off his helmet and said something in return.

"He's being polite," she said.

And there the conversation sputtered and died out. The man spoke to his mount, and the dragon said, in a rather thick accent: "We have come to bring peace."

"That's good. I hope you may also go in peace."

The dragon translated for the hag-rider. The man responded, through his dragon: "We seek allies in a great war. A war that unites dragon and man against their common enemy."

Hawks and mice uniting against the dogs and cats! The Copper didn't know what to make of it, but he was in the Imperial line and needed to answer well.

"If you are so united," the Copper said, "why do you need to speak the man's words? Why do you fly tied head and wing tip to the man? Answer me that, and don't bother saying anything to him."

The bronze looked nonplussed.

"I tell the man that, and he will be angry," the bronze said.

"All the more reason not to translate it."

The hag-rider yapped something.

"That was a 'What?'" Halaflora said.

The Copper smelled Nilrasha lurking somewhere. He suspected she was slipping around the side of the palace, next to the stairs.

"It is a great war," the bronze said. "We win battles."

"I'm happy for you, then. I'll welcome any dragon who wishes to come in friendship, parley, and leave in peace. Leave your men at home, though. It's bad manners to bring armed men into a free dragon's home."

The dragon said something to the man, but it didn't take long. The Copper suspected much of the wordplay had been lost. He hoped the meaning remained.

The man showed his teeth and raised his hand to his chin. He gave a twist of his hand, as though fixing his faceplate.

"We may return," the dragon said.

"Yes, I think that was it," Halaflora added.

The man climbed back up onto the bronze and took up the reins. He prodded the bronze with his pointy boots, and the hag-ridden dragon flapped up into the clean blue sky.

"I think I'm going to be sick," Nilrasha said, looking up. "The creature's riding him like a horse."

"If that's the great alliance, I think we should have no part of it," Halaflora said. "I'd sooner trust a dwarf."

That night the three of them talked the matter over across the feasting floor.

Nilrasha tore into her meal of kern-fattened pig, tearing off lusty bits and swallowing them, while Halaflora ate in her usual dainty style due to her trouble swallowing.

They presented a pretty contrast, the Copper thought. But he couldn't consider aesthetics.

"I think we'll have to tell Tyr SiDrakkon. This is a matter for him."

No one objected to the compound name, a serious insult had they been back at the Rock. At least in that respect, all three were alike.

"I'm going to send word through the bats. I'm afraid it will get confused, so I'll follow to answer questions," the Copper said.

"What if the rider comes back? Shouldn't you be here?" Nilrasha asked.

"I'm not even sure I'm the Upholder. The FeLissaraths have

moved to their lodge cave, but they still attend all the Anaean ceremonies, preside over them, in fact."

"I would go for you, your honor. But I cannot leave my post," Nilrasha said.

"You could leave it in my hands," Halaflora said. "I took the Firemaiden oath. I never did anything with the other maidens, but does that make the oath less valid?"

The Copper felt trapped between duty and need.

"No. I may need to argue, or even challenge. I'll beg the FeLissaraths to return to the palace long enough for me to return to the Lavadome. I can break tradition and fly to one of the *griffaran* cuts in the mountainside. This is important enough. I can make the journey at night and rest in the day and be there in two days."

"Will your wing hold up? You'll be far from help if that man's contraption fails," Halaflora said.

"If the joint fails after all this testing and trial, Rayg will wish I'd been on the other side of the world."

"Your blood certainly was up tonight," Halaflora said, as they settled into their sleeping chamber. His mate had turned several of the stone globes into rather comfortable backrests, thanks to cushions stuffed with bird feathers. "I've never seen you like this. Is this what war is like?"

"No. Nothing like this, and Spirits keep it that way."

"What way?"

"Far from here."

"You smell hot. I thought certainly you'd take your jade up tonight."

The world froze for a moment. "You thought *what*?"

Rhea finished cleaning out her mistress's ears and scurried out of the room. Had the girl put on weight? Ten other equally trivial thoughts washed through his head, so eager was he to avoid the consequences of thinking about what his mate had just said.

"I'm sorry. Am I being too direct? All those years with Si-Mevolant as a brother. Some time at night to relax and refresh, then."

"She's a Firemaid. She swore an oath. I swore an oath to you, for that matter. She's not . . . not my lover."

"Oh, RuGaard. My lord, I won't be hurt by the truth. I married a dragon, not some perfumed flower. There's nothing wrong with a jade for a dragon in your . . . in your situation. Because of my health."

"Have you gone mad?" He didn't mean it, but the words came out. Anything to stop her from going on.

"Our mating wasn't a real mating, after all. As much as it meant to me." She looked down.

"I had no idea you felt that way," he said at last. They each studied opposite corners of the room for a moment. What came out next was inspired by kindness, rather than love, but he meant every word of it. "Darling. Let's be mated again, then. Or mated for the first time. Whatever you call it. In tight spots, during wars and so forth, dragons have been known to mate underground. It's tactics, you know. Just a matter of position."

She looked up at him, blushing.

"Can we? Really? Would it be . . . proper?"

"Proper? Probably not. But it'll be exciting."

The sun rose in front of the mountains to the west and lit the night-curtains with its orange glow.

West? In front of the mountains?

The Copper's sluggish brain took its time apprehending the wrongness of the lighting. He opened another eye and righted himself, rose, and put his head out of the curtains.

Flames dotted the plateau, but they were nothing compared

293

to the conflagration below the temple. The city of the kern kings was a solid mass of fire.

He saw dragonwings silhouetted against the flames, and then another set, and another, flying in a line.

"What is it, my lord?" his mate said.

He pushed the curtains open with his tail. "War."

"RuGaard." He heard a dragon voice from above, soft yet insistent.

With a single soft wing-beat, FeLissarath alighted on the top of the temple, keeping to the shadows. His mate followed.

"We have terrible news," FeLissarath said.

"A moment." He turned to Halaflora. "Get the thralls and such meats as can be easily carried. Go to the Firemaid chamber. If they come into the palace, bring the roof down on top of the entrance and head down into the Lower World. Have Nilrasha fight and delay them; you just run. Leave the thralls behind if you must, but find the Drakwatch and tell them Anaea's been attacked by man-ridden dragons."

"I understand. Thank you for not treating me like . . . like . . ."

"I know. They may not come here. They may just be after gold." He wished he could summon a *prrum*, and instead rubbed his snout on hers. "Go."

As she left by the inner exit he climbed out on his balcony and up. Together the three dragons watched the flames spread.

"Less than a score, do you think, my love?" FeLissarath's mate said.

"They're causing confusion," the Copper said, watching a trio of dragons land. "Burning the city but landing at the palaces. I think they're after gold."

FeLissarath spoke: "They're man-ridden, RuGaard. We had a brush with one, but we lost him by going to ground by the river."

"I know."

"RuGaard, the Tyr must be told of this, the faster the better. Thank the Air Spirit for that clever thrall. Take the skyway to the plateau—"

"Yes, Upholder, I know."

"After this night you'll be Upholder, I fear."

"What do you mean?"

His mate spoke: "We need a prisoner or two. Find out who they are and where they came from." She stared into his eyes.

"The most dangerous game of all, my love? We must be careful. They'll be tougher than wild *griffaran*." He turned back to the Copper. "You must make the best speed you can to the Imperial Resort and come back with everything the Tyr can send. He should come himself, at that."

"Oh, for DharSii's old aerial host at this hour," she said.

"We'll try from above, dear. Don't frame against the moon—"

"Am I a wet-wing?"

The Copper only half listened to them talk. He watched another trio of dragons come in, landing on a triangular temple top. It was hard to see at this distance, but it seemed figures dropped off the dragons as soon as they landed. The dragons took off again almost immediately.

"This is for my benefit as well," FeLissarath said. "We may get lucky and snatch one out of the saddle. In case of trouble, make for the big smoke column and climb. Whatever happens, we shouldn't lead them back here. If we're separated, we'll go to the high pass lookout and meet there. RuGaard, are you still here?"

The Copper extended his wings. "Back in three days if I can. Four days at most. More means I'm dead."

"If you don't see us again, lad, remember us every time you take a wild bighorn," FeLissarath's mate said.

295

The Copper launched himself into the night.

It took time to gain altitude, and he did so on the dark side of the mountain backing up the temple. Curse the bright moon tonight!

He saw the FeLissaraths take off from their palace and wheel around north to keep the attacking dragons on the moon side. He saw them gain altitude.

Three shapes dropped out of the sky upon them, falling like hawks.

The FeLissaraths closed up on each other, with the male slipping a little below the female, guarding his mate's vulnerable belly.

Suddenly the old Upholders flipped over on their backs, practically bending their spines in half. Tails a blur, they struck their lead pursuer, one high and one low.

The Copper saw an object fall, turning cartwheels as it plummeted to the plateau. He suspected—no, rejoiced—that it was one of the hag-riders. The dragon they struck convulsed in the air and fell, limp-winged.

But the two following avoided their quarry-turned-hunters and broke, one high and to the right, one low and to the left, a terrible perfection in their evolutions.

The male swung under his mate again, guarding her, and the low-flying dragon passed under him. FeLissarath twitched in midair, turned sideways, and began a stiff-winged fall to the surface.

The female flew to the aid of her mate, diving, but that just gave the one who turned high an opportunity. It dove on her, claws extended like a hawk after a duck, and raked her across the back.

The Copper saw one wing rise, fluttering.

But she wasn't done yet. She lashed up with her neck, got her teeth in her opponent's tail, and folded her wings. With her

296

weight clinging to him, the other dragon couldn't stay aloft, and the pair began to fall, whirling around and around to destruction on the plateau. The female pulled herself up her opponent's tail and dug into his belly, trading bites as they went down.

So passed the Upholders of Anaea.

The Copper swung around toward the remaining hag-ridden dragon. He was descending to the aid of the other rider. But he saw another formation of three coming in, late to the fight but arriving before he could.

He couldn't match the flying of the FeLissaraths, let alone the guided enemy dragons working in concert. No flame, almost blind in one eye, and a bad wing. He wouldn't even get one. He turned east for the Lavadome.

But in his ascent, watching the aerial duel, he'd passed out of the shadow of the mountain and into moonlight. He realized it too late.

The three hag-ridden dragons flapped their wings in unison as they turned toward him.

Chapter 25

They made no great effort to catch up to him as he fled east. After closing to two-score dragonlengths, they seemed content to trail him.

The long flight exhausted him. He passed over unfamiliar country, dry and rocky and dotted with widely spaced patches of vegetation clinging precariously to what he suspected were seasonal water supplies. There was little sign of habitation in this waste.

Thanks to his injury, he couldn't manipulate his wing to take the wind at a favorable angle, and he suspected he was expending as much effort just to glide between beats as he would climbing. His strength would fail before dawn.

And on and on glided the pursuit. Didn't they have buildings to burn and gold to steal? Why didn't they close and put an end to him?

Painful beat-glide. Painful beat-glide. Painful beat-glide. On and on through the night.

A black scar broke the moonlit ground ahead.

Could it be the Tooth Cavern? He knew it opened to the sky not far north of the bridge at the Lower World. He altered his course a little south.

Fool! More the fool! The change proved to be a telltale to the pursuing dragons. They beat their wings harder, closing.

He expended what strength he had left trying to stay ahead; still they closed.

And still they fired no weapon, just kept him under observation.

At last the cavern was in his glide-path. No elegant flying, just a simple turn and descent. He closed his wings a little to hurry it, making for the canyon floor.

The leading two followed. The third stayed above, watching the action.

He looked frantically for some sign of the tunnel, the enclosure of the Lower World, but there was none. Columns of rock could be seen ahead; perhaps they were the beginnings of the teeth.

Reaching the stone columns, he swerved around one, the next painfully bashing his wing tip when he miscalculated his turn. Now the lead flier was closer behind, his companion a little farther back, and the Copper didn't dare roll his good eye toward the sky lest he hit the cavern's side.

There. Darkness ahead. As a dragon he could see well enough. He wondered how good the night vision of the riders was. Would they let their fliers choose their own path?

He whipped into darkness, and the first pursuer drew even closer.

These rocks he knew. He'd flown around them often enough in his practice flights as Rayg tested the joint brace.

The fat one ahead, in fact, had a deceptively wide but shallow route around the east side, and a narrow but deep channel to the left.

He approached the fat rock as though going around the east, then at the last moment rolled and shot through the west gap. But instead of continuing down the cavern he stayed in the turn, hoping to meet his pursuer coming around the other side—anything but nose-tip to nose-tip.

A flash, a thump in his wing, and they were past each other.

He found himself flying headlong toward the second hag-ridden dragon. The rider put a shimmering piece of metal to his shoulder and something whirled past his ear, turning tight circles as it cut the air—a crossbow bolt.

The Copper dove for the surface, and so did his opponent. He rose to turn and the opposing dragon lashed out with a *saa* as they passed, opening a wound in his belly.

He turned back south for the bridge.

Now the third dragon descended, its rider leaning over and struggling with his weapon. The Copper made for the tunnel, but the second pursuer banked in front of him. The rider hurled some kind of apparatus of chain and steel balls but missed, thanks to the tight turn his mount was making in the narrow walls of the canyon.

Ahead the Copper saw the first dragon shooting out of the mouth of the cave, the strapped-on leather chair hanging askew and reins loose and flying free in the breeze. He'd dismounted the rider!

Now in the cave he saw the hag-rider sprawled on the floor, unconscious or dead. He flapped into the canyon, the darkness promising safety, but still one dragon followed.

He didn't have time to wonder what had happened to the third.

The chasm descended sharply and he banked around a bend, and there ahead was the bridge.

He loosed a bellowing war call: "Firemaidens, cry havoc!"

He turned for the south side of the bridge and a crossbow bolt punched through his wing.

Under the bridge and up, he saw two shapes hiding at the openings of the short tunnel through one of the rocky "teeth" on the new bridge. As the dragon trailing him closed they loosed their flame and spread it.

The dragon closed its wings, and the rider crossed shield-elbowed in front of the Copper's face. They passed through flame together, the oily, burning mess sliding off dragonscale but clinging to the rider's exposed surfaces. The dragon flipped over, whether by orders, instinct, or accident, allowing the fire to fall off.

Until a stalagmite clipped off its rider from the waist up as neatly as a blade.

Now unguided, the dragon turned and fled, passing over the bridge this time.

A Firemaid spread her wings to pursue.

"No!" the Copper called, landing. "There's another waiting out there."

Alert Firemaidens guarded each end of the under-construction bridge and the tunnel in the center. The Copper felt confident they could deal with the remaining rider, even if the dragons assisted. They didn't seem like well-trained tunnel fighters, judging from their performance as soon as the walls closed in.

"What's your name?" he asked his rescuer.

"Asleea, your honor."

"Asleea, there's a rider down out there. If he's still alive, bring him back that way. If he's not, bring his body and whatever dropped weaponry you find. I'll fly above, close to the cavern ceiling, and keep watch. If they come down on you, turn tail and fly like the wind. Perhaps I can surprise them."

As it turned out, they retrieved the corpse without incident. Perhaps, having lost two riders, the remaining one flew back to wherever they came from to report.

He was a squatty sort of man, tanned and dark-haired, very different from the thin, darker, well-formed men of Anaea. His beard was almost as full as a dwarf's, and he had several layers of clothing on to protect him from the cold.

Rayg was most interested in the crossbow quarrels he found in a leather case strapped on the man's thigh. They were wooden, with nickel-silver tips, and two thin glass tubes to either side just behind the arrowhead containing a clear liquid.

"I'm guessing that's poison," Rayg said.

He carefully emptied the glass tubes on the ground, rinsed out the glass, then put them back in the sides of the quarrel. He wrapped his hand in a bit of leather and drove the quarrel into the dirt.

"Fascinating," he said, extracting the point.

"Yes?"

"When the head strikes it slides down the shaft, just the width of my thumb. But it's enough to shatter the glass, putting both vials into the wound."

The Copper thought back to the fight over Anaea. "I saw Fe-Lissarath pass over one. He died within a few seconds. I thought an arrow found one of his hearts, but it could have been one of these."

"A few seconds, you say? That's a deadly toxin, to bring down a dragon so fast."

"Perhaps it found a heart after all."

"You should take that into consideration when fighting these dragon-riders. The quarrels are light; I suppose every bit of weight counts when you're loading a dragon. Unless they were fired from a very close range, they probably wouldn't go through scale without a lucky shot."

" 'Close' and 'probably' are not exact enough that I wish to bet my life on it. I'm exhausted. I need a meal. Oh, and find one of my bats. I'll give him a nip of blood if it would hurry him down the tunnel in search of the Drakwatch."

The Copper sent messenger bats in both directions on the western road looking for Drakwatch patrols, bearing a request to hurry to Anaea and assist the Upholder's mate and the Firemaid at the cave mouth.

Upholder's mate. His mate. Sickly little Halaflora. So much depended on a cripple and a weakling. Whatever Spirit had put into dragons' nature the desire to contest every mouthful, with the weakest dying off, must be having a good, ethereal laugh at that.

Rayg found one other item on the dragon-rider and brought it to him before one of the Firemaids ate it. It was an odd little pendant on a thin chain, a tiny figure of a man standing with his arms and legs outstretched within a circle.

"I wonder what that could mean?"

"Man's first destiny," Rayg said.

"You know that symbol? Where does it come from?"

"The barbarians in the far north. I'm . . . familiar with them. They've got a few prophets and shamans who say life is like a great game between gods of each of the races, and we're all just pieces dropped into the world and taken up again when we fall to an opponent's piece."

"That's a grim way to think about life."

"The ones who wear this believe man is destined to rule the earth—worlds, Upper and Lower, as dragons think of it. Man will eventually remove all the blighters, the elves, the dwarves—"

"Dragons too?"

"They don't speak of it much, but I believe it's implicit in their philosophy."

"You get better with the dragon tongue every day, Rayg. You're an intelligent fellow. I'm glad you aren't wearing one of those."

"I was once," he said. "Now I'm just here to finish a bridge."

After getting landmarks from the Firemaid, the Copper scouted the mouth of the cavern as the sun set the next day. He took a short, circular flight. There was no sign of his pursuers—or pursuer, rather. It was hard to think of dragons as little more than brute service animals; he still couldn't quite get his mind around the idea.

Satisfied, he hurried west at the best speed he could manage. Luckily the wind here blew hard out of the northeast, a direction he vaguely knew to hold the Inland Ocean.

He managed to take down the smelliest, hairiest herbivore on four legs he'd ever encountered and, using the tiny gob of flame that was, as ever, all he could ignite, set fire to some brush to cook its skin off. Even the smoky scent didn't help the taste.

He saw the plateau a long way off, arriving in the late afternoon. It was an unusual sort of mountain range; all the peaks were so close to one another in height that from a distance they appeared identical. Only once you came closer did you see the variety in formations.

The plateau over the Lavadome was smaller, lower, and rounder than that of Anaea. Instead of being lush and green, it steamed and smoked.

He found one of the shafts the *griffaran* used and circled down toward it.

Two *griffaran* flapped up to challenge him, but recognized him, he supposed, by his bad limb.

"Good wind, egg saver!" one said, floating beside him effortlessly. The mixture of lizard and bird looked a little less strange aloft, thanks to its colorful wings.

"I'm on urgent business. I must use one of your shafts, and I can't be delayed. One of you, fly ahead and tell the Tyr I must see him as soon as I land."

"Follow, then."

The *griffaran* had to wait several times for him to catch up. He made the rather terrifying drop through the shaft—plummeting with wings folded into a shadowy gap was a bit of exhilaration he could do without—but it wasn't a far fall, and his eyes adjusted instantly to the tall cavern of the water ring.

He paused for water and to catch his breath, then went aloft again for the last, mercifully short leg to the Imperial Resort.

He made for the top of Black Rock and the *griffaran* swooped in front of him.

"*Yark!* No. No landings on Gardens. Through kitchens now fastest."

Next, he supposed, SiDrakkon would forbid flying in the Lavadome, or bathing in the river. The orange streams of lava, once so bright and beautiful against the otherworldly crystalline surface of the dome, seemed to have picked up on SiDrakkon's dour moods and now looked gloomy to him. Or maybe his eyes hadn't fully converted over to tunnel-sight yet.

He made for the red glow and smoke of the kitchens, and landed next to a pile of dead swine.

Thralls scattered.

He hurried past boiling vats and frying platters, smelling the sweat of the nearly naked kitchen workers. He knew the rest of the way to the Tyr's door.

NoSohoth, meeting him on the stairs, started babbling about Skotl and Wyrr, of course. "There's been a duel on almost every hill. The mating between SuUpshauant and Deresa—broke, now, and the Skotl blame the Wyrr, and the Wyrr blame the Skotl side. Hardly a moon goes by where we don't lose a dragon. Now there's a Wyrr Drakwatch and a Skotl, and they spend their whole time brawling with each other. CuTarin hill and the north side have threatened to burn each other's herds—"

"This is war news, man."

"War? The empire is cracking. After cracks, pieces crumble off. Then collapse. If the Kayai Uphold declares independence—"

"Flames burn in Anaea as we speak."

305

"Then you must speak to the Tyr. Except he's in his Gardens. He won't emerge until this evening, when the light fails."

"I know my way to the Gardens."

Though he knew the way, a wide-bodied Skotl, fully twice his weight, blocked the tunnel up to the courtyard and the gardens.

"Tyr level," the small mountain of scale grunted.

"Please, Skotl, let him pass," NoSohoth said. "It's war news."

"I have my order," the Skotl said.

Not smart enough to remember more than one, NoSohoth mind-spoke to him. The Copper thought it a rare intimacy.

"I'm mated to the sister of his mate. He can see me."

The Skotl's eyes narrowed as he tried to work out the family dynamics.

"You see Imfamnia, then," the Skotl said.

"Oh, very well."

NoSohoth led him, the Copper nudging him along whenever he tried to stop and talk politics. They found Imfamnia in Tighlia's old quarters. She'd mounted colored quartz and sheer fabrics in her balconies and galleries, bathing the room in a hideous watery color trying to be green.

"Tighlia lives with the Anklenes now," NoSohoth said. "She fell into a rage and started burning the silks and smashing Imfamnia's glasswork with her tail."

They found Imfamnia with SiMevolant. A thrall was painting her *griff*, and another slave was mixing colors for the one with the brush.

"No, dull as passwater," SiMevolant said as she lowered her *griff* and turned her head this way and that. "Would you consider having gemstones embedded?"

"But then my *griff* wouldn't close up properly."

"That may become the new fashion, then. Remember, as queen of the Lavadome you set the style."

Tyr's mate was always title enough for Tighlia, NoSohoth thought.

"Mate-sister," the Copper said, breaking in on the decorating. "I must see the Tyr at once."

"NoSohoth, I thought there were orders about guests without invitations," SiMevolant said.

The Copper came forward, the quartz-filtered light making the whole interview dreamlike. "Anaea has been attacked. By men flying on dragons."

"Ewwww. That must look a fright," SiMevolant said. "Skin tones."

Mother had warned him that he would have to overcome. But there were few foes as implacable as stupidity.

"Quiet, love," Imfamnia said. "You'll find my mate in his Gardens." She walked over to curtains dividing this chamber from another, opened them, and then stuck her head outside and said a few words.

"Not you, NoSohoth," she said as the Copper moved toward the gardens. "Family only."

The Copper passed out under two silver-clawed *griffaran* perched high to keep watch over the Tyr's privacy. He saw SiDrakkon in one of the warm pools.

One of his human females washed him behind the crest by sitting astride him, a blanket-sized piece of soft leather polishing Tyr SiDrakkon's scale, grinding her body back and forth. The rest of his human females bathed, or lounged, or ate, or anointed one another with oils taken from silver vials.

A muscular blighter brought forward a huge, polished turtleshell of wine. He grunted as he set it down.

"Idiot!" SiDrakkon roared. He knocked the vessel over. "Silver! I won't drink out of anything that isn't silver."

The blighter scurried away in the direction of the banquet entrance.

"The purity of silver! I require purity!"

The Copper approached and bowed. A few of the women covered themselves and cleared the way between the dragons.

SiDrakkon glared at him. "Everything around me is tainted and corrupt!"

The Copper didn't know whether it would be more dangerous to agree or disagree. One of the *griffaran* fluffed up his feathers and shifted his stance, leaning forward a little.

"Why am I being disturbed, RuGaard?"

"Bad news from Anaea. We've been attacked. Dragons, hagridden by men. I've seen it with my own eyes. They control them somehow."

Blighters extracted big river stones from his bath and disappeared as three more emerged and dropped the oven-hot stones in. "You can stop that now," SiDrakkon said to the blighters. "I'm climbing out."

He lowered his head so the females could dry his ears and *griff*. "I've heard these odd fables before, RuGaard. Men riding dragons come and take away young male dragons and insert logs into their—"

"No, they came with flame. They dueled and killed the FeLissaraths."

"My Upholder? Murdered?"

"They fell in battle. The riders use poisoned quarrels fired from crossbows."

"War, eh?" He climbed out of the steaming pool, and water cascaded off his scales into the tiles. It ran in channels down toward the lower Gardens. "War may shake the Lavadome out of the madness that seems to have crept in. I'll call for dragons and appoint a grand commander for the Drakwatch. Revive the title of aerial host commander. Perhaps I'll assume the responsibilities myself."

Whatever his faults, SiDrakkon could at least act decisively when it came to war.

"Will you come yourself, Tyr?" the Copper asked.

"No. Anaea may be a feint. The *griffaran* have reported strange dragons above the Lavadome, but they always flee north at sunrise. If I wanted to attack the Lavadome, I'd strike the most distant Uphold too, and draw our forces as far from the main blow as possible."

He shifted a little to let the women dry his underside, but he did it mechanically, grinding his teeth as he thought.

"You'll be host commander, RuGaard. You've seen me at war and know what to do. Strike fast and strike hard, and keep striking until the war is over."

"I've left my mate back in Anaea. I must return at once."

"Of course. You can take my personal flying guard with you; the Skotl bodyguard can remain. AuBalagrave is in charge of the flying guard. You remember him from the Drakwatch. I believe you served together. That'll give you an immediate force."

"Thank you, Tyr."

"Oh. I heard about this bat messenger service of yours. Let's talk again when this is over. I've an idea that we could expand it."

"They don't do it for love of us, sir, but the taste of our blood."

"Well, there are a few fat dragons here that could do with a little bleeding. Get back to your mate, Upholder, and keep me informed. Try to find out more about this enemy."

Chapter 26

He rested for a few hours in a spare nook Imfamnia offered him. With the numbers of the Imperial line dropping, and the increased space closing off much of the top level of the Imperial Resort, there were rooms and cushions to spare.

She even offered him a bowlful of gold. "For family only," she said, as though the gold could tell the difference. "Have as much as you like; my mate eats only silver these days."

He ate but a few coins, not wanting to have to fly with a chest's worth of heavy metals in his belly.

After checking with SiDrakkon one last time, to see if any additional orders or circumstances arose—"I'll try to send as many as thirty dragons," Tyr SiDrakkon promised—he departed with AuBalagrave and the other two dragons.

They were good fliers, lean and wide-winged, and he held them back the whole way. He wondered how many dragons would really be sent. Using NiVom's old formula, perhaps six or seven might make it all the way to the Uphold.

They approached the plateau at night. The Copper, his hearts pounding, crossed the mountain line and looked first to the Upholder's palace temple.

It looked intact.

"Have two dragons fly high. Just in case," he called to AuBalagrave using mind-speech. "You follow."

The words must not have come through clearly, because AuBalagrave took another dragon and gained altitude. Well, mind-speech wasn't a perfect form of communication among dragons who hadn't been long together.

If anything, the plateau was darker than usual at night. The hearth fires sometimes glowing out of windows didn't give the city its usual ghostly glow. But there would be time to survey the damage in daylight.

The palace temple had been scorched about the roof, and one of the stone globes had been knocked off the roofing. Another was missing entirely, and judging from the cracks in the long set of stairs it had been sent bouncing down to the fields and woods beneath.

"Halaflora! Nilrasha!" he called as he landed, ready to tear into any dragon but his mate or guardian Firemaid.

Fourfang waved from behind a stone.

"All sleep be—"

"We're in the lower chambers, as you asked, my love," Halaflora called, surprisingly loudly for her small frame.

He looked at his escort. "Tell AuBalagrave that I'd like one dragon to stay aloft, keeping watch. The others may rest, and I'll send food if there's any to be had. Don't go down into the valley to scavenge; the humans there are frightened enough."

The Copper descended to the mouth of the Lower World. Two members of the Drakwatch stood guard at the tunnel, now partly blocked with piled stone and timbers. Nilrasha slept atop the blockage, but she winked at him with an eye and fluttered a *griff*.

"Asu-ra, that kern king, was up here," Halaflora said. "He cried. He wanted to know why the dragons had loosed such fury on them."

"You told him it wasn't our doing, I hope."

"I said there are good and evil dragons, just like there are good and evil weather gods. I think he understood."

"That's a better reply than I could have produced, with half the valley floor aflame."

"They were after gold. They didn't even steal any women or children, which I thought warriors always did."

"What happened here?"

"They knocked down some statues and set fire to a few curtains. I believe they wanted to show their contempt for us more than to try to kill us. They never so much as ventured inside, though the upper level is entirely open, as you know."

"Don't forget the mess on the steps," Nilrasha croaked.

"What happened on the steps?"

"They used it as a toilet pit," Halaflora said. "Just a little water and scrubbing. Hardly worth mentioning."

"Are you well, dear?" he asked his mate.

"Better than ever, my lord. You know, I think all this stimulation agrees with me. I almost feel as though I could fly, if I found a high enough ledge and caught a good updraft."

"Let's put the Uphold back in order before dropping you off any cliffs, shall we?" he said.

"How were things with Tyr SiDrakkon?"

"War always seems to put him in better spirits. He sent three dragons with me and promised more, and a grand commander of the Drakwatch."

"Grand commander? I didn't know there were as many in the Drakwatch as that anymore. So few of the drakes from the better families volunteer. You must tell me all the news of my sisters and brother."

"Let's save politics and family news until I've eaten."

"I've been saving a fat calf the kern king offered just for you. Would you care for the liver, Nilrasha?"

The Firemaid yawned. "Very kind of you, lady. Yes, I could do with some dinner."

"Fourfang," the Copper said, "see about feeding the dragons who came with me. Where's Rhea? I'm caked with grit."

"Wonderful news, my lord. She and that clever man of yours are mated! She's going to issue, or whatever they call it!"

"Whelp?" Nilrasha asked.

"I think it's give birth," the Copper said. "All the more reason for a dinner. We should send her some stewed brains and the tongue. I've heard that's good for brooding."

"Oh, I'm saving those for me, my love."

"You don't think—"

"We may have hatchlings. Isn't it wonderful?"

"That could be dangerous for you. Your mother told me—"

"Oh, forget my mother. She's always looking at the dark side of things. I'll wager she's back in the Lavadome now, foretelling a loss in the war against these riders and lamenting the weaknesses of dragons these days. Our cause is just, so we are sure to triumph, are we not, my lord?"

Perhaps that is why Tighlia mated us, the Copper thought. *We both have what she called the simpleton's faith.*

Dinner passed in a more jovial mood than the Copper would have expected with destruction all around. Thanks to the guard overhead and outside, they ventured to the upper level and ate upon the feasting floor. Nilrasha made jokes, and Halaflora ate with unusual enthusiasm.

Or perhaps her expectations were forcing her appetite.

"A *griffaran* comes!" the watchdragon aloft outside bellowed. "He makes the signal-wing of bearing important news for the Upholder, from the Tyr himself."

"A message? But you just got here," Halaflora said. "Whatever could it mean?"

"I'd better see to that," the Copper said, rising and taking the exit that would bring him to the stairs.

The *griffaran* alighted on one of the globes-atop-squares flanking the long staircase down the mountainside.

"*Yark!* Upholder RuGaard?"

"Yes," the Copper said. Fourfang trotted up with a torch.

"Written message. Sent yesterday." The bird detached a tube from some sort of hook in its tail feathers and passed it to him.

"You must have flown straight here without a break. Have you eaten? Fourfang, go down to the pool and see if there are any fish there."

"Read message first," the *griffaran* said. "Then duty done."

The tube was one of NoSohoth's message tubes, certainly. He flicked off the sealing wax with a claw-tip and extracted the paper inside.

TYR DEAD. PEACE DECREED. TYR SIMEVOLANT RULES.
RETURN AT ONCE.

The Copper blinked, unable to believe his eyes. Each pair of words was harder to believe than the last.

Bwaaaaaaak!

He started. That was a blighter alarm horn!

It blew again, sounding from the dining chamber. His hearts froze for a second; then he spread open his wings and flew up to the balcony on the upper level. He crashed through the tattered, burned remains of the evening curtains and saw Halaflora, stretched out and twitching on the floor.

Blood ran from a corner of her mouth. A white-faced Rhea stood in the corner, gasping for air, the horn hanging loose in her hand. Over his mate Nilrasha stood, the claws of one *sii* bloody, scratched about her eyes.

"Away from her!" he roared, feeling his fire bladder well. He tripped on his bad *sii* and sprawled next to his mate, but he didn't care. He rolled her undersize head toward him, but Halaflora's eyes were white and sightless.

"She's dead, my lord," Nilrasha said, breathing hard. "There's nothing you can do for her."

The Copper shook his mate, struck her face, turned her upside down, and shook her until scales fell off and skittered across the spotless feasting floor. Finally he dropped her limp corpse.

"What did you do?" he asked Nilrasha.

"Do?" she choked.

"Shwok'd?"

"Am I not speaking clearly enough, you lisping lizard? Yes, she tore off a big piece of thigh—I think it had a bone in it—and lifted her head and gobbled it right down, smiling and happy as can be. It stuck. I tried to get at it with my *sii*, but I couldn't reach it without tearing her head off."

"How did you get wounded?"

"She panicked. She was flailing this way and that instead of letting me help her, and she scratched me."

"It's not like her to take such a big—"

"She's been delirious these last few days. She thought she was brooding, stupid thing."

"Get out of here!"

"But, Ru—I'm sorry about the lisping thing. You do it when you get excited. I shouldn't have said anything."

"Just go."

AuBalagrave and the other dragons arrived, looking for enemies, a fight, anything—but they just found the Upholder, lying against his mate. Nilrasha slipped out.

"Leave me alone!" the Copper said. "I'm staying with her until she cools! All of you, get out. No, not you, Rhea. Clear away this mess."

The dragons departed, and Rhea bent to pick up the spilled platter of spitted calf.

"Rhea. Please speak to me. For once in your life, don't be afraid and speak. Did you see this? What happened here?"

The pale girl—no, woman; she had a swelling at her midsection and the feeding sacs had enlarged—looked at him with terrified eyes. Then she fainted.

He buried Halaflora on the mountainside with a good view of the palace, the vale, and their sleeping chamber. Then he went to see Nilrasha and found her idling in her bathing pool.

"If I find that you had a *sii* in this, I'll kill you," the Copper said.

"You're upset, your honor. I know what you think. Put it out of your mind. She choked. It was a terrible accident."

"You're such a careful huntress."

"Wouldn't I have killed her long ago? I had opportunities every other day. I could have done it easily when we where hiding together, listening to those cursed dragons smashing the upper level. A quick pounce and—*snap!* She was so slight, you could practically poke a claw through her. What did the *griffaran* messenger want?"

The Copper couldn't decide whether she was being callous or just her usual practical self. She was a born warrior who left the dead behind and kept her regrets, if any, private. But maybe her instincts were such that when she had an enemy, she'd pounce. Grabbing a loin and shoving it down a rival's throat would be too roundabout a way of doing it. And if she wanted an accidental death, she would have just tossed Halaflora down that endless flight of steep steps as they took in the view, and then claimed she slipped.

"We have a new Tyr. SiMevolant. I'm to return to the Lavadome. I suspect his first edict will be that everyone paint themselves blue or add stripes."

"Si-SiMevolant? What happened to SiDrakkon?"

"He's dead. When I saw him last, he looked healthy enough."

"Is SiMevolant smart enough to execute an assassination?"

Would a killer be so ready to use that word? the Copper thought. His mind was turning quick enough circles, and he tried to put Halaflora out of his mind. "He may have just been pretending to be a fool so no one would suspect him. How did the title of Tyr fall on those golden haunches, I wonder?"

"Who will you leave in command here?"

"According to the message, there's to be no war. Which sounds like SiMevolant. He's just stupid enough to believe that it takes two to make a war."

"Challenge him if you get the chance," Nilrasha said. "You can defeat him. He's big and thick-scaled, but he doesn't know the first thing about fighting."

"I've never had much luck with duels. I always seem to come off the worse," the Copper said.

"Still angry with me?" she asked.

"Only if you killed my mate."

"Do you forget what you said? We can't be mated while she lives. She no longer lives. After a decent mourning period we can have our happiness. She would have died over your eggs. I can give you many."

The Copper snorted. "This is not the time for that kind of talk."

"I just . . . I just want to know that you don't hate me. What must I do to make you believe I tried to save her? Stuff a horse down my throat and choke myself?"

"You're too tough to choke on a horse. I must sleep. I've got a long flight tomorrow."

"I wonder what SiMevolant has planned for you?"

"Tyr SiMevolant," the Copper corrected.

"Not for long, I think. He won't last his name-year." She displayed her teeth and rattled her *griff*.

He left AuBalagrave at the Uphold, with instructions to defend the temple and inform the kern kings that he was in mourning over the death of his mate and would perform no functions, ceremonial or otherwise, until further notice.

Then he took to the sky. Thoughts of Halaflora took all the joy out of flying; now it was just a dull, exhausting routine. He broke his journey at the Tooth Cavern bridge to speak to Rayg and the Firemaidens and Firemaid.

"Supposedly there'll be no war," the Copper said. "But I want you watchful here nonetheless. I'm sure these hag-ridden dragons know of the existence of this bridge and this portal into the Lower World. They may use it to reach the Lavadome."

The dragons nodded their agreement. Then the Copper pulled Rayg aside, to the little bench where he kept his plans and designs.

"I understand you're to be congratulated," the Copper said.

"For what? Construction on the bridge has stopped ever since that fight in the cavern."

"Rhea. You're mated, I hear."

Rayg looked across at him, sucking on his fleshy cheeks. "I didn't know you paid attention to that kind of thing."

"I do. How would you like Rhea freed with you?"

"Nothing more, your honor. You would do that?"

"I just need you to turn your brain to one final project."

His shoulders dropped. "What's that?"

"You worked for the dwarves, I understand?"

"Yes, well, it was sort of an apprenticeship."

"They understand armor, I'm told. I want you to design some kind of armoring for the underside of a dragon. Enough to keep out one of those poisoned crossbow quarrels. It's got to be light, though. No layers of chain mail."

"It would help if I had one of their crossbows for a test firing."

"A few may have been lost thanks to those riders the Fe-Lissaraths downed. I'll have Nilrasha hunt for them." He reminded himself to send a messenger bat as soon as he finished with Rayg.

"Leather would be best, then," Rayg said, eyes rolling in thought. "Perhaps if it were stiffened and reinforced with wire. Or wood flanges."

"One more request. It's got to look like a regular dragon's underskin, at least from a distance."

As there was no emergency, the Copper returned to the Lavadome by the more tiresome—and cramped—south passage. The entrance was well hidden by a thick, multicanopied forest, and he'd never seen it from the air, only from the ground in his orientation hikes in the Drakwatch. So he had to cast around a little before he found the right waterfall that led to it.

He found Angalia and another maid guarding the door.

"I come at Tyr SiMevolant's request, Angalia, but I cry joy at seeing you again," he said, figures of speech being just that. "How do you like your change of scenery?"

"Warmer, your honor, but still terrible. The air is so heavy and moist. I feel it creeping into my lungs. I'll be dead of a fever in a year; mark my words."

"It would take a tall tablet to mark all your words, Angalia," her companion observed.

He had no difficulty learning about the death of SiDrakkon on the way to Black Rock. It was all anyone talked of, from the youngest drake to the oldest dragon-dame playing with some widower's hatchlings. He'd been found alone in his garden bath, dead of some sort of seizure.

"Alone?" the Copper asked.

He'd named SiMevolant as his heir some time ago, it seemed, though the news had escaped the Copper in his far-off Uphold. Everyone took it to be a kind of joke.

It was NoSohoth who explained it to him, as he ran himself ragged arranging for an audience SiMevolant had commanded for his line and the principal dragons of the six hills.

"I believe he thought of it as a sort of safeguard against assassination," NoSohoth said. "With the Lavadome the way it is, a fo—a personality like SiMevolant atop Black Rock would guarantee chaos and destruction. He figured we'd all be invoking the spirits every dawn and dusk, praying for his health."

"I'm told he was found in his bath, alone."

"Yes, by his mate and SiMevolant."

"Alone. In the garden bath. How likely is that?"

"If SiMevolant said it happened, that's how it happened."

"I'll challenge him on that."

NoSohoth placed a *sii* on his. "Don't. He's been unusually wise about things since he rose to the rank of Tyr. Let's wait and see. Things may work out. I expect he's going to announce a mating to Imfamnia at this audience."

"So soon?"

"These last years have been rather a whirlwind, haven't they? No one's had a chance to right their wings and glide for a bit."

"I'm worried about those hag-ridden dragons returning."

"They'll be handled. With diplomacy."

"I had a mouthful of their diplomacy over Anaea. It tastes like death and ash."

"I've no more time. There're details for a grand banquet to be arranged; the gardens are to be opened up again to the dragons of the Imperial Resort. . . ."

He hurried off down the tunnel, rounding up thralls to do his bidding.

———

The commanded audience was held just before a scheduled banquet of rumored magnificence, which showed some craftiness on SiMevolant's part. He'd speak to them in brief, and then dismiss them to go gorge themselves at length. No one could accuse the golden dragon of not knowing the most pleasant way to go about business.

Imfamnia, painted all in black—except for the sparkling jewels embedded into her *griff*—watched the dragons assemble from her bare widow's perch.

The Copper noticed that there were no *griffaran* above, and wondered. Either SiMevolant was extraordinarily brave or exceedingly foolish; both Tyrs he had known had found the implicit threat of a *griffaran* bodyguard useful.

The wooden arches above seemed cold and empty without their colorful feathers.

The audience chamber didn't look particularily full; perhaps some in the higher-ranking families feared reprisals. To fill the room NoSohoth began to shove in dragons of lesser lines. When a solid mass of dragonflesh stood before the Tyr's shelf, Tighlia foremost and eyes locked hatefully on her mate-sister, Imfamnia nodded.

"They're all assembled now, Tyr SiMevolant," Imfamnia called toward the curtains.

The curtains parted, drawn by thralls as though through sorcery, and SiMevolant emerged, moving forward on a sort of traveling perch that rolled both smoothly and almost silently, its wheels obscured by heavy fabrics, draped and corded. He had polished his scale to a bright sheen and purpled his eyelids and whited his claws, but other than that he looked like a fine, healthy, gold dragon. The Copper couldn't say what he was expecting—peacock feathers and snakeskins perhaps—but if anything, this mate-brother looked . . . kingly.

SiMevolant bowed, let his head rove across the audience, and let out with the loudest *prrum* the Copper had ever heard.

"I want to begin anew," SiMevolant said. "I've been distressed beyond words these last few years. Skotl set against Wyrr set against Anklene. Everyone may keep their current positions, but in the future I'm going to do my best to fill ranks based on merit, with the assistance of wise counsel.

"And I hate all this dueling. Is that really a way for dragons to settle differences? Can't we learn a new way that doesn't involve shedding blood? I don't have a solution, but I welcome ideas. I beg the assistance of wise counsel."

"Furthermore, I hate all this skulking around undergound. Dragons are the most glorious of all the Spirits' creations. It's time we started acting it instead of taking such pains to hide our existence."

"Bloody fool!" Ibidio hissed. The Copper hardly noticed that she'd slipped up next to him, shoving her way through a deputy of Firemaids.

"Also, I've thought it best to dismiss the *griffaran* guard, as you can see."

"Dismissed the *griffaran*?" NeStirrath asked, his tangled horns rising from the crowd. "Our stoutest allies?"

"And biggest appetites," SiMevolant said. "I've spoken to wise counsel, and, measure for measure, they consume twice what a dragon does. It's never been the greatest of friendships; there's almost no social interaction. We guard their nests and they guard our skies. The whole thing's based on some mossy old hatchling story of a *griffaran* egg and a dragon egg washed away in a storm, saved and hatched together by a wise old eagle. We're paying for it all these years later, in less for all of us to eat."

A few dragons raised their heads as though to object, but SiMevolant stared them down, his eyes full of power and certitude. The last time the Copper had seen eyes like that, they were attached to King Gan. It was as though SiMevolant could slay a dragon by thought alone.

"Let's hear how SiDrakkon died," the Copper said, not sure where the voice was coming from.

"Be silent," Ibidio whispered. "This isn't the time."

The surrounding dragons shrank away from the Copper as though he carried a new kind of parasite.

"I don't mind the question," SiMevolant said. "Not one little bit. He had some sort of seizure in his bath. His mate found him first; I arrived soon after. No one could say what caused it, or how long it took, but he did have a ghastly expression on his face. Accidents do happen, RuGaard. By the way, how is my dear sister? But back to our late, beloved Tyr. Perhaps it was an assassination; he had enemies enough, and there were no witnesses. Which reminds me—you'll enjoy the plumpest, most succulent, tastiest manflesh you've had in years at tonight's banquet."

"Look at you all! Lions led by a frothing hyena!" Tighlia said, stepping forward and rounding on the audience.

"Now, Granddam," SiMevolant said. "I thought I sent you some wine to keep you quiet. Why don't you go home and drink it?"

She ignored him, spitting a gob of flame at the audience. "The civil war killed off the good dragons. What's left? Brazen cowards, vain philosophers, mating deviants, and back-scratching scalemates adding to one another's hoards. It's the litter and detritus collecting in the shadows and corners that bred this, this . . . *farce*. This fool will get you all killed. Maybe it's for the best. We've earned our extinction."

"She's like one of those windup things the dwarves make. Same speech every time her tail is twisted," SiMevolant said quietly to Imfamnia, who giggled.

"Are you done, Tighlia?" Imfamnia asked.

"Yes. We all are," she said. She began to stalk out of the room, stumping out her own fire. She stopped and sent a sharp glance at Ibidio, who let out a startled gasp; then she moved on.

The crowd parted for her, bending back like tall grass before a strong breeze.

"Good," SiMevolant said. "I want to introduce some wise counsel who will guarantee our dignity and security for generations to come. Mmmmmm? I present our new ally, recently sent here from the Alliance of the Golden Circle."

A tall hominid in black scale armor stepped from behind the curtains and strode forward so he stood next to SiMevolant. He had gray hair flecked here and there with black, and a slightly darker beard hanging from a scarred face.

The Copper recognized the armor, the weapons, the face.

The Dragonblade stood before the audience.

Chapter 27

Tighlia turned again, knocking over two members of the Drakwatch.

"How dare you! How *dare you*!" Every scale stood straight up on her skin, her wings half-opened as they shook with fury; her *griff* rattled, and slime poured out each side of her mouth.

"On the shelf where my mate stood," she continued, hardly able to get the words out. "You bring a human arrayed for war? A spear and a drawn sword, atop the Black Rock? No man may dare stand on such hallowed stone!"

"Not any human, Tighlia," the Copper said. "He kills dragons for a living."

The Dragonblade tipped his spear forward just a little. Some of the audience squeezed out of the audience room; others shoved their way forward.

"I expected to be challenged," the Dragonblade said. "That it comes from an aged female surprises me."

"She's under the impression she's still a personage of consequence," SiMevolant said.

"Are you going to come down, man, or will I have to soil my mate's memory by spilling your blood where he used to stand?"

"I've no wish to kill. I made my peace with dragons years ago. But a wise man convinced me your kind can be saved, if properly led and channeled. I don't want to begin my governorship here with blood."

"*Governorship!*" Tighlia roared, shaking the timbers all the way to the roof, and jumped.

She jumped well for a dragon her size, and against an ordinary man, even a warrior, she would have turned him into pulp and black blood against the obsidian stone of the Rock.

The Dragonblade set his spear and she impaled herself upon it. He rolled out from under her, on his feet with sword out as easily as a falling cat righted itself. The sword flashed up once, and liquid fire spilled across the Tyr's shelf, a second time down and the Copper saw the gruesome white of the bones of her spine.

Tighlia collapsed, all of her going limp at once—save for her tail and twitching *saa*, which jerked and shuddered as though trying to fight on.

SiMevolant looked down at her. "What's that, Granddam? . . . Well, first, I don't believe in curses; second . . . Oh, dear, you're gone. I must learn to make my points more quickly."

"I wish she had stayed at home and enjoyed her wine," Imfamnia said.

Liquid fire ran off the Tyr's shelf. To the Copper, the events on the Tyr's shelf seemed a horizon distant, yet etched in vivid detail. His head whirled.

"Sand. At once—now," Imfamnia called, lifting a curtain out of the way with her tail to keep it from catching fire.

"Are there any more challenges?" the Dragonblade asked. A drake tried to step forward, but NeStirrath pressed his heavy *sii* on the youth's tail.

The Dragonblade retrieved a decorative, jewel-encrusted goblet from the Tyr's display of trophies and knelt beside Tighlia. He filled his cup with the blood leaking out of her neck and drank, smacking his lips afterward.

"Our future is in alliances, not war," SiMevolant said to the shocked assembly. "United with these men, no power in the two worlds may threaten us. Let all who doubt this truth remember the fate of Tighlia. Now begins a golden era, begun by a golden dragon. Light the beacons, NoSohoth."

"Hurrah!" shouted the Dragonblade. "The union forever!"

Ibidio slipped up next to the Copper. "I must speak to you," she whispered, then switched to mind-speech. *If you still live tomorrow, go to the hill of the Anklenes. Once inside, ask for the senior doorwarden. Tell him this: "Immortal Memory."*

The Copper was still too shocked to do anything but nod. The swirl of memories, of fears, of regrets, of pain brought by the Dragonblade's slaying of Tighlia, had left him clouded.

"*Immortal Memory,*" he thought back to her. *If I still live?*

In the lore of the Lavadome, the hours were afterward known as the Night of the Desperate Deaths.

To those who knew only vaguely of events within the Imperial Resort, the first sign of them was when two beacons were lit atop the Rock, burning a bright blue as though by magic—the Copper knew very well it was dwarvish chemicals, but what sort of mix the humans who lit the beacons used, he never could remember, despite all the pleadings and urgings of the Anklenes.

And with that, hag-ridden dragons flew into the Lavadome in two long lines.

Perhaps a score of dragons, knowing the war gossip that had been spreading ever since the Copper's arrival with the news of Anaea, realized what the invasion portended and took to the air to meet it.

No dragon who fought that night lived.

Black Rock was emptied of all dragons save for the Imperial line, who remained in the Imperial Resort in a nebulous role between leaders and hostages. The allies occupied the best caves and the best galleries, save for the top level and the Gardens, where SiMevolant, his widowed-and-mated Imfamnia, and the governor-general remained.

And the ubiquitous NoSohoth.

Atop the rock, as the hag-ridden dragons performed military evolutions, showing their skill, the most dispirited banquet in Lavadome history was held. The food—exquisite and tender. The wine—unparalleled by anything that had come before, thanks to exotic captured vintages brought in by the *Andam*, the Men of the Golden Circle.

It was a brave young drake who took the first bite. The rest of the company watched anxiously for signs of poisoning as they nibbled on bits of greenstuff, onions, and ores.

The Copper, never a fan of banquets and unable to enjoy the flesh of so many limbs and sides that looked like Rhea, sat in the garden and tried to think.

One thing the display of force and flying skill did offer him: a chance to count their numbers. Three-score dragons and riders, and another half-score of dragons on lines attached to the others, bearing baggage or supplies.

A few wings over forty, using the ten-count numbering system of the dwarves Rayg had been teaching him.

He did his best to overhear some of the conversation between SiMevolant and the Dragonblade. Evidently some kind of long-planned war had begun. They flew from a fastness in the north, and had just seized a sort of floating city on the Inland Ocean. Holding the Lavadome would give them a third hold for rest and organization in the south.

The Dragonblade filled SiMevolant's ears with praise about his foresight as a dragon and the heights his leadership would allow the Drakines to reach.

The Copper almost wanted to warn SiMevolant of the fine words that marched in front of betrayals, but when one gathered such snakes to one's bosom, one had to learn about being bitten.

He slunk off into the greenery and became violently sick.

The next day he did as Ibidio requested and went to the Anklene hill. He asked for the head doorwarden and gave him the signal phrase. The warden took him down a short ramp and stuck an odd metal spike into a crevice under a cast of a blighter's face, and the wall clicked.

He showed the Copper where to push, and soon he found himself in an underground chamber designed for dragon-sized creatures, with low ledges around the walls, fine sand on the floors, and a water cistern fed by a drip in the roof. There was also a tiled sanitary room with a gutter.

Rethothanna was already there, waiting with Ibidio.

"I don't understand," the Copper said. "Is this a conspiracy? If we packed this room with dragons atop one another, there wouldn't be enough to fight the hag-riddens."

"Well said, RuGaard," Ibidio said. "That's just what they are."

Rethothanna drew a claw across the sand, making a furrow. "This group was started . . . Perhaps you should tell him, Ibidio."

"After the death of my mate," Ibidio said sternly, "I suspected an assassination. He came back from the wars injured, yes, but he was a strong dragon who always recovered quickly, from even greater injuries than those I saw that last time. Then his wounds suddenly quit healing, became infected, and he died. Even the Anklenes said they'd seen nothing like it."

"No more than seven dragons ever belonged to this group," Rethothanna said. "One from each hill, and Ibidio from the Imperial Resort. We had Skotl, Wyrr, and Anklene members. All with one thing in common: love of my mate."

"And now you have an outcast of no particular line," the Copper said. "Even my name was once another's."

Others trickled in, at what seemed like long intervals. Finally NeStirrath arrived.

"Why, RuGaard too! You never seemed the conspirator type," NeStirrath said.

"We have two new members tonight," Ibidio said, with seven other dragons sitting around the edges of the room. "And we mourn the loss of UlBannesh in the fighting yesterday. A brave dragon. He will be missed."

"It's dangerous meeting so soon after yesterday," a Skotl dame said. "I'm sure I'm being watched."

"I will be quick. I have important news. Before she died yesterday, Tighlia and I exchanged our first mind-speech in . . . well, since my mate died. Yes, we used to argue or joke with our minds frequently, for our mates were kin and closer than usual for a dragon and his clutchwinner grown, but after AgGriffopse died—"

"Immortal be his memory," the others said in unison, save for the Copper, who just mumbled to join in, not knowing the group's habits.

Now I'm in league with the memory of a dragon I've never even met.

"But to go on," Ibidio continued. "RuGaard, this will be a shock to you. Tighlia mind-spoke and told me that just before he died, the Tyr—Tyr FeHazathant, my mate's father—said that he was appointing you heir and future Tyr. If you wanted the rank. That's what his words meant, the day he died. 'Ask Ru-Gaard to be Tyr.' I'm so used to looking for plots and hidden signs in everyday talk I couldn't puzzle out its simple meaning. What do you say to that?"

All the dragons were looking at him.

"What does it matter?" he asked.

"What does it matter?" Ibidio laughed. "If we ever gain back the Lavadome, I think you'll find it matters very much."

"If we are to do it, we must strike quickly," NeStirrath said. "Strike before they get organized, and before all here become used to submission to men the way these accursed foreign dragons are."

"I have a small force on the Western Road," the Copper said.

Others listed a few dragons who could be relied on. NeStirrath could bring together his best Drakwatch. But as they counted in their heads they knew it would not be enough. Not against the training and weapons that had been displayed last night.

"The men alone, we might be able to handle," Rethothanna said. "They're not much without their dragons."

"The dragons aren't much better without men," the Copper said. "I've seen them. They're not like us. They can't think for themselves very quickly; they either do what they're trained to do—"

"Perhaps we could convince them to revolt," Ibidio said.

"Fat dragons stuffing themselves with Anaean gold?" a dragon from the Wyrr hill asked. "You might as well ask a horse to fight its rider. I'm not sure they could even grasp the concept."

"Let us meet again tomorrow," Ibidio said. "Early, around the morning meal. I'll try to get in and get a feel for the hag-riddens. What's the matter, RuGaard, not feeling kingly?"

"I'm being hunted by an old nightmare."

The others nodded understanding, but the last thing he wanted was for them to understand.

The Copper walked back to the Imperial Resort—it didn't seem like a resort anymore, just a rather dark and forbidding rock—

with NeStirrath. They talked of unimportant matters, old memories of training with the Drakwatch.

He even returned to his old cave. There hadn't been a member of the Imperial line since him serving in the Drakwatch, and he even caught the faint smell of bats—wait.

A bat still lived, up in a shadowy corner. Something about the ears reminded him of an old acquaintance.

"You wouldn't be related to old Uthaned, would you?"

"I am Uthaned," the bat said. It stretched. "You've grown considerably, m'lord."

"It can't be. Mamedi and Thernadad's nephew? Bats don't live—"

"They do when they've been fed dragonblood. I even talk to Big Ear, Spike Hair, and Wide Nose, as you called them, now and again when they visit."

The Copper was relieved to be so pleasantly distracted. "But why are you still here, Uthaned?"

"The eating is good. These young drakes, they sleep hard after their days' hiking, and they dream better, down a little blood. They make it up quick enough. And that old one with all the horns and the stumps where his wings should be . . . well, he sometimes has a draft of wine to help him sleep, and with a bit of a nip he sleeps sounder still. I like to think I'm doing a service— Ah, soft. None have returned yet tonight. I don't suppose m'lord might spare . . . ?"

The Copper was thinking back to his own days with the bats. Sometimes they'd left him so listless, and in the mornings if he lifted his head high, he went dizzy. . . .

He froze. It was like the idea had a glowing aura around it, like the moon's halo in a mist. He didn't know exactly what the idea would look like once it took shape, but he knew its rough outlines.

"Are there any other bats still about?"

"Another of my cousins still lives near the kitchens, where it's warm. Then there's a son of mine, and his family. Oh, and of course—"

"I need more, many more. Can you go to your relatives and then send them out on the western road? Someone must know where that is."

"Yes, bats go to and fro all the time. That message system."

"Forget it. At least for now. I need every bat you can scrape up, big and small. But they've got to be smart, stealthy, sneaky."

"That's a good deal of flying on my part, m'lord." Uthaned smoothed down his hair and straightened his ears. "A bat setting off on such a flight needs a full belly, and at my age the wing joints pain me."

"Of course," the Copper said. "You can practice on me. I'll show you what to do."

The Copper walked in the Gardens, thinking. Some of the dragon riders, new to the rock, explored it as well, curious about the underground garden with its strange, spiked, low-light plants, or admiring the view of the lava streams against the dome.

He saw a glimmer of gold, and turned.

"Oh, RuGaard. No, don't sulk away. Your Tyr calls."

The Copper turned and approached SiMevolant. He bowed.

"What does my Tyr require of his Upholder?" the Copper asked.

"Just a chat. You looked so queer when the governor-general walked out, I thought you were going to keel over like SiDrakkon. Your face looked just like his. Shocked."

"I thought you arrived only after he died."

"I meant to say after he was dead, of course. Anyway, speaking of deaths, superb job on my sister. The more I think about it, the more brilliant it is."

"What do you mean?"

"The choking. I've heard all about it. I have my own sources and messengers, don't forget."

"It was an accident."

"Of course it was. And if it wasn't, you've got your jade set up to take the blame. You've got witnesses from two different species and three lines of dragons that can attest that you were nowhere near."

"She was my mate. She was your sister. How can you speak like that about her?"

"Because she was my sister. Sickly from the moment she came out of the egg and I sat on her while I dined on my late brother."

"I'm tired. I must beg your—"

SiMevolant flicked around the Copper and blocked his path. "Hold. Since you've shown such an aptitude for this, I've got a list. A tiny list, the briefest of lists; it'll take you no time at all to work your way down. The first is your old teacher, NeStirrath."

"I've got a list for you. Traitor. Cretin. Disgrace to—"

"Oh, please. Look, I've got a very clever weapon that will help you." He reached behind his *griff* and passed the Copper a silver tube, very much like the ones SiDrakkon had kept his oils in. "It's a dwarvish thing with a blade and a spring and a small vial of toxin drawn from—"

The Copper snatched it out of his hand before the tiny point projecting out of the end could be pointed in his direction.

He looked at the device. A little lever, a—what was the word?—trigger, was set into the side.

He pointed it at SiMevolant.

"Ah-ah-ah-ah," the new Tyr warned. "Am I stupid enough to hand you an envenomed weapon, or am I so clever I've given you a harmless point to test your loyalty, hmmmmm? Or, as a sort of a joke, have I given you one that in fact fires backward out of the thin metal on the bottom? And why am I even putting such doubts in your head? It's rather like looking at your image in a wavy pool, so many different possibilities in motion. Which do you think I am? Brilliant or an imbecile?"

"I think you're mad." He sent the tube spinning off the top of the Rock.

"You had your chance," SiMevolant said.

"We both did," the Copper said. "Let's see how we compare in surviving the consequences."

The next day the Immortal Memory group met, though it took twice as long for them to gather, and the Copper outlined his plan. NeStirrath improved on it, and a dragon from the Skotl hill promised to go up the western road and try to hurry things along.

"I've been to the stable caves," Ibidio said. "Off of the old spirit-caller's holes. Yes, I said stables. I can't think of what else to call them, dragons packed so close. They're well guarded, yes, and the men stay near. But there are vast galleries so several can take off at once, if need be."

"I might be able to get the men away for a few hours," the Copper said. "When the time comes."

"The sooner the time comes, the better," Rethothanna said. "A man and a drake crier came through the milkdrinker's hill today, looking for dragons to volunteer to be ridden, promising gold, food, a cave in the Imperial Resort, everything. With food stocks falling the way they are and dragons going without meat, soon half the dragons here will have nothing to look forward to but the saddle and a trough at the end of the day."

Chapter 28

Rethothanna got her wish. Less than a score of days later, the Imperial line and the leaders of the hill selected the hour for the battle. Of course, not everything could be readied on time. The bats were still gathering, and every day the Copper was making a trip to the river to explain to them what to do. But each day's delay increased their risk, for more and more dragons found themselves watched, and the Immortal Memory group could no longer meet except in twos or threes for a few brief words.

The Copper had spies of his own. The bats, out of hunger or curiosity, went so far as to do practice runs, trickling into Black Rock in search of nourishment.

There was a last-moment change in the Immortal Memory's calculations. A half-score more dragons had arrived, carrying several people each on them and more possessions. Some of the mates and babes of the *Andam* had arrived.

So the Copper stood, flanked by Rethothanna and NeStirrath, listening to SiMevolant speak. He was explaining to the high-ranking dragons that soon each of them would have a human "assistant" to help allocate food and cave space, ore rations, and exercise flights. Even grooming standards would be discussed, if there were health-threatening habits that needed to be broken.

The Dragonblade lounged on a golden chair, brought up and fixed on the Tyr's shelf. A rich fur lay before it, and another hung off the back. He also wore a fur cloak closed with dragonscale.

Imfamnia was not in the audience. She was inspecting a case of luxuries brought in on dragonback.

"I do not say you must follow the advice of the human assistant," SiMevolant said. "But they are wise, and I feel matters will go easier if we heed them."

"I say enough," a Skotl called.

"I say too much!" a Wyrr added.

The Copper braced himself and took a breath. This was worse than spreading his wings to jump, trusting to a bit of wood and leather and steel pin. "I say we have no Tyr. Just a dog too well trained to need a collar."

"That's a poor sort of insult, RuGaard." SiMevolant yawned. "I hope you didn't labor hard over it. You wasted your time."

"I challenge you to a duel, with the charge of treason against the Imperial line," the Copper said.

"You can't challenge a Tyr," SiMevolant said. "The rank is too exalted."

"I may. There are some who believe I am the rightful Tyr. Tyr FeHazathant named me as his successor after NiVom fled and before he died."

"I witnessed it!" Ibidio called.

"I was told in secret as well," said NeStirrath. Which was a lie, but a lie he gladly offered to tell.

"He told me the same," Rethothanna said. "There is even a secret testament in the archives." Another lie, but one she had made true with a bit of parchment and a forged scale-seal.

"That's three," NoSohoth said quietly.

"So, yes, I do challenge you," RuGaard said. "If you refuse, all will know you to be a coward."

"Yes, yes, yes, heroes taste death but once and all that. But the

337

coward gets a long time to enjoy all those deaths, bitter as the cup may be, and heroes die young. Still, you annoy me, RuGaard. I think I should like to kill you. I accept your challenge and name the Dragonblade as my duelist."

That startled the man out of bored daydreaming. He reached for his sword hilt.

"You get to kill a three-legged dragon," SiMevolant said.

"When I came down here, I was told I'd be acting as an adviser," the Dragonblade said. "I've had enough fights in my life. I'm old, my bones are easily chilled, and a hairy-rumped well digger would find this blasted rock uncomfortably cool."

"The alternative is fighting between the *Andam* and the dragons again," SiMevolant hissed.

"So be it. I'll kill the beast for you. What's one more to my tally? Ach, you're making me regret my chickens and coops."

"The deepest hour of the night, then," the Copper said. "When the new day rings."

Black Rock's dueling pit lay on its lowest level. An amphitheater had been dug out beneath a point of rock, and there was room for six-score or more dragons, though the air got closed-in and stuffy when it was that full.

Fewer than a score of dragons attended this duel. RuGaard was well liked (or at least not hated outright, as Tighlia liked to put it), so most of the audience was of the *Andam*. They would have preferred, perhaps, to see two dragons fight, but entertainments were few enough.

SiMevolant was there, of course, in his ridiculous bumblebee-painted scheme.

After a light dinner, the Copper took a last walk around the Rock. He wondered how many dragons—or men—noticed the bats flitting about. Every now and then one landed on his head to whisper in his ear.

Finally, it was time. He descended to the dueling pit with limbs that dragged reluctantly.

I've never had any luck with duels. From my first one out of the egg.

The Copper made a long, reluctant show of having himself groomed before the match, trying to make the contest last as long as possible. If he went onto the sand before the attack, in all likelihood he would be killed. The Dragonblade occupied his time sharpening his sword and testing his footing in the sand of the dueling pit. He picked up a bronze dragonscale shield—how odd, the coloring was much like Father's—and banged his sword hilt against it.

"Come on! It's late, beast, and I'll have this over with."

I've never had any luck with duels.

The Copper dropped into the pit and lowered his *griff*.

The Dragonblade put on a helmet featuring two wings rising up and meeting above his head, dropped his spiked face mask, and jumped into the pit. He took six paces forward so he couldn't be trapped against the wall. Then he waited, shield held ready and sword held loosely in one hand.

NoSohoth invoked the spirits, asking them to determine whose cause was just, and to offer strength to the combatant in the right—but took his time doing so, and had to go back and repeat several lines.

The dragon-riders began to shout and make venting noises with their lips and tongues.

At last NoSohoth finished the invocation. But then he improvised: "I give you one last chance to reconcile. You have both proved your bravery by stepping into the pit, knowing that only one will climb out again. . . ."

Where are they?

Neither offered to forget the quarrel. NoSohoth had difficulty making out the Dragonblade's reply, and finally asked him to step over and repeat his words, without the face mask in the way.

With that done NoSohoth droned on and on about the glorious traditions of single combat and how these two opponents set an example of courage to be learned from by eyes young and old. . . .

Never before had the Copper been so grateful for NoSohoth's ponderous speechifying.

"Enough, NoSohoth," SiMevolant cried. "Or I'll have a saddle made for the Dragonblade out of your hide. Begin!" he shouted, lest NoSohoth suffer another attack of deafness.

The Dragonblade dropped into a crouch. He whirled his sword, and it whistled an evil tune as it cut the air.

The Copper shifted stance and his wings opened a little and flapped, instinctively readying themselves.

"Now I know you. You're the little crippled traitor! Stupid of me!"

"Not finishing me when you had the chance?" the Copper asked.

"Thinking such as you might put up a fight."

Nothing to do but go forward. The Copper, for the first time in his life, made a show of limping.

The Dragonblade danced forward, deflected a bite with his shield, and cut the Copper in the shoulder. He moved as if he were made of air itself, a zephyr of slashing steel and stinking man-breath.

The Copper turned, swinging his stiff and broken tail, and beat his wings, kicking up a whirlwind of dust.

The men in the stands roared in displeasure, though whether they thought this was cheating, or just objected to not being able to see the action, the Copper couldn't say.

The Dragonblade was ready for the sand. Blocking it with his shield, he came forward and opened a cut in the Copper's vulnerable belly.

He's toying with me. He's going to let me die by scores of small cuts rather than a fatal blow.

Dribbles of blood made strange spiral traces in the sand beneath the Copper as he sidestepped, protecting his wounded underside. The man sliced a piece of skin from the Copper's haunch the size of his shield. Naked muscle gleamed red.

"I need a new shield-leather anyway," he said.

The Copper's fire bladder pulsed with his pain, and he vomited up its contents.

This, too, the Dragonblade was ready for. He crouched behind his shield and the thin liquid just splattered his shield, him, and the sand around. The liquid dripped off his shield like rain off a wide jungle leaf.

"Not even any fire? Let's end it; this is no contest at all," the Dragonblade said. He slashed the Copper's good leg, and the Copper collapsed face-first into the sand.

A man's voice shouted from the entrance. The Copper didn't understand the words, but the dragon-riders jumped to their feet and fought one another to the exit.

The dragons were coming at last!

He raised his head to see the audience in flight, and the Dragonblade kicked him behind the jaw. He saw stars and his whole neck went numb. He fought to regain control of his head and neck as painful, prickling electricity danced up and down his spine.

The Dragonblade planted himself in front of his snout, just out of reach. He pointed the tip of his sword at the Copper's eye.

If you died fighting, were you still vanquished?

A trickle of oily-smelling liquid dribbled out of the Dragonblade's scale greaves, spotting the sand. The Copper traced its source with his eye. It came from beneath the armor.

"Mercy," the Copper whispered, as Jizara had. Perhaps the

Dragonblade had changed. Perhaps this time he'd grant mercy to a vanquished foe.

The man just snorted and adjusted the aim of his sword tip. "Not to such as you. Last words?"

The Copper refused to waste his final breath in a curse. With what wind he had left he forced a gob out of his mouth.

A flaming *torf*. Pitiful. Hardly bigger than a lump of coal.

A flaming *torf* that struck the Dragonblade on the boot.

A flaming *torf* that struck the Dragonblade on the boot and set his whole leg aflame.

Which set his hips on fire.

Which crawled up his torso and yes, even flickered out the slits in his face mask.

He died rather more noisily than Mother.

A blur of gold and SiMevolant landed heavily in the sand. He stormed toward the Copper, shining like the sun itself come to earth. "What have you done? Don't you understand? Our age is over! We must ally with men, or our flame will be extinguished forever."

"Not yet," the Copper gasped.

SiMevolant raised his tail. Along with the strange black stripes, a silver barb had been added to the end.

It dripped.

Open jaws and claws bounded out of the darkness. Nilrasha seized SiMevolant's tail in her jaws and yanked, tearing a third of it off. She threw the dismembered tail away, and it rolled and twitched in the sand.

SiMevolant forgot about the injured Copper—someone had done that before, to his regret, the Copper vaguely remembered with a tickle of pride—and turned on Nilrasha, rising and spreading his wings a little, showing this backbiting female how big he truly was!

The fool. He should have kept to his cowardly ways. *Don't*

fight if you know nothing about fighting. He didn't even lower himself to protect his belly.

The Copper lashed out with a *saa* and opened SiMevolant wide and deep.

The would-be Tyr looked down at the coils spilling from his belly, writhing like a horde of unleashed snakes.

And then Nilrasha fell on him, pushing his neck to the sand, opening windpipe and blood vessels, and SiMevolant let out a gurgling protest as he died.

"Nilrasha, you've come again."

"I never thought I could fly so fast," she said, dropping beside him. "You're not badly hurt. Just cut up."

"You must go up. Help the others."

"I've no armor. Rayg had time and materials to make only three of the underside leathers. AuBalagrave and his dragons are wearing them."

"The plan could fail. We're deep beneath the Rock. You should leave, so you have room to run."

"In victory or defeat, I'm determined to die at your side, my love." She looked up. "Here! You! Bat. Get over here. I've work for you."

Uthaned himself, a gray mouse who could fit in the Copper's nostril, fluttered above his ear.

"The blood is in pools on the dragon-barrack floor, m'lord," Uthaned said. "The dragons rise just high enough to kill their men in their fall."

The Copper always regretted not being able to see it.

As Rethothanna related it to him later, like all well-fought battles, it was over before it was begun. The bats had opened veins on most of the dragon-rider mounts, numbing and cutting, numbing and cutting, and letting the blood run into the washing gutters.

In another cave it might not have worked—some attendant

might have noticed the blood pooling on the floor—but not in the shining confines of the Rock. The black surface concealed the damage done until it was too late.

So when the alarm was sounded and the men ran to their mounts, the woozy beasts slipped and bumped. Those who even beat their wings hard enough to rise soon passed out, crumpled, and fell to earth. There was a terrible toll in broken necks and backs on the dragons, but the dragon-riders had it even worse.

Of course, a healthy patrol was up over the Rock, as always, and it took many lives before the hag-riders were plucked out of their saddles and their maddened, confused mounts crippled. Even AuBalagrave, one of the few dragons with his belly armored against crossbow bolts, fell with a poisoned arrowhead in his jaw. But other dragons battered and swatted the flying hag-riddens, or plucked the men off while they were reloading their weapons.

There was bitter tunnel fighting against the *Andam*, but the Drakwatch distinguished itself. Old NeStirrath fell at their head when a wounded human plunged a poisoned blade into him. Of all the names of the fallen from that day, his glory lasted the longest.

The Imperial line had been reduced once again. Now only a handful remained.

Imfamnia fled. Some said she had chains of gold clutched in each claw. Others said she was heavy with SiMevolant's eggs. Or SiDrakkon's. Or a dozen other rumored lovers, earning her the title "Jade Queen" in the *Anklene Histories*. None could say where she went.

A small group of men and dragons barricaded themselves deep in the rock with a reserve of food and water. They refused all attempts at parley until the Copper tottered to their tunnel, supported by Nilrasha. He dragged with him a woman clutching a squalling babe.

He showed the pair to the men at the other end of the tunnel and issued the only offer he could to give to the poison-men, for it was the only one their savage, half-formed brains could appreciate:

He summoned his best voice. "Surrender and give your lives over to us, or we'll kill each of you, your wives, and spit your babes for roasting. The choice is yours, men: fair treatment as thralls, or death."

Two committed suicide in despair. The rest sensibly chose thralldom.

And it was only while limping out of the Imperial Resort, with dragons and thralls alike calling him "Tyr RuGaard" and Nilrasha "Queen Ora," that he realized what he had become.

Epilogue

An Anklene, with the assistance of two elvish thralls, stitched him up. His good *sii* soon functioned again, though the scarred hide on his haunch never grew a proper set of scale again, just a sort of scabby covering like a turtle's shell.

He had to make a great many decisions from the Tyr's shelf, but he grew used to much of the labor required of a Tyr, to the point where he looked forward to the challenges, such as rebuilding the alliance with the *griffaran*. He even made a sort of art of delegating authority. The real trick was matching the right sort of brains and brawn to each task.

"Rayg is a clever man. In the world I intend to build, clever men will do very well. As long as they understand their place in the Spirits' grand design," he said to Rhea as she scrubbed him one morning. He had to confess that he liked the smell of bathwater with a slippery woman in it. But all things in moderation.

"You might want to communicate that to him," Nilrasha said as she performed her own ablutions.

Rayg had been kept busy studying the dragon-riders' weapons and equipment in the hope of making improvements. Now and then he complained that he should be freed by now, but the Copper always reminded him that the bridge was not yet built.

"Release me from this trivia and I'll finish it in thirty days," he grumbled. But he'd grumble more in the ore mines, seeing to improvements in the hydraulics, the Copper reminded him.

Bath done and breakfast down, the Copper hooked his mate at the wing and walked her to the balcony overlooking the now-public Imperial Gardens. And yes, he had a review to do, then a short speech to give to the newest generation of Drakwatch and Firemaidens.

With his beautiful mate pacing behind, the Copper walked through the quarters of his tiny aerial host, still new and untested as a wet hatchling, but they were learning.

Instead of reins, the warriors fought chained to their saddles. For their own safety, of course. But it also established who guided whom.

He limped down a long line of dragons, with a few dragonelles sprinkled in, the red bands of the Firemaid oath around their necks. Each set of wings faced a rider, free thralls all—a fine-sounding status, as long as one didn't think about it too much. Dragon and rider stared into each other's eyes over a lance's distance. Their armor was variegated, their weapons according to taste, but at least they all matched in their red cloaks. Not all the men were former dragon-riders; some were thralls who showed great loyalty and promise and skill at arms. And not all the dragons had once been hag-ridden. Those dragons who'd been victorious in combat had the Tyr's *laudi* painted on their wings in inexpensive but long-lasting tones. The dragon-riders had the equivalent, called "tattooing" or some other odd-sounding Parl expression, on their arms and at the outer edges of their eyes and temples.

Maturing hatchlings—clutchwinners, for the most part, including AuBalagrave's own champion—stood between and behind the dragons and men they attended. Hatchlings bore food and carried wash water for the men, fetched boots and flying cloaks when called for. The human boys and girls polished scale, cleaned teeth with bristle brushes, and adjusted saddle pads with their nimble little fingers. The Copper hoped that in time a firmer alliance could be bred.

In time, as he often told Rayg, whenever he presented them with a tender calf, advising that the liver go to the swelling Rhea.

Imfamnia would have thought them poor work and too dreary-toned for words. So would SiMevolant, though he would have been arch about it. SiDrakkon would have approved, for the markings were grim-looking enough.

"Let's make it loud enough so the Tyr RuGaard hears it this time!" HeBellereth, the aerial host commander, roared.

"This is my rider," the ranks boomed in unison. "He is unique, an individual, and deserving of my respect."

The men recited the same speech as the dragons, switching *rider* for *dragon*.

"Without my rider, I am nothing. Without me, my rider is nothing. If I fall, he dies. If he falls, I will see to it he rests on the empire's ground. My blood is his nourishment. His sweat is mine. So be it until death or our Tyr releases us."

Of course, the men had to change the wording of the last, too.

The Copper passed through the Black Rock, limping past bronzed skulls and captured banners hung from cut dragon reins. Thralls, drakes and drakka, dragons and dragonelles, and even a watchbat here and there bowed—or crossed their wings, in the case of the bats—to him.

There was no more laughter at his awkwardness. A Skotl or two, and the odd Wyrr holdout or Anklene radical, glared at him hotly.

They can hate as hard as they like, as long as they fear.

He looked in on the workshop, and the thrall's meal room. Rayg and Rhea and their growing brood stood with the rest, though their textiles and footwear were of much higher quality.

He paused, and put his head close to his mate's.

"There's so much still to be done. I believe before long we will long for those quiet evenings around the feast floor in Anaea."

"We're in charge of the Lavadome now. We can do what we want," Nilrasha said, smiling. A little piece of him deep inside turned cold. He could still admire her lines, her cool courage, and her tenacity at getting what she wanted. And above all, be grateful for what she had done for him. But she was no Tighlia.

But at that moment, he would rather have had frail little Halaflora. Halaflora understood the burdens of rank and station. When his mood turned dark like this, part of him believed Nilrasha hungered for bows and scrapes as Imfamnia had once wanted expensive baubles.

Then they went back up to the top level, or "their level," as Nilrasha styled it. She nuzzled her head under his as he stepped out onto the platform overlooking the Gardens. What little was left of the Imperial line looked up at him. Lesser dragons lined the garden walls, drakes and drakka perched atop broken columns and darkvine arches.

A pair of hatchlings batted a dragon-rider's rotting severed head back and forth with their tails and had sport snapping at the flies seeking the putrescent flesh.

The Drakwatch and Firemaidens looked up.

Time for the words a Tyr had to say now and then, to remind everyone that life was more than banquets and hunts and mating ceremonies and discreet little intimacies.

"Our species is at the beginning of a great awakening. The blighters had their Age of Wheels. Then the other hominids began the Age of Iron with a slaughter of our kind. Never forget the betrayal and fall of Silverhigh, or the fate that we in the Lavadome so narrowly escaped. The malice of hominids knows no charity or reason.

"They must be subdued and tamed. Or they will do the same

to us, as the Dragonblade once tried. How many other Dragon-blades are there beyond our borders?

"Join me and look to our future. We need only master our-selves, and we can master the world! Today, here, atop this ancient stone, surrounded by the caves and egg shelves and trophies of our birthright, we dragons have inaugurated a new age. Let our enemies tremble, for now begins the Age of Fire!"

Drakine Glossary

Foua: A product of the fire bladder. When mixed with the liquid fats stored within and then exposed to oxygen, it ignites into oily flame.

Griff: The armored fans descending from the forehead and jaw that cover a dragon's sensitive ear holes and throat pulse points in battle.

Griff-tchk: An instant, an immeasurably short amount of time.

Laudi: Brave and glorious deeds in a dragon's life that make it into the lifesong.

Prrum: The low thrumming sound a dragon makes when it is pleased or particularly content.

Saa: The rear legs of a dragon. The three rear true-toes are able to grip, but the fighting spur is little more than decoration.

Sii: The front legs of a dragon. The claws are shorter, and the fighting spur on the rear leg is closer to the other digits, and opposable. The digits are more elegantly formed for manipulation.

Torf: A small gob from the fire bladder, used to provide a few moments of illumination.

Draconic Personae

(ALL MALES ARE NAMED USING MATURE DRAGON FORM)

AgGriffopse—Tyr FeHazathant's only male clutchwinner, mated to Ibidio, died years before the Copper's arrival at the Lavadome.

Angalia—Firemaid in Anaea.

AuBalagrave—member of the Drakwatch.

AuRon—the clutchwinner at the Copper's hatching.

Esthea—NeStirrath's dead mate.

FeHazathant—Tyr at the time of the Copper's arrival in the Lavadome.

FeLissarath—Upholder of Anaea.

Halaflora—sickly daughter of AgGriffopse and Ibidio.

HeBellereth—Skotl clan duelist dragon.

Ibidio—AgGriffopse's mate.

Imfamnia—daughter of AgGriffopse and Ibidio.

Jizara—the Copper's weaker sister.

Krthonius—member of the Drakwatch.

NeStirrath—chief trainer of the Drakwatch.

Nilrasha—Firemaiden.

NiThonius—Upholder of Bant.

NiVom—member of the Drakwatch.

NoSohoth—majordomo of the Imperial line.

NoTannadon—duelist.

Rethothanna—Anklene historian.

SiDrakkon—Tighlia's brother by mating to Tyr FeHazathant.

SiMevolant (golden drake)—AgGriffopse and Ibidio's surviving clutchwinner.

Tighlia—Tyr FeHazathant's mate.

Tyr—title for the ruler of the Lavadome, usually used in lieu of a name.

Wistala—the Copper's stronger sister.

About the Author

E. E. Knight graduated from Northern Illinois University with a double major in history and political science, then made his way through a number of jobs that had nothing to do with history or political science. He resides in Chicago. For more information on the author and his worlds, E. E. Knight invites you to visit his Web site, vampjac.com.